OSCAR MIKE
PAUL J. HALE

"MIND YOUR MANNERS."

PUBLISHED BY:

Paul J. Hale

OSCAR MIKE

Copyright © 2016 by Paul J. Hale

ACKNOWLEDGEMENT

I would like to thank the following for their contributions to my inspiration and knowledge and other help in creating this book:

My wife, Teresa, for letting me do this, and putting up with me through the whole process.

My kids, Lincoln & Brienne, for staying out of the office and being quiet while Daddy is working.

My mother, Kathleen, for never quitting and never letting me quit.

Brandon Scholes, for teaching me various cop stuff—like the whole blowing-air-down-your-chest-into-the-bullet-proof-vest-to-stay-cool-because-bullet-proof-vests-are-hot-as-hell thing. I totally used that.

Stephanie Sibley, for teaching me about guns, gun-lingo, and being an amazing support through the whole journey.

Rommy Driks, for being a friend, and helping me with the Spanish and Spanglish in this book.

Steve Mathis, for your encouragement, for keeping it real and telling me what I needed to hear, whether I wanted to hear it or not.

Terri Reid, for being there for me, helping me understand how everything works and welcoming Zarah into the O'Reilly family.

Everybody else who gave me their feedback and advice, you know who you are.

And finally, to all the A-holes on the motorways, for daily making me want to kill you the only way I legally can, thank you.

1

A GUN-METAL ACURA coasted down an empty south-bound highway. Jessica Devin, a sand-skinned, flaxen-haired valley girl, was returning home from a long day at work that had extended into a longer night—both of which she wanted to forget.

The air outside felt drier than ashes, but the sound of thunder and rain played through her stereo speakers. The satellite her stereo was tuned to had begun to play "Riders on the Storm" by The Doors. Jessica turned the volume up and rolled the windows down to let the night air, and Ray Manzerick's keyboard solo, surge through her. Jessica turned on the AC to give the broiling air outside some help, directing the vents straight at her.

The mixed current of fresh and warm with cold and filtered air flooded her car. Jessica smelled the bitter scent of smoke from burning weeds and leaves. It raised no alarms. Though winter solstice had happened weeks ago and the New Year was approaching, Southern California was as hot and dry as ever, and something was always on fire. Jessica relaxed and allowed her long hair to whip around, and she savored the freedom of the empty road.

The freeway between Valencia and the San Fernando Valley was calm during this period between late night and early morning. The black road weaved through a cluster of soft foothills, with few street lamps, and the light from homes twinkled from a high distance. Mercifully absent were the thousands of mechanical noise-makers that crowded the freeways in daylight. The sound of the road hummed through the car like the rippling murmur of a rolling river.

Jessica plucked an olive-green vape mod from the cup holder, put the mouthpiece between her glossed lips and drew a deep hit of mildly nicotined, Irish Cream flavored water vapor into her mouth. She enjoyed the taste for a moment, then exhaled a dense, white cloud that swept out the window into the night.

She looked forward to being home, watching something noir on late night TV, slipping into a deep sleep and dreaming of things other than work orders, deadlines and obsolete equipment.

In the web-development industry, marketing and I.T. never saw eye to eye, and Jessica's boss had become so sick of I.T.'s smugly delivered, techno-babble protests that he had commanded her to stay late, again, and badger them until they *"put it in gear."*

Jessica understood that I.T. was working in an impossible situation. Most of their hardware and all of the software was antiquated, and they did not have the budget to do anything significant about it. For them, everything was about stability. Tinkering with new and potentially unstable ideas on outdated software with a "let's-see-what-happens" attitude did not fly.

Jessica's mission was to chase the leading edge, the next *new thing*. To reach more people more quickly, she needed the right technologies.

Once upon a time, Jessica felt useful and respected, but someone upstairs decided that as head of online marketing, her job included working the bellows in I.T. like a feeble-minded, accordion monkey, blasting flames under everybody's ass to make the impossible possible. And no other department, in any company, had more hatred for marketing executives than I.T.

Jessica shook her head and forced herself to allow the commute home to do its job and relax her. She would be pulling into the parking lot of her townhome before "Riders on the Storm" ended, so she would stay in her car and let the song finish.

Her boyfriend, Scott, had called her several times during the day, but she had been too busy to take his calls. She knew what it was about. He wanted to come over to her place and spend the night. Some T.L.C. would be nice, but Scott refused to accept that she had a demanding career. He would put his arms around her, kiss her gently, rev her engine and then start bellyaching about her job and how much her hours sucked. Then they would argue, and Jessica had put up with enough recriminations for one day.

As much as she wanted to spend time with him, she could not afford to be anything less than an indispensable asset to her employers. An epidemic of layoffs was spreading through the web development industry and in the current anti-business climate, losing her job could cost her the future she had planned for herself—a future that did not necessarily include Scott.

She made another decision. She wanted to see him, feel him, but not to listen to him. She placed the vape mod back into the cup holder and lifted her smart-phone from its holster case on her waistband. Before she could call Scott to tell him "not tonight" she noticed that she had a voicemail. Jessica told Siri to play her messages but the electronic personal assistant inside the smart-phone refused, saying that it couldn't take the request at the moment.

"Sometimes you're as bad as I.T.," Jessica said.

"Well, I'm still here for you." Siri replied in her monotonic, fembot voice.

Jessica repeated her request and Siri did as commanded. It was a voicemail from Scott:

"Jessie, it's me. I would tell you this myself, in person, but as usual you're not picking up—too much of a big shot to take my calls. They aren't important, right? I mean, when something's important you make the time. You don't make it for me so it speaks pretty clearly about the deal between us.

"Nothing's happened, yet, but you should know there is someone else. I shouldn't be interested in her, but I am. When a guy wants a girl other than what he's already got… when that happens its cheat or move on. I don't wanna cheat.

"I wish I could do this in person but I can never get through till you want me to so…goodbye, Jessica."

He was pulling this crap on her now, *right before New Year's?* A wave of anger smashed her. She could not see straight. He never told her he felt that way. Or maybe she was not listening.

She spotted the sign for her exit and jerked the wheel, swerving her car into the right lane. She thought she was alone on the road and had not been paying attention, but there was another car with her. Its bright headlights seared her eyes through the rearview mirror. The pickup truck was forced to hit the brakes and yield the lane. Its driver leaned on his horn. It roared at Jessica loud and long.

Yeah, yeah I cut you off! Deal with it!

Jessica felt like driving straight to Vegas, picking up a bunch of young, sexy frat boys who just turned twenty-one and sending Scott a picture of her wearing that skimpy black dress he bought her, lying across their laps and being hand-fed those bright red cherries.

I don't wanna cheat either, douche bag! That's what I'll say!

Scott was lucky Jessica was not that kind of girl, because it would be too easy. She held the smart-phone to her ear, told Siri to dial Scott's mobile number but the bitch did not understand her.

The pickup behind her signaled and swerved into the lane beside hers. Then it sped up to pass her. She waited for it to be out of her way so that she could merge right again.

The driver maintained its speed beside her, blocking her.

"Move!" she hollered. "Jesus!"

She slowed so that the truck would pass her and she could change lanes behind it. It slowed and maintained its pace next to her. A hooded man glared at her from inside the pickup truck, trying to scare her.

Jessica sped up. He stayed beside her. She decided not to pay any attention; show him that his immature chest-thumping was not going to work. She waited. Soon this creep would speed off feeling manly and she could get off the freeway, go home and end this miserable day.

She tried to keep her teary eyes on the road but this guy would not go away. It made her furious. What was he hoping to accomplish by staring at her? What would he get out of it besides a nice view? She looked over at the driver to flip him the bird.

Then she saw the gun.

2

T HE MOON HAD risen bright and full, but the air was still as hot as if it was high noon. Strobing red and blue lights emblazed the dark as burning road-flares seared the asphalt. Three black-and-white LAPD squad cars were parked on the shoulder of the highway. In front of them was a fire truck, and in front of that was the forensic team's black SUV. A line of orange, reflective cones stretched down the road, slowing traffic and guiding it into the lanes that were still open.

Detective Zarah Wheeler pulled up in a filthy, purple Camry. She had ended her shift two and a half hours before and had been enjoying a cozy night in front of the AC, drinking Bacardi and watching a corny, made-for-TV romcom when the call-out came. She did not want to put the suit she had already taken off back on, so she changed out of her pajama pants, pulled on some blue jeans and a white t-shirt and, to appear semi-professional, a black 1-button jacket.

She shut off the engine, picked a strong-flavored mint from the pile in her cup holder and flicked it into her mouth. She grabbed her LAPD badge from the passenger seat and hung it around her neck by a ball chain. Still feeling warm and tingly, she flicked her wavy, black hair out from under the chain.

All right, she told herself. *Sober, poised...*

She took a breath, focused and strode toward the scene. A flat-bed tow truck was positioned sideways across the road. Its boom cable was stretched taut down a steep embankment, pulling a wrecked car up the slope. At first it looked like a common accident—a crushed Acura wrecked by repeated impacts as it tumbled into the ditch.

Her partner, Charlie Slocum, had already arrived. He noticed her and trotted over. It was enough to wind him. Zarah refused to slow down and made him pick up speed to catch up and meet her pace. The man needed exercise.

Charlie was six-foot-two with broad shoulders. He had excellent posture for a fifty-three year old, and his grayish, earthen-colored hair was high and tight like a proper soldier. But he weighed more than any cop free from a desk should.

Zarah could not figure it out. He had enough vanity to use contact lenses on his stony eyes. He kept his suits pressed and neat, but he did nothing to burn the calories off his rotund gut. Once upon a time, he had been a paratrooper, and a combat veteran at that. He had participated in *Operation Urgent Fury* and took the island of Grenada with the rest of the 82nd Airborne and received the Medal of Merit. Now he never exercised and would not bother with the shooting range unless he had an evaluation coming up.

Zarah refused to allow that to happen to her. Detective Zarah Wheeler was a razor, and she was going to stay that way until they hammered the last nail into her coffin.

"Road rage," Charlie said, catching his breath. "Good thing the call came after rush hour, or traffic would really be hell."

"Good thing..." Zarah said as she watched the coroners load a black body-bag into a white van.

"That's Jessica Devin", Charlie said. "Thirty-one years old... some kind of jobber for a web design firm, Syncope Interactive. She had one of those I.D. badges on her when they pulled her out."

"What's the story?" Zarah asked.

"Nothing sexy. DOA, shot a few times and beat up pretty good after rolling down that ditch. They were able to cut her out of the car and carry her up without mussing the body too much. Looking at her, I'd bet this happened sometime last night."

Zarah and Charlie reached the embankment and looked over the edge. The car was a quarter of the way up. The tow cable squeaked and groaned as the wrecked car plowed up dry dirt and dead foliage.

"What are we thinking?" Zarah asked. "Random?"

"We're thinking that Jessica Devin was probably a very nice young lass, but this isn't a Special case."

"Hey detectives," Swede, a small, round crime scene investigator with small, round glasses approached them holding a clear plastic evidence bag with a sheet of paper inside. "This was on the victim."

Zarah took it from him and looked it over. It was yellow legal paper with a message written in dark, sloppy ink, as if the author used a broken ball-tip pen—or a quill. It read:

Listen up Police!

This bitch had an entire empty highway, and still CUT ME OFF WITHOUT SIG- NALING!!! She was also TALKING ON HER CELLPHONE!! If I could've killed her twice, I would have!

Disrespect, rudeness, and arrogance on the road will NO LONGER BE TOLERATED!!! I will inflict BLOODY penalties on those who act inappropriately while driving!!! So pre- pare the morgues and hire more coro- ners because The Street Sweeper is going to work!

Zarah handed it to Charlie and he read.

"When first responders phoned it in," Swede said, "they said this has the look of a potential series or spree. I think that's why your section was called."

"That'll do it," Charlie said as he handed the note back to him.

Zarah shook her head. At least the psycho left evidence. The more he ran his mouth, the faster he would be caught, but each cry for attention would cost someone their life. Zarah rubbed her eyes. She felt the earth turning under her feet.

"What's wrong?" Charlie asked.

Zarah waved the question off with a flick of her hand.

"What, this your first series? 'Cause it's not a series till he drops three. You knew that, right?"

"No, Charlie," she answered, "it's not my first series. And yes, I knew that."

As far as Zarah could tell, her partner thought what the rest of Homicide Special Section thought. She was an attractive female and half-Arabic, so the brass must have sent her to Robbery Homicide to show folks that the LAPD was not a boys' club and that they were okay with Islam.

On the outside, Zarah's Arabic and Caucasian halves were well-balanced. She was five-foot-eleven, nearly a head taller than most women from Riyadh, and her skin was a sun-loved tan that one could mistake for a Malibu white girl's. But her curvy brows, sharp cheekbones, cognac-colored eyes and hair as black as a grackle revealed the imported Saudi in her.

Zarah had an Irish father and was raised in Illinois, and anyone who bothered to see past her DNA would learn that Darwin had been more religious, and Pope Urban II had been closer to being Muslim—not that she cared to volunteer such things.

She spoke with a subtle, North Chicago accent that placed emphasis on the short-A, and occasionally "th" became a soft D. She was close to shedding it, but sometimes Southern California became *"Suddern Calafornya"* as it exited her mouth. It may not have been one-hundred percent Midwestern, but it was nowhere near Middle Eastern. That, and her record as a detective should have been enough, but her age was her greatest flaw.

Zarah was thirty-seven, the youngest detective in the unit and one of three women. Her colleagues' skepticism was annoying, but she understood where it came from. She may have been a super cop in the common precincts, but in their elite unit, she was a green rook. And like a meddling parent, they could not stop themselves from trying to teach Zarah things she already knew.

"Our plate's gonna be stacked with bodies before this is over," Zarah told her partner.

"If he's gonna be gunning people down on the street like this," Charlie said, "he'll be exposing himself to witnesses and cameras. He'll be snapped up real quick."

Zarah was not convinced. Time would tell, but Zarah's working theory was that this *Street Sweeper* may not have had a plan, but he did have a mission. Now she and Charlie had one, too.

3

ON-SCENE, ACE REPORTER Carmen Sanchaz stood in front of a six foot, African-American mountain named Lamar with an HD video camera mounted over one shoulder. Carmen was five-foot-three with lustrous, auburn hair that ended above her shoulders. She spoke with an enticing Mexican lilt, "Los Angeles Police Chief Colin Masters said that both the police department and the community were *'angered and outraged'* over the attack on the chimpanzee, and *'it is indeed tragic that an innocent animal will be killed for defending itself from a lunatic.'* From the Los Angeles Zoo, this is Carmen Sanchaz, Channel Six Network News."

She grinned into the camera with a sassy twinkle in her inviting, brown eyes until Lamar said "clear." Then she relaxed and tossed her microphone to Gary Sterling, her skinny, spectacled producer and marched toward the blue news van.

"That was great," Gary said.

"*Gracias, papi,*" she replied, her poised and professional accent giving way to her natural, Echo Park street dialect. She withdrew her smart phone from its holder. "Big Boy's around here. Lunch time?"

"Who's treating?" Lamar asked.

"I treated *you* at breakfast," Carmen said.

"You got me a Snickers!"

"Aay, next time buy your own Snickers, *tacaño!*"

Carmen opened the Twitter app on her phone and tweeted:

Carmen Sanchaz @RealCarmenSNews6:

Man killed by chimp. If u missed, watch replay 2nite and learn Y Fight Club with monkeys is a bad idea. #LANews6 #LAZoo #CarmenSanchaz

Gary's phone rang. When he answered, he shot a look to Carmen and mouthed the name, *"Daniels",* the executive evening director for their network. Another assignment.

At first Carmen was wondering what state fair or arts & crafts show they would be covering, but as Gary nodded and smiled at the information he was receiving, her skin tingled. After Gary was off the phone, she braced herself for the news.

"Serial killer," Gary said. "A woman shot off the road."

"One dead lady, and it's a serial?" she asked.

"It's not *yet*," Gary said. "The killer left a note saying he did it because his victim was talking on her cell while driving, and he's gonna do it again. It's too late to cover the crime scene, and Daniels wants us back in the studio to talk, which pretty much means if this guy strikes again, it's ours."

"A serial killer with a gimmick," Carmen said, containing her excitement. "Interesting…"

"Can you call your friend at USC?" Gary asked.

Carmen nodded. "Let's go," she said.

"What about lunch?" Lamar asked.

"*Despues*," Carmen said. "Daniels wants us to come in."

And opportunities don't wait for lunch breaks.

4

AFTER A CUP of black coffee with an egg-and-bacon sandwich for Charlie and scrambled egg whites for Zarah, the sun rose and reminded everybody that in spite of the grass lawns and swimming pools, Los Angeles was still a desert. The detectives returned to Parker Center to confirm that Jessica Devin's murder was, in fact, their case.

When they had received the green light, they started building their murder book. Photos, sketches, autopsy and forensic reports, notes, transcripts and witness interviews would all go into a blue binder. At the moment, the book was anorexic, but as they investigated, it would thicken into a complete paper trail of their casework, from day one until they had the scumbag in a cell.

After that, they headed to Syncope Interactive in Calabasas to see if anything was going on there. The *Street Sweeper's* message could have been a ruse. Someone with whom Jessica Devin had personal contact may have committed the crime and then concocted some kind of character to deflect the attention.

They learned that Jessica Devin had been an ambitious go-getter who cared about her job. The word from Jessica's boss was that there were plenty of guys with ill will for the decedent, all of them in the Information Technology department. So Zarah and Charlie questioned everyone in the building trapped between rack servers and large screens.

They had all stayed after Jessica had left. They had computer logins, security cameras and I.D. badge check-in logs of their comings and goings—alibis in triplicate.

Jessica had no family in California and not been close with anyone at work. Zarah learned that all she did was work, and all she talked about was work. She was so intense about work that anyone who considered asking her out was too afraid of a harassment complaint to make a move, and she had a boyfriend, whose name one coworker hazarded as "Scott". Jessica had mentioned him in passing a scarce number of times, and the working theory at Syncope Interactive was that she may have conjured up a fake boyfriend to keep male coworkers from making her workday more tedious than it had to be.

She never took personal calls during work hours, did not subscribe to social media and kept her private life private, so there was no way for anyone to verify it one way or another. Zarah understood that discipline and practiced it herself. She expected to learn more about this Scott character from Jessica's family in Oklahoma—if they ever returned Charlie's phone calls.

After they had finished their canvass, Zarah and Charlie agreed that *the Street Sweeper* was no facade. The chances that they would apprehend him before he killed again were nil, but for the time being they had to continue investigating the possibility that this murder was personal, and the Street Sweeper was a dramatic smoke screen. All they could do was go through the motions.

5

DRAKE BARRETT MITCHELL sat behind the wheel of his stolen Ford F-150 looking for a target. He had spent the week before at home, peering between the curtains believing every chopper that buzzed overhead was out for him, the sound of every siren making him reach for his Colt M-16.

He had killed for his country honorably and had nothing to show except memories he was not allowed to speak of. Now, in the private sector, the pay was excellent, but the money did not buy anything that would help him fit into gentle society.

Drake had tried to live in the world, forgive people their trespasses, but when that blonde cut him off without signaling, yacking on her cell—*both of which were illegal*—acting as if she was not subject to laws…that was the end of that.

A week had passed, and the cops had not shown up. He returned to the hunt. He felt like a grizzly lurking on the edge of a waterfall, waiting for one of those idiot fish that swim the wrong way to spring into his waiting jaws and get what they never thought was coming.

It had taken time, but as he slowed to stop for a red light, his moment came. A silver Mercedes sped up from behind, weaved into the lane beside his and then swerved into his lane, cutting him off. Drake slammed on his brakes to avoid rear-ending it. He honked. The prick pretended not to hear, thinking that honking was all that was going to happen. The Street Sweeper pulled a dark brown hood over his head.

Right into the bear's jaws...

6

THE NAVY BLUE, Channel Six news van parked half a block from the crime scene. The entire intersection was closed, and Carmen Sanchaz did not know what the story was beyond the result of someone's homicidal road-rage, but she suspected that this murder was episode two of the series her boss had clued her in on. As Carmen approached the yellow tape surrounding the scene, she watched the police work.

According to her friend inside LAPD's forensics lab, Detective Charles Slocum had been given the Jessica Devin case with his partner, Detective Zarah Wheeler. Carmen never heard of her, but she assumed it was the tough-looking *chica* next to Slocum with the athletic figure, black hair and skin the color of the Gobi desert.

Za-da Wheeler, Carmen thought. *Interesting name. Probably could've been Miss Baghdad, but she became a cop. A good cop if she is in Robbery-Homicide. Hmmm…*

The H.S.S. detectives' presence meant the idea of this murder connecting to the first one had potential. If there was a series, Carmen was going to seize upon it and spearhead something real.

She approached the cordon, having left Gary and Lamar in the van to prepare their broadcast. A reporter with a simple pen and notepad was less alarming to Public Information Officers and skittish patrolmen than one sporting a crew with a camera.

If she could not get what she needed, fine. She would go on the air like everyone else and say "somebody was shot," but she wanted to use the electric words *"serial killer"* and open the ratings faucet— though the words *"potential series"* would be a good enough start.

The uniformed cops would know little, if anything. She needed to speak with someone in a suit. There were a lot of suits wandering around a wrecked Mercedes that had crashed into some gas pumps across the street, well inside the perimeter and out of her reach. Carmen had to lure one of those detectives into her orbit. She scanned the scene.

Carmen watched Detective Wheeler. She looked polished and self-possessed, not as severe as Charlie Slocum but still not one to be trifled with. In Carmen's mind the image took shape of an empowered woman who had proven herself a hundred-fold and would not take anyone's shit. *That could be useful,* Carmen thought, assuming her instincts were correct.

The detective was batting her lashes at a familiar face, CSI Adam Jamison. So, Carmen would not be able to channel her inner *Ellen,* flirt and charm information from her, but...

Carmen hatched an audacious plan. The reporter knew that she was pretty, and cops were horn-dogs who would jump at a chance to impress some Latina strange. If she could provoke a confrontation, play the intimidated, outnumbered and vulnerable damsel, *one* of these dicks would come to her rescue. Carmen fixed her sights on a young Public Information Officer and got into character.

7

CHARLIE AND ZARAH had come as fast as traffic would allow, but other detectives had arrived first and were processing the scene.

A silver Mercedes was crumpled into a gas pump outside a convenience store. The passenger side of the sedan was punched in. Fresh skid marks had been seared across the intersection and ended where a white Jetta rested a few feet away, the front end flattened as if a bailing press had gone to work on it.

Zarah spotted CSI Adam Jamison strolling her way, chatting with detectives Deon Woodley and Manuel Pérez—both from her squad in H.S.S. Adam was a head taller than Zarah and three years younger. His hair was an alluring bedhead the color of the Great Plains at sunrise, and his eyes were the sky before rain. When hers met his, instinct forced her to look away, but it was too late. She had been ogling, and the record would so reflect.

"Adam," Zarah said, offering her hand. Adam shook it and smiled.

Woodley was a rugged, forty-eight-year-old, African-American with the build of a tank. He wore a grey suit, shades with rectangular lenses, an ashen newsboy cap, and sported a sophisticated pencil-thin moustache. Wherever he went, the scent of aniseed, lavender and basil followed.

Pérez was a swarthy, brown-eyed Peruvian, and a former Marine in his early fifties. He was handsome in a weather-beaten, world-weary sort of way, with thick hair the kind of jet black that no human head could produce naturally. He had taken the jacket of his black suit off and had rolled the white sleeves of his dress shirt above his elbows.

"Hey, Zarah," Adam said. "Charlie. I heard you guys are working the girl from last week."

Charlie nodded, "Jessica Devin. Got anything that connects?"

"Almost," Woodley said. "Different kind of victim, different kind of locale, different gun..."

"We still think it's tied to yours," Pérez said.

"Between the clues and witnesses, I have a pretty good idea what happened here," Adam said.

"Let's hear it," Charlie replied.

"The victim was at a red light over there," Adam pointed to the far end of the intersection. "We got a thick skid mark, so I think when he saw his attacker point the gun, he burned rubber through the intersection just as the shooter fired. Shooter scores a hit, but not a clean one. We have a large concentration of scatter going into the dash, all diagonal-like, and blowing a hole in the windshield."

Zarah pointed to the passenger window of the car. "The passenger had her window open," she said. "The shooter jumped out of his vehicle, shoved the barrel into the open window, and when the driver took off it was deflected off-target."

"Right," Adam said. "So now the injured driver hauls ass through the intersection, right? And gets nailed by *that* car," Adam pointed to the Jetta, "which injures his passenger and alters his course into the gas station where he crashes into the pumps and passes out."

"And check this," Woodley said. "Witnesses say the shooter got back in his pickup, waited for a green light, crossed the

20

intersection, no rush, pulled next to the Mercedes, got out and pumped two more rounds into the driver, got back in and drove off."

"Okay," Charlie said, "but how does this connect to ours?"

Adam shrugged and looked at Pérez, who flipped open his notebook.

"He was wearing a long, brown, hooded robe, like some kind of monk," Pérez told him. "I got someone who says he may have been wearing body armor and thinks he saw a sidearm."

"Sounds like a man on the hunt to me," Zarah said.

Charlie thought for a moment and then nodded. "Okay," he said. "I'll buy that for a dollar."

"Some good news," Woodley said. "The passenger, Anita Nizamani, is banged up but alive, and what do you bet she tells us the driver of that Mercedes did some stupid shit before this went down?"

"Where'd the EMTs take her?" Zarah asked.

"Kaiser on Catalina and White Oak."

"Crap, she may be dead already," Zarah said. "Let's go."

As Zarah turned to head for the car, she found herself standing in front of a lanky, dark-haired Public Information Officer.

"Detective Wheeler," the P.I.O. said. "Carmen Sanchaz from Channel Six is asking to speak with you." He pointed to a pretty, Hispanic woman in a canary-colored blouse and blue jeans waving a notepad with a pen thrust into the spiral.

"I wouldn't have bothered you," the P.I.O. said, "but she said you know each other."

"I know her?"

"No," Charlie said. "And you don't want to, trust me. Let's go."

"Carmen?" Adam said. "She's okay."

Charlie, Woodley and Pérez fixed Adam with an incredulous stare.

"If your skin's thick enough," Adam added.

The detectives' stare became glassier. Adam cleared his throat and nodded to another group of detectives as if summoned, "… and if you're not a cop," he muttered quickly. "'Scuse me, guys." With that, Adam moseyed away toward a Devonshire division lieutenant.

"Anyway," the P.I.O. said to Zarah, "she told me you two had great rapport. I tried to help her, but she wants a detective."

Zarah scoffed. "Wow," she said.

That's something mother would've tried, right there.

Plotting, game-playing manipulators had maxed their credit with Zarah long before she had joined the LAPD. Her mother had spent it all decades ago, and of all the varied species of liars and schemers Zarah had confronted, on both sides of the prison bars, she loathed arrogant narcissists the most.

"We feel for ya, homie," Woodley told the P.I.O. "but you got played. Carmen hates cops every which way, so if you was thinking that helping her was gonna help you—"

"Fuck Carmen Sanchaz!" Charlie said.

"Well, yeah that's what I was—"

"Zarah," Charlie said, "we have a victim who's probably dying in Kaiser's waiting room! Let's go!"

Zarah nodded and the two of them started toward their car.

"What do I tell her?" the P.I.O. asked.

"Tell her to get her rapport somewhere else," Zarah said.

"Zarah!" the reporter shouted, "Hey, Zarah!"

Zarah stopped walking. *Did she just use my first name?*

"Come here," the reporter yelled. "I just want a minute!"

Did she just tell me what to do?

"Zarah," the reporter shouted, "over here!"

Zarah turned and advanced on the reporter like a batter who was hit by a wild pitch.

"Zarah, don't!" Charlie said, trying to keep up with her.

When Zarah was within a few yards, Carmen Sanchaz opened her notebook as if she were about to have pleasant discourse.

Wow.

When she reached her, the reporter opened her mouth to speak, but Zarah beat her to it.

"I don't know you," she said, thrusting a finger at the reporter's chest. "I mean, come on, you really expect that to work?"

Carmen Sanchaz's smile went from pleasant to crocodilian, and eyes that were warm and inviting turned fiendish. Zarah felt a chill, realizing that it *had* worked.

Charlie took Zarah's shoulder and tried to pull her away. She swept his hand off without taking her eyes off of the reporter. Instantly, she wished that she had not. She should have allowed Charlie to separate them, but she was committed.

"*Lo siento,*" Carmen said, sorry about nothing. "It's just…"

"*Just* what?" Zarah said.

"Well, I was *hoping* you'd be all like '*Have we met?*' And I'd be like, '*No, but it's really nice to meet you.*' And we'd make a little small talk and—"

The reporter spoke with a Latina dialect that Zarah was used to hearing from gangbanger *Lolitas* in East L.A., not what she expected from an educated broadcaster.

"Get to your point, Sanchaz," Charlie demanded.

"Come on, Charlie," Carmen said. "I mean fine, she's *un novata—*"

Zarah took an aggressive step toward the reporter. Charlie returned his hand to her shoulder with more force.

"Call me a rookie again!" Zarah dared, observing that with a slight widening of the eyes, a split-second lift of her eyebrow and a deepening of her insolent smirk, Carmen Sanchaz had mentally noted that Zarah understood Spanish.

"Charlie," the reporter said, "*you* know how this game is played."

"I know how you play it," Charlie replied.

"Well I had to try *something*, right? *You* at least know that, don't you?" Carmen pointed a finger at Zarah. "*She* looked like a nice person! I thought she'd be nice! *Perdóname*, I was wrong."

I am a nice person, Zarah thought. Zarah looked around and noticed that the drama had attracted attention. Onlookers, other police officers and other reporters were taking an interest.

Zarah took a calming breath. "Okay, you win. What do you want?"

"Whatever I want, I'll get from someone nice." Carmen raised her voice and addressed the cluster of detectives nearby. "I just need some info, no big deal. Anyone? Anybody *nice* here?"

Zarah burned with loathing for this woman, and the reporter knew it. It glittered in her eyes, daring Zarah to do something rash. Zarah snorted and bit down a curse.

"Zarah…" Charlie warned, as if he, too, thought Zarah might explode.

"Charlie," Carmen said, "I just wanna know if this murder was done by the same person who gunned down Jessica Devin on the fourteen-south last week? That's yours and Zarah's case, right?"

Zarah's nostrils flared, and her hands closed into fists.

Using my first name, again!

Charlie pulled Zarah back a half-step and stood between her and the reporter. Zarah glared sharp steel at Charlie, then at Carmen Sanchaz.

"Who the hell told you that, Carmen?" Charlie demanded.

"Okay," Carmen said. "I'm feeling a little ganged up on. I'm just doing my job, you're just doing yours. Let's start over, okay?"

Zarah heard Adam Jamison behind her. "You guys go," he said. "I'll talk to her."

"Ahh, Adam," Carmen said in a flirtatious, singsongy way that grated Zarah more. "Finally, someone nice."

"How on earth do *you two* know each other?" Zarah asked.

"Oooh, she's territorial, too." Carmen smiled and stroked Adam's arm. "Yes, we *know each other* pretty good, don't we, Adam?"

"All right, Carmen, you've had your fun," Adam said. He looked at Zarah and shook his head, dispelling Carmen's lie, and then placed a hand on the reporter's back. "Come this way, please."

"Seeya around, *Zarah*," the reporter said over her shoulder as she turned away, her arm around Adam's waist. She and Adam walked into the crowd of onlookers and were swallowed from sight.

"Well," Woodley said to Zarah, "the bell's gonna ring and I have to get to my locker for my pre-algebra shit, so..."

"Oh, shut up," Zarah said.

"Yeah, seeya in Glee Club." Woodley turned and walked away with Pérez next to him.

"Come on, Zarah," Charlie said. She and Charlie headed toward their car. Zarah took deep breaths and tried to calm herself.

"She ain't worth the skin off your knuckles," Charlie said.

"I know that," Zarah said, rounding on Charlie. "You, however..."

"Fuck did I do?" Charlie asked.

"I'm getting tired of you treating me as if I haven't been a cop for twenty years. You think I never had a civilian try to provoke me into a brutality case? I'm a professional, Charlie."

"A professional would have ignored the bitch," Charlie said. "You looked like you were about to go John Wayne, and I'm not gonna apologize for protecting my partner's job. Carmen Sanchaz is a biased, lying minion of the liberal media. One of the worst."

Zarah snapped, "I get it, Charlie. I've talked to reporters bef—"

"No, you don't get it, Zarah," Charlie said. "She *wanted* that scene. Take my advice and stay out of her orbit. And if you *have* to deal with her, learn from today and *don't* let her rile you like that again."

"Okay, okay," Zarah said, giving him a comforting rub on his back. "Point taken, lesson learned. It's just, people like that..."

"I hear ya," Charlie said. "But, you know, you're..."

"...a Homicide Special Detective," she repeated the mantra Charlie was so fond of chanting at her. "I hear you."

"Okay, then."

As they drove, she calmed herself, adjusted her attitude and refocused her thoughts to business. Carmen Sanchaz would never provoke her again, but if the reporter was indeed going to follow the case, the sooner it was closed the better.

8

ONE OF ANITA Nizamani's brown eyes was swollen shut, and a large laceration had been stitched below the socket. The hospital room was freezing, and though several blankets were tucked beneath her arms, she shivered.

"Hello Anita," Zarah said, smiling, "I'm Detective Wheeler; this is Detective Slocum. We're from LAPD Robbery-Homicide."

"Zarah?" Anita rasped. "Is that Syrian?"

"Saudi," Zarah said.

"They still let you carry a gun?" the girl joked.

She was in obvious pain, trying to put on a brave face, but no drug would erase the traumatic memory. After she related what had happened, it came as no surprise to Zarah that Adam Jamison's theoretical scenario was on the mark as was Woodley's assumption that the driver of the Mercedes had provoked the killer.

She did not have much to offer except that her attacker was a slim, athletic Caucasian, wore sunglasses, "like Elvis," and black leather gloves. Zarah and Charlie's murder book was still as thin as it was the week before, but there was no doubt that Jessica Devin, Ari Farhad and Anita Nizamani were all attacked by the Street Sweeper.

9

D RAKE BARRET MITCHELL popped the top off a can
of green beans and tossed the lid into the garbage as he
made his way from his kitchen to his living area, drinking the beans from the can as if it was beer.

His kept his living quarters so Spartan, Lycurgus himself
would have been proud. He did not have flatware or cutlery. He
had no furnishings, except for a flattened futon cushion and one
pillow. He had no décor, no landline, no luxuries. Most of his food
was pre-cooked, came out of a can or a bag, and he drank nothing
but tap water.

People who made food more than sustenance were the reason
thirty-three percent of civilians were overweight and why thirty-five
percent were obese. Those people were weak. Not him.

Drake always kept his blinds shut behind thick, black curtains. Night had fallen outside, but day or night his habitat was
dark. What lights he had were dim. Most of the illumination he
drew upon came from the TV and various electric devices.

When he was at home, there was never a moment when he was
not on the lookout for trouble. Along with the security cameras
he had installed on his front porch for all to see, he had hidden
tiny, wireless surveillance cameras around his street. They peered
at his neighbors' homes, their front porches and back yards. They

surreptitiously watched all comings and goings from the branches of trees, under storm drains, on rooftops and street lamps.

They all transmitted through a triple-encrypted router and into a six-monitor hub which rotated images from every camera he had installed. It had cost thousands and had taken a year to set up without being noticed, but his vigilance did not end there.

He had also installed motion sensors around the perimeter of his small house and sensors on his doors and windows. If an intruder was about, an alarm would sound, but it would not relay a distress call to any private security firms or police. Drake had his own, hands-on, protocol for dealing with intruders.

He sat on his hard, wood floor and watched the local news. A sexy, Mexican reporter on channel six had made the connection between his two kills. It appeared that Carmen Sanchaz was the one smart reporter on TV. She had reported that though the cops were not dismissing the notion that the two kills might have been done by the same perpetrator, they had no evidence to link them.

When he had made his first kill, it had been in the wee hours. The highway had been empty. He had plenty of time to write down what he wanted to say. The second time, too many witnesses had been on the street watching, and this was not North Korea. In America, anyone could have been armed, and he had no way of knowing who might have drawn a bead on him and escalated things.

Next time, he would mark his target and do them in their homes or a venue where there was less danger of being seen or challenged. He would kill quietly and give himself more time, but the message would be loud and clear. The Street Sweeper was for real.

10

THE DANZAN JUJITSU Dojo was Zarah's home away from home. The floor of the room was covered with blue folding mats, and the crown was trimmed with Japanese kanji and the names of fighting techniques in English beneath them. Next to the large, sliding-glass door leading to the park outside was a portrait of the founder of Danzan Jujitsu, a sturdy Japanese man named Henry.

The space was also used by the parks-and-rec, after-school daycare program, and amidst photos of men and women in martial arts attire, throwing each other, placing each other in chokeholds and joint-locks, their faces frozen in powerful shouts or taut with pain, there were crayon drawings of rainbows, butterflies, fire trucks and airplanes.

It was after hours, and the dojo was empty except for Zarah and her friend Sebastian. Zarah had managed to have a good class, but in the back of her mind, the day's events, and Carmen Sanchaz, were foremost on her mind. While she practiced freestyle ground-fighting with Sebastian, she tried to focus, but her thoughts kept returning to the Street Sweeper's victims and that smart-aleck reporter.

Why is it on me to be polite all the time? She was WAY out of line! I am nice! Ask anyone! Just don't ask my mother. She likes playing the vic—

"Jesus Christ, *MA-TE!*" Sebastian hollered.

Zarah snapped out of her trance and slackened the reverse shoulder lock she had managed to clamp onto Sebastian.

The pair lay flat on the blue mats. Sebastian was on top of her. She had twisted his arm near the back of his head and had locked him in her guard. She enjoyed having her legs wrapped around him, holding him close, imagining that he had not been trying to escape.

"You almost popped my shoulder!" Sebastian said.

Zarah released him, sat up and proceeded to rub his sore shoulder. Any excuse to stroke him was good on her. Sebastian was six feet tall with thick, dun-colored hair. His eyes were warm, deep, tawny pools of *Sebastian.* His body was rock hard and muscular.

It surprised her to find that she had put him in a submission. He was powerful and precise. He did not recognize her gender as weak or in need of special treatment in practice, so he was not as careful with her as the other men in the dojo. He used his strength, forced her to be crafty, decisive. If she gave too much away or did not seize opportunities, the consequences would be painful.

Her mind had been nowhere near the match. She kept visualizing autopsy photos and hearing Carmen Sanchaz's snarky, cat-purry, Julie-Newmar-from-the-barrio voice. She had not felt herself applying the submission, and she did not hear Sebastian submit until he was bellowing like a branded bull.

"Sorry about that," Zarah said.

"What's up with you?" Sebastian asked.

"Nothing," Zarah said.

"Just tell me."

"I'm telling you. Nothing."

"So you're preoccupied with nothing?"

Zarah put the squeeze on his shoulder as if she was trying to juice it, and her voice took a sharp edge. "Sebastian…" she warned.

"Okay. Letting it go."

Zarah eased off on the juicing. She understood his frustration, but she had to keep *some* distance. She had fallen far enough for him when he was single. Now that he was married, all she wanted was to climb out and regain her balance. It was an uphill battle that he kept steepening by being such a good man.

Besides, if Zarah wanted to talk about her day, she would go to some cop bar downtown, not all the way to Burbank to work out her anger and try to forget it all for a few hours.

"Anyway, don't feel bad," Sebastian said. "I didn't see it coming. It was a damn good move."

Zarah noticed how sweaty she was. Her ponytail was a mess.

"You wanna go again?" he asked.

"You bet." She wanted him to take her to the floor again just so she could squirm underneath him and pretend. She knew it turned him on, too. His heavy canvas gi may have been sturdy, but the material was thin and he did not wear a cup. She knew.

The glass door opened, and Sebastian's wife, Corinna, strode through with a pleasant bounce—the happy gait of a woman who had it all. When she saw Zarah and Sebastian sitting alone on the mat together, Zarah lovingly massaging his shoulder, she never blinked.

Why should she? She's got the ring.

Corinna was five-foot-nine, with some kind magical, Celtic beauty somewhere in her ancestry that Zarah wished had remained in Europe, or would at least go back there and give a Saracen girl a chance.

Her eyes were a dark, rich indigo that Zarah would have liked to pop out and use as beads. Her auburn hair had such tight, graceful curls it looked as if they had been spun by fairies. Her skin was the kind of creamy-fair that could turn Snow White green, and she had the body a woman who had a gym membership, and used it.

"Hey, guys," she said. Then she pointed to Zarah's hands on his shoulder. "What happened there?" she asked.

"Zarah snuck in an *ude garami* when I wasn't looking, that's all," Sebastian told her.

"Ahh," Corinna said. She had no idea what an *ude garami* was. Sebastian had a habit of using terminology his wife could not understand in an effort to make her curious enough to ask, or, Lord forbid, take a class. Mercifully, she never had.

"Well, right on, Z.," Corinna said. "He can use a good ass kicking. Good thing you're around."

I get it already. You trust me with your husband!

"You should join us," Zarah said. *Please say no,* she thought.

"Nah," Corinna said. "Wrestling's just not my thing."

"It's not wrestling," Sebastian said as though he was tired of saying it. "The *samurai* used Jujitsu for God's sake."

"Okay, okay" Corinna said, pulling him to his feet and kissing him. "My samurai." Another kiss. "You're so macho."

Zarah looked up at them. She wished Corinna was the one slumped over on the mat, watching hopelessly as Zarah smothered Sebastian with kisses. But Zarah had made her decision about him as soon as Corinna had loped into Sebastian's life, and she lived with it. Sebastian was a rare find indeed, but he was a meat-and-potatoes, man's man who liked his women stunning and submissive.

Zarah Wheeler was no effete damsel, nor would she allow herself to come under the thrall of a man, no matter how good he was to her, or how great his shoulders were, or how much she wanted to be his.

Never again!

Sebastian's wife looked deep into his eyes, as if Zarah was not even there. Zarah jumped to her feet, producing a loud *thud* on the mats, giving Corinna a start and snapping her out of it.

"Well," Corinna said to her husband, catching her breath, "are you about ready to go?"

"Zarah and I were gonna have one more match, actually."

"Oh," Corinna said. "Okay, well…the kids are still with…I'll just go get them and come back."

"It's okay, Corinna," Zarah said.

"No, no," Corinna replied. "I can grab something to eat with them and come back in, say, a half hour?"

Zarah wanted a reason to hate her, to punch the niceness out of her. She had what Zarah wanted, and that was all Zarah had on her. It was impossible to produce ill will against such an affable person.

Had Sebastian been out of the equation, they could have been close friends, but he was in it, and they both knew the score. Sebastian was Zarah's *one that got away.* Zarah knew that Corinna knew it, and Corinna knew that Zarah knew that she knew it. But Zarah had a rule about married men.

She knew the emotional wreckage that such a caliber of betrayal inflicted. She had been there; was *still* there. She would never subject it to another woman, especially one she admired. Zarah had her chance with Sebastian and took too much time to get real about her feelings. Her mistake.

No! You take your time, Zarah! Take all the time you need! You're not easy and you don't have to be! His rush, HIS mistake!

"Nah," Zarah said. "I have stuff to take care of downtown."

It was not a lie. Zarah did not want to go home and sit alone with nothing to do but bake in the heat, regretting past indecision and drinking rum until she passed out. And it would not hurt to work under the vents of Parker Center's free AC or have her case notes memorized.

Sebastian and Zarah went into the rec center's supply closet, which served as the dojo's locker room. They both removed their black belts, folded them neatly and put them in their gym bags.

"I'm gonna get you back for that shoulder lock," Sebastian said.

Zarah laughed, and peeled off her gi jacket. Sebastian's eyes slid down the sweaty, clinging neckline of her black, tank top and returned to her face in just below light speed before he turned his gaze to his wife through the open door.

Zarah pretended not notice and stuffed the jacket into her bag. *Ha! No salted caramel for you! Enjoy your vanilla, sucker!*

"You're cute," Zarah said.

They exited the locker room and walked toward Corinna.

"You made me tap once," Sebastian said. "Don't get a big head about it."

"I confess, I don't remember how I did it," Zarah said.

"Ah, you know what that is? That's *mushin.*"

"Mushin," Corinna mused. "I don't think I've heard that one."

"It means *'no mind',*" Sebastian explained. "It's when you've become so good at something it becomes automatic. Like when you're driving and someone in front of you suddenly stops, and you hit the brakes. You don't *think* about hitting the brakes. It just happens."

Zarah escorted Sebastian and his wife to the door. "That reminds me," she said. "Be polite driving home."

"Okay," Sebastian said. "How come?"

"There's a psycho at large who takes traffic laws and road etiquette very personal—two dead and one in ICU so far. So no talking on your cell, no cutting people off, no middle fingers..."

"That'll be hard," Corinna said, "cause I've become so good at that. Someone irritates me and..." she flourished her middle finger. "Mushin, right?"

Sebastian smiled and nodded while Zarah snickered, gave a knowing look at Sebastian, and thumbed at Corinna.

"Don't worry," Sebastian said. "Our birds will stay in the nest."

"Thank you," Zarah said.

Sebastian and his wife took their leave and left Zarah alone in the empty dojo. Zarah looked for her car keys inside her bag. She would go home, shower, head downtown and work alone. Then she would return home and sleep alone.

Zarah's soulmate and his wife were pulling away from the curb outside when Zarah realized that the mats under her bare feet still needed to be folded up and put away. The dojo needed to be locked up and the keys returned to the park office inside the main gymnasium. She would have to do all of that alone too.

Her phone rang inside her gym bag. She cursed when she saw Lieutenant Torres's number on the caller I.D. Another crime scene demanded her attention, and she felt in her bones that it was the Street Sweeper again.

THE PICKUP TRUCK used in the Ari Farhad murder had been reported stolen an hour before the crime. The Street Sweeper had abandoned it across from the Devonshire Community Police Station with all four doors left open—close enough to pique the curiosity of officers starting their patrols, but far enough away to avoid being caught on the station's security cameras.

January was passing the baton to February in a couple days, but the winter night air, which should have been downright frigid, was comfortably cool, bordering on lukewarm. Zarah had come straight from the dojo and had changed from her gi into what she had in her gym bag—wrinkled black denim jeans and her sneakers. She was still sweating from the workout, and as she exited her car, steam wisped from her hot skin as if she had come from the shower room.

She felt sticky and drained. Her hair was tied back in a greasy, kinked ponytail. Her heavy, golden LAPD shield dangled over her breasts, which were being accentuated by a tight, off-white, V-neck t-shirt with a blue outline of the state of Illinois with bold type that said, *License to IL.*

She had forgotten her work-jacket at home, and though it was unprofessional, enduring the male cops fondling her bosoms with their eyeballs while pretending to be reading her badge number was cheaper than the gas it would have cost to fetch it.

Charlie walked over to her, wearing a grey suit and a drab, grey-blue tie. Zarah expected a playful dig about her appearance, but he made no mention. In his hand was a plastic evidence bag with a sheet of yellow paper sealed within.

"The bastard wanted us to find this," he said, thrusting the evidence at Zarah. "It was on the driver's seat."

She took it and turned the small LED flashlight from her keychain onto it. It read:

Listen up Police!

YES! I KILLED the cellphone bitch in the Acura, and you KNOW WHY!!

YES!! I KILLED the Arab prick in his Mercedes, because he sped up behind me, WEAVED into the right lane WITHOUT SIGNALING and CUT ME OFF!!!

These assholes violated traffic laws that take NO EFFORT TO OBEY while demonstrating INTOLERABLE RUDENESS!! I will not hesitate to waste a driver who doesn't belong behind the wheel and I'm just getting started!! I don't care who is with them!! THEY WILL DIE TOO!! The girl in the Mercedes got LUCKY!!

Spread the word!! The rules of the road exist for the public's safety, now more than ever and POLITENESS COUNTS!!!
I am always Oscar Mike, always locked and loaded!!

THE STREET SWEEPER

Zarah gave a heavy sigh, handed the evidence back and rubbed her temples. "Don't tell me I came all the way down here just to read a rant I could've read tomorrow," she said. "I'm exhausted."

"There's a clue to who he is there," Charlie said. "Who he *isn't* is Jessica Devin's boyfriend, Scott. Talked to the girl's brother, he put me in touch with the gent himself, Scott Cattrall. He actually dumped her over the phone the day she was killed."

"Over the phone?" Zarah said. "Chivalry lives."

"Well, he was with another girl the whole night of Jessica's murder. I spoke to her. She alibied him. He's clear, so we can cut loose of that thread."

"So what are we thinking as far as who this guy actually is?" Zarah asked.

"This here," Charlie said, pointing to the note. "*'Oscar Mike'*. He's using the NATO Phonetic Alphabet—O and M. It means *'on the move.'* And that means he's probably military, maybe some P.T.S.D.ing, section-eight psycho or just some wanna be weekend warrior type."

"Well," Zarah said, "whichever it is, he's not concerned about us. Look where he left this."

"Under our noses," Charlie said. "Real dumb or real trouble."

Zarah suspected the latter. The Street Sweeper wrote like a man with a thought-out motive, and Zarah could not help but understand it. Zarah would have loved to chase down some speeding, lane-weaving jerk, but she knew there was no cure for fools.

People did not understand how unsafe they were. Even inside a suit of armor with wheels, moving at fifty miles per hour, actions still had consequences. It was too easy to cross the unseen lines drawn by perfect strangers who were capable of anything.

Zarah was no saint behind the wheel, and the knowledge that this Street Sweeper was out there—a man who could have been anybody—on the streets, looking for someone to do the wrong thing… It made Zarah's stomach flutter and it was a matter of time before this story hit the airwaves, raised a stink, and started a panic.

"Do you think the bosses will take this to the media?" Zarah asked. "That would make the killer happy; get his message out."

"Carmen Sanchaz put it together already," Charlie answered. "I'm surprised she's not on the air calling this a series already. But she knows it, and she'll run her mouth about it soon enough. If I could legally stop her, I would."

"Really?" Zarah said. "How come?"

"His *message* is *'do what I want or I'll kill you.'* We're supposed to think he's driven by some moral principle, but he's just a loser who wants attention." Charlie shook his head, thinking something bitter to himself. His face began to get a reddish glow that Zarah saw when something had brought his blood to a boil. "You know," he said, "I *hate* serial killers!"

Zarah knew. It was a well-known fact among detectives in H.S.S. Every murder that showed a hint of series potential produced volcanic anger in Charlie, and Zarah sensed an eruption coming.

"Here's a little prick with a monk's robe and some shades trying to be all scary," Charlie said. "His balls were cut off—maybe by his mommy, right? Or his boss, or his wife! Maybe the cool kids kicked his ass in high school, or the sexy redheaded cheerleader laughed at his pathetic love letters before wiping her ass with them! Now he wants to feel strong! No way do I give him the satisfaction!"

"Yeah, but if we tell people, tell them what his deal is, they'd be more careful. Wouldn't they?"

"Zarah, if by some miracle everyone in L.A. stopped acting like dicks on the road, he'd find some other reason. No way is this guy gonna thump his chest and make us all quiver like cunts."

Zarah gasped and jabbed Charlie in the shoulder, then she fixed him with a freezing glare and waited for an apology.

"Sorry," he said. "I forgot you're a classy lady." He gestured to her shirt. "But then, you *are* dressed like you're on a john-sting."

"I *came* here from the *dojo*," she said, slugging his shoulder two more times for emphasis.

Several yards behind Charlie, she spied Adam Jamison leaning into the stolen truck, wearing a pair of glasses with orange lenses and shining a green beam of light from a forensic laser system on to the steering wheel, dash and windshield— a cursory scan for latent prints and other trace evidence.

Zarah thought of Sebastian walking out of the dojo arm-in-arm with Corinna and leaving her to put the mats away by herself. Then she thought of the bottle of Bacardi 151 at home and knew what her plans were after she was done having her time wasted here. She could transcribe her current case notes tomorrow.

Woodley and Pérez stepped up to Charlie and her. They looked dejected and every bit as frustrated as she and Charlie were.

"I take it you guys have the same amount of nothing to tell Torres about yours that we have about ours?" Charlie said.

"Yup," Pérez said, "Security cameras from the AM/PM got us a hooded monk poppin' his shotgun into Ari Farhad's face. Witness statements say as much as the video."

"Dude with a *muhfuckin'* monk robe and a shotty," Woodley added.

"You have *something* to tell him," Zarah said.

"What's that, Wheeler," Pérez snarked.

"The Street Sweeper showed some tradecraft on the video," Zarah said. "He wore something that would draw people's attention to the outfit, not him. Like when John Gotti had Paul Castellano killed— his hit crew wore long coats and Cossack-style hats. It's all anyone noticed, right?"

Out of the corner of her eye, Zarah noticed Adam Jamison walking their way. "No faces, no height, no eye color," Zarah continued as she smoothed her hair, hoping she did not look as yucky as she felt. "Just coats, hats and guns."

"Well," Adam said as he approached the four detectives, "we have some prints, but no other trace that this could find." He raised the boxy hand piece of his portable forensic laser system.

"A man in a monk's robe is all we got," Pérez said.

"It's a Jedi robe, actually," Adam said.

"A *what*?" Pérez asked.

"Adam," Zarah greeted him. For some reason she felt heavier.

"Detective Wheeler," Adam returned her greeting, and then addressed Pérez. "A Jedi robe. I spotted it on the video."

"You spotted that right away, I bet." Pérez said, grinning.

"Right?" Woodley chuckled. "You wear that instead of a lab coat back at USC. Admit it."

Adam nodded and smiled, taking the ribbing in good humor. Zarah was not privy to the joke, and all she could do was watch from the outside in lonely frustration.

"At least I don't dress like I'm about to drop off Miss Daisy," Adam fired back at Woodley, drawing more chuckles.

"Seriously, though," Pérez said. "Do you think there's a reason the Street Sweeper's dressing up like Obi Wan Kenobi?"

"Zarah just explained why," Charlie said.

"Or because it's cheaper than the Boba Fett costume," Woodley joked, drawing chuckles from everyone but Zarah.

"Good grief," Zarah said, "What are you all talking about?"

"You don't know who Obi Wan Kenobi is?" Adam asked her.

"I've heard the name before," she said, her brain scrambling to find the most likely explanation. "He's a Buddhist Lama or something."

Woodley, Pérez and Adam all looked stunned, and then broke down in laughter. Charlie patted her on the shoulder in a sympathetic, condescending way that made her hackles rise.

"Screw you guys!" Zarah said. "Who is he?"

"That was a good call about the monk robe," Woodley said, "but now I gotta question your chops for detective work."

"Hey," Charlie stepped in, "Obi Wan didn't pass his Detective's Exam in the top two percent. He's a pussy next to Zarah, and so are you, Woodley."

"Great," Zarah said, "now I feel bad about punching you."

"Haven't you seen 'Star Wars'?" Adam asked Zarah as if he were asking if she had ever kissed a boy.

She shook her head. Zarah's mother had forbade her from seeing "Star Wars"— something about *sand people* had rubbed her wrong.

"Why not?" Adam asked.

Zarah shrugged. "I lived in Riyadh," she said, remembering her last day there—her father showing up at her school, out of the blue, taking her out of class. She remembered boarding the Lufthansa airplane that brought her to Chicago the same day, never to see her mother or her Saudi side of the family again. "Outside the West," she continued, "Star Wars isn't such a big deal."

"Infidels," Pérez quipped. Zarah gave him an irritated huff and shook her head.

"Wanna hang out sometime?" Adam said. "Come over and watch them?"

Zarah double-took. She felt a blush come over her and a fluttering in her belly. She visualized Sebastian leaving the dojo.

Say something! Everyone's looking at you!

She cleared her throat. "Really?" was all she could manage.

"You *can't* live your whole life without seeing it," Adam said.

"Man has a point," Charlie said.

"Really," Zarah said again, tucking her hands beneath her elbows. "I mean… What's the big deal?"

"No big deal," Adam said. "I just never met anyone who hasn't seen it. I'd love to watch you react. It might be fun is all."

"So," she paused, thinking. "You wanna watch me watch a movie? That's a normal date for you?"

Adam's posture straightened. He made an alarmed face as if he had felt something strange crawl up his back, and froze to avoid being bitten by whatever it was. Zarah realized her misunderstanding and fumbled to correct herself.

"By date I don't mean *date,* date," Zarah said. "I mean…"

"Yeah, no," Adam said, his cheeks starting to glow. "I mean a *normal* date is like coffee…"

"Then the *second* date you watch me watch 'Star Wars'… if the coffee date goes well."

"Right," Adam said.

"Adam," Pérez said, "there are less tedious ways to get oral."

Zarah gasped and slammed Pérez in a nerve cluster below his shoulder with a merciless knuckle-punch.

"Holy, shit!" Pérez said as he hunched over, grabbed his shoulder and paced, trying to walk the pain off or rub it away while the other two detectives laughed. "Christ alive, that fuckin' hurt!"

"You earned that, you pig!" Zarah said. "Between you and Charlie, I got chauvinism in stereo!"

"Fuck did I do?" Charlie asked.

"I'm pressing fuckin' charges!" Pérez said.

"See, now I really want a *date* date," Adam said.

Zarah looked up past Adam, at the sky. "Adam…um…"

'Yes', dummy! Say it! Not even 'yes'! Say 'sure'!

Her vocal cords refused to make the sound. She shook her head.

"Nice try, CSI guy," Woodley said, earning a dirty look from Zarah.

"Alright, well…" Adam said as he turned and moped away towards his SUV. Zarah felt a knot in her stomach.

"Maybe," Zarah said, too quiet for Adam to hear. "Sometime…"

Adam continued to his car without turning around.

Zarah's embarrassment must have showed. The detectives stood around awkwardly.

"The way you look at him," Charlie said, "I'm surprised you're not both getting in his car to go watch 'Star Wars' right now."

Zarah knew what was next. Woodley and Pérez would spread the word about that little scene like Nutella.

"I *did not* say 'no' to him," Zarah told the two detectives. "If someone besides you two talks to me about this, *you* will *pay*."

"Zarah, I'm sorry," Pérez said. "I was just fuckin' with him."

"Fine," Zarah said. "Now if we're done here, I have a bottle of rum that's been waiting for some oral since I got the call-out."

Charlie guffawed.

Zarah headed to her car, thinking about Sebastian. Wasn't it time to let go? It was not as if fantasizing about him all the time was taking her self-esteem to a healthy place.

"Wait," Woodley said. "If Pérez knew how to shut his face, would Adam have *actually* picked you up with *Star Wars?*"

"Goodnight, Woodley."

As Zarah walked away, she heard Woodley mutter, "Mm, mm, mm. That boy's my *muhfuckin'* hero."

12

CAROL STEIN WAS on the road with nothing but errands to run. She and her husband, Karl, were throwing the first Superbowl party to be thrown in their home. It was The Panthers vs The Broncos and neither she, who couldn't care less about football, nor her husband, an L.A. native, had a stake in the outcome. Still, anything less than the best experience for their guests was out of the question.

First she had bought new cookware. She had cookware already, but it was old, well used, and her girlfriends, who were mostly the wives of Karl's friends, would be helping with the cooking. Everything had to be perfect, as if Giada De Laurentiis was taping a show in Carol's kitchen. By the time she returned to Studio City she was exhausted, and she still needed groceries.

On most days, Carol would have participated in a mud run before stepping through the doors of a common Ralph's supermarket. But, it was closer to home, and she had already spent enough to make Karl blow his stack. She may as well make an effort to appear to be making frugal decisions.

The whole experience made her swear off Ralph's forever. First, there was a perfect parking spot right near the door, but she could not get in because some loser was putting groceries in his back seat and his car door blocked the parking space.

She honked her horn and yelled, "Come on, move it!"

He ignored her and continued loading groceries.

"Jerk," she said.

He smiled at her and moved even slower. There was a line of cars behind her with no way around her SUV, and this creep was going to make them all wait. Someone honked. She pretended not to hear.

Don't blame me. This idiot is blocking my space.

It seemed like an eternity before he closed his door and pushed his cart back to the line of carts near the entrance. Moron. They had *people* for that sort of thing.

When she had finally pulled into her spot, other shoppers gave her looks as they passed. She ignored them.

Ralph's was crowded, and they just *had* to put displays smack in the middle of the aisles so there was no room to maneuver. The checkout lines were long, the supermarket was understaffed, and the old lady ahead of her complained and did an item-by-item audit of her receipt.

After the cheap hag's problem was resolved, the bag-boy that was there took his break and was relieved by a retard whose top speeds were *slow* and *stop*. When she exited the supermarket, she felt as if she had been freed from a labor camp.

When she drove up the hill, into the Bird Streets, she called the nanny and ordered her to have Carol's two children prepared to unload her SUV. When she arrived, Carol popped the hatch-back, opened the doors, and the kids and the nanny got to work as she went inside.

When everything was in the house, she and the kids put all of her new cookware away. When she saw that the boxes were too numerous for her garbage cans, she squirreled them someplace out of sight so that it would appear to her friends that the beautiful new cooking tools had always been there. The old stuff was tossed into garbage cans.

Then it was time to whip up the marinades, prepare the meats and spices, and have everything ready to be made into delicious masterpieces. She and her girlfriends would only have to mix and cook while the men enjoyed their sport.

Carol loved that part—traditional wife and mother. When the whole thing was over, Karl would not care what the cost had been because she had played her part to a T. Nobility did not penny-pinch. But, to be safe, her receipts found their way into the garbage.

After many hours, the stage was set. Carol could relax. Karl came home knowing that his wife would be tired and frazzled, and he had brought home a pizza. Bless him.

It was a pleasant evening. She took a long bath before she went to bed, and it did not take her long to fall to sleep.

She did not know how long she had slept before something startled her from her slumber. She sat bolt upright. She could not put her finger on exactly what had caused it. She had sensed something, heard something. Was it a *thump?* Since the Northridge quake in '94, any small vibration in the house was enough to give her a start. Carol stayed still, trying to hear any rumbling or feel any shaking.

She thought she heard a voice—a grunt? She looked beside her and saw that Karl was not in bed. She looked at the clock. It was 1:00 am.

"Karl?" she called.

The house stilled and took on a disquieting quietness, as if the air itself had stopped breathing. Carol strained to hear anything. A shadow swept across the wall of the hallway outside.

"Karl, what's the matter?"

A hooded figure darkened her bedroom doorway.

13

CARMEN SANCHAZ HAD lived in Southern California her whole life and could not remember when it had been this hot in February. The day before, the Santa Ana winds had blown so torrid and strong, and because the past month had been so sweltering and dry, the foothills of Santa Clarita had spontaneously combusted and were now blazing like Hell on Earth.

It was nothing new, but it created spectacular drama: soot and flames, homes threatened and destroyed, sexy firemen in heroic, single-file attack lines blasting immense, overwhelming infernos with torrents of water, planes and helicopters bombing the burning hillsides with blood-red chemical retardant, hotshots and smokejumpers risking their lives, tears and tragedy. It was *great* television.

As soon as the alarm was raised, everyone working inside the Channel Six Network News studio had exploded into action, except for Carmen Sanchaz. She sat at a black, metal desk inside a small cubicle, trying to ignore the beehive of frantic energy swarming around her, trying not to be swept into it. As much as she wanted to get out there and work the disaster, she had committed herself to the Street Sweeper story.

Giant, out-of-control fires was a hard story to compete with, but if it bleeds, it leads. Carmen wanted to be ready to jump when the Street Sweeper dropped the next body. If the killer struck sooner rather than later, Carmen would have the story to herself.

Adam Jamison had made her a promise at the Ari Farhad crime scene to keep her informed. She thought back on that scene, the mangled cars, the brazen violence… and that haughty Arab detective.

Carmen was not a violent girl anymore. She no longer needed it. But *Zarah* was going to learn what being on the wrong side of *"Ojos Mariposa"* felt like.

Her smart-phone chimed. It was a text.

Adam: Hi Butterfly. Check your e-mail.

Sure enough, her phone chimed again and notified her of a message in her inbox. She opened it. It was a scanned image, another note to the cops from the Street Sweeper, with a caption by Adam explaining the circumstances under which the police found it. Carmen shook her head. Did this *loco* truly care if people were breaking traffic laws, being rude, or was it just a lame excuse? *Whatever.*

He did not have a prayer of changing anything, but his mission statement made sense. Even Gandhi would have wished death on some of the jackasses on the road if he had not walked everywhere.

L.A. had never been the hunting ground of a serial killer with a social angle, except in the movies. His name, though: *The Street Sweeper?* If he wanted to be taken seriously, his *nom deguerre* needed to invoke a more intimidating image than a municipal employee. There was no way Carmen Sanchaz was going to cover a maniac with a boring handle like *The Street Sweeper.*

What do I call him, then?

She looked at the image of the note Adam had sent to her on her smart-phone and saw something.

That's it!

She smiled, pressed her thumb and forefinger over the Street

Sweeper's new moniker, pulled them apart and enlarged it on her phone's screen:

Oscar Mike

Gary trotted up to Carmen wearing a yellow poncho. Lamar followed, eating a Hot Pocket with one hand and holding a camera the size of a Minigun in the other.

"They're evacuating homes in Canyon Country," Gary spoke fast, his eyes bright. He smiled at Carmen. "Daniels just told us if we get there quick we may have a shot at a live report tonight."

Carmen sighed and shook her head. She had explained to their boss that The Street Sweeper had killed two people, back-to-back, and she wanted to consult with her source in the crime lab and keep her crew available and ready on the chance that the killer would strike again soon. Daniels had nodded his head. He had told her "Okay".

Whatever...

Carmen held up her phone and showed Gary the image Adam had sent. Gary took the phone and squinted at the little screen.

"A new note," Carmen said. "He left it outside a police station."

"The Street Sweeper?" Lamar asked.

"Oscar Mike," Carmen said. "It's Oscar Mike now."

"*Oscar Mike.* I like that," Gary said. "Yours?"

Carmen nodded. "Well, technically his, but *sí.*"

"Nice," Gary said. "So, he *did* kill both those people."

"And he's gonna kill someone again. And I wanna be on *that* story, not in Canyon Country asking some stubborn, soot-covered *vieja* why she won't evacuate with the smart people! I told Daniels!"

"Okay, okay," Gary said, pulling his poncho off over his head. "Let's hope you're right again. Otherwise Daniels is—"

"*Papi?*"

"Hmm?"

"Why did you put on a poncho? It's a fire, not a rainstorm."

"Yeah, but if we'd gotten close to the action, the fire hoses and planes dropping stuff...never mind." Gary rolled the poncho under his arm and cleared his throat.

"You should be Geraldo's producer," Lamar told him. "He loves being in the middle of natural disasters and shit."

"He just wants people to be all like, '*Wow, he's brave.*'" Carmen snipped. "*Pendejo egoísta!* Always trying to *be* the story."

"Bitch," Lamar said, "you'd dance naked in a hurricane if you thought it'd get you closer to the main studio."

"That's not true! I'd never make the story about me!"

"You trying to say that you *never* showboated?" Gary asked.

"Trying? No, *papi.* I'm saying it. I never..."

Gary was looking her straight in the eye with a smug grin. She was busted. She could not remember when or how, but he had something.

"Okay," Carmen said, her cheeks flushing, "but—"

"You've done it before, and you'll do it again," Gary said.

"I'd...keep my clothes on."

Lamar chortled as Gary nudged Carmen's shoulder with a good-natured but still annoying victory-smirk on his face.

"*Cabron,*" she muttered.

Carmen's phone rang. She withdrew it from her pocket and answered, "*Hola?*"

Carmen listened for a voice on the other end. When the caller announced himself, she froze. She felt her heart pulsing against the inside of her rib cage. Her neck muscles tightened, and she stared straight ahead, stunned. Gary and Lamar's joviality was snuffed, and they gathered around her.

"Who is it?" Gary whispered.

Carmen waved her hand for Gary to be silent.

"Oh yeah?" Carmen said to the caller. "H—How do I know you're really him?"

14

ZARAH WOKE UP to a sunny morning and a ringing telephone. Her head felt as if it might split open; she had too much to drink the night before.

At first, she had done a few shots of rum to get to sleep, and it worked better than any over-the-counter drug had. Now she was waking up hung over every other morning. Zarah told herself that she had better rope it in before she became an alcoholic.

She opened her eyes and groped for the phone on her end table. She could not reach it. She groaned and pushed herself up. Her hair felt heavy. Her skin was tacky, and she smelled of fermented perspiration. She had not showered or changed her clothes from the night before. She felt as if she had slept in a landfill.

She answered the phone and tried not to sound drowsy. It was Lt. Torres. The Street Sweeper had struck again.

"This one's bad," Torres said.

"Text me the address."

When she was off the phone, Zarah took a shower and scrubbed the night before off. She wanted to look pretty enough to make up for last night, but tough and professional enough to be taken seriously. She put on a peach colored blouse with black slacks and a black blazer and kept her makeup simple. She would burn in the heat, but her presence would radiate authority.

On the better-than-average chance her colleagues had inhaled a sour whiff of her primal, off-duty scent last night, she rubbed a couple dabs of perfume onto her wrists so that when she wafted past, they would receive a tang of cleanliness packed with spices, rose, myrrh, cedar, sandalwood, cloves and plum.

She was still a razor. To reinforce that image, she holstered her service weapon, a Model 34 Glock, onto her belt rather than inside her jacket. Zarah checked the clip, slapped it into the magazine well and yanked back the slide, chambering a round. She made sure the safety was engaged and then shoved it into its holster. She attached her shield next to it. She may have been a mess of sweat and rum from the night before, but now Detective Zarah Wheeler was clean and sharp.

When she arrived at the crime scene in Studio City, Charlie was waiting for her on the landing of some brick-lined stairs.

"You smell good," Charlie said as they walked up.

Zarah grinned and thanked him.

The crime scene was a beautifully kept, ranch-style home. The stairs led from the sidewalk up to a path through the front yard, flanked by verdant and colorful flowerbeds that flowed upwards away from the street without a speck of soil visible. In a drought, their DWP bill had to be a nightmare. In the driveway there was a champagne-colored Lexus SUV and a black, convertible BMW with the top down. Both cars were waxed, shiny and spotless. There were CSIs crawling around the vehicles, looking for anything that would produce leads.

The scene worried Zarah from the onset. They were at a private residence, neither car had been shot full of holes or run down any embankments, no dead bodies inside them.

"This look like our guy to you?" Zarah asked Charlie.

"There's a note," Charlie said. "Beyond that..." He shrugged.

"God..." Zarah said. *He's evolving.* "That's just..." she bit back a curse. "Great, just great."

A few uniforms had begun spinning yellow tape around the perimeter. Neighbors were standing outside in bathrobes and slippers to stare at all of the cops milling around their neighbor's house. Zarah observed that most of the police on-scene were detectives.

"A lot of suits here," she said. "Where are the unis?"

"Most of them are in Canyon Country—the fires."

Zarah nodded as if she had already known about it.

There's fires in Canyon Country? I need to watch the news more. Ugh, and speak of the devil, there's Carmen Sanchaz.

The reporter was dressed in a red, cotton, button-down shirt and blue jeans, looking clean and pretty under a manicured orange tree on the front lawn. She was flanked by what must have been her news crew. On her left was an athletic, and decidedly good-looking black guy wearing a blue button-top shirt with the buttons open, a black tank top under that, blue jeans and a pair of expensive-looking Nikes. A large video camera rested at his feet.

On Carmen's right was a man, no more than five-foot ten, thin and waifish, wearing a sports jacket and khakis. He had a triangle-shaped head with coffee-colored, over-gelled hair that would not move if a tornado blew through it.

Pérez was talking to all three of them together and taking notes. The reporter glanced at Zarah and smiled the same cold-blooded, reptilian smile she had days before.

Be nice, Zarah.

"Why is Carmen Sanchaz the interviewee and not the interviewer?"

Charlie shrugged. "We'll ask Pérez later."

As Zarah and Charlie entered the house, Zarah saw the home-security panel next to the front door hanging by several wires. Someone had cracked it and wired it back on itself. Learning that the Street Sweeper was capable of stealth and possessed the ability to do more than noisily gun people down in public gave her a chill.

"Remember when you said he'd be an easy catch if he kept shooting people in the street?" Zarah asked. "I think he figured that out."

Charlie nodded and opened the front door to the crime scene. Not sure where to go, Zarah followed the bright flashes from a camera across a large kitchen with an Italian tile floor and an island stovetop. Out of a dining room with a regal, oak table and chairs that gleamed with cleanliness, the fetid, metallic smell of blood and death poured out, polluting Zarah's skin, her lungs. Fighting nausea, she proceeded inside.

She saw Adam, crouched low, taking photographs of a dead woman bound to one of the redwood dining chairs with duct tape. The corpse's skin was a pale, bluish color and from the smell it was clear it had been there for more than awhile. The victim's eyes were wide—frozen in pain and terror. She was in her pajamas. A blue wash rag had been stuffed into her mouth and lashed in place with a thin telephone cord. Her face was slashed and torn as if she had tried to kiss a three-point buzz saw, and kept trying.

Coagulating blood spilled from her wounds, over the front of her light-lavender tank top, down her pastel blue, Capri pajama pants, dripping from her polished toes and into a deep, red puddle around her feet that had flowed into the grout lines of the tiles like runoff from a slaughterhouse. A large kitchen knife was jammed into her throat, through her larynx.

Zarah turned away to compose herself. "Heavenly days," she said.

"No shit," Charlie added.

Adam stood up, hefting his DSLR Camera. "It gets worse," he said.

"How worse?" Zarah asked.

"Have you seen the other room?" Adam asked. "The kids' room?" There was no indication in his manner that he had asked Zarah out on a date hours before, or that she had turned him down.

I didn't turn him down. Maybe he'll ask again.

"Who's got the goddamn note?" Charlie's voice boomed through the house, rattling the walls.

"Pérez had it last!" Woodley shouted back from another room. "Charlie, is Zarah with you? I need her in here!"

Charlie and Zarah affirmed and started out of the dining room as Adam returned to his duties. Charlie called out for Woodley to tell them where he was. They followed his voice down a hall with a polished hardwood floor. The chubby CSI, Swede, was on his knees documenting small droplets of blood which led to the room they were looking for.

Woodley was standing over the corpse of an adult male in a bedroom that was adorned with playful, boyish décor. The corpse was face-down on the wood floor, blood pooled from his neck and around his shoulders. There were two, wood-framed, twin-sized beds on either side of the room. Each had a dead boy no older than eleven or twelve. Zarah gasped and recoiled, but quickly pulled herself together and refused to turn her head.

One boy's legs hung over the side of the bed as if he had tried to get up, but had died from the sharp force trauma to his midsection before he could even stand. His comforter was decorated with images from the movie *The Avengers*.

The other boy was on top of his covers. Likely it was too hot for him to use them. His blood-soaked bedclothes showed that the boy had been a fan of Disney's *Big Hero 6*. Cause of death looked to be a severed windpipe.

"So, what's up?" She asked, without looking at Woodley, forcing herself to study the scene.

"I dunno," Woodley said. "I'm trying to put my finger on how it all went down in here. You're better at this shit, so…" Woodley gestured to the carnage in the boys' bedroom, "do your thing."

Zarah looked over the room, then focused on the blood trail leading from the boys' beds, to the corner across from them, and then to where their father lay face down in his own blood.

"All right," she said. "So here's what I think happened."

Her partner and Woodley yielded the floor. "Let's hear it," Charlie said.

Zarah nodded. "He baited the father and killed him from behind."

"Where do you get that?" Woodley asked, unimpressed.

"The Street Sweeper said he was going to kill the *wrongdoers* and anyone with them," Zarah said. "And he's figured out that if he keeps shooting people out in public, he'll end up like Richard Ramirez, with an angry mob on top of him before the police even show up. So this time he followed his victim home and waited for the right time."

"Okay," Woodley said. "Keep going."

She continued. "He disables the security—"

"That he knew how to do that isn't comforting," Charlie interrupted.

Zarah nodded and kept going. "He sneaks around the kitchen, takes a knife, walks down the hall, checks this room and sees the kids, sleeping."

Charlie pointed to the boy with *The Avengers* décor on his bed. "He kills him first. Single slice to the throat." Then he pointed to the boy with his legs hanging over the side of his bed. "This one hears it, tries to get up. The killer keeps him there with a single, precise stab to the abdomen—finishes him in the heart—a hard target to hit from the front in one go."

"And the kid doesn't go quiet," Zarah added. "He makes a loud enough noise that The Street Sweeper decides to lay in wait behind the door in case the parents come to check it out, and sure enough, the dad comes in, sees what happened and rushes to his kid's bedside."

"Right past the killer who slits his throat from behind," Charlie added.

"Gotta clear your muhfuckin' corners, man," Woodley said to the dead man on the floor.

Zarah followed the blood trail out the door and down the hall toward another room.

"He doesn't clean his blade," Charlie noted.

The trail of blood led to a bathroom with blue tiles and some kind of cutesy boathouse motif with seashells, and pictures of sailboats on the Navy-blue striped walls.

"The washcloth he used to gag her came from there," Zarah said.

"He's going door to door," Woodley said, "sayin', *where's the bitch I came here for?*"

Zarah nodded, and Charlie grunted in agreement.

They followed the trail to the master bedroom. Zarah saw cast-off blood spatter on the door, on the eggshell colored wall inside and across the ceiling above the bed. Its directionality moved away from where the victim had been laying, as if the killer had flailed the knife or brandished it with theatrical bravado, throwing the children's blood from the murder weapon.

The king-sized bed with the cushioned head rest and down comforters and pillows was in disarray. The telephone had been ripped from the wall and thrown in front of a sliding glass door. It led to a landscaped yard with a swimming pool that resembled something from an island resort where only the one percent could afford to go.

"Damn," Woodley said. "These people spent more money on their decorating than they did on the house, I bet."

Zarah scanned the bedroom, walked inside and studied the state of things. Charlie did the same. Woodley watched them.

"After he killed the kids and their father," Zarah said, "he came in here, surprised the mother—"

"She was probably still asleep," Charlie said.

Zarah nodded and pointed to the telephone by the sliding glass door. "He gagged her, tore the phone out."

"The phone lines were cut already," Woodley said.

Zarah shuddered.

He knows how to disable phone lines, too? This guy is a nightmare.

"He just needed the cord to keep the gag in place," Zarah said. "After that, he took her to the dining room, taped her to the chair…"

"Why do that?" Woodley asked. "Why not just kill her in here?"

"I don't know," Zarah said. "Maybe he wanted to have some words with her before she got hers."

The three detectives headed back into the kitchen where the duct tape was being cut away from the woman's body and placed in evidence bags. Soon the coroner would place her into a bag as well and take her to a medical examiner.

Zarah left Charlie and Woodley and walked out the front door. She needed air. The pall of gloom inside murder scenes often took her breath. She saw Carmen Sanchaz, still talking to Pérez, and walked over.

"Hey, *Zarah*," Carmen said, trying to get a rise already.

"Sanchaz," Zarah returned the greeting and then turned to Pérez. "Charlie's looking for you. He's inside."

"Okay," Pérez said. "I got everything I need here."

"And what, pray tell…" Zarah said.

"Carmen discovered the D.B. Get this: The Street Sweeper called her cell phone, told her where to find it."

"When?" Zarah asked.

"This morning," Pérez said.

"This scene's gotta be three or four days old. *Nobody* else saw the front door and the jacked-up security panel?"

"Door's hard to see from the street," Pérez said, pointing down the sheer, sumptuous slope blanketed with colorful dahlias, lilies and other blooms to the sidewalk below. "I guess no one came to the door or whatever."

With that, Pérez headed off toward the house. Zarah looked at Carmen. The reporter met her stare. The cameraman looked over the two of them, concerned. Carmen tilted her head, crossed her arms and adopted a smug expression. The cameraman picked up his large video camera, mounted it over his shoulder and pointed it at Zarah as if it was a bazooka.

"So," Zarah said, "a serial killer calls you on your own phone, tells you where to find his latest murder, and you run here to shoot some spaghetti before calling us?"

"Something wrong with vetting a source's claims before wasting anyone else's time?" Carmen asked.

It was clear *Obstruction of Justice*, and perhaps even *Tampering* charges could have been pressed, but a piece of work like Carmen Sanchaz would skate, and their benign contempt for one another would descend into feudalism. Zarah did not need that on her plate. Besides, the reporter did have a point, and this could have been a chance to bury the hatchet.

"Put it that way, I guess not," Zarah said. "Still, it's pretty gutsy. If he had called me, I know what I would have done."

"Passed out from the shock of a man actually calling you?"

Zarah's face flushed, and she raised her chin and glared at the reporter. The cameraman took an instinctive step backwards, and the little man with the pointy chin put his face in his hands, shook his head and said, "Christ, Carmen."

Zarah took a deep breath, then pointed at the house. "You saw what he did to that woman?" she asked.

Carmen looked at Zarah with a face full of expectant smugness.

"The monster who did that," Zarah paused for effect, "has your phone number." She paused again to let it sink in. "If he got your number, it's a good bet he got your address along with it."

Carmen kept the arrogance clamped on her mug, but the tendons on her neck stood out and her eyes had become damp and bright.

"Sanchaz," Zarah put a hand on Carmen's shoulder and looked into her wet, russet eyes. "I'd start making friends here if I were you."

Carmen plucked Zarah's hand from her shoulder by her coat sleeve. "I have friends here," she assured her weakly.

"How many of them will attend your funeral?" Zarah asked.

Carmen scoffed.

"The next time he calls you," Zarah said, "you better call us. Because if you show up at a scene before we do again, it'll be an obstruction charge."

Zarah turned towards the steps leading to the sidewalk, grinning and feeling the pride of victory, the way she felt after making a righteous arrest or forcing Sebastian to tap out in the dojo.

She headed down the stairs to talk to the neighbors milling around below. She took a deep breath. She may have won one round with the reporter, but it was not going to make her day shorter.

15

DRAKE BARRET MITCHELL had planned on going dark after calling the reporter, but as he searched for a place to dump his vehicle and steal a new one, some jerk driving a red Yaris in the left lane decided to drive so far under the speed limit a squirrel could have outpaced him. When Drake signaled and tried to pass, the asshole floored it so Drake could not get around, sealing his fate.

Drake followed him to Santa Monica. His fuel status was becoming precarious, and assuming that the little car had a full tank, there was no way that a pickup truck could outdistance a small sedan.

Luckily, the Yaris entered one of the parking structures where beachgoers who knew better than to try parking on the beach would leave their cars and walk. It was busy, public—not ideal.

Drake promised himself that he would be patient. This guy could have been starting a shift at work or going to meet friends. Drake held himself back and watched the target exit his car.

He had short, messy, beach-blonde hair, was wearing non-prescription, Buddy Holly glasses, a brown t-shirt that had the word "DOPE" printed on it, and beige corduroy pants—though this clown would have probably called the color "otter" or some shit.

Drake did not want to wait all night, but this guy *had* to go. He chose to stay in the garage, and when the hipster returned, he would strike like a cobra. He took his M9 Beretta from the holster on his tactical vest, attached a suppressor to the barrel and waited.

16

ZARAH HAD ALMOST been able to leave Parker Center and head over to the dojo when the call-out came. She imagined Charlie's phone ringing as he was about to turn the key in his front door.

With rush hour traffic on the 10 freeway, the twenty-five minutes it should have had taken Zarah to travel fifteen miles between Downtown and Santa Monica took over an hour. When she reached her destination, the number of squad cars and news vans staging around side streets and alleyways, along with gawking rubbernecks who were driving slower than a pedestrian could walk on crutches, had clogged 5th street with so many vehicles that efficiency forced her to park on 7th and take a roundabout route on foot to reach the scene. She had touched base with Charlie, who was not far behind her, along with Woodley and Pérez.

The parking garage was surrounded by media crews trying to get the best angle for their reports as officers from Southeastern District tried to keep them away from the perimeter.

As she approached the gaping concrete entrance to the parking garage, Lt. Torres called out to her and trotted up from behind.

"Wheeler!" he said, "We the first ones from Special?"

"Yeah," Zarah said. "This is unprecedented. I don't know what to do with myself without Charlie."

"You take the lead on this," he said, "and talk to Carmen Sanchaz when you get a minute. A warrant's coming to monitor her calls. She can play ball or go to lockup for obstruction. You let her know."

Zarah shrugged. The last thing Zarah wanted was to deal with Carmen Sanchaz, but putting her in her place was time-worthy enough.

Zarah and Lt. Torres climbed the urine-scented, concrete staircase to the third level. The victim and his car were easy to find, a red Toyota Yaris with CSIs all over it. Lt. Torres made his way to the Southeastern detectives, and Zarah headed for the car.

Zarah caught a glimpse of Carmen Sanchaz from the corner of her eyes, and she could tell the reporter saw her too. Neither made an effort to speak, and Zarah kept her eyes forward as she passed. They would have plenty to talk about later. She crouched next to Swede as he photographed the dead victim in the front seat. She glanced over a gunshot that had been blasted into the victim's voice box.

Zarah nudged Swede. "What's that, nine-millimeter?"

"Hey, Zarah," Swede said. "Is it true you never saw Star Wars?"

Zarah gave Swede a glassy stare. "Nine-milli, yes or no?"

Swede nodded. "Hollow point. Look at the bite it took."

"Nothing else?" Zarah asked.

"Nothing cursory," Swede said. "We'll know more after the M.E. takes a pass."

Zarah raised her voice, "Witnesses, anyone?"

At the hood of the car, a stocky, grey-haired detective from the Southeast division spoke up.

"Nobody heard gunfire, but the attendant did see somebody drive out of here in a black GMC pickup wearing a brown hood and shades," he said. "We have guys all over this garage asking questions, and a BOLO out." He gestured to the dusty, dome-shaped cameras mounted in the ceiling. "We're also retrieving the video footage."

"Good work," Zarah said.

The detective gave her a sour look and returned to his business.

Yes. I'm half your age, I have boobs and I outrank you. Tough.

"What about the note?" Zarah asked.

"It was on his chest," Swede said.

"Who has it now?

"Here," Lt Torres walked around the Yaris and handed her the note, written on yellow legal paper, sealed in a plastic evidence bag. "I'll send you a copy for your murder book."

Zarah read the note aloud:

A turn signal is NOT a request!! It means that someone is COMING IN!! When someone tells you they are coming in, you SHARE THE ROAD!! You DO NOT speed up as if there aren't a thousand cars in front of you already!! This is why people don't use their signals in the first place!! I was on this Hipster hypocrite's six ALL DAY!! After I explained that he was being punished for refusing to share the road I put one in his VOICE BOX!! He DIED SLOW and in PAIN!!! And the same will happen to anyone who doesn't ACT RIGHT!!

Disrespectfully,

The Street Sweeper

"He's full of it," Swede said. "No one takes a hollow point to the larynx and dies slow."

"It's hard to believe that nobody heard the gun," Zarah said.

"This prick is military-trained, for sure," a gruff voice behind Zarah said. "Maybe his weapon had a silencer."

Zarah turned, and there was Charlie along with Woodley and Pérez. Zarah's time in the spotlight was over.

"What makes you so sure?" Zarah asked Charlie.

"*I was on his six all day,*" he said. "That's military talk.*"

"Right," Zarah said. "So where would he get a silencer?"

"I'm not saying he did," Charlie replied. "But if the canvass doesn't turn up an ear-witness in a place that echoes like this one, it could be the reason why. You could *make* a silencer if you wanted."

Woodley wandered over to the car, and Pérez discussed something with the Southeastern detectives. Torres was talking to Gary Sterling—not threatening to arrest him. He would wait for Zarah to do it. If it went bad, he could point at her and avoid getting chewed by the brass.

"Let's go talk to those guys," Zarah said to Charlie, pointing out several Southeastern officers. "See if they turned over anything."

"I got that," Charlie said. "Head on out if you want."

"Charlie, I could be in the office trying to generate leads on the six other victims at this moment, so next time I touch base with you on a call-out, tell me to stay put rather than letting me come all the way out to a scene just to blow me off."

"I thought you had your jujitsu class tonight," Charlie said. "Excuse me all over the place."

That's right, jujitsu! Zarah thought. *I didn't call and tell Sebastian I wasn't coming.*

"This isn't about my jujitsu—"

"We've all been called away from other stuff we'd rather be doing to drive a bunch of miles and spend five-minutes on a scene. That's the job, so don't be resentful, Zarah."

"I'm not resentful."

Charlie did not look as if he believed her.

"I'm *not*, Charlie!*"

"*Aaaah que la chingada!*" Carmen shouted from the edge

of the crime scene. "You cops gonna make me stand here all night?"

"Okay, now I am," Zarah said.

17

ZARAH'S INTERVIEW WITH Carmen Sanchaz did not turn up anything worth writing down, but she wanted the reporter to know that every one of her easy, snide remarks were going to be transcribed and filed. So she scribbled them into her notepad anyway.

Zarah expected huffing and puffing when she told Carmen the task force wanted to monitor her phone, and Carmen did not prove her wrong.

"You can't do that," the reporter said.

"We're not asking," Zarah retorted.

"Yeah," Carmen said, "asking would've been smart. And now you ain't gonna tap anything—until the hearings are over."

Zarah huffed like a bull with a fly in its nose.

"Oooh, sí! You'll win, but not without getting a black eye."

Zarah folded her arms and waited to hear the logic behind that little threat.

"You don't pay much attention to the world do you?" Carmen said. "The Justice Department spies on reporters. NSA reads people's e-mails. The FBI wants a backdoor to everybody's smartphone, and all the cops are becoming more racist by the second, profiling everyone—"

"Sanchaz," Zarah said with a half-chuckle, "saying all cops are racists who profile, is profiling."

"Not one Angeleno trusts you, *Zarah*. All I have to do is tweet '*abuse of power* hashtag-*LAPD*', and you'll have problems."

"I wonder what they'll tweet when they find out you're protecting a serial killer," Zarah said. "I bet it won't be pretty."

"And I bet the killer'll stop calling when he finds out you're tapping my phone. Now you got no reason to do it. Checkmate, *puta*."

"Look," Zarah said. "The bosses let it slide the first time you and your boys tampered with a crime scene—"

"We did not '*tamper*'—"

"The only thing stopping me from cuffing and stuffing all three of you *right now* is that you can help. If you do, they'll let it slide again."

Carmen scratched the back of her neck, looking over to her crew who were waiting by the stairwell. "Okay. Let's trade."

"I'm listening," Zarah told her.

"Get me one interview with the head of your taskforce."

"Torres?" Zarah said. "He was just chatting with your producer."

"He won't go on the record," Carmen said. "Give me that, and you won't need any warrant. You can tap me all night long."

"How about giving your career a rest for once and think of all those Angelenos you pretend to care about."

Zarah saw the veins on Carmen's neck throb, and she looked Zarah dead in the eyes. "You think you know me, *chica*. You *really* don't."

Zarah answered the reporter with her own steel gaze. "Don't I?" she said. "I remember hearing what *good* friends we are, what *great* rapport we have."

"If I stood behind the tape waiting to hear a fairytale from some fuckin' P.I.O. I wouldn't deserve this job," Carmen said. "Don't blame me for playin' you, Zarah. Blame yourself for gettin' played."

"You have a decision to make," Zarah said. "Think hard, and try not to hurt yourself in the process."

Carmen huffed and shook her head. Then she turned and marched toward her colleagues.

"The warrant is on its way, Sanchaz," Zarah called after her.

Carmen shrugged without turning or stopping. When she reached her two companions, they disappeared down the stairwell.

Zarah walked back to her car. She thought about jujitsu class, which was almost over. Zarah could not remember the last time she had forgotten to inform Sebastian when she had to go to a call-out. She thought of calling him after class had ended, but thought twice. She was not in the mood. She was more in the mood for peace, quiet and rum.

18

CARMEN SANCHAZ HAD always wanted to live next to a body of water, but she could not afford any beachfront property, yet. Instead, she compromised and bought a house high in the Silver Lake Hills overlooking the Ivanhoe and Silver Lake reservoirs—two large, concrete-lined basins divided by a spillway.

What made her decision brilliant was not the beautiful park with rolling, green lawns, running paths and views of the reservoir. It was because it was close to Echo Park where Carmen had grown up. But now, thanks to the heat and drought, most of it had turned a tarnished yellow color, and the reservoirs looked like two empty toilet bowls in dire need of scrubbing.

It was not posh, but Silver Lake was still one of L.A.'s hippest hoods. It had an energetic nightlife rife with bars, clubs and restaurants but was not so trendy that anyone from Carmen's old life would accuse her of putting on airs—though some had as soon as she left for college.

She was not in the best of moods when she returned home. Lamar did not want her to be alone until she cooled off, and Gary had invited himself along.

She plopped down onto a comfortable sofa covered in multi-colored, Peruvian alpaca blankets next to Lamar who immediately packed moist, pungent marijuana into a bong bowl made of jade-colored glass. Gary sat down in a brown Lay-Z Boy and thumbed over e-mails on his phone.

"Why don't you give your career a rest for once," Carmen said in a mock-Zarah-Wheeler voice. *"Pinche puta."*

"Don't let that get to you," Lamar told her as he picked a simple, glass water pipe from Carmen's thick, redwood coffee table and slid the fancy bowl into the stem. "They train to mess with your head." He handed the bong to Carmen. "Take this shit deep."

Carmen leaned forward and inhaled as Lamar lit the weed with a butane lighter. The bong bubbled and sputtered.

Lamar continued, "She knows you have a conscience, and she knew it'd fuck with you. Don't feel guilty about that shit."

Gary looked over to her and shook his head. "I don't know why I let you talk me into all of this. Now I'm going to jail."

"They can't do shit," Lamar said.

"Well, our injunction is coming down tomorrow, that won't please them. And the truth is, technically, they *can* throw us in the slammer."

"Mierda!" Carmen said. "We didn't go near that body! We shot it from a *billion* feet away, and then we called! We can prove that!"

"We can't prove what happened before or after Lamar was rolling."

"She's bluffing, Gary," Carmen said, taking the bong from Lamar and then taking a bubbly drag.

"Throwin' a mindfuck," Lamar added.

"That's possible," Gary said to Carmen. "Her solve in her last post was ninety-seven percent. In most of them, they confessed."

"Who told you that?" Lamar asked.

"Her lieutenant—Torres."

"So she's good at guilt trippin'," Lamar said.

"She's better than good," Gary replied, "and Carmen pissed her off enough that she'll throw us in a cell for any reason."

Carmen coughed. "Ay! You *pendejos* are supposed to be on my side! I mean, if we don't push our luck a little, how will we have any impact on the air?"

"I'm with you," Gary said, "but pushing your luck has risks. In Studio City, Detective Wheeler looked willing to let it go, but you kept poking that bear and here we are. Just be happy the station's okay with the injunction because—"

Carmen's phone rang. She took it from her jacket pocket and looked at the caller I.D. The caller was blocked.

Carmen's hair lifted on her arms and the nape of her neck. She felt her heart picking up speed. She tapped the ANSWER graphic on the touch screen and put the phone to her ear.

"Yes?"

A deep-pitched voice with a metallic tinge that no human being could produce without a computer, spoke. "Why is there only a story about the dead douchebag in the parking garage?" it said. "I've wasted seven people. Why aren't you on TV saying so?"

This was not the first time someone tried to intimidate Carmen. She was *18th Street La Aristocrata*, but in those days she had *familia* at her back. Now there was no one, and this *loco* might have been sitting across the street loading a gun at that moment. She cleared her throat. "I can start all of that tomorrow," she said.

If Zarah Wheeler doesn't put me in jail first.

"I'm thinking you aren't with the program," the voice said.

"No," Carmen said. "I was hoping for some quotes. I can go on the air right now, but without some corroboration, the cops will deny any of it is linked to a single killer. The story will lose momentum. We both know how scared they are of creating a panic."

It sounded like a good excuse, but it was not what held Carmen back. If she rang the *serial killer* bell, the police's job would become a waking nightmare of anonymous tips, dead-end leads and greater political pressure with each murder. The LAPD would be inclined to punish Carmen.

Any other time she could not care less how they felt, but at the moment they had her for tampering with a crime scene, even though she had tampered with nothing. Still, if they did not arrest her and get her fired, they would stonewall and shun her until the stars burned out. Her career path would be forever blocked, and she would be stuck covering county fairs, farmer's markets and surfing tourneys.

Those were not Oscar Mike's problems, and he made himself plain: "Tomorrow," he said. "Or you'll know where the next body falls without me telling you."

"Tomorrow," Carmen said.

He hung up.

Carmen lowered her face into her hands and rubbed her eyes.

"You okay, Carm?" Lamar asked.

Carmen looked up at Gary, her eyes dampening. She shook her head.

"Call the lawyer," she said. "Cancel the injunction."

"What did he say?" Gary asked.

"In so many words," Carmen answered, "if I don't start reading his notes on the air, I'm dead."

"Carmen," Gary said, "you just got a death threat."

"Not the first time, *papi*."

"Baby," Lamar said, "you gotta tell the cops about this."

"No," she replied. "That may just piss him off worse."

Gary and Lamar looked at Carmen, worried and disapproving.

Carmen said, "Look, we were gonna do this anyway. If I let the cops tap me, they'll be less pissed when I go on the air tomorrow."

"I don't know," Gary said.

"If we don't do it," Lamar said, "some other ace'll swoop in and take it from us."

"Well," Gary said, "it'll make Zarah Wheeler happy. Maybe we can start some bridge-building there."

Carmen felt her hackles rise. Zarah will probably think that she had put Carmen in her place.

Whatever, puta. Think what you want.

Zarah Wheeler had the upper hand, but Carmen resolved right there to seize any and every chance to make her sorry that she ever gave an ace reporter like Carmen Sanchaz an axe to grind.

"When you're done with the lawyer, call Daniels" Carmen said. "Let's get this party started."

19

DRAKE BARRETT MITCHELL cruised through Boyle Heights behind the wheel of a stolen, sky blue, Toyota Tacoma. It had a white decal of *Hello Kitty* sporting a mohawk in the rear window, so it must have belonged to a female—or a homo. After all, the Tacoma was the most pussified excuse for a midsize pickup on Earth, named after a hippie city in a hippie state full of worthless hippies.

After Carmen Sanchaz had taken his message to the airwaves, city officials were appalled, citizens were alarmed, and police were alert. As per his strategy, Drake had gone dark after Carmen Sanchaz had declared Los Angeles the hunting ground of a serial killer named "Oscar Mike."

At first he was not thrilled the reporter had changed the name of his alter ego, but over the weeks, the more he had heard it spoken on the news—"*Who is Oscar Mike?*" "*Where is Oscar Mike?*"— the more the name had grown on him.

He sat back, allowed the shock to dissipate and the rancor to die down somewhat. That is how effective whippings worked— they took time. Strike hard, let it sink in, wait for the sting to dull, then crack the strap across their backs again, and again. Make each lash count.

People believed that being cut off from other drivers by walls of steel and glass made rudeness and flouting traffic laws okay. A citation, a chiding and some online traffic school yielded nothing.

People had *no idea* of the things Drake Barrett Mitchell had done to protect the freedom they had to behave like entitled assholes— things none of them would have had the sack to do without a video game controller their hands. But Oscar Mike was going to introduce all of gentle society to the kind of inhumane wet-work warriors employed to accomplish their missions. His pointed message would penetrate deep into the limbic region of their brains and overwrite the existing pathology that was making them all such a barrel of tactless cunts, replacing it with a simple truth: When one may be made to answer for rude behavior with their life, politeness counts. And on Oscar Mike's streets, nothing mattered more than manners.

A month had passed, and Drake wanted to be different this time out. So, he looked for an example from outside the middle-class, 818 neighborhoods, and made his hunting ground in the 213—in an area where people were dark-skinned and dangerous.

Carmen Sanchaz's news reports were having an effect. In fact, it was becoming frustrating. He had expected to mark a target with relative ease, but people were obeying and cooperating. He remained calm. People in these neighborhoods had convinced themselves that they existed in some kind of social, racial autarchy, separate and better than everyone else. They did whatever they wanted on principle, went out of their way to break rules. On crowded streets with slow and difficult traffic, it would be a short matter of time before one of them did something stupid.

As if on cue, he heard tires screech behind him. Drake turned and saw a black sports car driven by a swarthy brunette. She had almost rear-ended someone one lane over. The woman and her elderly passenger looked relieved to have stopped in time.

Drake continued his hunt, driving around several blocks. He

patrolled for almost an hour without success. It was starting to grate on him. After a while it became ridiculous.

He was about to call it quits when the woman in the black car, who had already come close to nailing someone, charged into his lane, cut him off and slammed on the brakes. On instinct, Drake braked hard, pressing his hand to the horn and letting it roar a good long time.

She was holding a phone in her hand, talking while driving. It was probably why she had almost crashed the first time, and he was certain it was why she had changed lanes without signaling and was not paying attention to traffic lights. He had his target.

After Drake let off the horn, she flipped him the bird. At first, Drake had intended to follow them someplace more private, but he could not stop himself. This bitch had to go. Now.

20

WHEN ZARAH HAD been told that Carmen Sanchaz had chosen to play ball, she had been disappointed. She had been looking forward to visiting Carmen in lockup, but at least there would not be any courtroom drama.

A mixed blessing from all of it was that the word was out about the serial killer. Carmen Sanchaz had taken "Oscar Mike" to the big show, and now bigger names in broadcasting, up to and including Bill O'Reilly, Chris Matthews, Whoopi Goldberg and Greta Van Susteren were talking about him. Jimmy Kimmel, Ellen Degeneres and Stephen Colbert were cracking jokes about him, and Conan O'Brien, Chris Kattan and Kelly Ripa were trying to, with their usual level of success.

The downside to full media disclosure was public and political pressure. Now, thanks to the reporter's theatrical brio, the Street Sweeper Taskforce, which had been comprised of a handful of elite detectives, morphed into the Oscar Mike Taskforce, an army of investigators from Robbery-Homicide including H.S.S., and Robbery Special. In addition, if a tip produced a person-of-interest, which so far they had not, the Special Investigations Section were on tap to surveil them.

For the last four weeks, the killer had been quiet while Zarah and Charlie groped around for leads with almost nothing to go on. After receiving a tip about an ex-Marine upholsterer named Miguel Salgado, who had praised Oscar Mike's crusade a little too much for a fabric salesman's comfort, Lt. Torres sent Woodley and Pérez to question his friends and family while Zarah and Charlie paid him a visit at his upholstery shop in Boyle Heights.

Zarah tried to talk her way out of it. Miguel Salgado was a Mexican name. Boyle Heights was ninety-five percent Mexican, and it did not take a behavioral analyst to see that Oscar Mike's written rants were penned by a Caucasian male. It did not work, so off she and Charlie went to follow another dead-end lead.

After looking over Miguel Salgado's upholstery shop and asking some questions, the detectives took samples of his handwriting. His answers and penmanship were enough to convince them that he may have been a loudmouth, but he was not Oscar Mike. They thanked him for his time and left to grab lunch.

Zarah and Charlie pulled away from the Carl's Jr. drive-through in their charcoal-colored, police-issue Impala and headed towards East L.A. where another tipster believed that one Abel Hartog, an instructor at a traffic school, had raised suspicions by using Oscar Mike as one of many reasons to observe proper driving etiquette.

Zarah had one hand on the wheel while the other held onto a Double Western Bacon Cheeseburger. A sweaty, cold, diet Dr. Pepper sat in the cup holder. She knew that her body mass may suffer for the indulgence, but she owed herself a burger now and again, sure to include bacon. Zarah relished the idea of what her mother's reaction to that would have been.

On the radio, a news program was talking about a congresswoman who had announced that she would be working to put forward a law that would make punishment for disobeying traffic laws more stringent—steeper fines for citations, mandatory traffic school and perhaps jail time for repeat offenders. She also wanted an effective enforcement strategy, undercover highway patrol officers in unmarked vehicles, and hiring more of them to keep people honest and safe.

"How are they going to pay for that?" Charlie grumbled, "By raising *our* taxes, that's how. Fucking Liberals."

"Will you please turn that off?" Zarah asked.

Charlie turned the radio off and turned up the police band. After listening and driving for a few quiet minutes, Zarah became acutely aware of all of the crime around them.

"I'm so sick of this, I can scream."

"Are you okay?" Charlie asked.

"Yeah," she answered. "I'm just thinking. Would we have an Oscar Mike if everybody could just be civilized? You know what I mean?"

Charlie nodded and thought for a moment. He took a deep breath. "Civilization is bullshit," he said. "Nobody's civilized."

"What?" Zarah said. "You're civilized. I'm civilized."

"Zarah, if you think you're civilized, you're living in Fantasyland, okay? Civilized people don't live in reality. They don't even *believe* in reality."

"What do they believe in then?" she asked.

"Disbelief."

"What?"

"Look," Charlie said. "How many times have we heard wives, husbands, parents and stuff say '*we never thought this could happen.'?* They think they live in a civilized world. They think that they've evolved so high up the food chain that nature no longer applies. They don't *believe* in violence, right? But every day they're protected *from* violence *with* violence. They don't believe in killing, so they sit back and let other *civilized* people do it for them. It's a sad joke."

"There's nothing misguided about placing a premium on peace," Zarah said, "or the sanctity of all life."

"Zarah, you can't sit there and tell me you believe in the sanctity of all life *and* eat a cheeseburger with bacon on top!"

"Okay, okay!" Zarah said. "I'm trying to see your point."

"The point is people are so focused on the accomplishments or ideals of civilization that they've forgotten what they are."

"And that is?"

"Human. The same as we were fifty-thousand years ago. No more intelligent and no less savage."

"I think the fact that we can forget such a thing does make us better than some monkey in the woods."

"You're missing the point."

"Whatever."

"Yeeaah! Just what I thought. Another schizophrenic Liberal with blinders on."

"Oh, heavenly days, Charlie, give it a rest."

"Yeah, you know it's there, but you don't wanna know."

"Your point is that we're the same apes we were when we first crawled out of the *ick* and smacked the first chimp with the first stick, snatched his blueberries and ran. Having a peaceful, law abiding society is a pipe dream, so let's all grab our knives and guns and rumble without even *trying* to be more than animals. I get it."

"No, no. That's not—"

"*Suker khaljic!*" Zarah commanded in Arabic. *Shut your mouth.*

It had worked when her mother yelled it at her, and it was worth a try. It shut Charlie up and unnerved him at the same time.

Since 9/11, the sound of Arabic being spoken on American soil made people's hackles rise like an angry cat's. Poor Charlie had to act like it had not bothered him. He scowled and gripped the overhead grab handle, likely wondering what Zarah had said, too abashed to ask.

Zarah finished her bacon-cheeseburger in peace as she and

Charlie drove, both sulking, until Zarah sucked the last rattling sip of her beverage through the straw. Charlie looked at her.

"You're so sexy when you're like this," Charlie said.

"So that's why you like pissing me off so much," Zarah replied.

Charlie chortled, and they both relaxed and let go of their tizzy. They continued to drive through Boyle Heights. Stucco houses with flat roofs lined the street like shoeboxes separated by driveways one car wide, most with yards the size of trading cards. Bikes and toys had been abandoned in the driveways, and more than one yard sported a deflating swimming pool, wilted and lifeless in the radioactive sun.

Hard looking guys were sitting in parked cars or standing in small groups as if they were immune to the heat. Most wore white tank-tops and jeans baggy enough to hide a dead puppy, and most were heavily tattooed. They eyed the Impala with studied indifference.

"A lot of bangers on this street," Zarah said.

Charlie picked up the radio mic and called a casual code-one to tell the dispatch officer their twenty, "Bridge and Echandia, by Prospect Park in Boyle."

"Copy," dispatch crackled back through the radio.

Zarah looked at Charlie expecting an explanation for the call.

"What?" he asked. "I want em' to know where we are."

Zarah flicked her gaze upward and shook her head.

"Hey," Charlie said, "you're not the white-and-hated one here."

"Right, I'm just the half-Arab, hated-more one."

The resentment and hatred the War on Terror had brought down on the Arabian side of her bloodline was hurtful and difficult at times, but it was a small matter compared to how she had been treated in Riyadh for being half-*American*— most of it coming from her own kin. The shame of bringing a white, Catholic, westerner's child into the world was a disgrace Zarah's mother was still trying to live-down, and likely never would.

As Zarah's thoughts drifted back to Riyadh, a week after her eleventh birthday, her father sweeping in and absconding with her to the United States, something interesting crossed her line of sight outside, and piqued her interest.

She peered at it. Across two lanes in a pale-blue pickup truck, a lean man with short, ashen-brown hair was wearing something with a thick, deep brown, woolen hood that hung across the back of his shoulders.

21

ZARAH FOCUSED ON the man in the blue pickup truck. The thick hooded garment did not look like a common hoodie or a jacket, but she was too far away to be sure.

Is that what a Jedi robe looks like? God, why didn't I ignore Pérez and just watch Star Wars with Adam? It's been four weeks. Should I call him? If he was gonna call me, I think he would've by—"

"Zarah!" Charlie shouted.

Zarah snapped to attention and saw red brake lights in front of her. She jammed her foot down on the brake pedal like a steam piston. The Impala screamed to a halt inches from the car in front of it.

"What the hell, Zarah?" Charlie said.

Other motorists turned to see what the commotion was, including the man in the blue Tacoma. He had on dark sunglasses with big lenses.

Like Elvis, she remembered Anita Nizmani's description.

"Over there," Zarah said, "two lanes over. The blue pickup."

Charlie leaned forward. "I can't see," he said.

The Tacoma had passed them, but from behind she saw the thick folds of the driver's hood across his shoulders. Zarah signaled and changed lanes trying to get closer, but the truck's cab was elevated, making the driver difficult to see.

"Call in the plate," she said.

"Come on, what are the chances?" Charlie asked.

"Charlie?" Zarah said. "He's in a blue pickup, wearing a brown, thick *something* with a hood in a hundred degree weather. Just check."

Charlie hesitated. Zarah huffed and snatched the handset from the radio, called in to dispatch and recited the car's plate number. It came back as registered to a Moira Lawrence in Sherman Oaks. It hadn't been reported stolen.

"Not stolen," Charlie said.

"Or not reported yet," Zarah said, "If it's him—"

"Zarah—"

"If it's him, Charlie, this wouldn't be the first blue pickup truck he's stolen from Sherman Oaks would it?"

Zarah watched the truck as logic played tug-of-war with instinct. Millions of people, millions of places, and Oscar Mike chooses this street, this city and this time after a month-long absence?

"Let's just watch him for now," Charlie said.

Charlie then called into dispatch and advised that they had possibly sighted Oscar Mike, described the truck and driver and let them know that he and Zarah were tailing him.

Dispatch called out a Code-Two for units to respond to Zarah's location, no lights or sirens. The traffic light turned green. Zarah stayed in her lane, and with one car between her and the Tacoma, she followed. His route was erratic, as if he was lost. Zarah stayed with him, through Boyle Heights and into City Terrace. The Tacoma kept driving as if the shark was circling prey but unable to zero in on it.

"Okay, this is fucking weird," Charlie said. "What do you think?"

"Let's bait him," Zarah said.

"Okay, but wait for the other units to catch up."

"Why?"

"You want a fight on your hands with no backup?"

"If it's him, he'll follow us," she said. "That's been his M.O. since the Stein family, twice in a row. We'll lead him to our guys, right into custody."

"He's gunned someone down on the street twice in a row, too, Zarah. You don't know what he'll do."

Zarah stayed with the Tacoma, looking for an opening.

"This is a bad idea," Charlie said.

"Charlie, I back your plays. For once, back mine."

Charlie radioed backup one more time. Then he removed the safety from his Glock and checked the chamber. Zarah did not check her weapon. She did not have to. Oscar Mike had figured out the foolishness of public shootings and changed his M.O. Besides, she was always ready—a razor.

"Okay," she said speeding past the blue pickup. She took her phone out of her pocket and held it to her ear. "You ready?"

Charlie shook his head. "This is stupid."

With one hand, she yanked the wheel left and barged into the lane in front of him making sure not to signal. The suspect braked. His horn roared at Zarah as the truck's tires screamed to a stop.

Zarah looked in the rear view at the driver and rolled her eyes at him. Wanting him to get a good look at the phone in her hand, she raised her middle finger and gestured at him as if he were a benign nuisance. Through his dark shades, Zarah felt his eyes lock onto her.

"Come on," she said. "Follow us."

The driver whipped his hood over his head and leaned towards the passenger side of his car, reaching for something.

A gun!

"Oh, Crap! Charlie, it's him, it's him!"

Zarah hit the brakes and dropped the phone. She slammed the gearshift into park and unfastened her seat belt. Both detectives were out of the car and in the middle of traffic as the driver opened his door. They yanked open their backseat doors for cover and leveled their guns at him.

"LAPD!" Zarah yelled, "Step away from the vehicle!"

"Show us your hands," Charlie shouted. "Now!"

Pedestrians were staring. Traffic stopped to watch.

The hooded man thrust a pistol-gripped, sawed-off shotgun around the pickup's door and fired on Zarah with an ear-splitting *BOOM*. The two detectives ducked. The blast pushed the door of the Impala into Zarah, and jagged pieces of glass drizzled into her hair. She knew if she had been hit, she would have been shorn into a wet, ragged pulp.

Charlie hollered, "Everybody get down! Get down!"

Some did as commanded. Others screamed, ran and took cover behind anything larger than them, or fled into whatever doorway was closest. Motorists who would have driven away were trapped by the ones who were too frightened to. They all hid in their vehicles.

Zarah and Charlie's pistols popped loudly as they returned fire. Oscar Mike ducked behind the Tacoma's door as it was studded by nine millimeter rounds. He fired one more huge blast from his shotgun, spraying buckshot into the door protecting Zarah. He bolted towards the back of the truck. Behind him sirens were sounding, and LAPD patrol cars sped around every corner.

"Cover!" Charlie yelled across the Impala at Zarah.

She cracked off a few more shots at the gunman. Zarah scored a hit in the back that should have severed his spine at that range, but he did not fall. He winced in pain and spun. The skirt of his robe whipped around, and Zarah saw his body armor. With one hand, he thrust the shotgun at Zarah and fired. Zarah took cover. She heard Oscar Mike's buckshot pepper the Impala's door.

Zarah lunged from behind the car door and ran towards him, planning to take cover behind the front of the truck. The gunman pulled a dark, round object from inside his robe. A slender piece of metal flipped away from it through the air.

"Grenade!" Charlie yelled.

Oscar Mike bowled it towards Zarah. It tumbled past her and rolled underneath the Impala.

Charlie cried, "Run! Run! Run!"

They sprinted from their car in two different directions and dove for cover. The thunderous explosion shook everything. Car alarms cried out, glass from the Impala scattered, and the windows of storefronts on the sidewalk rattled and cracked.

Panicking motorists jumped from their vehicles and fled in all directions. Zarah rolled behind a deserted VW and pulled herself to her feet.

Oscar Mike lobbed another grenade down the opposite end of the street at the patrol cars barreling towards him. Then another. Policemen threw open their doors and tried to flee.

Explosions rocked the street, and men cried out in pain. Zarah heard someone shout, *"Man down! Man down!"*

The gunman raced across the street towards the mouth of an alleyway. Zarah fired at him but missed by miles. The slide on her Glock sprang back and locked in place. She was empty.

Oscar Mike turned and raised his shotgun at her as she fumbled to load a fresh magazine. He held his fire. He stared at Zarah through those large, dark shades, pointed his sawed-off shotgun with one hand and wagged it at her. Then he fled down the alley.

Zarah was not sure what he had meant by the gesture, but it gave her a chill all the same. When she had managed to lock a fresh magazine into her pistol, he was gone. She knew she should have been giving chase, but her ears rang and she was trembling uncontrollably. Instead, she found Charlie. He was sitting against a blue USPS mailbox. His jacket was bloody, ripped and torn at the shoulder.

She tried to help him lay flat, but he slapped her hands away and shoved her backwards. "What are you doing?" he yelled, gritting his teeth against the pain. "Go get him you stupid bitch! Go get him!"

She tried to still her shaking, but it was no use. She tried to stifle tears, but she did not have the energy. She stood on uneasy legs and lurched towards a trash bin and vomited.

She heard the ambulances howling towards them. Several young, Latino gangbangers knelt by her partner.

"Dog, you okay?" one of them asked him. "It's a fuckin' war, eh!"

Charlie tried to stand, but his feet slackened and he collapsed backwards. The young vatos steadied him back onto the sidewalk. "Just chill here, eh. The ambulance is coming."

Zarah sat on the curb next to Charlie, trying not to tremble, unable to stop. Charlie kept his eyes forward, refusing to look at her, refusing to speak. Zarah did not press. She had nothing to say.

A fleet of ambulances were on the scene in minutes. As the paramedics helped Charlie onto a metal stretcher, she wondered what progress had been made. Was Oscar Mike in custody? She hoped to God he was. She cursed herself for causing Charlie to be injured.

Charlie was right! We had him! You should have waited for backup!

Zarah knew she was going to answer for it. If the brass did not fire her, they would suspend her, remove her from the taskforce. Then she would be banished to a desk to review reports, or sent to train rookie detectives, or worse, transferred to Valley Forgery to chase identity thieves in North Hollywood until she retired early. Her haste would set her career back years.

Before Zarah had come to her senses, the E.M.T.s had loaded

Charlie into an ambulance and sped away. She wanted to go with, but it was too late.

She looked down the alley where Oscar Mike had fled. She watched her colleagues in uniform head in after him. She did not join them.

Charlie...you were right.

22

D RAKE MITCHELL RAN through the alley. A helicopter was coming. It would not take long for the cops to shake off the firefight and come in full force. He had to find a point of egress, or create one.

Drake reproached himself. He should have tailed the Arab woman. At some point he would have figured out she was a cop. How they had found him in the first place was a question for another day.

He stripped the robe and rolled the shotgun into it. It would have hair and sweat on it, but so what? He was not in any databases. He had cut all labels from the robe. Serial numbers or RFID chips from the shotgun, if it still had any, would most likely trace back to some character in Eastern Europe who never existed to begin with. When it came to covering his tracks, Drake's arms dealer was nothing if not exceptionally scrupulous, and none of it would trace back to Drake himself. He ditched the sawed-off and robe into a dumpster. The chopper was circling the alley, so he walked casual, hoping that they were still looking for a Jedi hauling ass with a shotgun. Still, cops and K-9s would be on his scent soon. He needed transpo.

He made his way to a residential street. Three young bangers were hanging out in front of a Lincoln Continental. He walked over to them.

"We ain't doing nothing man!" A svelte, bald soldier said. He looked to be a member of a gang called the 18th Street something-or-other from what his tattoos displayed. On his neck under the left ear was a small design, the letters "LA" drawn in the cap logo style of the Los Angeles Dodgers baseball team and a large number "18" underneath.

"You are now," Drake told them reaching into his pocket. He produced a thick roll of hundred dollar bills and tossed it to him. Without waiting for an answer, he opened the rear door of the Lincoln and sat down inside.

23

WHEN CARMEN SANCHAZ heard that a shootout involving Oscar Mike had touched off in City Terrace, she had to move fast. Gary was in a meeting, and there was no time to lose. She grabbed her purse, laptop, press credentials, a pen and note pad, told Lamar to grab his gear and headed to the nearest broadcast van in the motor pool.

When she arrived on the scene, the street looked like Fallujah. Police cars smoldered, and smoke darkened the air. The acrid smell of burning rubber gave Carmen a headache.

She was wearing a black and white pinstriped blazer with cuffed pants to match, and they absorbed the heat. She saw several police and firemen milling about, talking when there was work to do. Carmen pulled off her blazer and tossed it into the back of the van.

"Lamar," she said, "get shots of these cops doing nothing."

Lamar studiously aimed his camera and recorded the scene.

"*Oscar Mike...*" Carmen narrated while scribbling onto her notepad *"makes a daring and violent escape... after killing two and wounding five... and the maricón cops... stand idle... as City Terrace burns."*

"I thought we weren't fuckin' with cops no more," Larmar said.

"*Oye,*" Carmen said. She pointed to a group of uniformed officers that resembled a social circle more than lawmen invested in catching a cop-killer. "That's them asking to be fucked with."

Lamar panned his camera over the scene. "Zarah Wheeler's here," he said, pointing down the street.

Carmen looked and saw Zarah in a dark blue pantsuit similar to her own. Her posture was weak. She was shaking her head, scrubbing her hands over her face. Lieutenant Torres had both of his hands on her shoulders and appeared to be speaking gently, comforting her.

Carmen ducked under the yellow crime-scene tape and trotted over to two officers and a sergeant in the midst of a discussion.

"Excuse me," she said, dropping her barrio accent.

"You can't be in here!" a large sergeant said.

"I would really appreciate some details of what happened, and could anyone tell me what that discussion is about over there?" Carmen pointed at Zarah and Lt. Torres.

"None of your business!" a young cop told her, seizing her roughly by the arm.

As he was about to pull her back behind the yellow tape, Lamar shouted, "Yo, po-po!"

The cop shot an angry glance at the cameraman and opened his mouth—probably to tell Lamar to watch his—but when he saw the red tally-lamp atop Lamar's video camera blink on, he released Carmen and took a nervous step away.

"It's police business," he said, trying to put the wind back in his sails.

"*Entiendo*," she said, the barrio returning to her dialect. "So you want me to just report what I see?"

"What?" the sergeant asked.

"Because I see an army of cops standing around looking like Oscar Mike pimp-slapped them up and down the street. I'll report that, *sí?*"

"How about I arrest your ass for violating a police cordon?" the sergeant said.

"Fine," she said. "After I make bail, I'll go on the air and publically forgive you."

"What the hell are you talking about?" The sergeant demanded.

"Oscar Mike whipped you all like red-headed step-children," Carmen said. "You took your frustration out on me, and I forgive you."

The cops stood there, not sure how to respond. The sergeant opened his mouth to speak, but Carmen beat him to it.

"*Mira*," she said. "Obviously something happened that Detective Wheeler feels guilty about. You can tell me what it is, and I'll let you get back to doing nothing. *Or* I can report that Oscar Mike made you all his bitch, got away, and you're doing nothing."

"We'll have Oscar by the end of the day," the sergeant promised.

"That won't be news until it happens. Zarah is getting the daddy treatment from Torres right now, and I wanna know why."

"She couldn't keep her shit in her pants," the young cop said. "He should be firing her ass!"

His superior barked his name in a way that meant "*shut up*."

"*En serio*," Carmen said. "Continue."

The young cop looked at his companions, their jaws tight and shaking their heads at him. "Let Wheeler tell you," he said.

Carmen smiled, but there was a dark warning in her eyes. "Tell me what's happening with Wheeler," she said, "or I'll report what's *not* happening with you. And I do mean, *you*."

"We're discussing road-blocks and closures, likely routes the killer may have taken, oh, and the *two friends of ours* that he murdered here not ninety minutes ago!"

"So, Oscar Mike evaporates after killing two of yours, and you're talking about maybe catching him. I'll report that instead of how *she's* involved." Carmen pointed at Zarah. "Last chance."

The sergeant looked as if he wanted to eat her liver. He shook his head and spoke. As Carmen listened, she looked over at Zarah. The detective's face looked stressed out and anguished.

Carmen smiled.

24

DRAKE BARRET MITCHELL dropped a garbage bag containing his flak jacket and utility belt onto the floor of his empty, hardwood living room and crashed onto the futon.

The three bangers had taken him to Griffith Park. He could have forced them anywhere by gunpoint, but he did not want them talking to cops once they found out who he was, so he used a carrot instead— seven grand. He also let them decide where to cut him loose when he was well away from City Terrace, so if they did snitch, they would have no idea of where his base of operations was.

The driver had dropped him off in a large park with plenty of people around. He found an empty waste bin that had been recently given a new liner. He put his gear inside it and pulled the garbage bag out. He used the bus system to make his way back to Toluca Lake, carrying it over his shoulder.

When he arrived, he turned on the TV and channel surfed. Every news report was about his fight with the LAPD. Soon he came to channel six. Carmen Sanchaz was interviewing a female merchant who had witnessed the battle.

"When I saw the police pointing guns," the merchant said, "I ran inside. Then I heard the shots. Everybody got down on the floor, and next thing, I hear this really loud *boom* and the whole front window broke all over the place. It was frightening, very frightening."

"Yeah, yeah," Drake said to the TV. "Try living in Kabul."

A photograph of a female officer in a LAPD dress uniform standing in front of an American flag and the seal of the city appeared on the screen as Carmen Sanchaz's gentle, Latin-accented voice-over said, "The shootout started with Homicide Detective, Zarah Wheeler…"

Drake sat up and leaned forward. He studied the image of the bitch that had set him up, given him the finger, and would have crippled, or killed him if not for his armor.

"…who acted without support or authorization in an over-zealous act of glory-seeking, which resulted in the injury of her partner, four other officers, and the deaths of two more that had arrived on the scene, too late to be effective. Several civilians trapped in the crossfire were also injured."

It was a shame about the civvies. Drake never intended for innocents to get hurt when he began this mission, but he took comfort from the fact that he did not choose the battlefield. This *Detective Zarah Wheeler* did. That blood was on her hands.

The scene on the news program cut to Carmen Sanchaz trying to get Zarah Wheeler to talk to her. Drake felt his temperature rising as he watched the bitch stride away, ignoring Carmen Sanchaz's questions, with her head high, dignified and defiant.

That's right. Act like you didn't just choke on my cock!

"Is there a reason you had to arrest him then and there, Detective Wheeler?" Carmen Sanchaz asked. "Why did you attempt to apprehend an armed and dangerous man without adequate backup? Please, just a comment."

Zarah Wheeler passed between two officers who blocked Carmen Sanchaz from following her any farther. Behind them, Zarah Wheeler climbed into the back of a grey Chevy

Impala—similar to the one that she and that old man had ambushed him in—and was driven away. Then the scene cut to a mid-shot of the pretty Latina reporter, not a speck of dirt on her, standing in front of a smoking police car, holding a mic under her chin with a somber yet satisfied expression.

"Details are sketchy," she said, "as the manhunt for Oscar Mike continues into the night, and the LAPD struggle to recuperate from the botched arrest in this, the latest of an ever-escalating climate of violence, fear, and police incompetence. This is Carmen Sanchaz, Channel Six Network News; back to you Leon."

Drake wanted to track Zarah Wheeler down, and who better to help him than Carmen Sanchaz? He picked up his pre-paid cell phone and attached the scrambler, plugged it into his laptop, and turned on the voice-distortion software. Carmen's line went directly to voicemail.

Was the little spic being insolent now? Did she think he was one of her fans, that his authority could be defied? Or had she put her conscience before her career, and her own life, and gone over to the cops? Drake still could not figure out how the police were able to ambush him in City Terrace, what they knew, and where they were getting their information from. Could it have been Carmen Sanchaz?

No. Drake had gone dark for a month, and he had not called her in that time. There was no way to trace him through her. He tried calling again. Same result.

"Okay, bitch," he growled. "Time to die."

Then he looked at the TV. The picture was cutting back and forth between the anchor, Leon Mandel, and Carmen Sanchaz. He was asking questions, and she was giving answers. On the lower right hand corner of the TV screen was the word *"LIVE."*

"Oh," he said. "Right. Okay then."

He would have to wait a while if he wanted to use Carmen

for this job. He could not sit still. He wanted to find out every-thing about Zarah Wheeler as soon as he had escaped her cross-hairs. He could wait for Carmen and terrorize her into doing his bidding, but she probably would not accomplish much, and whatever she could manage to procure for him probably would not be worth the wait.

You get what you pay for.

Drake began making plans in his head for Carmen after he had what he needed regarding the detective. Drake activated his SAT phone and punched a few keys. He heard the other end pick up. No one spoke.

"Kobe Bryant," Drake gave them his keyword.

"Go," a woman with an Eastern European accent said.

"I have a pest."

"Vhut kind?" she asked.

"Badger," Drake said.

"No badgers."

"I'll do it myself. I just need documents."

"Vhut kind?"

"Everything."

"High reesk eentel. Vee get docs, but no morde."

The welt on his back where Zarah Wheeler had shot him throbbed. "Understood," he said.

"Chennel iss open." she hung up.

Drake opened a browser on his laptop and entered sev-eral numbers separated by decimals. When he hit *ENTER* he received a *"404 Page Not Found"* error. He refreshed the browser, and the screen went white and empty save for a long rectangular text input field. He typed:

Wheeler, Zarah – Los Angeles Police Department, Detec-tive, Homicide

After he hit enter, the detective's name disappeared. When

he refreshed the browser again, he saw "*404 Page Not Found.*" Then he accessed a bank account that he kept in Grand Cayman and wired ten-thousand dollars to his contact's account, also in Grand Cayman. Now all he had to do was wait.

25

ZARAH HURRIED DOWN the cold, brightly-lit hallway of White Memorial Hospital's Emergency Care Department. She had to see Charlie, tell him he had been right. She needed him to hear her say it.

Still dirty and shaken from the firefight, she weaved and squeezed her way through a crowd of uniforms, detectives, and to Zarah's deepening dread, the brass. She kept her eyes forward, refusing to meet the sad, angry and accusing faces of her colleagues.

Before she reached the room where he was being kept, she was intercepted by Woodley and Pérez. They both had sympathy in their eyes, but they blocked Zarah's path with their hands raised in the firm, cautious way that riot cops were trained to.

"You can't," Woodley said.

"Why?" Zarah asked. "He's okay. Tell me he's okay!"

"He's okay," Pérez said. "You just can't see him right now."

"He's my partner," Zarah said. "He needs to know I'm here for him! Please, get out of my way!" She tried to pass between them.

Woodley threw his granite arm across her chest and grabbed her shoulder. "We get it, but you *can't.*"

Zarah yanked herself free and tried to shove past him, but she may as well have been trying to body-check a sequoia.

"I'm sorry, baby, but I can't let you," Woodley said.

"Out of my way or I'll tear this place down, starting with you!"

"You caused enough drama," he said, stripping off his jacket, "but if you want some of that ol' discipline, try and get past me."

"Come on, guys," Pérez said. "Let's take it easy."

"Naw, man," Woodley snapped. "She don't know when to step off!" He glared at Zarah. "Charlie don't wanna see you, he needs to relax, but you don't give a fuck! You think you're gonna lay me up, too? Come on then!"

The news smashed Zarah. It had never occurred to her that Charlie would not want to see her. "He really said that?" Zarah asked, tears forcing their way out of her eyes. "He doesn't want to see me?"

Woodley nodded, "That's right! He told us to keep you the fuck away from him, and we are, so don't be mad at us!"

"I'm not, I'm just…" Zarah shook her head, and put her face in her hands and rubbed her eyes as if to shove the tears back. She looked at the two veteran detectives. "I know what I did, okay? Tell him I'm sorry." She turned and walked back the way she had come.

"Zarah…" Pérez called after her.

"I know!" she shouted to everyone without turning around or breaking stride in her walk of shame toward the exit.

The following morning, Zarah reported to Captain Sheridan, a tough old cob with salt and pepper hair, shoulders like a linebacker, and a stomach like a sumo wrestler. Torres had quietly accepted her badge and service weapon, so she knew that the Captain had not summoned her to clear her for duty.

When the meeting was over, Zarah walked out of his office on unpaid suspension, having been advised to seek counsel and informed that her return would be a matter of when the bad press died.

26

ZARAH KATHLEEN MADANI was born in Riyadh, Saudi Arabia, on October 13, 1978. Her mother, Kamillah Zaheeruddin Madani, had been educated at the University of Westminster in England, likely with permission from a male guardian, and worked for the Saudi Ministry of Education. The detective's father, James Howard O'Reilly, had started his career as a Chicago cop, and then, for one reason or another, bailed out of that life and became a journalist for the Chicago Tribune. He was likely on assignment when he met Kamillah. Why Zarah had retained her mother's surname was not in the files, but Drake Mitchell suspected a Western name like *O'Reilly* would have stood out in Riyadh, and not in a good way.

Zarah had lived in Saudi Arabia for eleven years. In 1989 James returned to Chicago with Zarah. Who knows why? Maybe because Saudi Arabia is a sweltering hellhole where an Illinoisan, Irish-Catholic and his half-breed daughter were treated like shit, Drake guessed.

Now living in Mount Greenwood, Chicago, Zarah adopted her father's surname, *O'Reilly*, probably because *Madani* would have stood out in the predominately Irish-Catholic Mount Greenwood, and again, not in a good way. She did more than hold her own in the abominable public school system, having never received a grade below A, she skipped twelfth grade, and gained acceptance to attend the University of Chicago, on the fast track to achieving the American Dream of success and fortune. Then, in May 1998, she dropped it all into the toilet, and flushed.

Twenty years old—too young to legally drink champagne— Zarah dropped anchor and tied a poor bastard named Seth Wheeler into marriage. She then took the name Zarah Wheeler. In February 1999, her new husband was stabbed to death in Humboldt Park, in an alley behind a sports bar—probably after going into it to escape that bitch wife of his. The crime remains unsolved.

Zarah held fast to her married name, and with a Bachelor's degree in Communications, moved to Los Angeles and was accepted at the Los Angeles Police Academy in Elysian Park.

After twenty-eight weeks of training, she was on patrol. Her performance reviews were positive, though one training officer wrote that she was *bullheaded*.

At age twenty-seven, she made detective. For three years she bounced around several bureaus and stations, finally landing in the Hollywood Homicide Division. After five years there, she was promoted to Detective III and sent to the Homicide Special Section of LAPD's famed Robbery-Homicide Division.

Drake concluded that Zarah Wheeler was a dangerous adversary. He realized that stalking her was comparable to poking a coiled rattlesnake with a twig—still, the rush it gave him had no familiar. He was smarter than most cops, but not all of them. Zarah Wheeler may have been one of the exceptions. He still could not figure out how she had caught onto him in City Terrace.

Drake followed the news about the detective. Weeks had passed since their battle, and though Drake had put his mission on hold again, Zarah Wheeler still had to answer to Oscar Mike.

Three times a week, he had trailed her to a small Jujitsu dojo at a parks and recreation center in Burbank. The vantage where he parked was decent, but not great. Through the sliding-glass door in the front of the bungalow, he could see people in white martial arts uniforms rolling around on blue mats. Zarah was wearing a heavy, white judo jacket with black bottoms while the rest wore all white.

Zarah Wheeler passed in front of the glass enough times for Drake to mark her, but from across the street he could not see well enough to study her movements. He decided to leave the safety of his vehicle, risk detection to make ingress, and watch Zarah Wheeler up close.

Being the last person inside, every eye turned to him, including his subject's. He tried to ignore it and sat in the back of the dojo. His heart pounded inside his ribcage. Every kind of winged insect fluttered inside his stomach.

The head instructor, a well-built, tall man with shaggy, brown hair glanced over at him more than once, as did the pretty detective. Drake's skin tingled every time her brown eyes met his. It happened more times than he was comfortable with, so he fixed his gaze on the head instructor and studied her through peripheral vision.

Drake thought that the fighting techniques they were practicing were useful—against a clown who telegraphed like a U-Boat. One week in Bragg would have had them breaking limbs and suffocating enemies in ways that advanced students would wait years to learn here. Two weeks would have taught them killing methods that so-called *masters* considered advanced secrets that only the most dedicated students would be permitted to learn. They were all origami samurai who would crumple in real combat when forced to kill or be killed.

Zarah Wheeler was a different story. Drake could see that much by her enthusiasm for what she was doing. Her behavior during their battle may have been like a chimp at its first fire, but the precise shot to that upper-third section of his spine said it: her skills are sharp. And in the dojo, she was moving causally but with control and accuracy. There was a hurricane of violence concealed by calmness in her face.

This one doesn't train people to win fights. She trains them to destroy enemies.

She continued to teach, demonstrating basic techniques to the wide-eyed, lower ranked students with different colored belts sitting in a neat, rainbow line, like Skittles, Drake thought—pieces of soft candy looking up at their sensei with awe and respect.

Her black belt was rough, frayed and stringy along the edges and turning grey with wear—physical evidence of practice and experience, symbolizing that she was returning to her White Belt innocence. All it meant in truth was that she needed a new belt.

When the class ended and he stood up to leave, he smiled amiably at an attractive woman, a single mother who gave him a shy "hi" and a flirtatious grin. He made his way to the door.

"Excuse me," a female voice said.

He turned, expecting to see the single mother, but felt a chill run over him when he looked into the face of Zarah Wheeler. She was smiling at him.

"I saw you over there," she said, indicating the spectators' section, "and I haven't seen you here before."

He felt relief fill him. She did not recognize him from their first meeting, with guns and grenades. Though she *had* seen him without the hood, it was through a mirror, and he was wearing sunglasses.

Drake relaxed. "Uhh," he said, "yeah, I was driving by, and I thought I'd check it out."

He turned to leave, but she spoke again. "Are you interested in lessons, or..." She gave a casual chuckle. "I'm sorry. I'm just used to the same faces over there. A new face can mean a new student."

"A new student, right," Drake said. "No, I don't need lessons. I was just curious."

"Are you sure?" The head instructor asked, walking up to them. "This is a non-profit class. It's not expensive."

"I'm Zarah," she said.

"Nice to meet you both." He shook their hands.

"What's your name?" the head instructor asked.

Oscar Mike, bitches!

He imagined whipping out his shotgun and doing both of them right there. But he did not have a weapon on him. His handgun was in his car. He was out of character.

Why'd I put myself in this situation? What's wrong with me? But what would happen if she knew?

He would tickle her nerves a little, push his luck.

"Seth," he said in a casual, yet sly tone.

Drake saw the briefest flash of *something* in her eyes, but a split-second later they were warm and friendly again. She said, "Nice to meet you."

"You, too," Drake said. "Have a good evening."

Now she knows! Now she must die!

He left the dojo and made a beeline for his stolen, white Toyota Tundra. He yanked open the door and found his nine-millimeter hidden in the pocket. He retrieved it and pulled back the slide to chamber a round.

"Hey!"

He turned and saw the detective jogging up to him, still smiling, with a sheet of paper in her hand. He stashed the gun inside his waistband at the small of his back. When she reached him, she thrust the paper at him.

"Class schedule," she said. "Come back if you change your mind."

"Thank you," Drake said, taking the paper in his right hand and reaching around his back with his left, pretending to scratch an itch. He felt the grip of his gun.

"See ya," she said, then turned and jogged back to the dojo.

What did she mean by that?

He should kill her now, but she would not know why. Or

would she? He reached for his nine again, but when he looked to the dojo, the head instructor was watching with clear and present jealousy.

If Drake killed her, he would have to go in there, waste the big guy and everyone who had stayed behind. Too risky. The craving to spill blood stirred within him. While he was goofing off with Zarah Wheeler, people were on the streets, without control, without regard.

Not tonight. He started his engine and drove. The busy streets were about to become busier.

27

*Z*ARAH AND SEBASTIAN sat across from each other at a coffee shop on a corner of Magnolia Boulevard at the outermost edge of the *NoHo* arts district, a small community of artists, musicians, dancers and actors between North Hollywood and Burbank. The crowded coffee shop was situated between a series of small boutiques, beauty parlors, an acting school and a quaint café.

White lights twinkled in the branches of the fragrant magnolia trees along the sidewalk that made the street smell like perfumed soap combined with blends of brewing coffee. They were lucky to have the table they had, outdoors and private, flanked by two potted ficus trees with braided trunks. The aroma wafting on the cool breeze should have produced serenity after the physical strain and pain involved with Jujitsu practice, but this night it did not.

Hanging out at one of the coffeehouses or tearooms near the dojo was a common practice for them, but this night Zarah preferred to be home. It had become a mental labor just to go to Jujitsu class. Over the past few weeks, she had been afraid to show her face in public thanks to Carmen Sanchaz. Carmen's report on the LAPD's skirmish with Oscar Mike, which she had coined "The City Terrace Shootout," had been carried online by The Huffington Post, and the bellicose underbelly of the Internet was unleashed.

On Twitter, there had been a smattering of goodwill for Zarah that had been smothered by an alarming torrent of foul invective, vulgar, sexual wisecracks and unabashedly racist put-downs. Not much had been said about the news article or what she had done wrong. It was cruelty for its own sake, and Zarah had come to discover that "trolling" was a favorite pastime of the fainthearted. Millions of people, it turned out, hid behind anonymity and kicked others when they were down—or up—or sideways.

When Zarah had contacted Robbery-Homicide's Special Assault Section to discuss the tweets describing all of the creative ways people wanted to rape her, they treated her like an out-of-touch senior citizen who should have known that the internet was like this.

Zarah could not feel bad about that. Before she had been suspended, she had been too busy protecting these plankton from the likes of Oscar Mike to familiarize herself with cyber-culture.

Zarah decided to avoid the internet as best as she could and stay away from social media altogether. She still did not think she was doing herself any favors by being out among the plethora of amateur paparazzi with their smartphones, any one of whom could have recognized her and kept the report alive.

She also felt off balance ever since Torres took her badge and gun. Unlike civilians, she was permitted to *carry concealed*, but to Zarah, packing heat without her badge was like walking on a wet sidewalk in socks. It was okay to do, but uncomfortable and potentially messy.

"What are you thinking about?" Sebastian asked her.

She rested her hand over her large, blue and grey suede purse on top of the table. "My gun," she answered.

"You carry a gun?"

Zarah nodded. "Always," she said.

His disapproving look made Zarah's hackles rise. "Go ahead and judge me then," she snipped. "Everybody else is."

"I'm not," Sebastian explained. "It's just, you never told me."

"A billion times you said you hate guns," Zarah said. "Every time guns come up—" Zarah deepened her voice and straightened her posture to impersonate Sebastian. "*A gun is a coward's weapon. A phony's weapon. People kill too often because guns make it easy.*"

Sebastian gave a wry chuckle. "I got that from a Batman comic," he said. "And I'd never think of you as a coward."

"Thanks," Zarah said with biting insincerity.

"So why are you telling me now?"

Zarah shrugged. She knew why. Sebastian's approval was not the hot commodity it was before he married Corinna.

She thought about Adam Jamison. She was too embarrassed to call him, though she felt constant urges to. Adam had not spoken to her since the night he had asked her out, sort of. Zarah did not know the protocol anymore. She had survived full-blown, life or death combat. A grenade had been thrown at her. Why was she so afraid to try and make a date with Adam?

Now was not the time to consume her mind with boy-drama. Charlie was still not speaking to her, and she still had a hearing with the review board to worry about. Her direct superiors seemed to be on her side, but there was P.R. and politics…

Carmen freakin' Sanchaz.

She considered trying to make peace with the reporter, but it smacked too much of surrender. Her dignity would not permit it.

"Everything okay?" Sebastian asked.

Zarah smiled. "Fine," she said. "Why?"

"A second ago you were all chilled out. Now you look upset."

"Just stuff," she said. "You know."

"Tell me."

She exhaled deeply, and then leaned forward and rested her head on the table, using her large purse as a makeshift pillow.

"Just so much crap to deal with," she said.

"The hearing?"

"The hearing, my career, my future…" *You,* she thought.

She perked her head up. "What did you think about that guy who came to the dojo tonight?"

"You're changing the subject," Sebastian said. Zarah made no reply. "Okay," he said. "I think he's from another dojo, checking us out. Checking *you* out. You know him?"

She sat up. "Why do you think he was checking me out?"

"Some guys in the dojo do this *thing*. Ogle you, trying not to look like it. That guy was doing that."

"He was checking me out?" she asked. *Because he couldn't wait to get away from me,* she thought.

"The whole time. Why, do you know him from somewhere?"

She put her head back onto her purse. "He's probably on Twitter right now," she grumbled, "telling everyone how rape-able I am."

"You gonna answer the question?" Sebastian asked.

"I don't know him, Sebastian," Zarah said.

"So, were you checking *him* out?"

"Ugh!"

"Yeah, I guess not," Sebastian said, "cause it's normal for you to chase men down and give them schedules."

"Fine," Zarah said. "I checked him out. Can we drop it now?"

Zarah tried to be unsympathetic about Sebastian's jealousy. He had made his choice. Zarah suspected there were times when Sebastian wished he made different choices, but regret would change nothing.

Her thoughts wandered to the stranger—*Seth.* He had given her a strange feeling when she made eye contact with him. He looked nervous and shifty. It was his name that had affected her most. She tried not to think about her late husband. She had to let that go as well.

"You have a lot on your mind tonight," Sebastian said.

Zarah nodded her head on the purse.

"I wish you trusted me."

She looked up at him. "I do. Don't ever think I don't."

"Then tell me what's weighing your head down on that table?"

"You think I'm keeping something from you," Zarah said, "but I just don't like talking about this stuff."

"Just try."

She took a deep breath. "That guy from the dojo."

"Seth?" Sebastian asked.

"That's my husband's name."

Sebastian made no effort to hide his shock. "You're *married*?"

Zarah nodded. She felt her anger rising.

"So what happened?" Sebastian asked. "Where is he?"

Zarah took another deep breath. She remembered when the Chicago Police came to the small apartment she and Seth had shared, delivering the death notification. She felt the grief of his loss again, the pain of his betrayal. Any ability she possessed to formulate words about it was scorched and incinerated by heartache and unquenchable rage.

"Sebastian, I *don't* want to talk about this." Zarah said.

He shook his head. "Why do you always shut down—"

Zarah pounded her fist onto the table. "Why can't you just let me live in the damn now?"

Sebastian lurched backwards in his chair. "I'm sorry," he said, raising his hands. "I just want to close this gap—"

"Well I don't!" Zarah shot out of her chair and snatched her purse from the table.

"Zarah, what the hell is going on with you?"

"Don't follow me," she commanded as she marched away, her eyes filling with tears.

"No problem!"

Zarah stormed down the sidewalk. She wanted to flip tables over, break glass. People saw her advancing their way and stepped aside as she passed. She turned the corner onto a side street where she had parked. She looked for her car, taking deep breaths, trying to calm herself. She located her vehicle, disarmed the alarm. Before she stepped into the street to get in, a man's voice spoke.

"Detective Wheeler."

Zarah turned and saw a man sitting at a wrought-iron table across from her car, outside a boulangerie. He was younger than Zarah, rugged looking with a tan face, smiling. His hair was a thick, Malibu beach blonde, styled into a neat mess. The rest of him was all business—a dark suit with a white shirt. On the table, next to a white plate with a pie crust and some crumbs was a folded, badge-holder wallet. He was law enforcement without a doubt.

"Hi," he said.

"Who are you?"

The stranger picked up the wallet, unfolded it and presented FBI credentials. "Special Agent Sherman Singer," he said. "Please, sit."

Zarah eyed him warily. He gestured to the chair across from him.

"Please," he said.

She looked over to her car.

"Don't worry," he said. "The meter's fed. We need to talk."

117

28

SPECIAL AGENT SHERMAN Singer had been watching Zarah Wheeler all night, waiting for an opportunity approach her in private. He would have made contact outside the Jujitsu dojo, but the only time she was without that big guy was when she was talking to that other dude in the white Tundra. She and her friend had taken separate cars, so expediency forced him to wait outside for her.

He expected a long wait, so he was surprised to see Zarah Wheeler arriving at her car when he did. When he asked her to take a seat and talk, the detective sighed, lowered her head into her hand and rubbed her temples the way one does at their wit's end.

"Listen," she said. "I'm not trying to be rude, but I've had a *really* bad night. Can we do this later?"

Singer softened his countenance. He had an inkling of what she had been through lately, but he had orders.

"You've had a bad *month*," he told her. "I know. But we need to have words. We don't do this tonight, we don't do it. You may find yourself regretting that later."

Zarah exhaled, set her purse down on the table, plopped into the chair and fixed Agent Singer with an expectant stare.

"Okay," Singer said, "I'll get right to the point. The FBI would like to work with you."

"Come again?" Zarah asked, "Why?"

"We started a file on you a few years back," Singer said.

Zarah jerked her head back. Her nostrils flared, and her eyes began to smolder.

Singer put his hands up. "Detective…"

"What the hell is wrong with you people?" she asked. "Have you *seen* my record on the job?"

"We have," Singer said. "A Saudi-American female who rose to D3 and joined RHD at thirty-seven years old. It's awesome. It's mythic enough for the conservative chauvinists in my office to be in wonderment about how such a thing could have happened."

"If the FBI wants something from me, they should've sent a better representative, 'cause you're scoring *zero* points here."

"Relaaaax," Singer said, slacking his posture and settling into his chair. "My boss ordered me to approach you about bringing you into the bureau. We think you'd work well with us."

"Why?"

"I'm not privy to his motives," he said, keeping quiet about his suspicions that his boss' and Captain Sheridan's polite hatred for each other played a part.

"Why right this second and not, I don't know, *tomorrow?*"

"You've been running around all day," Singer explained. "This is the first chance I've had to approach you alone, and since Braden Wade isn't the kind to be kept waiting, here I am, in North Hollywood eating pumpkin pie when I could be in West Hollywood eating ricotta gnocchi with sunchoke purée."

"Wait," Zarah said. "You work for Braden Wade?"

That secured Zarah's attention. Special Agent Braden Wade was a legendary law enforcer. He was a lead investigator in the search for The Olympic Park Bomber, had led investigations that stopped an Al Qaeda cell from destroying the U.S. Bank Tower in Los Angeles, foiled a plot to bomb the port of Oakland, and prevented an attack on a Pacific Gas and Electric Company power grid that would have blacked out all of Silicon Valley.

"What makes him so interested in me?" Zarah asked. The question seemed addressed more to herself than Singer.

"I already answered that," Singer said. "Now I'm thinking you wanna hear me say what a great investigator you are. And since your agency is tossing you—"

"No one's *tossing* me, Singer."

"After they find out we had this chat... could go either way."

"And when's that gonna happen?" Zarah asked.

"As soon as you get in your car and drive off."

"What is it that the FBI wants me to work with them on?"

Sherman Singer smiled. "There's this terrorist in town, calls himself Oscar *something-or-other*. Ever heard of him?"

Zarah smiled back.

29

CHARLIE SLOCUM, DRIVING a new, dark grey Impala, snaked through light, early morning traffic and exited the San Diego Freeway onto Sunset Boulevard. The sun was rising, but foreboding, autumn clouds muted its ascension.

He cruised east through Bel Air, past the estates of Beverly Hills, and then headed up Benedict Canyon, climbing the slick winding road past cascades of pink and white bougainvillea lulling over fences. He sped past steep, drab olive hillsides, sheathed in brush, studded with oak trees.

The homes about the canyon roads were bordered by towering bluffs, shaded by sycamores, cypress and an occasional sequoia, ringed with thick stands of bamboo, palms and Joshua trees. He knew he was approaching the scene when the sides of the road were dotted not only by mailboxes and running sprinklers but also with onlookers.

He found what he was looking for, flashing squad-car lights and yellow tape lined with reporters and their crews—all of them gesticulating like moths caught on flypaper. He parked his car by the curb, behind a line of unmarked squad cars, opened the door and exited.

"Charlie!" Carmen Sanchaz trotted up to him with a bright look on her face. The big cameraman slid up behind her.

"I just *got* here," the detective said, slamming the car door shut. "I know as much as you. Now get lost."

"I'd already be gone if I didn't have public info officers in my face and stonewalling detectives telling me to *get lost*."

"You brought that on yourself."

"Come on, Charlie," Carmen said. "Throw me a bone."

"You wanna fix shit between us, get in front of that camera and issue my partner an apology." Charlie said.

"*Ay,* she did what she did and has to answer for—"

"Do you think that maniac was out there joyriding in City Terrace?" Charlie asked. "He was looking to kill someone!"

Carmen opened her mouth to respond, but Charlie knew what she was going to say. "Yeah, he got away," he said. "But on that day someone on that street got to keep on living because of Zarah Wheeler!"

"And two cops died to save that *someone*," Carmen said.

"Any cop worth a damn will tell you that's a fair trade, you ratings slut! Now fuck off! I got a real job to do."

Carmen Sanchaz stood still, her mouth open—probably caught up by being called a slut. Good. Maybe she would leave Zarah the hell alone. Charlie left her there to chew on it.

He made his way to the yellow cordon tape stretched across an open, gothic style, wrought-iron gate of a large, creepy, grey stone building that looked like a miniature castle with a thick portico about the front door, several stained glass windows, and arrow slits. A murky pond littered with lily pads of various sizes and bordered by reeds took up much of the front yard. The whole thing was shaded by several weeping willows.

The corpse of William Capucilli, a successful partner of a tax attorneys firm, lay stomach down on the red-brick driveway, half his body on the thick, green front lawn, the door of his black Ferrari still open. The license plate read: *LESTAT1*.

A puddle of blood had formed around a stump where his hand used to be and had started to jell. The hand was nowhere to be seen. Charlie could not get too close to Capucilli's body while the coroner's investigator examined him.

The air was heating up, and beams of morning sunshine were thrusting through the soft branches of the willows. The gray evening clouds were surrendering to daylight.

Six West L.A. detectives and two H.S.S. detectives were moving efficiently about the crime scene for evidence to collect when Charlie had arrived. Several criminalists were scanning the Ferrari for fingerprints and tape-lifting fibers and hair.

"Neck is bruised," the coroner's investigator noted out loud. "He was probably strangled—a rear naked choke maybe."

"What, no fang marks?" Charlie said as he crouched onto the balls of his feet and cocked his head to get a look at the victim's face. An expression of surprise and fear clouded the victim's eyes, his mouth agape in agony.

The coroner's investigator called over a colleague, and the two of them rolled the corpse onto its back, then cut a small incision just above the waist and plunged a thermometer into its liver.

"Rigor is set," the investigator said. "Liver temp says..." he looked up in thought and counted numbers with his fingers. "I'm gonna say he died about twelve hours ago."

"He's been laying here since rush-hour *yesterday,*" Charlie said, "and nobody phoned it in till this morning? Who found the body?"

"Landscaping crew," the investigator said.

The LAPD photographer set up his camera and began shooting. Lieutenant Torres strode up to Charlie.

"Guy was an introverted loner," the lieutenant said, "or just had a really shitty personality. Lives in this little castle by himself—no wife, no kids, only contacts in his phone and computer look like business and clientele. No friends, no family, and no fucking witnesses..." He looked down at the corpse. "You think this was Oscar?"

Charlie shrugged, "He's been inactive for a good while, and he didn't call Carmen Sanchaz, though she may have already served his purpose by opening her big yap and starting this circus."

"Well, it's our case either way."

"How come?" Charlie asked.

"William Capucilli's one of those rich, silent, political-donor-philanthropist types, and West L.A. is already in the process of shoving their heads up their asses. Nobody put a Post-It on the dead guy's forehead saying *'I did it'* and gave an address so..."

"Am I solo or what?" Charlie asked.

"I'll find you an assist," Torres said.

Charlie nodded. "How about Wheeler? She's been in the penalty box long enough."

"I was under the impression that the two of you are on the outs," Torres said.

On the outs?

Zarah had felt guilty enough to make a scene in the hospital, trying to beg his forgiveness, but Charlie knew himself too well to grant her an audience at that time. He was furious, and would have answered her heartfelt apology by lashing out, telling her that she was too full of herself. She did not listen, or think things through enough. He would have told her that, whether she knew it or not, she was a closeted house-drunk and nobody was fooled by her breath mints. He would have told her, whether she knew it or not, that she was lifted to D3 and sent to RHD because of her Arabian ethnicity, and her gender, not because she was any-where near Robbery-Homicide material. He would have told her that her recklessness was fucking up Homicide Special's reputation worse than the O.J. Simpson investigation. He would have dressed her down and chewed her out in anger, without believing most of what he'd have been saying.

Zarah would have, of course, forgiven him. It confused Charlie, but she was able to let go of beefs, no matter how galling the other party had been. She sure as hell would never forget, though, and it still would have destroyed what equilibrium they had. He needed time to get his anger under control to preserve their working relationship, but "on the outs"? No way.

They were so close to having a fully-functioning partnership. The dynamics of it were not entirely ideal, but it could have been much worse. They could have loathed each other. It had happened before, in both of their careers. And after some reflection, the way Charlie saw it, City Terrace was as much his fault as it was Zarah's.

Zarah was still working at a Hollywood Homicide, case-a-week pace, and in H.S.S. things did not have to move that fast. Charlie was the lead detective, the senior, the mentor, and had allowed Zarah's youthful zeal to rub off on him. He should have taken charge and commanded her to stand down.

He wanted to believe that he had forgiven her for City Terrace, but he still could not bring himself to reach out and say so. When Zarah did decide to join the feds, Charlie wanted to see her off as a friend, but that did not mean he was going to get all sappy and fall to his knees.

"We have serious issues," he told Torres, "but if we were on the outs I wouldn't be asking you to bring her back."

Torres breathed out of his mouth and looked up into the branches of a large live oak in thought. "Sheridan said she was out until after her hearing," he said.

"Come on, Lieutenant," Charlie said, "We both know how that hearing is gonna turn out."

"And how's that, Charlie?"

"They'll give her a reprimand, and she's back here, though I admit I'm giving the brass more credit for brains than most people."

"I'll think about it," Torres said.

"Well, think fast and be prepared to stroke her."

"Why's that?"

"I had a phone call from Sherman Singer last night. About Zarah."

Torres lulled his head back with a flustered huff and looked up into the overcast sky. "*Why?*" he implored the heavens. He shook his head and looked back at Charlie, "Don't you love how he sends Singer to sneak up the chain of command like a fucking earwig?"

In H.S.S., the words *Sherman Singer* automatically translated to *Braden Wade*, the FBIs Special Agent in Charge of their L.A. field office. Charlie looked back at his boss, waiting to hear about how much the captain was going to love finding out that the only man in the FBI he hated more than an Internal Affairs probe was sniffing Zarah's ass, but Torres bit his tongue and answered Charlie's look with an expectant stare.

"You gonna tell me the fucking gist of it or what?" he asked.

"Really?" Charlie answered.

Torres squeezed his temples. "After all of the press—"

"They don't give a damn. They've seen her record."

Torres shook his head again, thinking something nasty. "What does Zarah have to say about it?"

"Haven't talked to her," Charlie said. "But Singer says she's thinking it over. Still, given the fact that she's a hothead and on suspension without pay…"

"Next time we talk to her she'll be sporting Federal creds, and her ass'll be puckered for us to kiss it," Torres said. "I'll make a call, and if the brass is on board, she'll work *this* case. But until the hearing decides her fate, she's not going near Oscar Mike."

"Something tells me she'd be fine with that," Charlie lied.

"In the meantime, start your book on this one. Check clients, business associates, *anybody* who may have known this guy well enough to have a motive for this. "

"Will do," Charlie said.

Charlie watched as Torres stalked away with his phone to his ear. Charlie shook his head. Zarah may have asked for time to think the FBI's offer over, but she was not stupid. She was waiting to see if Sheridan valued her enough to make a case for staying. What she did not know was that being a pawn in Sheridan's and Wade's little cold war could yield massive dividends for her career.

After Sheridan had groveled enough, pleaded with her to *come home,* offered her the return of her badge, her gun, back pay and a raise, just to deny Braden Wade the satisfaction of acquiring one of his big hitters, she would choose the federal-jurisdiction side of the argument. And why not?

She deserved to be courted and wooed by the LAPD after the way they buried her in the back yard, as if her presence was evidence of some colossal screw up. She may not have been experienced enough for Homicide Special, but she *was* special, and she knew it.

Sorry, Captain. Zarah's moving up.

30

WHEN CARMEN SANCHAZ entered the studio offices, the rush she usually felt was not present. The electric chaos of the broadcasting life that quickened her blood had no effect. She had nothing to report on the William Capucilli homicide. The cops shunned her as if she had been wearing a scarlet letter.

Usually Carmen was more tenacious. She knew that success depended on her ability to entertain her audience and satisfy their hunger for information. Talent and skill alone would never be enough for her to succeed. It took a certain amount of business smarts and determination, not to mention serendipity and star quality.

Perhaps Carmen was lacking in the business smarts department? People wanted to see the police humbled, and Carmen gave it to them. But cops were also her greatest source of information on the Oscar Mike story, and Detective Slocum's scolding had struck a nerve.

Zarah Wheeler likely did stop another murder. Carmen kept asking herself why that had not occurred to her. Zarah could not have known things would have turned out the way it did.

She did create a situation that ended with two deaths. Who

cares what her self-righteous partner thought about it? *Still, it stuck in Carmen's mind.* She could not shake it loose.

As she approached the snail-mail cubbies, she was intercepted by Stacie Wynes and Aiden Daniels, the two executive directors of Channel Six Network news. Carmen, whose stories usually aired in the afternoons and evenings was used to dealing with Daniels, a bottle brunette in his late-forties with a business-class haircut and square glasses over tired, hazel eyes. Wynes was in her early forties, a tall, dishwater blonde wearing casual business attire in contrast with Daniels's executive level suit. Carmen rarely saw her in the offices unless she was on her way in or out.

"We were just coming to see you," Daniels said.

Now what?

Carmen searched her memory for something she must have done wrong, but could not find anything. Then it occurred to her. If she were in trouble, she would have been summoned to one of their offices. The executive directors had come to her. This was a good thing. Carmen forced her excitement away and turned on her cool.

"Oh yeah?" Carmen asked. "What's up?"

"We'd like to have you in the main studio tomorrow morning," Wynes told her. "Think you and Gary can put something together?"

Carmen had picked a bad day to be downcast and lazy. "So far all I have is that murdered tax-lawyer in Benedict Canyon," she lied.

"Was it Oscar Mike?" Daniels asked.

"Doesn't seem like it," Carmen said. "West L.A. cops made Robbery-Homicide take it, but no note, and no *loco* phone call to tell me about it."

"Hmmm," said Wynes. "We'll need a little more."

Carmen's heart sank, but she sucked it up and shrugged.

"Day's young," she said. "If I get something good enough in time, I'll give you a call."

Wynes nodded, "Fair enough," she said. She gave an approving smile before strutting away.

Daniels stayed behind. He grinned. "Keep it up," he said, patting Carmen on the shoulder before following Wynes.

"Thank you so much," Carmen said calmly while her insides held a jubilee.

She needed a story, and she had phone calls to make. She found her snail mail cubby and checked her box. Inside she found a heavy cardboard mailer. It had been sent by one-day mail and had no return address, but there on the label she saw her name. It was written in a familiar, sloppy scrawl that made her heart stop:

CARMEN SANCHAZ Channel 6 Network News

The entire law enforcement community would have recognized that penmanship. Her own name, written by that man's hand…

Carmen's stomach fluttered again, but this time it felt like a stone had been dropped in it. Her first impulse was to call the police, but she hesitated. She had to see what Oscar Mike wanted with her this time. She would tell the police after and say that she had not realized who it was from until she had already opened it.

She placed the envelope on her desk and took a small package of Kleenex from her purse. With the tissue between her fingers, she carefully opened the mailer and poured the contents onto her desk, the way she had seen it done on "Criminal Minds." It was a thick stack of documents clipped together, all of which seemed to be about Detective Wheeler. A small, white, business envelope fell on top of it. It read: Detective Zarah Wheeler

Inside, on a sheet of yellow, legal paper he had written:

Carmen,

I know what good friends you are, so deliver this to Detective Zarah Wheeler.

The next time I see you on TV you'll be spreading the word. The damage she has done will be visited back upon her. Zarah Wheeler will pay for City Terrace.

Oscar Mike

Carmen slowed her breathing and resisted the urge to cry. Oscar Mike could have been outside in the parking lot with a ream of paper about *her* sitting in his lap. If she did not obey, he might send a different message by lacing her up with bullets and letting Zarah find this stuff on her corpse.

She needed Gary. She left a message on his voicemail. Gary did not respond right away unless his curiosity was piqued, so she kept it vague and told him she wanted to discuss something that she would rather not talk about over the phone.

In the back of her mind, she entertained the idea of taking this to Stacie Wynes and doing exactly as Oscar Mike had told her—from a big chair in the main studio. And then she heard Charlie Slocum's voice calling her a *ratings slut* and telling her to *fuck off.* If Carmen did as Oscar told her, she would win the ratings but forever lose the cops. Every feeling revolted, but to fix that situation there was only one cop she could appeal to.

31

ZARAH PLUNGED A fork into a half-frozen turkey breast that she had been defrosting in the sink—nearly missing it, as buzzed as she was. She hated waiting for it to thaw, but she could never defrost things in her microwave without half-cooking them on accident.

Ordinarily, she would be leaving the dojo right about now, but she thought that distancing herself from Sebastian was a better idea. He had tried calling. Eventually they would make up. No rush there.

She would have liked to review casework to fill the time, but Lt. Torres would not have it. And she was *done* trying to connect with Charlie.

He wants to hold onto his anger? Screw him.

Agent Singer had followed up with her about working for the FBI, but Captain Sheridan had also called. He must have found out about Singer's little chat with her, as Singer had promised he would. But instead of raging on her, he told her that her hearing was a formality for the press and no one wanted to fire her. He promised to return her to active duty, but she would be off the Oscar Mike taskforce, not because of any wrongdoing, but because Carmen Sanchaz was still milking ratings from the case. Keeping the reporter away from her was in everybody's best interest.

Zarah thanked him for the call, hung up, and then reached out to Agent Singer. She expressed her interest in joining the FBI and told him that she hoped she could get to work right away.

Singer told her to hold her horses. He had to talk to her superiors, and if there were no obstacles, she would have some red tape to cut, some documents to sign, and some questionnaires to fill out. She would be vetted. Her friends, family and colleges would be asked questions about her habits, her personality—no worries there. Nobody in her Illinois family would say anything negative, and though she knew the feds would hear the word *"sharmouta"* used once or twice if they spoke to anyone from the Saudi half of her bloodline, Zarah had no fear.

She was a top-shelf detective. Defense attorneys were wary of her, juries liked her, and a high percentage of her cases lead to convictions at trial. These truths must have had factored into the feds' decision to recruit her. Beyond the City Terrace fiasco, which they were overlooking, Zarah was an immaculate razor. So, in the interim, Zarah opted to wait for the good news, and drink rum.

She poked the turkey again as she considered setting her oven on broil and roasting it already—though it had staggered across her tipsy mind that in her condition she would probably overcook the thing and bring her house down in flames around it.

She turned her oven on. *You're gonna cook it eventually. Right?*

She had completed every tedious, domestic errand that work had given her a reason not to, and now there was nothing to do. She thought about calling Adam.

She looked at her ring finger. The mark where her wedding band had once been was now long lost, but Seth's memory persisted. She poured another shot of rum, downed it, and slammed the shot glass down on her cherry-wood coffee table.

God damn him!

Her doorbell, followed by an authoritative knock at her door, jerked her mind back to the present. She walked to her door and peered through her peephole. Her skin felt hot. Rage flooded her mind.

Carmen Sanchaz.

The reporter had a large purse over her shoulder with a thick folder sticking out. That triangle-headed producer stood behind her almost as cocky and dignified as his ace reporter, but they were both fidgety, and Zarah smelled fear. Zarah stood silent at her door, beaming a sharp evil eye through the hole.

"Your car's in the driveway, detective!" the reporter said. "Your lights are on!"

Zarah remained still.

"*Oye!*" Carmen said. "I *feel* you looking at me! I know you're home!" She hammered harder and rang the doorbell twice more.

Zarah leered at her through the door, waiting for Carmen Sanchaz to go away or spontaneously combust.

"Well," Carmen said, "you must want *ALL YOUR NEIGH-BORS TO KNOW—*"

Zarah jerked open her door, whipped her arm out and seized Carmen by the lapel of her stylish wool jacket and the blouse underneath, and yanked her inside as if she were a three year old. The news diva shrieked.

"Hey!" Sterling croaked in shock. Zarah slammed the door on him and shoved Carmen into it, tearing the blouse under her jacket. Zarah made a fist. Carmen raised her hands in surrender as the producer pounded on Zarah's door.

"Shut up!" Zarah commanded. "She'll be out in a minute!"

The pounding abruptly stopped. Carmen took a few rapid breaths. "Okay," she said squeezing her eyes shut, bracing herself. "Bring it! *Vámonos,* punch me! I'm ready!"

Zarah relaxed her grip on the reporter's jacket.

The reporter was decked to the nines—all black and white and classy, while Zarah, barefoot, wearing violet yoga pants, and a black tank-top with no bra underneath, held her against the door with a raised fist.

Zarah noticed a colorful monarch butterfly tattoo fluttering above Carmen's left breast. Zarah was able to make out a word inked in fancy cursive, "*Mariposa*", *Butterfly.*

There was more inked underneath, but Zarah could not see through Carmen's lacy bra, which probably came from Victoria's Secret and cost more than Zarah's whole outfit.

"No?" Carmen said, opening her eyes. "Then let go!"

She slapped Zarah's hand from her lapel with surprising strength. Zarah could not believe her nerve, and it must have shown because Carmen swallowed and jammed a finger in Zarah's face.

"Touch me again," she warned, "and you'll be way fuckin' worse than suspended! Got it?"

Zarah could not tell if the threat was physical or litigious, and since the room was beginning to sway, she lurched a half step away from Carmen. The reporter cocked her head to the side, and her eyes narrowed. She scrutinized Zarah's face.

"You're drunk aren't you?" she asked.

"No," Zarah said. "And what if I am? What's the headline gonna be, *Off Duty Cop Gets Drunk?* Good luck getting me fired for that. That's like...*half* the force does that!"

Carmen's face tightened as she examined the rip in her shirt. She tried to straighten and smooth it out, but it was no good. It was a tit-exposing eyesore, now and forever. Carmen exhaled and shook her head. She frowned at Zarah and opened her mouth to say something sassy but thought twice.

"Whatever," she said instead, taking the folder out of her purse and offering it to Zarah. "This is for you. It was mailed to me."

Zarah took the folder. It almost slipped from her grasp, but she quickly caught it. After making sure she was holding onto it, she flipped it open. Clipped to the top page was an envelope with

Zarah's name on it. The handwriting was unmistakable. She tore it open. Inside was a single piece of note paper and a message:

Dear Zarah,

You came close. Now I'm closer.

Love,

Oscar Mike

An ice floe of adrenaline washed over Zarah. She squinted and looked over the note again.

"I bet you're sober now," Carmen said.

"When did you get this?" Zarah asked.

"This morning."

"And what's this?" Zarah raised the thick folder.

"If you weren't half blind on *Arak* you could see for yourself."

"A *what?*" Zarah asked. "Just shut up and sit down."

Zarah tottered into her living room and dropped the file next to the bottle of Bacardi and the shot glass on her coffee table. Carmen followed her in.

"This is off the record, Sanchaz," Zarah warned her.

"No one cares if you're a drunk, *Zarah*. It's cliché."

"That's not what I mean! I mean—"

"I know what you mean," Carmen told her with some amusement.

Zarah gestured to her sofa.

Carmen dropped onto the couch and zipped her jacket over the torn blouse as Zarah staggered to her front door and invited Gary Sterling in. He looked as if he wanted to chew Zarah out but had decided that silence was wiser. He entered and took a seat next to Carmen.

Zarah plopped into the armchair across from them and rubbed her eyes, trying to sober herself up. "Have you had any other communications from him?" she asked.

"No," Carmen said.

"He hasn't called?" Zarah asked.

Carmen shook her head. "He hasn't killed."

Zarah could not figure Oscar Mike's logic in this move. Zarah was certain that he was too intelligent to do something this stupid. To threaten a cop this way, even a suspended pariah, would make it beyond personal for the LAPD.

"Why…?" Zarah mused out loud. "What on Earth is he thinking?"

"He wants me to go on-air and tell everyone that he's gunning for you, the cop responsible for the City Terrace Shootout, and he's gonna punish you for the damage you did to—"

"The damage *I* did," Zarah chuckled. "So, he's starting to believe his own press."

Carmen shuffled in her seat and smoothed her black skirt, but her poker face remained.

"And I guess that's what you plan to do, isn't it?" Zarah said. "Tell everyone that he's gonna do them all a favor and kill me."

Carmen scowled. "No," she said. "How could you think—"

"You've been gunning for me since the day we met!"

"Detective, detective," Gary said, raising his hands. "The pressure Carmen puts on the LAPD is incentive for the police to be more pro-active about catching him. That's all it is."

"I'm not talking about the LAPD," Zarah said. "I'm talking about me. You chased me down, flinging mud the whole way, and you didn't stop until I was suspended and almost *fired* for being *pro-active*. So you'll understand when I tell you that's a load of self-serving crap."

"Aay, I'm not saying I didn't exaggerate, but my reports will help bring him down in—"

"How are your reports supposed to help bring him down when you're too busy telling everybody what a screw up *I* am, how incompetent the police are?"

"Oh, so when the police make mistakes, the public is not allowed to hold them to account?" Gary asked.

Carmen rubbed her forehead, "Gary," Carmen said. "Just leave it."

"No. *We* didn't botch that arrest. We just reported who did."

Zarah shot out of her chair onto her feet. Carmen and Gary flinched away from her. Zarah picked up Oscar Mike's message from the coffee table and flourished it.

"And now, the killer is sending me love letters!" Zarah tossed the note onto Carmen's lap.

"We did our jobs," Gary said. "You should stop looking for other people to blame for your mistakes and just accept responsibility."

Zarah nodded. "And after he kills *me,* I wonder if you'll accept responsibility for getting me killed."

Zarah walked to her front door and opened it. Carmen stood up with a tired groan. The sass and contempt had left her face. As Carmen walked towards the door, Gary stood and followed. Carmen stopped in front of Zarah. The reporter's face softened.

"I didn't consider…" Carmen said. "I'm—"

"Stop trying to act human and just get the hell out," Zarah said.

Carmen headed for the door. "Whatever," she said.

Carmen and Gary turned to leave. Before she crossed the threshold, she lurched backwards and let loose a horrified yelp that filled the room. Gary slammed the door shut. Then he turned around, scanning the room frantically.

"What is it?" Zarah said.

"Holy God…it's, it's a…it's…someone's…"

Zarah ran to her purse and found her .9mm.

"Get away from the door!"

Gary, green-faced, eyes bulging and cheeks filling like a chipmunk, ran into the small kitchen and puked into the sink—reminding Zarah of the turkey breast she was defrosting in there.

Carmen pulled her phone from her pocket as she turned from the door. She dialed 911.

Zarah jerked her .9mm from its holster and cautiously moved toward the door. She opened it, leveling her gun. There was no one in her line of sight. She looked down.

On her doormat was a severed hand, its middle finger extended. Its other digits save for the thumb had been cut off at the knuckles, flipping the bird to whomever stumbled across it.

32

CARMEN SANCHAZ SAT on Zarah's blue couch. She took in the detective's home environment. The many green ferns and other houseplants, the thick pillar candles, the light and fruity smell of incense and the half-burned sage smudge-stick leaning into a kind of seashell bowl made Carmen conclude that Zarah was overly aggressive in her attempts to relieve stress. Considering that Zarah had been home alone doing rum shots, the new age stuff must not have been working.

Zarah seemed to have sobered up somewhat. She was trying to look stoic, but Carmen saw through the act. Zarah could burn sage until every evil spirit in Pacoima rethought their afterlives. That severed hand coupled with Oscar Mike's message would cancel out any stress relief techniques she employed for all the days to come.

Carmen could relate. Oscar Mike had spoken personally to Carmen, exchanged vocal dialogue. They had *a relationship*, and Carmen felt a powerful urge to get her hands on a gun.

Police were on the way. Zarah had escorted Gary from her kitchen sink to her bathroom. Then she shut herself up in her bedroom, talking on the phone, probably with Detective Slocum or Lt. Torres. She had given Carmen a dirty, mistrustful look as she left the living room.

Puta. Like I care what you and your friends have to say to each other. Like any of that is news.

Carmen held her phone in her hand, looked at the tiny camera lens. She should shoot some filler, just in case.

Is a dead guy's hand too gross for the morning news? Carmen wondered. *Just leave Zarah out of it. Fuck Oscar Mike.*

It had been one thing to get Zarah in trouble at work, but putting her in the crosshairs of that *loco* was unintended. If Oscar Mike smoked Zarah, the LAPD would blame Carmen, and her chair in the main studio would be yanked from under her. Carmen had to turn that around.

Maybe she should scrap the idea of a severed hand story? There was not much sizzle there anyway. But Carmen was first on the scene. Was she supposed to pass that up over a guilt trip? She had a job to do, nothing to show to Stacie Wynes for the morning broadcast and Zarah's quaint abode had become scoop city.

Then something snapped in her mind, and her skin goosed up. The murder scene she had covered in the early morning, William Capucilli. His hand had been severed. Could that be William Capucilli's hand? Should she tell Wynes that it could be—maybe?

She activated the camcorder on her phone and crept over to the open door. She hit record and shot some footage of the ashen hand. The extended finger was beginning to look like the product of some unholy tryst between a breakfast link and a slice of Graukäse.

Carmen kept it together. Her bosses would give her big-time kudos for improvising and shooting it on her phone, regardless of how crappy the picture was. No one else would have footage like this.

Main Studio, here I come!

When she heard sirens approaching, she raised her phone and shot footage of the police cars pulling up to the curb in front of the house from both sides of the street. She heard Zarah emerge from her bedroom, still on the phone. Carmen quickly switched off her camera and went to her car, a strawberry-colored convertible. In Zarah's neighborhood it stood out like a rosebush in a junkyard. She leaned over the passenger's side door and dug through her file bag on the seat until she found a legal pad.

When she looked up, she noticed that a black pickup truck with a shell over the bed was parked a few yards in front of her. She remembered it when she and Gary had pulled up to the curb. It should not have mattered except this vehicle was pristine, like hers. In this environment of dirty clunkers, the truck did not belong.

The truck rocked. It was slight. A blast of hot, Santa Anna wind could have done it, but—*was there a blast of wind just now?*

The windows of the shell over the truck bed were tinted, but she thought she sensed a presence behind them. Her heart wrung itself inside her chest. She was being watched.

She averted her eyes and pretended not to notice. She struggled to remain calm, resisted every urge to get into her car and drive away. If she fled he might follow *her*. She was safer with the cops.

Mariposa from Echo Park felt eyes on her, as if she had crossed into another crew's turf without any *soldados* to back her up. She wanted to get out of there and surround herself with 18th Street muscle, stat. But she was Carmen Sanchaz from Channel Six Network News now, and Carmen Sanchaz wanted to tell all the cops inside Zarah's house what her instincts were telling her. She wanted to see Oscar Mike arrested or killed, and she wanted to be shooting it all on her phone as it happened.

This is a bad idea, Carmen!

You have to, chica, this is your job.

He could jump out and kill me!

He won't do that with all the cops around here.

Are you fuckin' kidding me? Remember that little thing called the City Terrace Shootout?

Carmen acted casual, as if she was going through her contact list for a number on her phone. Then she held her breath and braced herself as if a bomb might explode. She hit record.

I'm going to die!

No, no. Would he risk his freedom, his life, to stop you?

He's fuckin' with Detective Wheeler, leaving sick shit at her door, hanging around cops who want him dead a few feet away! What do you think, estupida? We're done, let's go!

Carmen stepped out of her car and walked back toward the house, trying to make haste without looking hasty.

She did not look back. As she came closer to Zarah's front door, her breathing became harder, and her pace quickened until she was running into the house. She did not care if it alerted the killer. Carmen did not want to be on the street anymore.

Zarah was in her living room with Gary, answering questions for Lt. Torres. She had changed out of the shoeless, braless, *lazing-around-the-house-and-getting-wasted* outfit and had brushed her hair, put on a pair of cross fit sneakers, black jeans, a blue, LAPD t-shirt and, noticing a marked lift and increase in the size of Zarah's tits, Carmen assumed a push-up. The reporter also observed that the bottle of Bacardi and shot glass had vanished from atop Zarah's coffee table.

Carmen must have looked as if she were in a panic. Even Zarah appeared to be concerned. "What is it?" Zarah asked. "Are you okay?"

"I think," Carmen said, gasping for breath, "he's outside."

The cops all jolted at once. Hands went to guns, radios went to mouths, and all eyes shot towards the door. Zarah had the same lupine, hyper-alert look.

"Where?" Zarah asked.

"The black pickup across the street, with the shell."

"Are you sure?" Lieutenant Torres asked.

Carmen nodded her head and clutched Gary.

"Okay," Zarah said with a low growl in her voice. "Wait here."

Carmen wanted to be far away. She also wanted to record everything. The inner debate ended when Zarah stood up and joined the gang of cops at her front door and Carmen found that her camcorder app was active and recording.

33

THE OCCUPANT OF the truck must have known he had been made when a legion of police poured from Zarah's front door onto the tiny, gravel lawn, but there was no movement inside it.

The officers took cover behind their vehicles and leveled their guns at the pickup. Zarah ran across the lawn and hid behind a squad car. Carmen was right behind her, her cell phone raised in her hand, the lens pointing at Zarah.

Zarah whispered, "You've got to be kidding me!"

"Pretend I'm not here," Carmen whispered back.

If Carmen Sanchaz was injured or killed, the finger of blame would point at Zarah, again. "Get back in the house," Zarah quietly demanded.

"No, this is *my* job! You do your thing!"

Zarah looked around. The producer was nowhere to be seen. "Where's Sterling?"

"He's inside," Carmen said, "calling the network."

"Oh, heavenly days. I swear, you people…"

"You *people?*"

Zarah resolved to keep Carmen Sanchaz from harm at all costs. Squad cars had pulled across both ends of the street and sealed it off. If there was to be a pursuit, it would be on foot.

An officer called in the truck's license plate over the radio.

"If he's not in that truck…" Zarah warned.

"I know," Carmen said.

"If you raised this stink for nothing…"

"I know."

The dispatcher returned with a Burbank address for the truck, *"registered to a Sebastian Michaels."*

"Sebastian?" Zarah said, the shock in her voice amplified by the look of horror on her face. She peeked over the rear of the car. It *was* Sebastian's truck.

"You know him?" Carmen asked, with her phone raised, recording every moment. Zarah ripped the phone out of Carmen's hand.

"Ay, qué chingados?" Carmen squeaked.

Zarah turned off the camera and accessed the dial pad. "No, no, no…" she prayed.

She dialed his home number. No answer. Not even Corinna or one of his kids. She pictured him dead in his home, his hand chopped off at the wrist. His wife, his children…

She dialed his cell. It rang—then a voice.

"Hello?"

"Sebastian?"

"Uh, hey Zarah."

Zarah went slack as horror gave way to relief.

"Are you okay? Where are you?"

"Uhh…"

Zarah tightened up again.

"No," she said. "You're *not* in your truck."

"Well… Yeah, I am but—"

"Are you *kidding* me?"

"No, wait!" he said. "Hold on a second, Zarah. I was just gonna ask to hang out, talk… but you had company, so—"

"Why? What happened?"

146

"Corinna's…she's a little upset, and she—"

"She kicked you out, and you thought I'd have a warmer bed than a Best Western?"

"Why is it whenever I come to you as a friend your first thought is—"

"We are *not* having *this* conversation on Carmen Sanchaz's phone!"

"Nice," Carmen grumbled.

"That's right, Zarah," Sebastian said, "tap out when you don't—"

Zarah spat a few Arabic curse words and tossed the phone back to Carmen. The reporter held it to her ear, and Zarah heard Sebastian saying *hello*, trying to figure out if he had been hung up on.

"Mr. Michaels?" Carmen asked.

Zarah went rigid.

"This is Carmen Sanchaz, channel six network news."

Zarah lashed out for the phone, but Carmen pulled away.

"Why are you stalking Zarah Wheeler? Are you some kind of thrill-seeking freak? Do you have a death wish or something? My viewers and I would like—"

Zarah managed to pull the phone away from Carmen and disconnected the call. "You're a nutcase!" Zarah said, handing the phone back.

Carmen shrugged and shoved the phone into her jacket pocket.

Zarah leaned against the car and looked into the sky, confused as the order of her world unraveled.

34

CARMEN COULD NOT tell if Zarah was reproaching herself or asking silent questions of God and getting no answers. The gossip center in Carmen's brain was firing a few questions of its own. She wanted to know who Sebastian was. She stood up and looked to the pickup truck.

Police officers pulled Sebastian Michaels from the bed, frisked him and cuffed him. Carmen snapped a crappy picture with her smart-phone. The man was tall, cute, messy brown hair, athletic and definitely macho. He was looking around for Zarah, but she stayed behind the squad car she was leaned up against. Sebastian called out for her, but she did not move.

"He's a friend?" Carmen asked Zarah. "Or is it complicated?"

"Is he gone?" Zarah asked. Carmen told her no.

After Sebastian had been driven off in the back of a black & white and Carmen gave the *all-clear*, Zarah stood up with a far-away look in her eyes. She plodded toward her home, weighed down by a heavy mixture of woes. Carmen did not know why she gave a damn, but soon the cops would clear out and Zarah would be alone—with that bottle of rum. Carmen trotted after her.

"Hey Zarah," she said, "you hungry?"

"Not since your buddy yakked all over my—crap, my oven's on!"

Zarah quickened her pace into the house. Carmen kept up.

"Fresh air then," Carmen said. "We'll go somewhere."

Zarah cocked her head and looked at her. "You and me?" she asked.

"Uh huh."

"Why?" Zarah continued into her kitchen.

Carmen shrugged, "Why not?"

"Because thanks to you, I can't go places without getting *looks*."

"You're a hot *mamacita*," Carmen said. "You've been getting looks all along."

"Carmen," Zarah said as she turned her oven off. "No con you pull, or stratagem, or whatever you want to call it, is going to get you an interview with me."

Carmen felt her blood warming up. She should leave her here to get drunk, pass out and drown in her own puke.

"I don't want an interview with you," Carmen said. "I want it with him." She pointed to Lt. Torres. "All I was hoping was for us to get some equilibrium, but you wanna be alone and booze it up."

Lt. Torres and several officers turned their heads toward the conversation. Zarah's eyes darted around each of them.

"Okay," Carmen continued. "Dive back into that bottle, and—"

"Let's go," Zarah said, seizing Carmen's arm and pulling her towards the door.

"Not without protection," Lt. Torres said. He gestured to a pair of uniformed officers. "Keep an eye on Wheeler," he told them.

Zarah nodded her thanks to him and nudged Carmen toward the door.

"Who's driving?" Carmen asked.

Zarah's gait skipped a beat, and her lips tightened. But she recovered and walked on, shaking her head. "I swear to God..."

35

CARMEN HAD DRIVEN with Zarah several blocks from her home, to a small Mexican cafe across from Hansen Dam. It was almost closing time and empty, save for the two of them and the two uniformed cops seated at a table by the glass door with large writing in yellow, red and black tempra paint, advertising meal deals in Spanish. From there, they watched the comings and goings outside from a large window.

A million questions were swimming in Zarah's brain, as Carmen sat across from her, pecking at a tostada and communicating nothing beyond a few amiable grins whenever Zarah made eye contact.

A text from Lt. Torres informed Zarah that Sebastian had been brought to the Foothill Station, and Charlie was on his way there to conduct the interview.

She called her estranged partner, but he did not pick up. Carmen sipped Horchata through a straw, her eyes averted, pretending to mind her own business. However, a subtle lift of her eyebrow, after Zarah pleaded with Charlie's voicemail to go easy on Sebastian, indicated that the reporter was paying rapt attention. Zarah hung up, hoping that Charlie was in a giving vein. Sebastian had to have a rational explanation for what he was doing.

Carmen poked her tostada a few more times, thinking *something*, judging.

"There's nothing to charge him with," Zarah told her. "He wasn't stalking. There has to be an established pattern of behavior... You know what? I don't have to explain."

Carmen raised her brow again and nodded, stirring the contents of her tostada with a fork.

"All right," Zarah said, "it's creepy, but not illegal."

The reporter nodded again. Zarah sighed and shook her head. Carmen must have noticed that her impartial silence was getting on Zarah's nerves, and she finally spoke.

"I got this death threat once..."

"Just once?" Zarah asked.

Carmen smirked at the wisecrack and continued. "Homies from Echo were watching my back for weeks before I found out."

"One day you have to tell me the reason."

"One day I will," Carmen said. "The point is, they were just lookin' out. *Your* boy had no reason to be all sneaky unless he was having impure thoughts."

"He's not that kind of guy," Zarah said. "He's a grown man."

"Whatever," Carmen said. "Speaking of being threatened, did anyone tell you about the thing in Benedict Canyon this morning?"

Zarah nodded. "Tax lawyer found in his driveway, right?"

Captain Sheridan had told her as much, right before telling her that H.S.S. would take her back, but only to investigate that particular dead-end, whodunit—and with Charlie of all people, who has not spoken two words to her since the City Terrace Shootout. Oscar Mike was off limits to Zarah, and the reason for it was sitting across from her pretending to eat a tostada. Zarah felt her blood heating up.

"This morning nobody thought it was Oscar," Carmen told her, "but I'm thinking they do now. I do, anyway."

"How do you figure?"

"The dead guy's hand was chopped off," Carmen told her.

Sheridan had *not* told her that. So even if Zarah had turned down the FBI and returned to duty to work this murder, the investigation would likely lead to Oscar Mike, she would be snatched off of yet another case, and she would find herself investigating officer-involved shootings and other vanilla crap.

It did not change the reality that Zarah had to work. She could not sit around all day, especially with Oscar Mike, who had just put *her* at the top of his hit list, running around out there. Plus her savings would not last forever, and she needed a paycheck. But she was relieved that she had hesitated to give Sheridan an answer, and took the FBI up on their offer. Sheridan and the rest of them would consider it a betrayal, but she would be allowed to hunt the man who was hunting her. Then she thought about Sebastian again, and what he may have witnessed outside her home. She folded her hands together, "Sebastian, *please* tell Charlie you *saw* something."

"Y'know," Carmen said, "when we met, I never figured you to be the…"

Zarah gave her a glassy stare. "To be *the* what?"

"The *other* woman. "

"You're so arrogant," Zarah said. "If that's the way it is, why would he hide? He's a grown man. There's some feelings there, I admit it, but he's a grown man."

"You're chanting '*he's a grown man*' like a Buddhist prayer," Carmen said. "But a *grown man* wouldn't stalk you from behind tinted-glass. You *know* I'm right."

"If you're such an expert, where's your lineup of boyfriends?"

"Like I need *that* shit," Carmen snarked.

"That's what I thought."

"A *real* woman doesn't need a man in the first place," Carmen said. "In the second, she *knows* a real man when she sees one."

"Oh, so you think I'm not a *real* woman?" Zarah asked.

"I think you're a real *confused* woman."

"I swear to God... *Where* do you get off?"

"I'm just sayin'."

"No," Zarah said. "You don't get to insult me and skate from it with that adolescent, passive-aggressive, '*just sayin'* crap. No way."

"Okay," Carmen said. She thought for a moment, bobbing her straw inside the plastic cover of her cup, creating an irritating squeak.

"Your physique tells me you work out," Carmen said.

"Does it, now?" Zarah snipped.

"*Sí,*" Carmen said. "But Barcardi One-Fifty-One, straight up... That's a one-way ticket to the toilet, the hospital, or your deathbed. And the empty neck and shoulders of the bottle I saw—"

"Your point, Carmen."

"You work hard to be healthy, but you're good friends with *el ron*— the kind that's only good for lighting shit on fire, or guaranteeing you'll wake up wondering where you are and why there's a dick on your face. That's *un*healthy."

Zarah huffed and rolled her eyes. "Please..."

"Okay..." Carmen said. "You work at Homicide Special where rational, slow, steady investigating is the pace. *You* jump out and throw down with *pinche loco* terrorists in the middle of the street without backup. The *viejos* you work with will break their fuckin' hips trying to keep up with you."

"Do you ever just get to the point?" Zarah asked.

"The Zarah Wheeler *I'm* acquainted with would've marched right up to that Sebastian fool's truck, yanked him into the street and smacked the shit out of him, that's my point. But here you are, all distant and indecisive and soft.

"So, is Detective Zarah Wheeler a tough, purebred bitch you best respect or she'll rip out your heart and feed it to her wolf pups?"

Zarah scoffed.

"*Or* is she an uptight poser," Carmen asked, "frontin' behind a pretentious, tough-bitch smokescreen? Nobody can tell, Zarah, because you *yourself* are so fuckin' confused."

"I'll admit it," Zarah said. "You see a lot. But you know nothing about me and less about Sebastian. He's a *good* man, a good husband."

Carmen scoffed. "From what I've seen tonight, I hope his wife isn't lying in a ditch somewhere."

"Shut up, Carmen."

"I know you're sprung, but—"

"I am not sprung!"

"Are you prettier than her?" Carmen asked. "I bet you are. When's the last time you saw her?"

Zarah stood up. "All right," she said, at her wit's limit. "You know what?" She gestured to the one of the police officers. The cop nudged his partner, who was looking outside, and both stood up.

"Aay, don't be that way!" Carmen said, grabbing Zarah by the arm and tugging her back. "I'm just teasing."

"You're a sociopath!"

"Am I blushing?" Carmen said. "Look, I'm sorry. I didn't think you'd get all mad."

"I'm not mad," Zarah lied. "I have to go check up on something."

"Sebastian's wife, right?"

Zarah ripped her arm from Carmen's grasp and grabbed her purse.

"Oh, come on!" Carmen called after Zarah as she stormed towards the exit. "I'm winning you over!"

36

DRAKE BARRET MITCHELL was sleep deprived and felt its effect, but he stayed frosty. He had kept himself awake for more than fifty-four hours on several missions. He had often resented the thanklessness of serving The United States. Just looking at the entitled assholes he crossed paths with every day was reason enough.

He had barely made it through *The Crucible* in Marine recruit training, but he overcame it. Through the skills he had honed from the trials of military service, his intrinsic talent for clandestine murder, his relationships across the pond and his reputation for discretion, expedience and efficiency, Drake Barret Mitchell had forged himself into a highly vendible asset in the private sector.

Anyone who had need of quiet wet-work had to pay his overseas handlers just to offer him the job, and every job paid enough for him to live in luxury if he so wished. But he was a warrior, and the money he did not spend on his spartan living expenses went right back to his guys in Kirov to keep him stocked in the tools of his trade.

Business had been slow recently, but Drake had set more than enough dough aside to survive the lull. Still, he needed action as all warriors do. He needed blood, and the motorists of L.A. along with Detective Zarah Wheeler had given him more than enough elective work.

He wished he could have stuck around to see her reaction to that Ferrari-driving douchebag's bird-flipping hand on her welcome mat. It must have been priceless. If Carmen Sanchaz had delivered the package he had sent to her, *priceless* would not have been the word for it.

Alas, he did not know how long it would have taken her to make the discovery, but he knew when she did, cops would come running in droves. It was not worth the risk to wait around and see, so he returned to Toluca Lake, but he was restless.

Taking the Ferrari guy's hand had not been planned. It was improvised, out in the open, and with the time it had taken to do the *surgery*, there had been none left to write a communiqué. Drake may have been a serial killer, but he was not an obsessive-compulsive one. He did not have to do the exact same thing every time. *But still...*

Drake had enjoyed making that fat fuck pay for cutting off a college girl in a Jetta, and coming within an inch of causing a pileup, *several times*. It had been rush-hour, and there had been construction on the road leading into the hills. People had to go slow and inch along, but apparently driving a Ferrari gave this prick the right to penetrate every opening and force the plebs, whose lives and safety mattered not, to hit their brakes, and nearly each other, making way for his majesty.

Drake did acknowledge that the guy had technically signaled every lane change, but engaging one's turn-signal *as one turned* was not signaling, it was being a smartass—and in Drake's book, that was reason enough. Drake knew he could not grease every asshole who failed to signal. He would have to fly over the entire 405 freeway in a B-52 and carpet-bomb the length of it from Ventura Boulevard all the way to LAX to make that point, but there *had been* a point to be made with "LESTAT1". *Jerkoff...*

What amused Drake the most was that in spite of the guy's success of barging his way in and out of the lanes, he had been easy to tail without having to mimic that behavior, even in a rush-hour traffic jam. Ferraris did grow on trees in L.A., but they were not so common as to be hard to spot, and the fool's personalized license plate had made it even easier. Oscar Mike was darkening his driveway seconds after the dimwit had pulled in.

But still... The hurried improvisation of that kill... it was weak-sauce. What was the point of making an example when he did not have time to leave a message giving the reason he did it? There was no lesson to be learned there, just another corpse, and Drake was dissatisfied. The goal *had been* to send Zarah Wheeler a message, but it would have been a *great* statement to everyone with a car: signal your fucking lane-changes properly.

I should have left the note with the prick's hand at that bitch's house.

The next night, his juices were flowing hard. He wanted to deliver justice, and make a righteous hit, one he could savor, and one the city would remember. But where to hunt? As he thought back to hacking off that rich prick's bejeweled fingers, he had an epiphany: Rich people.

If he wanted to find easy pickings, some arrogant ass who acted above the rules and everything else, he need only drive over the Holmby Hills. Bordered by Beverly Hills, Wilshire, Westwood and Bel Air, elitist, pompous, Benz-driving, road-hogging one-percenters were coming and going all over the place. And after dropping off his message to pretty, little Zarah, he left Pacoima for the hills.

Beverly Glen Boulevard passed over the Holmby Hills and through a wealthy section of Bel-Air, lined with large homes and gated communities. It was unbelievable how stupid the people here were.

He observed a man in a Hummer resting at a red light over the left hand turning lane. This macho shithead had decided not to turn when the arrow had gone green. People behind him needed to turn, but no, they had to pay for his mistake. They honked and hollered. He pretended not to hear.

When the two right-hand lanes were given the green light, he stomped on the gas, raced ahead and swerved into the intersection, without signaling of course, brazenly cutting people off, one of whom was driving a minivan with three kids inside.

A traffic camera's flash pulsed several times, and the driver would receive a five hundred dollar citation from the city, but so what? People like this spent that much on bottled water. Drake's way yielded results, and by the time some ineffectual ticket arrived in this moron's mailbox, he will have already paid with his life.

37

THE MORNING AFTER visiting with Zarah Wheeler and the horror of finding that hand, Carmen and Gary put together a little vignette about how Oscar Mike was taunting the LAPD with severed body parts. Carmen did not think it was necessarily the best thing to be showing people at breakfast—but hey, *Main Studio*.

Carmen stood up from a comfortable chair behind a sumptuous, backlit desk made almost entirely of glass in front of an enormous television camera. After receiving some pleasant congratulations from the crew on her first time, and compliments on her performance from Stacie Wynes, Carmen left the main studio for the offices.

Carmen was well aware that Leon Mandel, who had been an on-scene ace like her, had gone through the same grooming before becoming the primary anchor. Carmen did not dare to dream of becoming that big, but occupying a seat in a flagship news program was not too lofty a goal.

She could have reported on the excitement at Zarah Wheeler's house after the hand, but she chose to hold that back. Carmen could have attributed it to journalistic integrity brought on by the dignity and professionalism of reporting in the main studio, but it was not that.

Fuck Oscar Mike and what he wants, was what it was. It had been one thing to feed Carmen scoops but to *use* her to threaten and terrorize someone else was too far. Playing along with that would not help catch him, and considering what Zarah had said about shifting attention from the killer to her, she needed to recalibrate her position with law enforcement. It was time put the focus back on Oscar.

She had given the Capucilli murder some sizzle by suggesting that even though it was not his usual M.O., Capucilli was likely another Oscar Mike victim according to a source inside the LAPD. Carmen had been her own source this time, and when the cameras were down and the lights faded to dark, Carmen reproached herself. She *had* to stop doing things like that if she wanted to be recognized as something other than a ratings slut.

As she made her way to Gary's office, the energy of the newsroom washed over her, and she wondered if she deserved to be there. She had painted a good, honest woman as an ambitious, trigger-happy renegade to get this far. It was no wonder the police hated her.

And Oscar Mike's campaign of terror was working. Traffic had improved. People were playing it safe, careful not to break the law or show unnecessary rudeness. The number of accidents had decreased, and fewer moving violations had been cited by the Highway Patrol.

Buses were overloaded, the trains filled to capacity. The number of students on bicycles and skateboards tripled in high school and university campuses. California legislators were leading a crusade to raise the minimum legal driving age from sixteen to twenty-one, as teenagers were the craziest, rudest drivers of them all.

A web poll taken by her network showed that 66.6 percent of Angelenos thought that Oscar Mike had a point. The symbolism of the triple sixes shook Carmen. Now she was no longer a mere enabler of a terrorist. She was in league with Satan. *I have to reverse this,* she thought as she stormed into Gary's office.

"Hey Carm," he said. "What's wrong? You should be over the moon."

She folded her arms. "Over half the city agrees with the crazy killer. What are we doing, Gary?"

"Not the whole city," Gary said, "just the ones on the website."

"You mean the website that gets over six-million hits a day?"

"Well," Gary said, "a *hit* is misleading. A *hit* is when a file is opened. That's image files, video files. I mean, you go to the home page once, and that's like fifty hits right there, so—"

"It was a stupid poll! 'Do you think he has a point?'"

"Well cheer up," Gary said, "'cause in your next broadcast *you* are gonna take a new poll, asking if people think he's wrong."

"No way!"

"I have the directive right here," Gary said pointing to his computer monitor.

"I'm not doing that!"

"Jesus Christ, Carmen," Gary lowered his head and massaged his sinuses. "You're in the main studio two seconds, and already you're a pain in the ass."

"Gary, he's massacring little kids in their beds while they sleep! And you're telling me I'm supposed to ask people if he's *wrong,* like there's two sides to that?"

"I get it, Carmen," Gary said.

"Do you? Does reporting from the main studio mean I'm not a reporter anymore? Now I'm a fuckin'... *poll-reader girl?*"

"You're exaggerating, as usual," Gary said, "and if you don't want to go along with the plan upstairs, that's fine. I just hope the junior college you end up teaching remedial reporting in pays better than this job."

"I'll read the goddam poll, Gary!" Carmen said. "I just...I wanna do a *real* report."

"What do you have in mind?" Gary asked.

"Getting crime scene photos, conducting intense interviews and putting together something provocative. *Sixty Minutes* type stuff."

"You're not a correspondent. You are an on-scene ace."

"So was Leon, and I can write circles around that *analfabeto cabrón!*"

Gary looked up and scratched the back of his head.

"Gary, they put me behind the desk."

"One time in the big chair is not a promotion," Gary said. "They are trying you out, that's all."

"And I wanna show em!" Carmen said.

"Show them what?"

"I'm more than a sexy, token Chicana who reads polls and covers chimp riots at the fuckin' zoo, that's what! I wanna show em' the bodies and the blood, and say '*this is what Oscar Mike will do to you and yours.*' Then we can ask people if they think he's *wrong.*"

Gary thought about it, and after a moment nodded his head. "I'll take that upstairs and run it past them," he said. "At the very least, they'll see how seriously you take being in the main studio." Gary reached for his phone, but before he could pick it up, Carmen's rang.

Blocked number. Carmen entertained the idea of ignoring it, but the cops were monitoring. If it was Oscar Mike, which she had no doubt it was, this could help them. She answered.

38

BY THE TIME Carmen, Gary and Lamar had arrived in
Bel-Air, the police were already working the scene, which
answered the question of whether or not they truly were
listening to her phone.

Oil-black body bags, sealed and strapped atop stainless metal
stretchers, advanced through the side-entry gate of a two-story
home. A train of corpses and coroners moved down the sumptuous, curved driveway to the open rear doors of the white and blue
coroner's vans as if they were on a conveyer.

Carmen Sanchaz's news van was parked a block away from the
crime scene where the Public Information Officer directed her to
stage. Residents of the wealthy neighborhood were watching from
their windows. Several lined the yellow tape. Officers were asking them questions, and Carmen, too, approached several onlookers to ask them what they knew about the residents of the large
home, and whether or not they would consent to being recorded
on camera.

Some liked the family that lived there—they seemed like
decent people—and some did not know them at all and preferred
to have their own questions answered. Only one man in the whole
bunch really had anything negative to say, which figured because
everything about him was dark. He a was tall, strapping white

guy with charcoal colored hair, wearing silver, Nautic sunglasses, a black tank top and trousers with a lot of pockets, and black workman's boots. He must have been a landscaper with clientele in this hood, or some kind of handyman.

When Carmen asked him how well he knew the family, he said he had only known the man who owned the Hummer.

"What can you tell me about him?" Carmen asked.

"He drove a gas-guzzling monstrosity and thought it gave him dominion over the road," he said. "The kinda guy Oscar Mike loves."

"Why *loves?*" Carmen asked.

"'Cause he loves killing people like that."

"Okay," Carmen said. "What's your name?"

"Seth."

Carmen shook his hand. "Seth, can you hang around so I can talk to you on camera?"

"Hell no." The man turned and walked away.

Pinche pendejo, Carmen thought as she returned to the news van. Only a handful of residents who knew the family were willing to show their face on TV. When she returned to the van, she was aghast at what she saw. There was Lamar, high aloft on the fifty-six foot antenna mast as if it were the crow's nest on a ship, sitting on the retracted satellite dish and shooting down into the scene.

She wanted to scream at him to come down, pronto. If Lamar fell and hurt himself, they would all catch hell from the network, but if he hurt the broadcast van, there would be a true and terrible reckoning. Carmen sucked up her fear for Lamar's safety, and elected to keep quiet and pray. If she hollered at him, he could lose his concentration and fall, or make some sudden movement that could damage the mast. She doubted that she could have convinced him to come down anyway.

Carmen exhaled in surrender. For the first time in the frenzy for Oscar Mike's ratings, she had been defeated. By the time Lamar came down from there, anyone she wanted to interview would be snapped up by other aces. Still, watching those bodies being loaded was more important, optically.

Other on-scene teams were closer to the action, but Carmen had to work with what she had rather than make trouble over it. Ever since her violation of their cordon after the City Terrace Shootout, the LAPD made sure that Public Information Officers arrived at every murder scene hinting at Oscar Mike's M.O. before the detectives had. They took special care to make sure that Carmen's crew was far away. It made no difference that she was the one who provided the location of this scene straight from the horse's over-modulated mouth. And when she asked if the trace had worked or if they had gleaned any useful information from the phone call, the answer was *no comment*.

Why did I let those pendejos monitor my calls? Oh right, jail.

Carmen's next move would have been to try to get a chopper from the network to hover over and shoot down on the scene, so Lamar could document her interviews, but the FAA had issued a temporary flight restriction at the FBI's request. The PIO, of course, had no idea why and told her to ask them.

Now Carmen pulled open the doors of the van and put on a headset with a microphone protruding from it. She sat in the rear of the van, legs dangling over the bumper as she listened and scribbled notes.

Carmen spoke into the microphone. "You hear anything good, *papi?*"

On the other end of the wireless line in her headphones was Gary, somewhat concealed in an ivy patch behind a thicket of bushes on a neighboring property, aiming a parabolic microphone at Lt. Torres.

"You're just starting to listen *now?*" Gary said.

Carmen heard Lamar chuckle.

"Yeah," Carmen said. "I was talking to lookie loos, trying to line up some interviews."

"Jesus Christ…"

"Whatever, Gary! There's only fuckin' *one* of me!"

Lamar chuckled some more.

Gary had agreed to sneak up, but he refused to record anything on the better-than-average chance they would be discovered. Carmen could not blame him. Parabolics were a serious affront to the integrity of crime scenes and active investigations. They did not need any more enmity from the LAPD, and if the cops caught Gary, they could all find themselves barred from every future crime scene.

"You know I wanna cooperate," Carmen heard Lt. Torres say.

"I don't even think that," A man said. "Not that it matters."

"Sherman…" Torres said, defeat in his voice.

"Robert…" the man responded, warning in his.

"Who's he talking to?" Carmen asked.

"Some dude named Singer, " Lamar answered. "Probably a fed."

Carmen wrote the name *Sherman Singer* in the margin of her notes. There was a long silence. Carmen twisted around to look at the monitor in the van. Lamar was still shooting the coroners, the bodies. That was *the shot*, and since she figured her interviewees were not going to pan out, Carmen was not going to sacrifice it to watch Torres and this Singer guy stare at each other or whatever was going on in their non-verbal drama.

"Did you talk to Wade about this?" Torres asked. The silence from Singer suggested that he knew that Torres already had the answer.

"Okay then," Torres said. "Just tell her she still has a hearing, but we all want her back."

"You tell her if you think it'll make a difference," Singer said.

Torres gave a wry laugh. "You're a bitch with bone."

"Don't be like that," Sherman said. "If you put up a big enough fight, it could still go either way."

"Who're they talking about?" Carmen asked.

"Dunno," Lamar's voice answered in her headset, "they haven't said a name."

"I don't know that she's worth fighting for," Torres said.

"Then don't," Singer replied. "She's too young and dumb for your *special* section anyway. Let her play with kids her own age."

"Whatever," Torres said. "Anything else I should hand over without an argument?"

"Photos, evidence log, the note especially, oh, and your murder books for this scene and the William Capucilli murder, for now."

"This is great!" Carmen said into her microphone. "We should do this more often!"

"Can I please come back now?" Gary begged.

"Just a minute longer, *papi.*"

She returned to her notepad. "How many body bags have come out?" she asked Lamar.

"Six," Lamar said. "A couple were little, like kid-size."

Carmen had a sudden sensation of cold dread. When Carmen went on the air and did what she was planning to do, the monster who just massacred this family would have a sudden craving for Mexican. But, Carmen had hope that going on the air and attacking *him* personally would be just what the police could use to capture him.

The *carbon* loved to hear his own voice, Carmen could tell. When Oscar watched Carmen's poignant, contemptuous, burning of him and his *mission,* he would call. He would want to let her know how dead he was going to make her. The cops would be tracing. The curtain would fall. His reign would end, and Carmen Sanchaz would take a bow.

167

ETER DRAKE BARRET Mitchell had gone from room
to room, killing that Hummer-jackass and every member of his household, he called Carmen Sanchaz. He was
immediately suspicious. She had not gone on TV and reported
that Oscar Mike had marked Zarah Wheeler for death, and when
she spoke there was something in her voice that waved a red flag.
She had no fear. He decided to stick around and wait for her.

He parked his truck far enough away to safely watch his suspicions be confirmed. The on-scene ace and her crew had arrived
thirty minutes after the police. Carmen Sanchaz was out of play.

After the police had taped off the house, the neighborhood
awoke and gathered around the cordon. He decided to approach.
He removed his BDU coat, put on his sunglasses and watched.
When the cops asked him what he knew, he told them that he
lived up the street and knew nothing. Soon he found himself talking to Carmen Sanchaz. It felt right, and he relished the adrenal
rush as he returned to his vehicle and left the scene.

As he exited Sunset Boulevard to Beverly Glen, he rolled down
the passenger-side window and took the pre-paid cellphone he had
used to contact Carmen Sanchaz from a pocket in his trousers. He
checked his review mirror, making sure there was no one behind
him, and he flung it out the window. The burner sailed over the
edge of the steep foothill and disappeared.

ZARAH HAD FINISHED an exciting day. At about noontime, as she had left her house for the first time all week, she was armed, alert and scanning her surroundings. The tight feeling in her stomach loosened some when she saw the dark blue Chevy Impala resting to the left of her driveway. Its engine started, and the woman behind the wheel, Officer Wilster, gestured a stoic greeting. Wilster was a tall, sharp-featured Valkyrie, whose platinum hair had been pulled back so tight Zarah wondered if her scalp might tear loose from her skull.

Torres had asked S.W.A.T. for help protecting Zarah, and Wilster, the only female in S.W.A.T., had volunteered for the post. She had been accepted to C-Platoon, a special unit in Metro that was all about quelling violent crime. Her expression was serious without a spark of warmth in her cobalt eyes. Zarah approved.

Zarah entered the freeway and drove south to the FBI's Los Angeles Division in Westwood, with Wilster in her Impala behind her. She had to fill out some paperwork and make her provisional position with the FBI official. While she was doing that, Agent Singer had gone to meet Lt. Torres and inform him of the FBI's official involvement in the case, and of Zarah's official involvement with them.

Zarah still could not work the investigation. She had to wait until the LAPD sent the FBI paperwork that would make Zarah a liaison of sorts. She was not quitting her job with the LAPD—not yet—but everyone would see the writing on the wall.

Zarah wanted to clear her old life from the board as soon as possible. For that to happen, Oscar Mike had to be put in a box—whether it was steel bars and high-security locks or timber planks and nine-inch nails made no difference.

She wanted to maintain her distance from Sebastian, but on the night he had spied on her house, he had an opportunity to see the killer in the flesh. The problem was now he was the one doing the avoiding, even after she reassured him on his voicemail she was not angry. She did not want to fight. She just wanted to talk.

No callback. No text. No e-mail. Nothing. Zarah had even called Corinna several times, but she was not talking to her either.

Sebastian had embarrassed Zarah in front of her boss, her colleagues, *and Carmen Sanchaz of all people.* Why was he acting as if she was the one who had done something wrong? And *Corinna*... she should have been *happy* Sebastian had stayed in his truck.

Zarah held fast to her standards, and *"No Intimacy with Married Men"* was in the top five, but had Carmen Sanchaz waited until morning to make her surprise visit, had Sebastian come knocking on Zarah's door in need of consolation, and had Zarah answered it—vulnerable, lonely and far from sober—*anything* could have happened.

It was all becoming too much, and Zarah considered that if things did not pan with the feds, perhaps it would be time to go somewhere else—maybe to Texas and become the small-town sheriff from *Los Angeleez.* Or maybe she would return to Illinois, live in Freeport, partner up with her cousin Mary and become a ghost-whispering P.I.

After Zarah had finished her business in Westwood, she jumped in her Camry and headed back towards the valley. She checked her rear-view and spotted the Impala and the poker-faced Viking woman driving.

She considered trying to touch base with Charlie, but he, and the rest of them, had all shunned her like a bad smell. If she had met Agent Singer a month before, the decision would not have been as easy, but now? She was only showing them the same species of loyalty they had shown her, and though she relished the idea of strutting into Parker Center, shoving federal credentials in their faces and douching all over them, the FBI had field divisions all over the country, and she was feeling only too happy to pull up stakes and start fresh somewhere new.

41

L IEUTENANT ROBERT TORRES sat in his office and read over the file that the FBI had e-mailed, though he did not have to.

At the bottom were the signatures of Zarah Wheeler and Special Agent in Charge, Braden Wade. Zarah was going through with it. He felt his blood pressure rise. Time stopped for a one-count, but then he rationalized. The pay was better, the power was greater.

The brass may have sent her to RHD to promote the image of a gender-equal, racially, and religiously, tolerant department, but she was a highly-skilled and dedicated detective, and was as qualified as anyone else in Special. She would be a bigger pain in the ass than any fed he had to put up with before, but she would get it done for them.

The FBI had copied the file all the way up the chain of command. Clever. Torres could almost hear the locomotive that they were going to railroad her on pulling into the station. When it was over, Zarah would have nowhere to go *but* the FBI.

He paid a visit to Captain Sheridan. He, too, had read the request.

"Wade's making sure," the captain said. "When she's gone

from here, she's gone for good. It sure as hell isn't because she was suspended. Shit, I've been suspended. You've been suspended."

Torres chuckled. "Twice," he said.

"Good cops take calculated risks sometimes," Sheridan said.

"You're not pissed?" Torres asked.

"At Wade, sure, but not Wheeler. She's doing what anyone would. Especially after all this."

"If Carmen Sanchaz had just kept her mouth shut…" Torres said.

"Yeah," Sheridan said, "but it can't look like the Blue Wall is still standing. It's political. It's optics and all that. I told Zarah last night: *Just take your medicine and come back wiser.*"

"I think she just wants to work the Oscar Mike case," Torres said. "We took her off it. They offered to put her back on. When it's over, she'll come home."

"Why the fuck would she do that?" Sheridan said. "There's prestige, she'll be able to fly with her firearm without any paperwork, she'll have the job of a detective and make as much as *you* do, and you're an L.T. And if she's reassigned to another state… shit I make *more* than a special agent and I have a two-bedroom apartment in La Brea. Wheeler can go pretty much anywhere but here or New York, and she'll be able to afford a four-bedroom house with a fucking *pond,* with fucking ducks and shit."

"She'll never have time to enjoy it," Torres said. "Besides, an LAPD dick will catch more bad guys in a month than she will in a year," Torres retorted.

"The bad guys she'll catch will be more interesting," Sheridan said.

"You sound jealous."

"Fuck you," Sheridan said. "Anyway, it's all moot. Zarah's gonna be boxed in, especially after the commander reads—"

The captain's phone rang. He looked at the caller I.D. and then gave a knowing glance to Torres before picking up.

"Sheridan," the captain said.

Someone on the other end barked something at him.

"Yes, sir, I did."

More barking.

"It's provisional," Sheridan answered. "Her lieutenant and I—"

The barking was less loud, but barking nonetheless.

"Sir, I would ask you to rethink that. She's still—"

Loud bark.

"Yes, sir."

Sheridan hung up and looked at Torres with an expression that prophesied some troublesome news for Zarah Wheeler.

42

ARAH WAS ON her couch, poring over the taskforce's notes and reports that she had splayed across her coffee table. Singer had brought them by earlier, complements of a begrudged LAPD. Her attention was fixed on Charlie's interview with Sebastian.

She inserted a small thumb-drive into the USB port in her laptop and opened a video file. The harsh picture displayed Sebastian, looking weathered and weary. His posture was rigid, his arms crossed in front of his chest in a defensive posture.

Zarah watched Charlie sitting across from him, exhaling white cigar smoke, taking his time. He leaned back into the steel swivel chair as if it was an Edinburg and all that was missing was a glass of cognac. The chair creaked and moaned under his large girth.

"I thought smoking wasn't allowed in here," Sebastian said.

Charlie looked him over, took another long draw, nodded his head blissfully, and exhaled over Sebastian's head.

"So, you had a fight with your wife, right?" Charlie asked.

"Yes."

"Why haven't we been able to confirm that with her?"

"When she's like this, she turns off her phone."

Zarah wondered what they had been fighting over.

"That's okay, some guys are on the way over there. We'll get that straightened out."

Sebastian's face did not convey fear, but the way he shifted in his seat hinted at a guilty conscience.

"Okay," Charlie continued, "so you have this fight. You leave your apartment in Burbank and drive all the way to Pacoima to visit with Detective Wheeler—a friend of the family?"

"That's right."

"I've worked with her close to a year, and I never heard of you."

"Because it's none of your business," Zarah said to her laptop.

Sebastian shrugged. "Haven't heard of you either. Zarah isn't much of a name-dropper."

"Because it's *none of your business,*" Zarah repeated.

"I'll give you that one," Charlie said. "Anyway, you saw that she had company, a man and a woman?"

"Yes, and I didn't want to intrude. So I waited."

"You waited."

"I waited," Sebastian said.

Zarah's mind raced. *In the bed of your pickup truck?*

"Okay," Charlie said. "So, it's what, almost eighty-five degrees tonight? And rather than sit in the cab with the AC running, some tunes on the radio, light to read a book by or anything like that while you wait, you say *no.* Better to crawl into the bed of the truck with no AC, no comfort at all?"

"Have you even *looked* back there?" Sebastian asked. "It's not that hot."

"It's Cambodia out there tonight," Charlie said. "Under the shell of a pickup bed, it's Hell."

"I was just waiting," Sebastian said. "Zarah will tell you. I'm welcome there any time. I don't have to wait in my truck."

Then why did you?

"I was just being polite."

WHAT? Zarah's mind continued searching for a logical explanation and came up empty.

"*That's* where you politely wait for Detective Wheeler," Charlie asked, "so after she's had a good time with her company you can piss in her ear about your marriage, your clothes soaked in sweat and you smelling like a Cambodian's armpit?"

"How sweaty was I when I came out of the truck," Sebastian demanded. "How sweaty was I when I came in here, and how sweaty am I now?"

"You both have phones," Charlie said. "Why didn't you just call her?"

"I wanted to ask if I could crash on her couch. And in person it's harder to say no."

That was the one thing Sebastian had said that was consistent with his personality. He had always advocated asking for big favors in person rather than e-mail, text or by telephone.

"Is that against the law?" Sebastian demanded

"To ambush her into giving you a sympathy lay? Not at all."

"Charlie!" Zarah yelled. She thought it was too bad that Charlie would not have felt it if she had punched him on her laptop.

"I'm married!" Sebastian said.

"Relax." Charlie took a pull on his cigar, gave Sebastian a moment to calm down, and then exhaled the smoke in his face. "Were you watching the house closely?"

"Yeah, I wanted to see when her friends left."

"Between the time you arrived and the time the cops came, did you see anything else?"

Now we're getting to it.

"About ten or fifteen minutes before all the cops came, someone pulled up. I think he left something at her door."

Zarah leaned forward.

Charlie put the cigar between his teeth and took a healthy draw. He exhaled, away from Sebastian this time, Zarah noticed.

"Tell me about him."

Zarah felt her heart rate speed up. Her skin tingled.

"Not much to tell," Sebastian said, his voice shallow. "Just some guy, stopped in the middle of the street, jumped out, went to her door, came back and took off."

Zarah observed that when Sebastian spoke he had not moved or made any gesture. Charlie jotted down what Sebastian told him. The suspicious glance he had given him before he took his notes told Zarah that Charlie had seen the same thing she had. Sebastian was lying.

Zarah's phone rang. She quickly glanced at the screen. It was Lt. Torres. It would keep. She sent it to voicemail and continued watching the interview.

"That's it?" Charlie asked. "That's all you saw?"

"That's all I saw."

Repeating the question asked, Zarah thought. *Lie number two.*

"Was he white, black?"

"White."

"What was he wearing?"

"A grey hoodie and dark cargo pants."

"What was he driving?"

"A black pickup truck like mine, except his was a Dodge."

"Did he walk to Detective Wheeler's door? Did he run?"

"He moved fast, but I wouldn't call it running."

"What would you call it?"

"How should I…" Sebastian shrugged. "Casual, okay? Like any guy from UPS dropping off a package."

But he was not any guy, and the way Sebastian lowered his gaze to Charlie's notepad and sat back told Zarah, and likely Charlie as well, that again, he had told less than the whole truth.

"Did you recognize him?" Charlie asked. "Anybody you know? Maybe you've seen him somewhere before?"

Zarah nodded, "Good question."

"I'm done answering questions," Sebastian snapped. "What's he got to do with any of this?"

"Take it easy," Charlie said.

"No!" Sebastian said, slapping his hand on the table. "This guy comes, leaves something for Zarah, then a thousand cops show up and I'm being grilled just for sitting outside."

"Relax, son. The woman with Zarah was Carmen Sanchaz."

"Who the hell is Carmen Sanchaz?"

Awesome.

"She's involved in an investigation. She saw you watching the house and thought you were watching her."

"What about the guy with the package?" Sebastian pressed.

"That guy wasn't just caught watching Zarah's house under suspicious circumstances," Charlie said. "That's you, Mr. Michaels."

Oh, no, Charlie.

Zarah was ashamed of her partner. She had told him that Sebastian was a close friend. If Charlie had told Sebastian that it was Oscar Mike threatening her, he would have come forward with everything he knew, to protect her. It still begged the question of what the whole story was, why Sebastian did not reveal everything, and why, oh why, he had been watching her in the bed of his pickup.

"Now, you can go," Charlie told Sebastian. "But if you pull any shit like this in the future, we'll be seeing each other again, and it won't go well for you."

"You have no idea how long Zarah and I have known each other," Sebastian said. "She's going to call me, and I wonder how well things will go for you after I tell her how you treated me."

Pretty well since you haven't picked up the phone once!

Charlie shrugged. "If you *really* know her, you'll spin a better bullshit yarn for her than the one you just did for me."

Zarah scoffed as she watched Sebastian leave the room without a drop of perspiration. Sure, she had asked Charlie to go easy, but Charlie had barely sweated him. Zarah picked up her phone from the coffee table and dialed for Sebastian. If she was shot down by his voicemail one more time, she was going to crash land right on top of him.

43

SEBASTIAN HAD SPENT two nights in the covered bed of his pickup truck, sleeping on top of a folded gymnastics mat from the dojo. Corinna had been furious. After the police let him go, he tried to reason with her on the phone, but she was having none of it. The detectives that the LAPD had sent to check on her had been too happy to tell her every detail of his detention and their cause. Sebastian expected that Corinna had been calm and courteous, the beautiful, dignified and accommodating woman she was to all who did not know her better.

She had been strong enough to tolerate Zarah's presence in his life for all these years, but it had never been beneath her to complain behind closed doors. The seals which contained her resentment and jealousy had been eroding for years.

The humiliating experience with the detectives had shaken the bottle, and when she had relented and taken his call, the cork burst forth and the hot torrent of wrath and invective that followed was a sound he had never heard before. He imagined his two children cowering in a corner, horrified as she roared into the phone at their father.

"All this time I thought *she* was crushing on *you,* but it's *you!*" she had yelled. "I don't know why I kept denying it, kept refusing to admit it to myself! Every day it's *Zarah, Zarah, Zarah!* 'What's *wrong with Zarah? Why's Zarah so pissed off? Why doesn't Zarah talk to me? Boo hoo hoo!'* Now you're watching her *house?* When will you get it through your head? She friend-zoned you! I *married you!* And by the way, for the first time in a decade, she called *my phone,* probably to tell me how innocent *she* is in all this, or to tell you to grow the fuck up!"

To the police, Corinna had stood by him, defended and alibied him. Between swear words, she had told him as much. But she would not let him set foot in their home until she had cursed him thoroughly, which she had accomplished with aplomb, and cried herself empty, which she needed privacy and time to do.

They both needed time—time for her to calm herself and for him to put together an honest and eloquent explanation for what he had been doing outside Zarah's house. The reasons were as complicated as their friendship, but they were still innocent. The storm had to subside before he, his wife and Zarah could discuss things rationally.

Another mistake.

Sebastian had returned home to a dark, empty apartment. A large, rectangular, clean spot was on the living room floor where the kids' toy-chest used to be. Corinna's half of the bedroom closet was empty, save for a few bare hangars. Many of the plastic ones were broken in half. The metal ones were stretched and bent, their hooks hanging onto the pole by a fingernail after she had torn her clothes from them.

The sliding glass door to the balcony on the far side of the living room was open. When he investigated, he saw that she had taken her grandmother's wind chimes and her potted plants. He slid it shut.

When she cleared out the master bathroom, she must have been pulling herself together. Her nail polishes, hairbrushes, makeup, shampoos, soaps and perfumes had been removed with deliberate calmness. Nothing was knocked over or in disarray.

In the kitchen, everything seemed in its place until Sebastian opened the fridge. The beer was gone. He opened the liquor cabinet above it—empty. Corinna had taken all of the alcohol from the apartment, and she did not drink.

Sebastian crossed the living room to the phone on the end table next to the sofa that had been picked clean of the kids' stuffed toys, pillows and blankets. He saw Corinna's wedding ring. As if she had known what he would do, she had placed it next to the phone on top of a small, white card. Sebastian picked up the diamond ring. On the card, Corinna had written:

All hers now. ~C

Sebastian picked the card up and turned it over. It was Zarah's LAPD business card. It was from the time when Zarah was still working in the Hollywood Homicide division, when Sebastian and Corinna were barely a couple. Zarah had given it to her as a gesture of friendship. Corinna had always regarded it as an insincere act of misdirection.

There was a time when Corinna believed that Zarah was in love with him but she had been bested by the better woman. Corinna knew that Zarah and Sebastian had chemistry and feelings were there, but when she had come into Sebastian's orbit, Zarah never stood a chance.

Back then, that was not exactly the case, but it did not matter. Whenever Sebastian intimated, tried to get close, Zarah withdrew. Then he met Corinna. She had become the game-changer.

While Zarah hesitated, Corinna pursued him with no emotional fetters. When she and Zarah crossed paths, they were civil, mature. But when push came to shove and Corinna made her intentions known, Zarah backed off and played the friend card.

Zarah was always ornery, always tight-lipped about anything approaching intimacy, but in recent days, she had become more withdrawn, more anxious, more preoccupied and pissed off. She had stopped showing up for jujitsu class with no explanation. Her phone would ring one and a half times before her automated greeting answered, which meant she had heard the ring, looked at his name on the caller I.D. and *sent* him to voicemail. And then she did not return the damn call!

They had their ups and downs, as true friends do. Yes, there were times she made him feel like the most important person in her life, but there were also times when she placed him so low on the totem pole he could taste dirt in his mouth. Yet, for all of her guardedness, when she was angry, that was one thing she would not have kept quiet about. She had been proactively avoiding him. He deserved to know why, and since Zarah's voicemail had become an oubliette where his calls went to die, yeah, he watched her house.

Would Corinna buy that? All she saw was her husband pining for what he had lost when he chose her, but being in Zarah's friend zone meant they were friends, didn't it? Aren't friends allowed to care about each other, worry about each other, know each other?

She's been married all this time?

Why Zarah had hesitated to become more intimate with him before made some sense now, but he deserved a little more information than *"that's my husband's name."*

Are they divorced, separated? Where is he? What happened?

Was she being vague to make him jealous and piss him off? Forget about love and romance; Zarah was his *friend.* Didn't he deserve to know a little?

He *still* would not know about her husband if that Seth twit had not come to the dojo to watch, looking down his nose at Sebastian's class as if he was so tough. And Zarah had made certain not to mention she was seeing him.

It's none of my business. I know that! But why can't I know anything? Why can't she give me peace of mind? I'M HER FRIEND!

Sebastian decided.

He took a few deep breaths and calmed down. He would put this behind him. He may have been innocent of infidelity, but Zarah's presence had become unhealthy. Corinna was right. He had to grow up. It was time for him to accept his decision, restore his honor and win back his wife and family.

His cell phone rang.

Zarah's ring tone.

If Sebastian had accomplished anything by being caught watching Zarah's house, it was getting her undivided attention. Sebastian considered ignoring it.

It kept ringing. Soon his voicemail would pick up, and she would demand to see him for the umpteenth time. She wanted answers that he already gave at the office.

One more ring.

Sebastian had to deal with her, or she would not stop. He put the phone to his ear and answered it.

"Yes?" he said.

"Sebastian," Zarah said, surprised that he had picked up. "... how are you?"

"Capital," he answered.

"I *really* need to talk to you," she said. "Can we meet?"

"Why don't you just talk?"

Silence. Was she actually shocked he did not want to meet her? Did it hurt her feelings? *Who knows, with her?*

"You're angry with *me?*"

"No, Z," Sebastian said.

"Then what?"

He was tempted to tell her about his empty home, Corinna gone, her ring left behind with a scornful blessing for Zarah to take her place, but it was bad enough that he was caught snooping on her like a little boy. He could not let Zarah know that his benign concern for her had wedged between him and his wife.

"I'm just not in the mood for this," he told her.

"You think I am?" she asked. "You think I'm happy my dearest friend is snooping outside my home like an obsessed creep and won't tell me why?"

"You could have asked me that night," Sebastian said, "but you sent your cop-partner to—"

"I *sent* him?" Zarah said. "Get your facts straight."

"Whatever."

"Look, I'm suspended in case you forgot. I didn't *send* anybody. But I saw the interview—"

"Interview?" Sebastian scoffed. "You mean *third-degree*, 'cause the only thing missing from that was a rubber hose."

"Call it what you want," Zarah said. "We both know you didn't tell the whole truth. I wanna sit down with you and talk. My cop-partner probably wants to run you through the wringer again."

"I don't give a crap."

"Alright," she said, "y'know what? Forget it. Just forget it."

He heard her take a deep breath. Sebastian envisioned her huffing and puffing, pacing. Nothing smoldered quite as beautifully as Zarah's brown eyes when her blood was up, but having those daggers pointed at him was yet another reason not to see her.

"Just tell me what you really saw the other night," she said.

"I already went through this," Sebastian answered.

"Go through it with me."

"No."

"Sebastian—"

"I'm done with this, Zarah."

"Sebastian—"

He disconnected and jammed his phone into his pocket. He stood in the middle of his apartment, waiting for her to persist, but the place remained still, dismal and empty, like him.

ZARAH JERKED THE door of her purple Camry open, slid into the driver's seat and then yanked it shut. She jammed her key into the ignition and revved the engine. She had considered being a persistent ring on Sebastian's phone, but knowing him, he had already shut it off.

The sky was painted an array of violet, orange and yellow, the clouds spread thin and long, offering the promise of a calm, peaceful evening, but Zarah knew better. Oscar Mike was likely out there at that moment. Zarah looked in her rearview mirror and could not tell if Wilster was behind her. Zarah was not alarmed. With the setting sun blazing through the mirror, all the cars looked the same.

As she inched toward Burbank with the rest of the rush-hour traffic, she reminded herself that she had her chance to be with Sebastian and did not take it. The moment he came strolling into the dojo with Corinna on his arm, she should have strolled out, found another dojo to train in and saved herself years of torture, but she had wanted him in her life and still did. If there was a way to remedy the toxicity of this relationship without excising him from her life, she would take it. Zarah lacked any faith that such a cure existed.

Zarah took the exit to Olive Road and steeled herself for the only kind of fight she had never trained for. She decided whatever happened this night would be what had to happen.

CARMEN SANCHAZ KNEW what she had to do to put together a gut-wrenching report. The problem was that when she tried to get the pieces she needed to make it more than just words on paper, something jerked the rug out from under her feet.

She had failed to acquire crime-scene and autopsy photos from the police through official channels. Now she needed to find someone willing to leak them. Adam Jamison had explained to her that he had been okay dropping her crumbs here and there out of friendship, but he refused to risk the case and his career by giving her the whole meal. Zarah Wheeler was out the question. Torres would not have just said no. He would have put out a memo or some shit, and she would have no chance with anyone. Woodley and Pérez had told her off, and the one hope Carmen had left hated her guts and her liver, but she had to try.

The word was that Detective Slocum spent his days off at Disneyland, which struck Carmen as a little weird, but more importantly, it was a terrible place to approach him. How would she find him there? It was huge and crowded, and it cost two arms and a leg to get in.

She opted to wait for him outside his home, a quaint little place in Westlake just a few miles southwest of Echo Park where

Carmen had grown up. She felt a pang of nostalgia, a throwback to tougher times.

Carmen had Detective Slocum figured for a closet-bigot, no shortage of those in the LAPD, but he chose to live in an area populated mostly by Latinos and Koreans. Carmen did not know how much money Slocum, a Detective III, made after taxes, but Zarah lived in Pacoima. It was a humble area, kind of rough, but not nearly as scary as this barrio.

Westlake had once been the place for illegal immigrants to go if they needed a fake driver's license, work permit or social security card. When Carmen was a teenager, Latino gangs owned the whole place, but now there was a surge of middle class businesses. More genteel elements were gentrifying Westlake, backed up by the cops, who wanted to shed the taint of the Rampart Scandal of the late 90s from their division. They pushed the more hardcore sets further and further south of Sunset Boulevard.

But the fresh graffiti on the walls around the commercial areas indicated that it still may not be safe to be in a shiny convertible after dark, and the sun was already sinking into the horizon.

This was where the straight-laced detective chose to hang his hat? There had to be a story here. Maybe he chose to live close to the scum to keep his cop instincts sharp, or to remind himself of how much cleaning L.A. needed or something.

She had to work out a strategy to get him to help her, and it could not be the same attitude she had given Zarah Wheeler. With Zarah she could be herself, a strong and proud career woman, but Charlie would not respond to that. With him, Carmen needed to have her hat in her hand. What would she say?

"*Oye, mami!*" A Latino voice spoke from behind her.

In her side view mirror she saw a heavily tattooed man in a white tank top and Khakis. She twisted around in her seat to get a good look at him. He was bald and had the kind of rippling musculature that came from lifting in a prison yard. An "18" was inked onto the side of his neck with "LA" drawn like the Dodgers baseball team logo above it. With him were four other men from 18th Street. The big, bald one stood in front of them, the clear leader.

"*Oye, papi!*" Carmen said. "*Como estas?*"

"Where you from lookin' so fine like that?" he asked.

"From Channel Six," Carmen said. "Carmen Sanchaz."

She offered her hand.

The gangbanger hesitated and scrutinized her face, trying to decide if he believed her until one of his vatos said, "Holy shit, man! *Oye*, that's *her* man!"

The bald one stared harder. "You're *Aristócrata*, right? Show me."

Carmen opened the door and got out of her car. The top of her head ended just beneath his collarbones. She looked up at him and pulled down the front of her sweater above her left breast, revealing more skin than she preferred to but also her gang ink.

An exquisite and colorful monarch butterfly, the words *Ojos Mariposa* inked in fancy cursive arching above it, and below it, *La Aristócrata*. It indicated that not only was she from around the way, but also that she was *Aristócrata*, a member of a small, all-girl Echo Park set that used to carry respect in this barrio.

She silently prayed that her gang was still influential. If they were not, then Carmen hoped that the fact that she came up in *el barrio* would be enough for them to have mercy and just take her car.

The leader had a lustful, predatory look. It was something Carmen recognized, something that tougher gangbangers pick up in prison. If *Aristócrata* had lost its juice, it was more than possible that this guy would beat her down, drag her someplace private where he and the rest of this little clique would run a train on her.

Carmen reminded herself that she was a news personality standing in front of a cop's house, so her cool stayed in check. The bald guy's four henchmen leaned forward to get a peek at the ink.

One of them whipped out a mini Mag-Lite and shone a bright light onto her breast.

Carmen yelped and yanked her sweater back up. The gang-bangers laughed and slapped *Mag-Lite* on the back. The bald one loosened up and smiled.

"*Carmen Sanchaaaz,*" he said in an oily way that made her feel dirty. "You look *way* better off the TV."

"Yeah," said Mag-Lite, "like super-duper-*duper*-high-def, eh!"

More laughter.

Carmen smiled. There was no way to get rid of them until they felt like leaving.

"*Su nombre?*" She asked.

"*Diablo,*" the bald one said. The others introduced themselves as Shadow, Jarhead, Grim, and the one with the Mag-Lite called himself Looney, which did not surprise Carmen in the least.

"So whatcha doin' on this street?" Diablo asked.

Carmen gestured to Detective Slocum's small house, "Waiting for the guy who lives there to get back."

The gangbangers shared suspicious looks with each other.

"He's *la chota,*" Diablo said. "What the fuck you wanna tell him?"

Diablo squared his shoulders and pushed out his chest, the posture of a man getting ready to throw a punch.

"*Está bien, Papi,*" Carmen said, "I don't wanna tell him anything. You know about Oscar Mike, right?"

Diablo's face took on a disturbed countenance. After a moment he nodded his head.

"The cop who lives in that house is the one—"

"That got fucked up bangin' with Oscar," Diablo said. "I know all that shit, so what?"

"Right," Carmen said, relieved that the street remembered the City Terrace Shootout. "I'm doing a story on Oscar, and there's shit he can tell me to help."

"Don't be talkin' to cops about that shit," Diablo warned.

The gangsters shared some anxious looks, each maintaining a forced casualness that made Carmen nervous, and curious.

"What do you mean?"

"You been gone a long-ass time, *Mariposa*," Diablo told her. "Remember where the fuck you come from. *Recuerda tu familia!*"

"Why? Do you know something *la chota* should?"

"Man, *fuck you!*" Diablo took a threatening step toward Carmen. Her street instincts kicked in, and she fixed Diablo with a defiant glare and held her ground. She had no chance against them, but it was Diablo who had reminded her—Carmen was *Aristócrata*. They would have their way without a doubt, but not without a fight.

A pale blue Ford Taurus cruised up the street. It slowed as it passed the five gangbangers and Carmen on the street. It was Charlie. His eyes narrowed when they met Carmen's. Relief warmed her skin and flooded her mind. She exhaled and closed her eyes, thanking God.

"You fuckin' lucked out, bitch," Diablo said.

Carmen pushed her luck farther. "Diablo, if you know something—"

"Oye *Carlito!*" Diablo said, smiling and waving to Detective Slocum.

Charlie nodded suspiciously at Diablo's greeting and pulled into his small driveway. Diablo shot a hot, menacing look at Carmen and leaned in close. Looney grabbed his shoulder.

"*Es hermano Aristócrata,*" Looney said. "Chill!"

Diablo angrily shrugged Looney's hand off him. "If any fuckin' pigs start asking us shit," he told Carmen, "I don't give a fuck who you are. I'll smoke your ass."

Diablo turned his back, and he and his boys strutted away. Carmen watched Diablo and his crew leave. She could not guess what they knew, but there was something. Why else would Diablo react with so much anger and fear? It was not fear of getting in trouble with the cops. That kind of fear resembled mild nervousness. Diablo had shown full-blown anxiety. Something juicy was there.

Charlie barked her name, "Sanchaz." She squeaked and spun around.

"Sorry," she said giving an embarrassed chuckle. "You scared me."

"What are you doing here?" Charlie demanded.

"Huh?" Carmen said, watching Diablo walk down the street. "Um… I wanted to ask you for something."

"There's no story here," he said. "And a girl like you shouldn't be in a neighborhood like this."

Carmen was amused by that. It was true that Carmen stood out in *el barrio*, but not in the way Detective Slocum concluded. She was a bigger star here than she was anywhere else in Los Angeles. Her name opened doors here that would be slammed shut in the face of any detective.

Carmen continued to follow Diablo and his crew with her eyes, and pondered their connection to Oscar Mike as they rounded the corner, out of sight.

"In neighborhoods like this," she said, "there's always a story."

46

AFTER ZARAH PARKED down a residential avenue beside Sebastian's apartment building, she strode to the gate of the parking garage and looked between the bars. She saw his pickup truck, the Danzan Jujitsu decal on the back window, and recognized the plate. He was home.

When she reached the glass door to the lobby, she looked through. The lobby was empty, well lit, with brass mailboxes and a clean, polished, marble floor, and a closed, metal elevator. The door was locked. She found his apartment number on the directory and pushed the button for Sebastian's apartment. No one came to the intercom. She buzzed again. And again.

If Zarah still possessed her badge, she would have rolled the dice, called the building's manager and demanded to be let in without a warrant. She returned to her car and scanned the street for Wilster. She would be in uniform and could perhaps get Zarah what she needed.

Where is she?

Zarah returned to her car and looked up and down the street for any units. She saw none. They were supposed to be protecting her. Where were they?

Zarah walked back to Sebastian's building and pressed the

buzzer a few more times. If she kept this up, somebody would call 911, but Zarah was not leaving until she and Sebastian had words.

Eventually a group of young people, headed out for an evening on the town, exited the front door. After they had all passed by, Zarah slid in. She took the elevator to Sebastian's floor, found his door, and hammered away with her fist.

"Sebastian, open up!"

Maybe he had gone somewhere with Corinna's SUV? Perhaps it was Corinna who refused to answer. Zarah's mind raced with all the scenarios that could have been taking place. She felt guilt, nervousness. Why? Zarah had been nothing but nice to Corinna. She had shown her nothing but respect. She was guilty of nothing. *Screw this!*

She pounded some more.

"Corinna!" she said. "I need to talk to your husband, now!"

The door opened.

It was Sebastian. His face looked drained and haunted.

"Corinna left," he said. "I was hoping I'd be gone too. I knew you'd be coming."

"You can't ignore this," Zarah said, pushing past him into the apartment. A quietness hung over it. It was not the kind of silence one hears, but sees—a scarceness of familial accoutrements, like some kind of gloomy bachelor pad.

The walls were barren, though the clean-spots they had left told Zarah there had been some photos and art. There were round indentations on the beige carpet where houseplants had sat, and a rectangular impression next to a wood and glass entertainment center, where some kind of chest must have been. Across from it, an oaken coffee table was empty; no knick-knacks, or magazines, or coasters.

By "Corinna left", did Sebastian mean Corinna left *him?* Zarah was as single and alone as it gets—hardly ever home for more than a few hours at a time—yet *her* place possessed a homier, more lived in-quality than Sebastian's, in the state it was in.

That fight with Corinna must have been more serious than Zarah thought. The air was dead, and Sebastian looked so downtrodden and defeated. Zarah wanted to hug him, comfort him, and help him through it, whatever it was.

No! Answers, now!

"You have no idea how important it is that you tell me everything that's happened," Zarah said. "I'm always straight with you. I'm just asking that you return the favor."

Sebastian gave a wry snort and closed the door.

"What, I'm *not* straight with you?" she asked.

"Mulholland Drive is straighter than you," Sebastian said.

"OHH! When did you *ever* ask me a question and *not* get a straight answer?"

"See," Sebastian said. "I gotta *ask* you something before you tell me anything! Unless you don't want to, in which case you dig your heels in and clam up, or just throw a public bitch-fit!"

Zarah's eyes widened in bewilderment. She shrugged with her hands open toward the ceiling.

"Good friends don't keep stuff buried, Zarah!"

"What have I buried?"

"You're married! And you don't think I should have known that?"

Zarah gave an incredulous laugh and shook her head. "I do *not* believe this."

"You don't think I deserve some explanation as to who this guy is—*where* he is?"

"I'm supposed to spill my guts to you," Zarah asked, "while you stand there refusing to tell me why you were snooping outside my house the other night?"

"Who is he?" Sebastian demanded. "Where is he?"

"He's *DEAD!*"

Zarah's eyes watered, and her anger at having to think about it again must have been obvious. Sebastian's expression went from authoritative to guilty. "Why didn't you tell me?" he asked.

"I just—"

"Do *not* say *'I just did!'*"

"*Sorry* I didn't give you my autobiography up front!" Zarah said. "But unlike *you*, I don't live in the past! Unlike *you*, I consider my friends' own burdens before adding mine to theirs!"

"Gee, thanks," Sebastian said. "'Cause, truly, it's much easier to feel as if I don't rank enough to know anything about you!"

"I don't treat you like that!"

"Yes you do! And the second you started dating someone, you threw me off!"

Zarah gave another chortle of disbelief. "I'm *dating* someone now? When did that start?"

"Don't play like you don't know what I'm talking about!"

"Okay, let me get this straight," Zarah said. "I step back from you for two seconds, and you get it in your head that I've *thrown you off,* because I'm *dating* someone?"

"Zarah, I just mean—"

"You wanna know how many men I've *dated* since my husband died?"

"No, I—"

"*One!*" Zarah said. "You wanna know his name?"

"Zarah, I really—"

"*YOU!*" she roared.

"Zarah, will you please calm—"

"I guess I should've just put out and married you the next day, because that worked *so well* for me before!"

"Zarah—"

"But I'm glad I was careful, because now I don't have to worry about *my* husband lurking across the street from the woman he *really* wants!"

"How long did I have to stay in limbo with you, Zarah?" Sebastian said. "You told me nothing to help me understand what you were thinking, or feeling, or going through! So how long was I supposed to wait for you to get serious?"

"I was serious," Zarah said, "but I needed time! I needed to be sure! It had to feel right, but *you* didn't feel like waiting! Corinna, though... She was just your speed, wasn't she?"

"Corinna wasn't fast," Sebastian said, "she just isn't the mixed-up train-wreck you are!"

The outrage on Zarah's face; her widened eyes, flaring nostrils, clenched jaw, and closed fists took Sebastian aback, and he retreated a step away from her.

"Hey," he said, with his hands raised, "you could have *told me* about your husband! You could have told me why you needed time, but it was none of *my* business, right? I didn't deserve to know any of that! I have *never* known where I stand with *you*, but Corinna knew what she wanted, and made it clear! *You* had every chance!"

"Oh, I know it!" Zarah said. "Wanna know why I never took it?"

"Yeah I do," he said, bracing himself for a cruel insult.

She had one all lined up, but something in his face changed her mind. He was right about her, and this was looking more and more like the end of their friendship. Maybe Sebastian had not loved Corinna when they had started, but it was clear he loved her now. He should not be made to regret it, but he also deserved to know the truth.

Zarah shook her head and sat down on his couch. "I would have," she said. "I wanted to. I just... What else can I say? I needed time."

"Time for what?" he asked.

Zarah shook her head and shrugged again. "Does it matter?

You chose her. The stuff I had to work through to be with you didn't have to be worked through after that."

"You should've said something," Sebastian said.

"You're acting like *I* screwed up. You made your choice, and I dealt with it like a grownup. It wasn't me spying on you, Sebastian."

"I *wasn't* spying!" Sebastian said. "At least not the way you and your friends think."

"Then *please* explain it to me."

"I…" he began. He looked absently into Zarah's eyes, searching for the right words. "I just want to understand you."

Zarah scoffed. "I'm a *mixed-up* train-wreck! What's not to understand, Sebastian?"

"Will you please..?"

Zarah put her hands up in surrender.

"You've been more preoccupied," Sebastian said, "more detached, and frankly more short-fused than ever. The only time we ever see each other is at Jujitsu class, but you stopped coming, you stopped calling, and you stopped answering your phone. So I wondered what was causing this… this tense, mean-as-hell version of you. And like our doomed romance, if you had just said *something,* none of this would have happened. Corinna would still be here. She wouldn't have done this."

Sebastian pulled a white business card from his back pocket. He sat down next to Zarah and handed it to her. Zarah read it. She turned it over and saw her old Hollywood Homicide business card.

"Her wedding ring was on top of it," Sebastian said. "The message is pretty clear."

"I'm sorry," Zarah said. "I'll talk to her."

"It's on me. I'll handle it."

"Sebastian, I can understand you not coming to my door that night. Waiting, whatever. But you were hiding. You didn't want to be seen. I need to know why."

"I was *not* hiding," Sebastian said. "I was waiting!"

"In the covered bed of your pickup truck, with tinted windows."
Sebastian nodded. "I have a mat folded up in there, Zarah," he said. "I have a sleeping bag, audiobooks on my phone. I have a battery pack and a fan. I camp out in the truck *all* the time. You know this. You know I take trips to Joshua Tree, or Angeles, or Point Magu to think, and get away, meditate. It's not at all weird for me to go back there and hang out, lie down, think. It's a little man-cave I made for myself. It's where I planned on staying if you didn't let me crash."

"It sounds so great," Zarah said. "Why did you need to crash at all?"

"It is great, but it doesn't have a shower, or a toilet, or someone to talk to. And yeah, I'll admit to it being kinda stalkerish, and I'm mortified by how it looks, okay? But it doesn't come close to what my intentions were, and I'm sorry that it hurt your opinion of me."

"What did you and Corinna fight about?"

Sebastian's eyes cast down, hurt that she did not accept his apology. "Zarah," he said, "I talk to my wife about you. When it comes to you, I have to be totally transparent or I'll feel guilty. I've complained about you. I've wondered about you. She doesn't blame *you* for my feelings, and she understands yours, but she can't stand you, Zarah."

"What?" Zarah said. Her stomach felt heavy.

"I guess recently, worrying about you like I have, and after the other night, me outside your house like that. That just tore it for her."

"If I knew that…" Zarah said, tears threatening to spill. She knew that she and Corinna would never have been besties, but there had always been a friendly respect. "I'm not glad about that, but I'm glad I know now. And I get it. She knows I love you as much as she does."

In her thoughts Zarah had said it many times, but saying it out loud, and with him there to hear it, her whole body tingled.

Sebastian's head jerked back, his breath hitched. "Zarah, I..."

"If you were my husband," she continued, "I wouldn't have tolerated *her* this long, that's for damn sure. She's very special."

He wanted to know what you feel. Now he knows. Change the subject.

"I'm sorry Charlie gave you a hard time," she said. "This wouldn't have computed with him."

"I know cops look out for each other," he said.

"He means well, but if you really were stalking me, I mean criminal, *love-me-or-I'll-kill-you* stalking, he'd find a way to say it was my fault. He didn't tell me anything about his interview with you."

"I doubt I told him anything interesting," Sebastian said.

"You didn't," Zarah said. "But when he told you that Carmen Sanchaz thought you were out there watching her, the truth is Carmen thought you were Oscar Mike watching me. He *is* stalking me, or so he wants me to believe. You wanna know why I'm keeping you at a distance? There it is."

"And you all thought I may have been him that night," Sebastian said.

Zarah nodded.

"Are you okay?" Sebastian asked.

"I'll be fine. But that's why I've been after you like this. I know there's more to what you told Charlie. I saw video of the interview, and I know you. You didn't tell him everything."

Sebastian sat back. "Okay, no," he said. "I didn't."

"What is it?"

"Well..." Sebastian said, "okay, look. First, Detective Slocum was being *real* antagonistic, blowing this noxious cigar in my face—"

"What is it, Sebastian?"

"I thought I was looking out for the guy! I thought you were dating him or whatever. And I'm not gonna be all like the *jealous* guy. Why put *him* through all that crap?"

"Who was it, Sebastian?"

"May I first reiterate that if you didn't compartmentalize every little aspect of your life—"

"Sebastian…"

"It was dark, but I remember that asshole well."

Zarah leaned forward, her adrenaline rising. "Who is he?"

"That guy. The one who came to the dojo that time. The night you told me you were married and then P.M.S.ed all over me, remember?"

For the sake of appearances Zarah pretended to wrack her brains.

"Remember?" Sebastian said. "You chased him down and gave him a schedule?"

"I didn't—"

"*Fine*," Sebastian said, "you didn't chase him. But I was inside. I don't know what passed between you two, but I do know you sure as hell weren't gonna tell me if I asked."

"I gave him a schedule, Sebastian! *That's* what passed between us!"

"*Okay*, Zarah! But back then I thought maybe your phone number was on the schedule—"

"Wait," Zarah said, "I '*compartmentalize every little aspect*' of my life, but I'll give my phone number to a total stranger if he's cute enough?"

"*Or*," Sebastian continued, "maybe he gave you *his* number. I don't know, but that's why I thought maybe you were dating him. I thought he had stopped by to drop in, say hi or whatever, but since you had company, he left something there and bailed. Anyway, it was that guy."

Zarah remembered being intrigued by him. She had found him nearly irresistible.

Seth!

47

"SO I'M JUST supposed to hand over our murder books so you can put them on the air?" Charlie said. "You're off your damn rocker!"

"I don't need everything!" Carmen begged. "Just crime scene photos, autopsy stuff like those little drawings that the doctors do."

"Medical examiner's notes."

"Yeah," Carmen said. "Nothing that's gonna give away anything except what this *pendejo* has done to people!"

"And what do you get out of this?"

"*We* get to watch it supremely piss off this city! Watch it become *uncool* to root for Oscar Mike. Then the people who go online or on the air in favor of him are dismissed by everyone else!"

"I know you mean well here, Sanchaz, but—"

"Come on, Charlie!"

"You and your ilk are what made him a rock star in the first place," Charlie said. "Now you're trying to take back what you did."

"Yes I am," Carmen said. "I put Zarah Wheeler in danger, and I want him caught before he does something to her! I'm trying to help!"

"Okay," Charlie said with a heavy sigh, "just forget for a minute that you're asking me to risk my job. Forget that any leaked information can jeopardize the investigation. Forget that it can hurt our case at trial, and forget that I just don't like you—"

"All right," Carmen said, standing up and grabbing her purse.

"Carmen," Charlie said, warning in his voice.

"What, Charlie?"

"Zarah provoked him, and he went on a rampage that killed two cops; almost three," Charlie said, gesturing at his wounded shoulder. "If you attack him on TV like you did Wheeler—"

"He'll do what," Carmen said, "leave chopped-off hands on *my* welcome mat?"

"The only reason he hasn't killed Wheeler already is that she's dangerous. She's a veteran cop, a fourth-degree Black Belt and an expert markswoman. You're just a biased reporter with a big mouth!"

"I am *Ojos Mariposa, 18th Street Las Aristócratas,* mother-fucker! You think my life ain't been threatened before? You don't know shit about me!"

"Neither does Oscar Mike," Charlie said, "and take my word for it, neither of us gives a fuck!"

Carmen marched out of his house without closing the door and headed down the walkway towards the street.

Charlie called after her, "After you're *dead,* it won't matter what happens next, will it? Sanchaz! Don't do anything stupid!"

He slammed the door.

Her Oscar Mike exposé was dying fast, but it was not over yet. Her *Aristócrata* sisters would help her out. Carmen had lost some of her street-cred by raising herself out of *el barrio,* but *Domita* always had time for her. And after her run-in with those 18th Street *vatos,* she knew that *Las Aristócratas* still had respect.

Carmen whipped out her phone and dialed.

48

S HERMAN SINGER ENTERED Papoo's Hot Dog Show in Burbank, an old-fashioned, urban style dog-flaunter that went all the way back to 1949, if the sign was to be believed. It was not Singer's style of restaurant, and it did not serve his kind of food.

The bright red walls with white scalloped trim and black-and-white checkered floor made him wince. The gingham curtains and tablecloths, heart-shaped chair-backs, and red booths with cow-print table tops all screamed like Amityville for him to get out, but he was there for a reason, which thankfully was not to eat.

He looked around. To its credit, the place was crowded. While looking over the room for Zarah, he noticed that every plate on every table had burgers, sandwiches, fish and chips, but no hot dogs.

It was no surprise. Forty years ago, people ate lots of hot dogs. Today they did not. To stay afloat, Papoo's Hot Dog Show must have been selling more of everything other than hot dogs for nearly that long.

At least they did it well enough to keep their business alive and had not been overtaken by a tacky chain restaurant, and the Department of Public Health had given it an A-Grade, which was posted proudly over the pick-up station.

Tin signs of vintage cars dotted the walls alongside one of Marilyn

Monroe pushing *Lustre-Crème* shampoo. Singer saw an arm rise above the crowd waving him over. It was Zarah, sitting halfway out of the booth with narrow eyes and a down-to-business expression.

Across from Zarah, Singer saw a blue-eyed man with dark, messy hair. That must have been Sebastian Michaels, Zarah's witness, among other things, if the cop-gossip he had heard was accurate.

He was twisting in his seat to get a look at Singer. If he and Zarah were an item, he could see why. He was sufficiently hunky, though he looked strung out.

Singer smiled and headed over. He introduced himself to Sebastian, tapped him on the shoulder to slide over and began to sit down. Sebastian pulled himself deeper into the booth, narrowly escaping from having the Special Agent in his lap.

Singer took off his sunglasses and tossed them onto the table and fixed Sebastian with a curious stare.

"Singer, I—" Zarah began but was cut short by a gesture from Singer. He continued to look Sebastian over.

After an awkward moment he said, "One stalker identifying another. That's one for the books."

Outrage flashed in Sebastian's eyes.

"This whole stalking thing has gotten really stale," Zarah said.

Singer turned his gaze to Zarah. "Why aren't you two talking to sketch artists," Singer said, "and why isn't Braden Wade chewing me out about a call he took from Captain Sheridan, bragging about how the LAPD just scooped the FBI?"

"I didn't tell them," Zarah said. "I thought I was working for the FBI."

"Right now you're working *with* us," Singer said. "Don't burn any bridges. If you become one of us, you'll always need local enforcement agencies in your corner."

"You want me to call Torres?" Zarah said, withdrawing her phone from her jacket pocket.

"In good time, my lady," Singer said. "They just earned themselves a federal kick to the nuts, so I'll grant you one."

Zarah's eyes narrowed, and she tilted her head to the side.

"What?" Singer said. "No one told you?"

"Told me what?" Zarah asked.

Singer glanced at Sebastian, who along with Zarah was all ears. "We'll discuss it later."

"Why?" Zarah asked. "What did they do?"

He glanced at Sebastian again. "In private," Singer said.

"I trust Sebastian," Zarah said. "We can talk in front of him."

"No we can't," Singer said, brooking no debate.

Zarah exhaled and flicked her gaze upward. "Whatever," she said. "I'll fill the taskforce in."

"Okay," Singer said.

"Okay, what?" Zarah demanded.

"Okay, *okay*," Singer said. "Jeez…"

Zarah's cell phone rang. She looked at the caller ID. She jerked her head back. "It's Charlie," she said, surprised, before sliding out of the booth.

Singer heard her bark "What do *you* want?" before the sound of the crowd muted her on her way out the back door.

"Poor Charlie," Singer said. "I'd hate to be on her wrong side."

"If he was really on her wrong side," Sebastian said, "she would've ignored the call."

Sebastian looked tired, weighed down, sad. Singer decided to refrain from making him more uncomfortable.

"What's got her so agitated?" Singer asked.

"She's pissed. Oscar Mike made her feel stupid. So when she talks to you, it isn't you she's mad at, it's herself."

"How did Oscar Mike make her feel stupid?" Singer asked. "Last I checked she had gotten the drop on *him*."

"A while ago, he came to our class and watched."

"Jujitsu," Singer said, "correct?"

Sebastian nodded. "Thing is, when class was over he would've just left with the rest of the parents and students and stuff, but Zarah stopped him. There was something about him that made her curious. When Zarah asked his name, he gave her dead husband's name."

"Seth Wheeler?" Singer said.

Sebastian scowled and shook his head, as if he did not believe what he was hearing. "*Seth*, was all he said," Sebastian told him. "She didn't put it together until a few hours ago. It pissed her off good."

"I've only known her a couple of days, but I can still see the cork is in there pretty tight."

Sebastian nodded. "I've seen her pissed, you know, about her job? When she's frustrated, she gets kinda mean."

"Noticed," Singer said.

"Now, Zarah's *really* pissed," Sebastian said, "so when you find Oscar Mike, try and keep her from doing something she'll regret."

"Sounds like you know her pretty well."

Sebastian gave a wry chuckle and shook his head again.

Zarah weaved through the dinner crowd and sat down.

"So?" Singer said. "What's up?"

"It's nothing," Zarah said. "More Carmen Sanchaz nonsense."

"What about her?" Singer asked.

"Charlie says she wants to put some kind of anti-Oscar thing on TV, and she's asking for photos and examiners notes so she can shock everybody and make herself famous. She can't get what she wants legit, so she asked Charlie to leak it. And she must be pretty desperate to be asking him."

"What's the angle?" Singer asked.

"I don't know. It's some half-baked notion to show Oscar Mike for what he really is. *Turn everyone against him,* she told Charlie."

"That's not such a bad idea," Singer said.

"Please," Zarah said. "Like the *whole city* eats out of her hand.

207

Every time I start thinking she's cool... An *exposé*, as if nobody knows this guy is scum. The news media thinks people are so stupid."

"You sound an awful lot like Charlie right now," Singer said. "It's actually a viable idea. We *should* help her. The media is a big part of our strategy."

"Why are you sticking up for her?" Zarah snipped.

"Hey, go online," Singer said. "People have made fan-pages, blog posts. Oscar has a following. Some crying widows and kids, a few spaghetti shots on TV... That'll shut em' up."

"It doesn't matter," Zarah said. "Charlie isn't giving her squat, and the only reason he told me is because he wants me to talk her out of it."

"What difference does it make?" Singer asked.

"Carmen Sanchaz can't speak without irritating someone. If she turns that charm onto Oscar Mike, she's doomed. I'm gonna call her right now." Zarah thumbed the screen of her phone for her number. "All I did was flip the guy off, and now he's...just *no*."

"Put your phone away, Detective," Singer ordered. He had already decided to give the reporter what she needed. There was no point in arguing about it, especially in front of Zarah's civilian boyfriend.

Zarah looked at him with a raised eyebrow and blanched expression, suggesting she did not comprehend who the boss was. Singer's expression did not change. She shook her head and put her phone away.

Singer continued, "Let me get a forensic artist on the line so we can get this started."

"Wait a minute," Sebastian said. "Do you want him to know that you know what he looks like? I just remember something about The Night Stalker throwing his sneakers off a bridge when he found out that cops knew what kind of shoes he was wearing."

"We're not holding any press conferences," Zarah said.

"Not immediately," Singer said. "It's the hounds to the hunters. First, we get the sketch. Then we give it to law enforcement agencies, transit authorities, border patrols, airports, etcetera, all over the place. Then we use the media—"

"Not Carmen," Zarah interjected as if she had say-so.

"We flush him out," Singer said, "and make him run right into our waiting paddy wagon."

Zarah exhaled her relief, tears filling her eyes. "Thank God this is almost over."

"Don't get excited," Singer said, trying to straighten his grin and look reserved. "We don't have anything yet."

"I gotta make this call," Zarah told Singer. "Carmen works fast, and Charlie said she left his place like he wasn't her last resort."

"Listen, Zarah," Singer said. "I didn't wanna pull rank, but we're giving her what she wants. Leave it be."

Sebastian sat down in the booth and pretended to read a menu.

"Ugh, now you're kicking *me* in the balls," Zarah snapped. She looked intently into Singer's eyes. "I get it. You're in command. You wanna help her. You wanna jeopardize everything including her life. There's nothing I can do."

"Precisely. Now follow orders and leave Carmen Sanchaz to me."

"Just give her the stuff *with* the sketch," Sebastian remarked from the booth, still looking at the menu. "She does her story, ends it with the sketch. Now she's turned everyone against him, and they all know what he looks like. While he flees toward your 'waiting paddy wagon' trying not to be recognized by anyone, you and Carmen Sanchaz both hide out until he's caught."

Singer thought about it. It was an impressive strategy, but it would not work.

"It's a good idea," Zarah told him gently, "but it's too slow."

"What do you mean?" Sebastian asked.

Zarah explained, "If we give it to her and wait a day or two while she produces some dramatic exposé, more people could get killed in the meanwhile."

"And if his picture is leaked online or sold to reporters before then, it'll look like we were dragging our feet," Singer said. "We can't wait for the sketch to help Carmen Sanchaz."

"Then why give her anything?" Sebastian asked.

"Thank you," Zarah said. "Exactly."

"Because, you two haven't read his profile," Singer said.

"Tell me then," Zarah said.

Singer exhaled impatiently and sat back down. Zarah followed.

"Mr. Michaels," Singer said. "This is privileged information. Could you wait outside?"

With a forced chuckle and a hard smile, Sebastian stood up and left, shaking his head.

"Okay," Zarah said. "Let's have it."

"Well", Singer said, "he's ex U.S. military."

"We know that," Zarah said. "Charlie thinks he was in some kind of Marine recon unit. *"Oscar Mike"* means *"On the move."*

"Charlie's right. The profile suggests a soldier, well-schooled in war strategy, tactics. Well trained in combat, perhaps Special Forces, somewhere in the middle of the chain between lieutenant and captain."

"A leader of men," Zarah said.

Singer nodded. "And his authority matters," he said. "Rules and regs are important. At some point he left the military. We don't speculate as to why or how. Now he's likely a soldier of fortune."

"A hit man?"

"More like a mercenary," Singer said. "Someone who does freelance missions for clients in the private sector, and is good at it. He demands a high fee and has contacts around the globe."

"How do you figure that?" Zarah asked.

"Frag grenades are expensive, and you can't buy em' at Wal-Mart."

"Give them time."

"Also," he continued, "and this is what prompted us to bring you in, one of the computer geeks noticed when our FBI file on you was accessed. She ran a trace. A virus chewed the network up so bad that we'll never know who it was. But we know who paid for the intel."

"What are you talking about?"

"That epic ream of papers Oscar Mike sent to you, full of information about Zarah Wheeler... He checked you out thoroughly, didn't he? And not just government files, everything. Police records, FBI, etcetera."

"So he hired a hacker or somebody?"

"Oh, it was a hacker all right," Singer said, "but not some nerdo in his mommy's basement. We traced it to Lithuania before it blew up in our face. I doubt it's the real source, but it does mean you were being reconnoitered by someone with reach, and cash. Someone who ain't exactly on a budget if you know what I'm saying.

"This is a guy who knows how to lay low, avoid patrols, complete his missions and escape. He's a highly-skilled, experienced predator. So if we just have a sketch, great, we have a sketch. That will likely get us his name. And great, we'll have his name. And his training will tell him to stay out of sight and wait for things to calm down and then slip away.

"But when Carmen Sanchaz whips people into a lather, and he has a whole city mad as hell and looking for his ass, his training will tell him that he *must* run. He'll know that we'll be getting tips, lots of calls, and most of them will be wrong. But *one* won't. He'll need to get out before that *one* tips us. And so he'll run, right into our trap."

"So I'm right back where I started a minute ago," Zarah said. "And, fine, give Carmen what you think she needs, but I wanna go on record that I should at least try to cool her jets."

"Noted. So where can I find her when she's not on the air?"

"What, you're asking me?" Zarah said.

"Zarah…"

"I *don't* know. Now screw already, I have a lot of nothing to do with Sebastian."

"Where will you two be? Parker Center?"

"Sure," Zarah snarked. "And after I tell them why Sebastian is with me, because they'll ask, I'll tell them why you aren't with me, because they'll ask me that, too. And when they hear that you're handing their murder books to Carmen Sanchaz—"

"Alright, Zarah," Singer said, giving up. "Just keep your phone turned on. We'll touch base in a little while. And Zarah?"

"Yeah?"

"Stay alert," Singer warned.

Singer left the restaurant, walked past Sebastian Michaels without a word, and headed for a black, Ford Mustang parked directly across from Zarah's Camry. Inside was Agent Louis, a young, athletic man with brown, cropped hair, wearing a black polo shirt. Singer leaned into the open window.

"I have another job for you," Singer told the agent.

"But I thought I was supposed to w—"

"No buts," Singer said, "just track down Carmen Sanchaz. When you find her, I'll take over, and you come back to Zarah."

"Are you sure this is wise?" Louis said.

"No," Singer answered, "but Zarah's a tough chick. And you two are all I have at the moment, so find the reporter and do it fast."

49

ZARAH AND SEBASTIAN both had appointments with two different FBI forensic artists in the morning. Since forensic sketching is more about psychology than art, they agreed to take the evening to calm down and clear their thoughts.

Their memory from the night that Oscar Mike came to the dojo was a fragile piece of evidence. It needed to be treated that way. With luck, they would have a general description of Oscar Mike before the late afternoon tomorrow.

A tightness she felt inside was loosening. Zarah and Sebastian drove toward Sebastian's apartment. She imagined he was going to try and patch things up with Corinna. It was a touchy subject, one she avoided since their last big talk. Zarah had pushed her feelings for him deep inside herself, but Corinna had given Zarah an opportunity. The only thing stopping her from taking it was his wedding ring.

A wedding ring that she, literally, gave to you, Zarah thought.

Histrionics. She didn't mean it.

Probably. But still...

The revelation about Oscar Mike's identity gave them both an excuse to distance themselves from the issue and return to a kind of equilibrium, but Zarah still sensed a smogginess between them. The air needed to be clear.

Zarah parked in front of his building and pulled over.

"Don't go up yet," she said. "I think we should talk some more."

"Okay," Sebastian said warily.

She thought about where to begin. She needed Sebastian to understand why she behaved the way she did, but she was not sure that she understood herself. She stared off into space, looking for words.

"Are you okay?" Sebastian asked.

Zarah nodded. She was thinking too much. She had not even started talking, and her eyes started prickling with tears.

"After Seth..." Zarah said. Sebastian turned in his seat and looked at her, making steady eye contact, his pupils large, his mind open. Zarah was afraid, but she had to make him understand. And she had to do it now.

"After Seth was killed, the murder investigation led to some information..."

"He cheated on you," Sebastian said. "Right? I mean, why else—"

"He didn't just cheat," Zarah said. "A small cheat, I could've handled. University of Chicago was a campus full of hard partying people. So, reckless, irresponsible behavior was par for the course."

Zarah started to relax, and reminisce. It was not all betrayal and angst. While tears were building in her eyes, a tiny smile crept to the corner of her mouth.

"My dad used to write for the newspapers in Chicago, before he met my mother in England. After they split, he went back to it. He was so happy, and I learned so much from him that when I got to UChi, all I wanted, all I gave a damn about really, was getting a degree in communications and broadcasting. Take a step up from the papers and report for CNN. I thought being half Saudi and knowing Arabic would give me a leg up at CNN."

"I bet it would have."

"Well, then along came Seth."

"Ah."

"Yes. And keggers, drugs and generally stupid behavior. Have you ever tried to make a Margarita with Crystal Light and tequila? Don't."

Sebastian chuckled.

"And Seth had the same major, the same ambitions. He was handsome and funny...the most beautiful girls would ogle him all the time."

"That must have been tough," Sebastian said.

Zarah nodded. "So, I took up Judo."

"That explains why your throws are so good," Sebastian said.

"Yeah. But I ran, too, played basketball. I exercised like a fiend and barely ate anything but tuna and eggs, mostly to compete with this blonde chick from the tennis team that used to come onto him. If Seth had ever strayed, gotten drunk, been taken advantage of, I could've forgiven him."

"I can't see why you would."

"I'm not saying it wouldn't have hurt, but under those circumstances... I don't know. Living in Saudi Arabia, with my mother's family... it gave me a pretty thick skin when it comes to men having their little weaknesses, making their little mistakes."

"'Weaknesses'?" Sebastian said. "'Mistakes'? A guy betrays you, commits outright adultery, and you blow it off as a little—"

"Sebastian, when I was a kid I witnessed men getting away with... I mean, America's idea of adultery, it's sensibility about what adultery is... It's much simpler than what goes on where I'm from, so yes, if Seth strayed, but *admitted* the mistake..." Zarah cocked her head and shrugged. "I'd be pissed, and he would be on the couch for a while, but... My mother and father both had a moment of weakness and here *I* am, so..."

"How did your mother and father get together in the first place?"

Zarah chuckled and shrugged. "Neither of them talk about it. Mother says it *just happened*. My father says it happened because

I was *meant* to happen, but I suspect my conception was a less than convenient for them. I know that my mother and I are both lucky my grandfather didn't kill her when she went home and told them."

"Why go back at all?" Sebastian asked.

Zarah shrugged. "Her fear of God runs deep," Zarah said. "But God forgives. If she repented, owned her sin, Allah would be merciful. But just in case grandfather was thinking of killing me in the womb, she waited till she was four months along to go home. My father went with, to protect her, to man up, marry her and take responsibility, but he went back to Chicago, I think, six months after I was born.

"So how did you end up in America?" Sebastian asked.

"I was in school," Zarah said. "I had just turned eleven, and this tall white guy shows up, pulls me out of the classroom and pushes me into a car, without a word. Drives me to the airport and boards a plane with me."

"He didn't tell you who he was?" Sebastian asked. "You didn't ask?"

Zarah shook her head. "I was a girl who'd been trained from birth not to question men," she explained. "I wasn't stupid enough to start doing it at that moment. I kept my mouth shut and sat there wondering *'what's gonna happen to me?'*"

"He didn't say anything?" Sebastian asked.

"He talked to me on the plane, but I didn't understand English. His eyes though, his face, his voice… It was kind and loving. I wasn't used to that at all."

"So eventually you started to trust him." Sebastian said.

"Oh hell no," Zarah said drawing laughter from Sebastian. "Yes, I had my own bedroom in a high-rise overlooking Lakeshore Drive, and Lake Michigan beyond, it was the most beautiful thing. It was autumn, there was rain, cool weather, and warm, vibrant colors on the trees. But women walked down the street next to men, no hijab, no burqa, holding hands.

"Four times a day, I begged Allah to protect me from these sinners and devils all around me. Then, maybe a week after he took me from Riyadh, he brought me to a mosque, and the Imam told me that the tall, white guy was my father."

"That must've thrown you for a loop," Sebastian said.

"Oh yeah," Zarah replied. "But what stunned me the most was when the Imam told me *my mother,* a woman whom I was convinced would push me in front of a speeding train if she thought it would make my grandfather happy, contacted him, and begged him to come rescue me."

"Rescue you?"

"Yeah," Zarah said, "as soon as I turned eleven, my grandfather had arranged to sell me into a *Mut'a*. That's a temporary marriage."

"*Temporary* marriage?"

"Yeah. My grandfather made a contract with some guy to marry me. My grandfather would collect my bride price, I'd be married to the guy, we would *consummate* the marriage—"

"He'd rape you, you mean," Sebastian said.

Zarah nodded. "And a couple weeks later the contract would expire, the marriage would end and we'd go our separate ways. Here, it's called 'child prostitution' and will get you ten to twenty-five, but there it's all religious and legitimate. Sunni Muslims, like the guys my father took me to learn English from, don't hold with it, but Shias, like my grandfather..." Zarah shrugged.

"So," Sebastian asked. "How much would your grandfather have gotten for it? A lot, I bet."

"I don't know," Zarah laughed. "His mistake was that he needed both my parents' permission to make it legal. My *mother,* didn't want to go against him openly, so she gave her permission, but then she snuck a message to my father, and he swooped in and saved me."

"They never tried to get you back?"

"My father went to the Saudi Consulate in Chicago, told them why he had absconded with me, and if they made a fight about it the whole United States would know why, and they had no reason to doubt his word, 'cause my father was a reporter for the Sun Times."

"So they didn't make a fight," Sebastian guessed.

"My grandfather let it go," she said. "I wasn't worth the trouble I guess." Zarah chuckled. "But as soon as I was an adult, by American standards, my mother was after me to go back, be Muslim, marry some rich, Saudi import-export dude, but there was no way that was gonna happen. I'm American. I know what the premedieval job of a wife over there is. It's criminal, and on top of it, I'm nobody's cuckquean."

"Unless it's Seth," Sebastian quipped, "and he shows a 'little weakness' or makes a 'little mistake'."

"Hey, there was no mistake there, Sebastian! He didn't just get drunk and forget himself! He was proactively deceiving me till the day he was murdered!" Zarah's tears had returned. "He was lying to my face, daily! You know the other woman? He got engaged to her!"

Sebastian's eyes widened. "And you were his wife?" he asked.

Zarah nodded. "Out of the two years we were married, he was faithful for six months, give or take. My parents, who can't agree on the color of an orange, both thought that my marriage was a petulant act of rebellion. My mother thought it was just a stratagem to shut her up about me coming back to Riyadh and marrying Mr. Rich Guy. She told me that even if she could leave Saudi Arabia, she'd still refuse to come to the wedding because it wasn't a *real wedding*, and I wasn't entering into genuine, holy matrimony. And that made everything extra humiliating. Nothing grates me worse than when my mother is right."

"Well," Sebastian said, "in retrospect, it sounds like she knew something you didn't, but that's not true. Seth may have been faking it, but your feelings were very real."

"I guess," Zarah said. "Maybe Seth married me on a whim. Maybe he proposed thinking I'd say no and he wouldn't have to go through with it, or maybe just to see if I'd say yes."

"I'm not defending anything," Sebastian said, "but after everything that went on between us, I still kept teaching with you because I didn't want you to leave. Maybe in some twisted way Seth just wanted you to stay, whatever the circumstances."

"Maybe, but I'll never know," Zarah said. "Seth was murdered, gone, like that, and *then* I found out the truth. I was never able to make him explain himself, make him answer. Look at me, Sebastian. It makes me a wreck just to think about it. Why would I want to expose you to that? How do you get closure from a situation like that?"

"By talking about it," he said. "Why bury it? It's not treasure."

"I just don't see how burdening anybody with my—"

"Zarah," Sebastian said. "You wear this invisible armor, trying to convince everybody that you're invulnerable, but you're already hurt. You tore into me for not letting you *live in the now,* but you don't. You think holding onto these old wounds, never letting them heal, gives you some kind of strength, but all you're getting from your past is a past."

"So I should just trust everyone?" Zarah asked.

"Wouldn't you rather believe that most people are good and be wrong occasionally? It's better than locking out everyone because you're afraid one of them is a fake. Zarah, you're smart, and funny. You're the kind of beautiful that scares lesser men."

Zarah turned away. "Don't say things like that. That's just—"

"Look at yourself," Sebastian said. "You could have more *real* friends than you're aware of, but you gotta let 'em in. I mean, I don't know of *anyone* who doesn't admire you. All of our students are in awe of you. It was pretty damn clear to me that you're family to your partner, Charlie. I could tell he would have enjoyed turning that camera off and going to work on me with a nightstick. Even Corinna admires your dignity, and she's never denied that you're a class act."

Zarah looked at him. His eyes were so intense, so sincere. Zarah became angry at herself for allowing him to think these things. This woman he saw—she was not any of it. Her demeanor may have been honorable and self-respecting, but her nature was cowardly— weak, bitter and egotistical. She was the fake.

"I *know*," Sebastian continued, "part of what makes you the admirable woman in front of me is what that ass in Chicago did, and I'm glad. Without that, you wouldn't be—"

Zarah seized Sebastian by the head, pulled him to her and kissed him. She could not let him believe these lies anymore. He knew that she wanted him. He needed to know how much.

And there she was, kissing a married man, subjecting his wife to the same humiliation and heartbreak she had felt all those years ago— and she did not care. She burned to be with Sebastian, and no code could put out the fire. He pulled away, tried to say something. Zarah jerked him back and pressed her attack.

He tried to speak but did not get a chance before she was forcing her tongue into his mouth.

Sebastian pulled away harder this time. She let him have his mouth back, and began kissing his neck.

"Zarah," he said.

"Don't talk," Zarah begged as she kissed him.

Sebastian shoved her away roughly. "Stop, Zarah!"

Her passion fizzled. She sat back and faced him, breathing heavy. There was not confusion on his face. It was anxiety, guilt, sadness.

What have I done to him?

"I'm sorry," she said. "I had no right. Just go. I'm sorry."

She sniffled and wiped tears from her eyes.

"Zarah—"

"Please just go! Go now! I can't handle this!"

"We'll talk later," he said.

He had a glimpse of the real Zarah, and now she was at his mercy. As she watched him walk toward the glass door to the lobby of his apartment building, he turned, smiled softly and waved goodbye. Zarah tried to smile back. Wiping away tears, Zarah resolved then and there to leave L.A. and start over somewhere else—FBI job or no FBI job.

Zarah pulled away from the curb and headed for the freeway. As she drove, she reproached herself for what she had done. Zarah wanted to take a bath, drink rum, crawl into bed, fall asleep and wake up to learn that it had all been a nightmare.

As she approached the onramp her phone rang. She checked her caller I.D. It was Sebastian. Zarah took the call.

"Sebastian," Zarah said, "let's talk about this tomorrow, okay?"

He did not answer. Zarah looked at the screen of her cell phone to make sure that the call had not been dropped. The line was open.

"Sebastian?" Zarah asked.

She heard something but could not make it out.

"Hello?" she said.

There was rustling, then a dull, wet thud with a gasp.

A cold current ran up her body. She listened.

Again, the plunging sound—but this time no gasp. No breath.

Zarah pulled to the side of the road, cutting off traffic and creating a din of angry horns and curses.

She stomped on her brake. The car skidded, and all four tires cried out as they burned before the car halted with a jolt. She shoved the gearshift to park.

Tears filled Zarah's eyes, and she sobbed.

"Sebastian?" she could barely breathe the words. "Sebastian?"

Nothing.

"Please...please answer me...please."

"Zaraaaaah." It was a raspy, sinister whisper. *"Driving and talking on your cell phone again?"*

"No…" Zarah whimpered. "No, no, no…"

"Haven't you learned?"

"No…no…"

He hung up.

50

ALL OF THE blood in Zarah's body froze. She could not breathe. Her lungs heaved, and she sobbed with such aggrieved, wrathful fury that her throat began to ache.

She had to pull herself together. Sebastian could still be alive. She rammed her gearshift into drive and peeled into the street. As soon as the road was clear, she spun her car into a U-turn and sped back towards Sebastian's apartment building.

She tried to relax her breathing—*think*. Oscar Mike would have to flee. He had to know Zarah was coming, and if he was still in that apartment when she arrived, he would be a dead man.

She dialed 911 and told them her name and badge number. "10-31, 10-31! Off-duty officer needs assistance! Ambulance and EMTs required! It's Oscar Mike, do you copy? It's Oscar Mike!"

She gave them the address, dropped her phone onto the passenger seat and stomped on the accelerator.

When she arrived, she weaved into oncoming traffic, causing drivers to slam on their brakes and swerve aside. Horns roared as she pulled in front of the building where she had dropped Sebastian off, where minutes before she had revealed her true self to him.

She drew her .9mm from her purse, jumped out of her car and ran to the glass door of the apartment building. She fired into all four corners of the door. Shattered glass cascaded to the cement in a heap of small, crystal shards.

She stepped through the ingress and entered the lobby. She passed the elevator, made her way to the stairwell and ran up the three flights to Sebastian's floor. When she reached the hallway, she leveled her gun and checked both ends. Empty.

She stepped inside the corridor. Continuously checking her front and rear, she approached Sebastian's door.

She tested the doorknob. It was unlocked and ajar.

Zarah took a deep breath, raised her weapon and rammed the door with a hard, flat-footed kick. It swung open with powerful velocity, and Zarah quickly took cover beside the doorway with her back flattened against the wall.

No movement. No sound.

She leaned sideways and peered into the doorway. The hallway was well lit, the apartment shone no light at all, and Zarah could not see inside beyond a foot or two.

"Sebastian?" she called.

No answer.

With her gun in front of her, she entered the darkened apartment. When she crept past the small kitchen and looked into the living area, she saw that Sebastian's coffee table had been flipped onto its side. Then she saw Sebastian, bound to one of his dining chairs with his hands behind his back. Blood from several stab wounds flowed from his chest.

His heart's still beating!

Zarah ran across the room to him. She knelt in front of him without regard for the blood pooling around him on the floor.

"Sebastian," she said, desperately scanning the living room for anything she could use to staunch his wounds. "I'm here! You'll be okay! Help is coming!"

She heard the front door slam shut behind her. She twisted around and saw a dark figure advancing on her. Before she could raise her weapon and get to her feet, she was looking down the barrel of a handgun held in a black, gloved fist.

"Stay," he said.

Zarah froze, and slowly raised her hands.

"Drop the piece."

Zarah let her .9mm fall from her grip. It splashed into Sebastian's blood.

Inside his black hood, she looked upon the stony face of Oscar Mike. His features were burnished by the soft illumination from the street lamps outside the large glass door. In this light, his complexion was pale, almost gray, as if his skin was preternatural or undead. His cheekbones were steep and chiseled, and his jaw line was strong. He glared at Zarah with deep seated and intense blue eyes that pierced like sharpened steel, and there was no doubt—he would show no mercy.

He looked like the same man Zarah had engaged in friendly dialogue with outside the dojo, but it was not that person. That person had soft eyes, a handsome face, and a mild manner. The predator before Zarah now was frigid and immovable, as if all of his life he had never smiled, never laughed, and never felt an emotion outside of rage.

He wore all black, mostly military battle dress except for his hooded sweatshirt, zipped up under a long coat. Underneath it, he had a utility belt full of martial hardware. Bulges on his hips suggested grenades. The handle of a large fighting knife jutted from his belt. There was some blood on the shaft—Sebastian's blood.

"This is it, Zarah," Oscar Mike said.

Zarah's anger boiled over. She wanted to tear his throat out, but he had the gun, and Sebastian's life was pumping out of him. She heard distant sirens outside. Oscar Mike heard it too, and Zarah knew he would see her and Sebastian dead long before help arrived.

Take his mind off the gun— just for one second.

"You don't have to do this," Zarah said.

Oscar Mike snarled. "People do things they don't *have to* all the time," he said. "Like flipping off a perfect stranger from their car."

"You're gonna to kill me for that? That's nothing!"

"You deciding it's nothing doesn't make it *nothing!*"

His grip tightened around the handle. His finger jumped from the side of the gun to the trigger. "You don't tell strangers, people *you don't know,* what matters to them and what—"

Zarah seized the weapon with both hands. One hand snatched the barrel and pushed it aside, and as the other cupped the hammer block and frame, she jerked it down toward her. In shock, he tried to yank his gun back with terrific force, pulling Zarah to her feet.

She kicked him between his legs, again, again and again. Her kicks were having little effect, and she felt her foot connecting with something solid protecting his groin.

She tried to tear his gun away from him, but his grip was too strong.

He growled, throwing the elbow of his free arm into her jaw. The blow rocked her hard, and her grip loosened. Her vision blurred, and she felt the gun slipping away.

He must have sensed it. He yanked, and the two of them struggled over the weapon, pivoting and spinning, both of them trying to get enough leverage to unbalance the other.

He jerked her into him. With a ferocious roar, Zarah used the momentum and lunged with her whole body, throwing her knee into his abdomen. Zarah felt armor under his clothes, and a blow which should have winded him did nothing but make him angrier.

He smashed Zarah's temple with another elbow. She felt the gun slipping away and quickly engaged the magazine release with her thumb, dropping the magazine from the well. Zarah felt it bounce off her foot and onto the carpet. She slid her thumb into the gun's trigger guard and yanked the weapon up past her head. She pushed Oscar Mike's finger into the trigger and fired the chambered round into the sliding glass door. The blast rang in her ear as the door split and cracked.

Maneuvering to throw him, she pressed the side of Oscar Mike's finger into the metal trigger guard, trapping it there. She pivoted her feet, pulled his elbow toward her and twisted the gun his wrist with it. He grimaced and gnarred. The sharp pain would have forced him to his knees, but the overturned coffee table stopped Zarah from completing the movement, thwarting her attempt.

He jerked back. Zarah released the gun, and Oscar Mike stumbled backwards and crashed into the front door.

Her attacker's vicious blows and the concussion of the gunfire in her ear was catching up to her, and Zarah's vision began to blur. She could not tell if Oscar Mike had returned to his feet with uncanny speed or if she was slowing down. She charged him, trying to remain conscious long enough to take him down with her.

He raised the gun and squeezed the trigger. Zarah was on top of him as he realized that his weapon was dry. He tossed the handgun aside, but before he could raise his guard, Zarah slammed an open-palmed strike under his jawbone, snapping his head back.

She threw a left cross at his temple with all of her weight behind it, but he weaved out of its way and Zarah stumbled. He seized her by the hair with both hands, yanked her head down and threw up his knee, ramming it into the bridge of her nose. She heard a crunching pop in her ears as pain seared her face. She wailed in agony as her knees buckled. Tears flooded her eyes. She felt her blood running down over her lips, tasted its metallic salinity.

He released her and slammed his fist into her temple, dropping her with a pained grunt, onto her hands and knees. His leather glove had torn her skin and blood spilled from the open wound. She sluggishly reached up and grabbed his jacket, trying to pull him down, but her strength was fading.

He bent low at the knees and rammed his fist into her again, and with another agonized grunt, Zarah collapsed.

Breathing heavy and groaning in pain and anguish with each heaving breath, Zarah tried to get to her feet. The floor rocked and swayed beneath her.

Oscar Mike stood over her, taking a moment of gloating self-satisfaction, and watching Zarah on all fours, fighting to stand. She wobbled and lurched like a deer just out of the womb, with blood streaming from her temple down the side of her face, spilling from her ear and running from her nose and mouth. Oscar Mike unsheathed the large knife. It had a vicious, black blade, already soiled with Sebastian's blood. He reached down and seized a fistful of her hair. Zarah did not have the strength to resist, and all she could do was accept defeat. Her last thoughts would be of her love.

"...Sebastian..."

"Was that his name?" Oscar Mike said. Then he jerked Zarah's head up. She cried out in anguish, raising herself to her knees to escape the pain. Zarah sobbed in dismay, her tears mixing with blood.

Her breathing quickened with panic as Oscar Mike pulled Zarah's head back, raising her chin and exposing her throat. She squeezed her eyes closed tight, took one last, deep breath, and braced herself for the end.

BANG!

Gunfire.

Zarah opened her eyes, and saw Oscar Mike's sharp knife in front of her face. He released her and she dropped back down to her hands and knees. She looked up at him and saw him feeling the side of his head with his fingers, looking past Zarah in shock.

Then he cursed, turned, yanked open the front door and fled down the hall.

With all of her strength, Zarah raised herself up and turned to see what had frightened Oscar Mike off. Sebastian was lying on his stomach, propped up in a puddle of blood by his elbows, free from his restraints, with Zarah's smoking gun raised in his hands.

He looked at her, but did not speak. Zarah's vision was too blurred to see his face. His arms slackened and he dropped.

Zarah lowered her head, went limp. And darkness took her.

51

S HERMAN SINGER HAD relieved Agent Louis almost an hour ago and was regretting it. Carmen Sanchaz had been tailed to a small house in Echo Park, and had not emerged for hours. From what Louis had told him, there was some kind of gang meeting taking place, and Carmen had been warmly welcomed—curious, but not surprising.

While he waited, Singer used his phone, accessed several databases on his laptop and scraped together some info. The more he knew about someone before making contact, the greater his advantage would be in dealing with them.

The house belonged to one Domitila Espinoza, a.k.a. *Domita,* who according to the LAPD's gang database had not been active in criminal behavior beyond suspected harboring and conspiracy. The only skinny informants had given them was that she was the den mother of a group of women known for providing succor and assistance to several gangs of the Echo Park region, and that their participation in gang violence and other crimes occurred after the fact.

Domita's gang, La Aristócrata, *The Noblewomen,* were some kind of Latina mix between *The Pink Ladies* and a M.A.S.H. unit. The only serious crime that law enforcement could attribute to them was smuggling prescription medications into the country from Mexico to use to treat their injured, gangbanging patients. Of course, the police had no proof of this yet.

The Noblewomen did not fight with other chick-cliques, did not sell drugs, rob or steal, or had simply never been caught. Having much bigger problems with more visible and violent gangs in Los Angeles, LAPD's Gang and Narcotics Division let The Noblewomen be.

The police did have a benign file on Carmen Sanchaz, a.k.a. Carmen Sanchez, a.k.a. *Ojos Mariposa/Butterfly Eyes.* She had come up the hard way. But crimes she had committed as a youth were mild, and she had been held to account. Beyond theft, assault and possession charges, her rise to success was as mythic as Zarah Wheeler's.

Since Carmen Sanchaz was seventeen years old, she had stayed out of trouble. She dropped out of gangland to pursue a career in broadcasting even though her entire family was involved with EPD-18, the 18th Street Echo Park Drifters, one of the most powerful L.A. gangs. Carmen Sanchaz appeared to be the first of her family to rise above.

She had paid off her student loans, which told Singer that she did not take money from her gang friends to put herself through school. If she had been using dirty money, Singer doubted that student loans would have been necessary.

On the face of it, Carmen Sanchaz was an educated and accomplished woman, worthy of respect—an example to follow. Whatever the issue was between the LAPD and the reporter, it was not the FBI's problem. The saucy Latina wanted to destroy popular opinion of Oscar Mike, she had the reputation of a person who was hard to stop, and that was where Singer stopped caring.

She had been arrested once for refusal to cooperate, true to *La Aristócrata* form. She was never charged, but the reporter's dislike of the police seemed to be more like a way to stay connected in the street than a genuine animosity.

She disguised her opportunistic cries for attention as righteous confrontation—the old Al Sharpton excuse. Sometimes that did some good and kept authorities honest, and none of it changed Singer's mind about helping the reporter get what she needed.

But what was the deal here on Kent Street? Since Carmen had struck out with the LAPD, was she looking to the street for information, or was this meeting about something else? The street did have eyes and ears, and Charlie had told Zarah that Carmen had behaved like he was not the last stop in her quest for intel. But how could Latino sets in Echo Park help?

Singer was tempted to go to the door, but he vetoed that notion. That could have ruined the reporter's reputation in the barrio. Best to stay on her trail and approach her in more friendly territory.

There was time. Tomorrow morning they would have a description of Oscar Mike to go with Carmen's smear piece. He sat for a little while longer, contemplating what Charlie's and the rest of the LAPD's reaction to him leaking this info to one such as Carmen Sanchaz was going to be. It was not going to be pretty.

After a while, Singer became bored. It was dark, and the neighborhood was dangerous. He could have been enjoying a meal in Westwood. As he started his car, he saw movement at the door of the house.

He counted ten Latino men and boys. They were laughing and acting casual. Singer could spot an ex con in an instant by how they carried themselves. Most of these guys had *joint-bodies,* like gorillas, and they walked with a prison strut.

Carmen Sanchaz was at the door of the house waving goodbye. Next to her was a taller woman, covered in tattoos, with bright red hair and clothes clinging so tightly to her curvy form, they almost looked as if they had been painted on. The two women began talking as they stepped back inside the house and closed the door.

"Goddammit!" Singer said.

He decided that Carmen Sanchaz could be there all night and was preparing to leave when his cell phone rang with the news about Zarah Wheeler and Sebastian Michaels.

52

CHARLIE SLOCUM HURRIED down the freezing cold, sterile corridor of Providence Holy Cross Medical Center. In his anguish over Zarah's uncertain condition, he forgot to demand answers from Torres, from Singer, from anybody who claimed to be on Zarah's side.

Where the fuck was the follow-unit?

When Charlie turned the corner to the trauma center, he saw Lt. Torres and a number of detectives standing outside the door leading to the ICU. Charlie stopped short before meeting them.

The mournful and despairing look Torres cast at him, his face absent of any anxiety or worry, told Charlie her condition. Zarah was gone. Charlie did not need to be told. He turned around and walked away. He had work to do.

"Charlie!" Torres said. Charlie allowed him to catch up.

"I should go to the crime scene," Charlie said.

"It's okay, Charlie," Torres said giving his shoulder a sympathetic squeeze. "Woodley has it."

"Woodley fucks up his own signature. I gotta go there."

Torres put his forehead in his hand and squeezed his temples.

"Show some respect, Charlie."

"It'll do no good... no good."

"You selfish pussy!" Torres said. "Remember City Terrace,

Charlie? Remember *your partner*, who wanted to tear the hospital walls down with her bare hands to be by your bedside?"

"How's me going in there going to do her any good? She's gone!"

"She's not gone, you simple fuck!" Torres said.

"She's not?"

"No!" Torres said. "Who told you that?"

Charlie started towards the ICU again with Torres alongside him.

"How is she?" Charlie asked.

"She got her ass kicked pretty good," Torres said. "Broken nose, two black eyes—she looks like a fucking raccoon."

"Was it Oscar?" Charlie asked.

Torres nodded. "She called it in. Go see her. She's unconscious, but she might sense your presence, take some comfort."

"What about the other victim?" Charlie asked.

"D.O.A.," Torres told him. "Sharp force trauma; multiples."

"Shit," Charlie said. "I.D.?"

"Sebastian Michaels, the guy we pulled in the other night."

"Goddamn," Charlie said.

It would have taken a lot of skill to bring both of them down with just a knife. Sebastian Michaels was a sixth-degree Black Belt in Jujitsu. He was Zarah's teacher.

Charlie shook his head. "I hope they got some good licks in."

"Michaels may have," Torres said. "Zarah's off-duty piece was in his fuckin' hand when they found them. GSR on him and a spent shell nearby. He shot at someone."

What the hell happened over there?

"Any blood that ain't theirs lying around?" Charlie asked

"We'll know in a few hours. Go see Zarah."

"Listen," Charlie said. "Where the fuck was Wilster?"

"Don't ask."

"I'm fuckin' asking!"

"Zarah signed a paper," Torres said. "She's with the feds now. Command got pissed and ordered Sheridan to yank her protection."

"They can't just fucking *do* that!"

Torres shrugged. "It's fucked up," he said, "but Zarah never formally requested protection."

"That's bullshit," Charlie said. "What is that, a joke?"

"Hey, I'm on your side," Torres said, "but that's command's story and they're sticking to it, besides, Singer said he'd look out for her."

Charlie shook his head. "Fucking, command cocksuckers," he said. "And now I'd like to ask Singer why Zarah's protection wasn't there. Wouldn't you?"

"I'll make a call," Torres said. "Now go see Zarah."

Charlie nodded and asked a nurse to bring him to Zarah. When the young woman asked if he was member of her immediate family, he told her that he was and did not brook any argument. She looked skeptical but led Charlie into the ICU.

The space was cold. Large, fluorescent lights blazed down on Zarah. Her arms were at her sides, a heart rate monitor clipped onto one of her fingers and IV tubing taped to her wrist.

Her long, black hair had been bunched into a plastic, disposable cap. Her forehead was wrapped in a bandage. Both of her eyes were swollen and dark. The corner of her left eye had been stitched and dressed. She was covered by a white sheet with a blanket atop that, below her shoulders.

Charlie looked at the patient monitor. "Her respiration is low," he quietly told the nurse.

"It's from the pain meds," the nurse said. "It's normal. The doctor thinks she'll recover quickly."

Charlie nodded and accepted it, not wanting to step on any toes.

He looked at Zarah, remembered the first time they met. She did not fit in among the other Homicide Special detectives in their squad, most of whom were nearly twice her age. But they all wanted her on the team anyway. She was amiable. She listened, most of the time. She was a good investigator. She was one of them.

"You're a damn fine human being, Zarah Wheeler," Charlie told her, unsure of whether she heard. "You matter too goddam much, so snap out of it fast. We need you."

The nurse told Charlie it was time to go, and he did not argue. Seeing Zarah like this, her eyes closed, brows furrowed in a kind of catatonic wince. She was in pain.

The words he wanted to say he would save for when she was awake. He wanted those first words to be that Oscar Mike was dead, and that he had suffered greatly before he got his.

53

CARMEN SANCHAZ'S ALARM clock rang in her ears like a bomb-raid siren. She groaned, pulled a pillow over her head and squeezed it shut over her ears, but it did not go away. She gave up and slapped the top of the screaming clock-radio on her night table, silencing it.

She did not feel like getting out of bed. She did not feel like taking a shower, or brushing her teeth, or getting dressed, or putting on her makeup. She wanted to stay in bed until the next day.

After her meeting with the leadership of 18th Street, Domita called a few of the newer *Aristocratas* together to meet her, party with her, and hear her success story—though Carmen was honest enough with herself to know that taking any job that could raise a woman out of *el barrio* was a success story to Domita. Carmen could have been a meter maid, or worked at UPS and Domita would be proud. Carmen was off the street, and that remained her greatest achievement.

Still, *familia* was what Carmen had needed. Recently she felt as though nobody liked or respected her, needed or wanted her, but she came to realize that she did not need friends. She had *familia*.

Carmen forced herself out of bed. The clothes she wore the night before were in a disorderly heap on the floor next to the mirrored closet door. Carmen could still smell weed smoke coming off of them. She looked in the mirror at herself, wondering what made her think it was a good idea to put on her black, satin peignoir instead of her usual cotton pajamas.

She shook her head and chastised herself. She was supposed to be a responsible professional. She had no regrets about catching up with the *hermanas*, but Gary and Lamar knew a hangover when they saw one. They would not bring it up. They would share *looks*, and smirk, and nod to each other when they thought she was not watching.

She would have liked to call in sick, but amateurish alchies pulled that kind of thing. Carmen Sanchaz was a veteran ace, and would remain visibly so. Her head yelled at her when she turned the light on in her bathroom and the vent fan roared to life. It sounded like a leaf-blower between her temples, but she had no one to blame for that but herself, so Carmen resolved to push through it and set about her morning routine.

She washed away the previous night in a cool shower. She wanted to dress empowered— something classic but simple. She picked a form-fitting, merlot-colored skirted suit out of her closet, hung it on her bathroom door and started brushing her hair.

"Hello?" a man's voice shouted from Carmen's living room, giving her a start. "FBI! Miss Sanchaz, are you home?"

Carmen was naked except for a yellow towel around her chest when she hurried into her living room to investigate. In her doorway, a man with a bed-head of blonde hair thrust his gun at Carmen and took an authoritative step toward her.

"Don't move!" he commanded.

Carmen shrieked and raised her hands.

The man wore a polished, black suit. He looked Carmen over with a suspicious expression and then scanned the room with alert eyes.

"Miss Sanchaz," he said. "FBI. Everything okay?"

"No," Carmen said. "There's a *pinche federale* in my house pointing a *gun at me!*"

The man holstered his weapon inside his black suit jacket but still looked worried. His eyes continued studying the house. He withdrew his credentials and displayed it to Carmen.

"'*Knock, knock!*'" Carmen said. "You know? '*Come in!*'"

"Your car is parked *into* the wall in your garage, and your keys are still in the doorknob." He pointed behind her to Carmen's open door. "The judiciary calls that *objective reasonableness.*"

Carmen rubbed her eyes and shook her head. "I had a long night."

The agent backed out of Carmen's doorway with a sardonic look on his face, reached around the door, took the keys out of the knob and tossed them onto a wooden bar top looking into Carmen's kitchen. Then he stepped outside and closed the door in front of him.

Carmen was confused—until she heard three polite but strong knocks at her door.

"*Puto gringo,*" Carmen grumbled as she walked to the door. When she opened it, the agent was wearing a serious expression and hefting a box full of folders and documents. Carmen did not understand. He entered and placed the box at Carmen's bare feet.

"Now," he said, "before I leave, I have to make it clear: You heard a knock at your door. When you answered it, this was on your doorstep." He pointed at the box on the floor. "We never met."

"Why didn't you just leave it there then?"

"You mean besides finding your keys still in the door?"

Carmen flushed again. "Yeah, besides that."

"When you go through it you'll know why."

She narrowed her eyes, and her brow wrinkled. "Okay..." she said, looking down at the box.

"If you cross me, *Butterfly*, if you tell *anyone* where you got this, I'll pull your pretty little wings off, for *starters*."

"What the hell is this?" Carmen demanded.

"Your career. Gift wrapped."

The agent gave a polite nod, backed out of the doorway and left.

Carmen closed the door, picked up the box and put it on her glass and wrought-iron coffee table.

She reached down and withdrew a folder marked "STEIN" and opened it. Inside it were handwritten notes, typed documents and photographs. She pulled out a photo of a playfully decorated bedroom, the kind that kids would have slept in. There were two wood-framed, twin-sized beds across from each other. In each was a boy, still in bed.

"Oh my God…"

Carmen's stomach heaved. She returned the picture to the folder and took out another. This one was of a woman in a kitchen, her hands bound behind her in a chair. She had been savaged. It was the first murder scene Oscar Mike had ordered her to go to.

She understood why Charlie Slocum wanted her to stay out of it now, but all it would take was that single crime scene photo of those little kids, murdered in their beds as they slept, to smack people out of the shallow paradigm they were stuck in. And she had a whole box full of Oscar Mike's work.

A plan took shape. She had to act, now. Carmen dressed in her suit, loaded the box into her drunkenly parked car and wondered what that FBI guy was getting from this. No way did he give it to her out of the kindness of his heart. This favor was going to cost. Carmen headed for the studio wondering what the price was going to be.

54

CHARLIE STOOD IN the apartment of Sebastian Michaels, inches from where he had bled out. The scene was not telling Charlie anything that the other detectives did not already know. Neighbors had heard two gunshots. Swede had pried a .9mm slug from the front doorpost. The other round would be harder to find, judging by the translucent web of cracks spreading out from a neat, oval bullet hole near the upper edge of a sliding glass door on the far side of the living room. A spent .357 SIG shell casing had been found near the foot of the couch.

The theory was that the intruder—an average-sized male, as evidenced by a partial, bloody boot print on the carpet—had disarmed Zarah, but with her melee training Zarah is never truly disarmed. And being Zarah, she fought back.

Only Zarah could connect the dots, but her desperate call-in to dispatch for backup and EMTs, her car parked on the curb facing the opposite direction of traffic, the four reported gunshots in the lobby and the shattered glass door, her friend bound to a chair and repeatedly stabbed, all gave rise to a scenario in Charlie's mind. Oscar Mike had lured Zarah here and ambushed her.

Except Zarah isn't some weak-kneed housewife, you fuckstick!

The perpetrator left his gun behind, a single-action P229, but it did not have prints. The weapon had been fired, and the magazine had been found on the floor a couple feet away from where the gun had been laying. No bullets had struck Zarah or Sebastian.

"Charlie," a familiar voice said. Charlie turned and saw Sherman Singer. His eyes were soft and sorrowful. Charlie turned away.

"Get what you came here for and get lost," he told him.

"Is she okay?"

Charlie rounded on him. "If she were *okay,* she wouldn't be in the hospital, would she?"

"I'm sorry," Singer said. "Is she going to be okay?"

Charlie nodded. "Now that *we're* protecting her."

"Is that the same *we* who stood down her detail in the first place?" Singer asked. "I spoke with Wade. *We'll* double the guard."

"Double the guard?" Charlie said. "What does that mean? What's two times zero?"

"I know it's my fault, Charlie," Singer said. "It was just for a few hours. I didn't think..."

"Yeah, well, you and Zarah have that much in common."

Singer was not catching Charlie's drift. It showed on his face.

"If she bothered to think," Charlie explained, "I wouldn't have spent three weeks on medical, and that scumbag would be in prison right now. If *you* had used any part of your brain, she would still be upright, and her friend would be alive. This case has been one catastrophic fuckup after another because nobody thinks."

"You're right," Singer said. "Mistakes were made. But Zarah and I were both doing what we thought was right under the circumstances. Sometimes you have to act fast, Charlie. What I did was impulsive, but strategically correct."

"Okay," Charlie said. "What strategically correct thing did you do that got Sebastian Michaels killed?"

"I located Carmen Sanchaz."

"What the fuck for?" Charlie asked.

"Charlie," Singer said in an even tone, "I was sitting in a restaurant with Zarah when you yourself told her that Carmen Sanchaz was acting like she had other leads to follow for her story. If she knows something that we don't about this case, *we* need to know what that is, but I don't have the authority to detail new people. All I can do is move the pieces I have around the board. I called my SAC, and he agreed to assign some more guys to put on Zarah. But it takes time, Charlie. So I pulled Zarah's guard off of her long enough to find out where Sanchaz was, and then I personally took over that surveillance and sent my agent *back* to Zarah. But by the time he reacquired her, *this* had already gone down."

"Why pull her guard at all?" Charlie demanded. "Why didn't you locate her yourself?"

"I was at my office, trying to decide what details were safe to give to the reporter and what to hold back to protect the case. In my experience, reporters don't tell you what they know unless you put something on the table."

"Zarah and I agreed," Charlie said, "that was a bad move."

"I *disagreed*," Singer said. "I spoke about it with Wade. He gave me the nod with the caveat that it's my ass, and it's done. Now she has just enough to achieve the effect she desires."

"And what information did you glean from the know-nothing attention whore?"

"It was…" Singer stammered, "She was… Look, I'll just say it wasn't an ideal situation to be having a dialogue with her, okay?"

Charlie's face went crimson with rage. "In other words, *nothing!*"

"Charlie," Singer said. "I just trusted you with my entire career in law enforcement. So take a breath and promise me—"

"You didn't *think!*" Charlie said. "I get it. If this blows up, it'll be in your face and no one else's—except Carmen's after Oscar Mike sees that report!"

"That's not true," Singer said. "When that report and Oscar Mike's composite sketch hit the airwaves, he'll be too busy running for the border to put anyone in danger."

"That's a stupid, arrogant and dangerous assumption," Charlie said. "He's a lunatic! You have no idea what he'll do, and need I remind you, it was Carmen Sanchaz who exposed Zarah on the evening news? It's why we're standing in this crime scene! And when Carmen Sanchaz gets in front of that camera and turns on him, what do you think he'll do? And last, but not least, Zarah Wheeler and Sebastian Michaels had that I.D.! One's in a coma and the other's dead! There's no fucking *sketch!*"

"Shit!"

"You didn't think!" Charlie said.

"Fuck you, Charlie!" Singer said. "I didn't know until an hour ago! Oh dammit! Without the I.D., the news report is worthless!"

"To us, but not to Carmen Sanchaz or her network," Charlie said.

Singer whipped out his phone and headed out the door.

Charlie followed him down the hall. "What are you up to now?"

"I'm gonna tell her to hold her horses," Singer said.

"Trust me," Charlie said, "when she turns her horses loose, there's no holding them."

"Protective custody then!"

"Sherman, think dammit! You really think she'll accept that?"

"What can I do, Charlie?" Singer said, on the edge of panic. "I'm not trying to get her killed!"

Charlie thought for a moment. "All right... She kinda regrets putting Zarah on Oscar Mike's radar. She told me as much. If we can lure her to the hospital, let her see Zarah, explain why we need her to wait on her story for two seconds, she may agree. But that's a ginormous, fucking *'if'.*"

Charlie retrieved his phone from inside his jacket. "Give me her damn phone number."

55

CARMEN SANCHEZ WAS riding a wave of optimism. She had just secured an interview with the widow of one of the valiant police officers who died in the City Terrace Shootout. After Carmen had stated her case, explained her intent, the woman confessed that she was disgusted by all of the pro-Oscar Mike nonsense she had been hearing. The truth needed to come to light, and she would share her pain if it would help people find their humanity.

Carmen had crime scene photos. She had medical examiner's documents. She had a victim's brave friend, and to complete things she needed a brave survivor. There was but one.

Carmen knocked on the thick, oaken door of Anita Nizamani's home in Woodland Hills. She had not returned Carmen's phone calls. By now Carmen was sure that most of the news hawks had given up on her and moved on, but they did not have what Carmen had, which she relished more each time the thought crossed her mind. Also, their motives were not Carmen's motives.

"Who is it?" A woman's voice asked through the door.

"Carmen Sanchaz. I left a few voicemails. Is this Anita?"

After hesitating moment the woman said, "No. She moved to Atlanta."

Bullshit! I know your voice after all those voicemail greetings!

Carmen summoned up what little patience she had and willed

her tone to be gentle. "Anita, please just hear me out. I don't have a camera or a recorder or even a pen and paper. It's just me. After we talk I'll go away, and you'll never hear from Channel Six again if that's what you want."

The big door opened wide enough for Carmen to see Anita Nizamani. She was a slender brunette, not much taller than Carmen. Her head was lowered, and her brown eyes looked over Carmen and studied her. The wounds to her face had left scars, which she tried to obfuscate with cover cream. It worked, to a degree, but she would never be as beautiful as she once had been.

Carmen spread her arms out. "See," she said, "I have nothing. I even left my purse in the car. I'm just here to talk."

"But I don't—"

"I'm not here to ask questions. I need you to hear *me* out."

"Fine," Anita said. "What is it?"

"May I come in?"

"I thought you said no questions," Anita snarked.

This was becoming annoying, but Carmen let it slide.

"Okay," Carmen said. "By now I'm certain you've noticed that the man who killed your boyfriend—"

"Fiancé!" Anita said, thrusting a hand out and flourishing her diamond engagement ring in Carmen's face.

"I'm sorry, your fiancé…the man responsible has garnered something of a following on the internet, and the news programs, such as mine, are doing more to justify and glorify his deeds than to report the true nature of these crimes."

"Why do you need me?" Anita asked. "People know he's a psycho. They're just talking stupid 'cause they think it's funny!"

"Exactly," Carmen said, "because the only reports about it discuss why he's killing, without considering what the human cost is."

"I still don't know how I could help," Anita said.

"What he does and how he does it is more important than the *why*. People need to *see* it with their eyes and hear the truth from the people who have suffered. In the trunk of my car, I have photographs of some of his crime scenes. I have autopsy reports, investigator's notes. I want to show them reality, nothing romanticized. You *can* help."

"Why, so he can come finish me off? No thanks."

"We won't talk about *him*, just the attack, show people the true impact these murders have. People won't be so flippant after that. I can pre-record your sound bite, show the crime scene photos of your attack, not your face, no pictures of you at all. Then as the photos are on the screen, you would be describing what happened in voice over. I can disguise your voice electronically and give you a false name or omit names altogether. Your identity will be safe."

"I don't know..." Anita said.

Carmen's phone rang. Carmen withdrew it from its case and looked at the caller I.D. It was Gary.

"It's my producer," Carmen told Anita. She took the call. "What's up, Gary," she asked as she strode a few feet from Anita.

"Carmen," Gary said. "I need you to meet me at Providence Holy Cross Medical Center."

"Why?" Carmen asked. "What is it?"

Carmen glanced back at the young woman. Anita stood with her arms crossed, her head turned and tilted, trying to hear Carmen's half of the conversation.

"Oscar Mike," Gary said. "Carmen..."

"What is it?"

"It's Detective Wheeler. She's been hurt."

"Oh no," Carmen said, her chin quivered. "How bad? Is she okay? Don't tell me she's dead. Don't tell me that."

"She's not dead," Gary said.

Carmen let out a huge breath and pressed a hand to her stomach. "What happened?"

"Not sure," Gary said, "but the LAPD is giving us access. You need to come here now."

That seemed strange. After everything that happened, why would they give her access to anything?

"Are you sure?" Carmen asked. "Who told you this?"

"Detective Slocum."

Carmen smelled a rat. Charlie Slocum hated her, and the feeling was mutual. He would never let her near Zarah without some ulterior motive.

"I don't know, Gary," she said. "What do you think?"

"It's a little odd, but Zarah *is* in the I.C.U. We have the story, and we have someone on-scene, outside the hospital. But so does everybody else. They just don't have the access we've been offered."

It stank. There was something going on between the lines that Carmen was not clever enough to figure. Slocum was up to something.

Carmen also noticed Anita kept glancing inside her home.

"Someone's already there?" Carmen said. "Give them the access."

"Yeah, but they asked for—"

Carmen disconnected and returned her phone to her jeans pocket.

"I'm sorry about that," Carmen said as she walked back to Anita. She was not interested in playing Charlie's game, whatever it was. Anita had been eavesdropping, she was clearly interested in the case and Carmen was fed up trying to convince her to play ball. So she bluffed.

"Listen," Carmen told Anita. "If I had your story it would make a big difference, but I'm out of time. Oscar Mike just attacked someone else. If I can't get you on the record, I have to go."

Anita mulled it over. As she thought about the decision, all Carmen could think of was how badly she was going burn Oscar Mike on the air, with or without Anita Nizamani. When Carmen was finished, *Oscar Mike* would be a synonym for *piece of shit,* and if he came for her, he could bring it to 18th Street and see how long he lasted. Carmen glanced at her watch. "I'm sorry. I need an answer."

Anita bit her lower lip and looked antsy. She nodded. "I'll do it."

56

GARY STERLING WALKED down the sky-blue halls of Providence Holy Cross Medical Center. Another producer, a young, dark-haired, hazel-eyed charmer named Rachel Cooney, along with Ronnie Young, Cooney's tall, tan, on-scene ace with the sun-bleached hair followed behind with a brawny cameraman in tow.

They were a solid and consistent unit, but from where Gary stood, they were no competition for Carmen, Lamar and himself. Carmen and Lamar were fearless, inner-city veterans, willing to follow SWAT into a crack house with nothing but a camera phone and Bluetooth.

Ronnie Young was a pretty-boy who used hairdressers. Stacie Wynes usually sent him to Malibu or Venice to cover beached porpoises and folk-art. Gary had no worries about handing this story over to them.

Gary had never been to this hospital and was not sure whether or not he was going the right way until he saw the large figure of Detective Charlie Slocum advancing on him. Beside him was a sharply dressed man with blonde hair. He had seen him outside of the crime scene in Bel Air, talking to Lt. Torres. He did not remember his name, only that he was FBI.

Gary tried to introduce Rachel Cooney but was cut short by Slocum.

"Where's Sanchaz?"

"She's working on another story," Gary explained. "But this is Rachel Cooney, also from our studio, and she and Ronny'll be covering this."

"With all respect and dignity," Cooney added.

"Like hell they will!" Charlie said.

"Why didn't Carmen Sanchaz come?" the FBI agent demanded.

"She was in too big of a hurry to tell me that, Mr..."

"Singer," he snipped, shoving his FBI credentials in Gary's face. "We need to get in touch with her, now."

"You want her and only her to cover *this* story?" Gary asked. "Is there a reason for that?"

"We're giving her a big story," Singer said. "Why ask why?"

"Because she's my ace, and I want to know."

"And *my* ace," Cooney chimed in, "has places to be, so if we're not going to shoot anything..."

"Talk to Detective Slocum," Singer barked at her.

Charlie gave the agent a reprehending look but did not fight it. He escorted Rachel Cooney and her crew down the hall toward a mob of police uniforms and casual looking feds wearing jeans and blue windbreakers that said *FBI* in big, yellow letters.

When the crowd of police swallowed them up, Singer moved in close to Gary and spoke quietly.

"Listen," he said. "I know what Carmen's up to, and I need her to hold back on it."

"We've been over the material," Gary argued. "Nothing is in that information that would hurt the investigation. It's all gross pictures and crime scene notes. I don't see any reason to sit on it."

"Fine," Singer said. "The important question is, is she gonna be as blithely arrogant and provocative as she was when she reported the City Terrace Shootout?"

"That's a strong possibility," Gary said.

"You realize that Oscar Mike will thank her for it by hunting her down and killing her slow?"

"You'd just let him do that?" Gary asked.

"You think he'll ask for permission?"

"So you're saying Carmen's on her own?"

"For now," Singer said. "Detective Wheeler's seen his face, and Oscar Mike could be here, right now, trying to stop her from waking up. *Nobody* is leaving that post for a snarky, anti-establishment reporter, especially the one whose reporting put Zarah in this position."

Singer was beginning to make a lot of sense.

"If you wait for a green light from me," Singer continued, "we'd be willing to look out for her. Air it now, and you can accept the Emmy yourself and bury it next to Carmen's butchered corpse. It's that simple."

"I'll talk to Carmen," Gary said.

"Thank you, Gary," Singer said. The agent walked away toward the pack of cops outside of the I.C.U. and disappeared into the crowd.

Gary was not sure about this strategy, but it sounded good. Still, Zarah was in a coma, and those things could last forever. Gary would ask Carmen to give it a few days, and if Zarah didn't come out of it by then, they would run with what they had and take their chances.

57

CARMEN'S DAY HAD been unexpectedly productive. Though Carmen had been taken aback when the bereaved Pakistani girl asked to see the crime scene photos from her attack, they had a profound effect that would soon reverberate through the airwaves and touch everyone.

A gruesome photo of her fiancé, slumped at the wheel of his BMW, half of his body shredded by shotgun blasts and the trauma that Anita Nizamani had suffered, the pain and horror that she must have buried deep within herself to carry on with her life, had come crashing back like a flood tide and sent her into a grief-stricken rage.

When she calmed down, Carmen produced a digital recorder. What followed was a sorrowful and horrifying, enraging and heartbreaking monologue that made Carmen teary. It was so powerful and so real. Carmen thought it was a shame no cameras were there to see it.

Now Carmen was in her convertible with the top down, heading up Lucretia Avenue toward *Las Aristocratas'* summit house on Kent Street.

Domita's political clout with EPD-18 had paid off. Domita had texted her that the O.G.s had found what she had been looking for.

Carmen was feeling stupendous. She was successful, powerful

and doing right for the forces of good. She was reaffirming her connections to the street and climbing the career ladder.

The air was warm with a gentle breeze, and the setting sun in the smoggy sky highlighted the palm trees. Even the evening rush hour traffic had a soothing sound. Norteña music blasted from a local street vendor's boom box, filling the street as she slowly passed by— the sound of L.A., of home. It soaked Carmen's entire being.

One lane over, a Jeep signaled a lane change and was allowed in by the Honda behind it. Carmen thought of Oscar Mike. She knew that a day was coming when the driver of that Jeep could illegally merge without signaling a damn thing without fear that a killer might follow him home. When Channel Six aired Carmen's exposé, the fun and games would be over. Nobody would have a good thing to say about him.

She turned onto Kent St. and saw many vehicles in front of Domita's old house. The lights were on, and the driveway was empty. Carmen pulled in and heard Domita's Dobermans raising the alarm inside.

A bald Latino with a goatee peered out of a window and regarded Carmen as she parked in the carport. He looked her over with forced indifference, gave her a casual nod and turned away, probably to report that she had arrived.

When she reached the door, it opened, and she was greeted by a crowd, mostly men, mostly in khaki trousers, white t-shirts and tank tops. Some of them had on flannel shirts with only the top button fastened. There were some crude jailhouse tattoos and some elegant and masterful studio pieces. All the ladies sported *Aristocrata* tats.

Some of the partiers were holding forty-ounce bottles of beer. Some were smoking weed. Some were doing both, and there was festive, Spanish hip-hop playing from a stereo.

To Carmen, no one carried Latina sex appeal with more swank than *Las Aristócratas'* matriarch, Domita. When she approached to greet Carmen, she looked sexier than ever with smooth, copper skin, fiery, brick-colored hair, which she had fashioned into pig-tails, and sumptuous, bright red lips. She wore a white, cropped shrug with thin vertical blue stripes tied tight around her ample bosoms, and tight blue jeans. Almost every inch of exposed skin was decorated with colorful tattoos. Her ink was not haphazard or random, and to understand Domita's body art, one would have to see her nude and spend hours pondering. Many men were willing to try. None were entirely worthy.

Domita had kept things casual, and Carmen realized that Domita had arranged for her to have another long night, which if Carmen played her role too well, would be followed by another brutal hangover.

Just Chronic, Mariposa, she told herself. *No cerveza!*

Carmen had been on the go all day and was still dressed like a professional. The first thing that had to go in the stuffy, smoke filled room was the jacket, so she took it off and tossed it to some-one by the door.

She gave them all a bright smile and greeted them each with hugs and kisses on the cheeks, and when she reached the center of the room she yelled, *"Hola, familia!"* which was answered by smiles and a din of Spanish greetings with some applause.

Domita pushed her way through to greet Carmen. After hugs and kisses, the tattooed matron got down to business, never losing her smile. "Diablo and his bitches are in the other room," she said.

"He doesn't get to party?" Carmen asked.

"Little *niño* has a fuckin' attitude," Domita replied. "I had to call some *Coronas* up in there to make him behave."

Domita pulled her by the arm to escort her to a quieter room in the house. Carmen pointed to a bong sitting on a folding chair and addressed the revelers. "Pack that for me. I'll be right back!"

There was laughter and applause as Domita pulled Carmen into a dark hallway. They entered a room with some folding chairs up against the wall, but it was otherwise empty, save for the group of 18th Street *Coronas,* high ranking gang members, standing behind Diablo and his crew who were seated on folding chairs in front of them.

"*Hola*, Diablo," Carmen said, looking down on him, smiling.

Diablo hung his head and stared at her feet.

"What?" Carmen asked. "You like my shoes?"

No answer.

"I'm sad now," Carmen said. "When we first met you were so friendly. Now you're too much of a fuckin' *chido* to talk to me?"

The gangster standing behind Diablo cracked him hard upside his head. "*Cual es tu pinche pedo?* Answer her!"

"What!" Diablo said. "Shit, man!"

"Oye, Looney," Carmen said to the vato to the right of Diablo, looking like a Chihuahua that was caught peeing on the floor without an exit strategy. "I remember you, too. *You* wanna talk to me, right? Or you wanna shine your flashlight on *mi bubis* again?"

"What the fuck!?" Domita roared. "He did *what*!?"

The five gangbangers stiffened in their chairs, their *Coronas* leering at them with reprehending expressions. Carmen had seen this show before. None of the higher-ranked gangsters really cared what their soldiers did, but the relationship between Echo Park gangs and *Las Aristócratas* was a beneficial one. When a soldier got rough or was disrespectful, an act of contrition was in order, or they may have found themselves out in the cold when it really mattered.

"Carmen," Domita said. "You know who Looney's *papi* is?"

"Who's his *papi*?" Carmen asked.

"Flaco."

"Flaco?" Carmen asked, surprised. "You mean, *Carlos?* Flaco from Mohawk Street?"

"*Sí*," Domita sang with a mischievous shine in her eyes. "You remember Flaco don't you?"

"Oh, *sí, sí, sí, sí,*" Carmen said. "I remember Flaco! He didn't *need* no flashlight!" The two women burst out laughing. "He just wink and smile and—" Carmen mimed ripping her blouse off and made a tearing noise. She and Domita continued cracking up.

Looney appeared to be taking pride in that slice of his father's history, and the room loosened up. Some of the gangsters were grinning, chuckling. Carmen was indeed *familia*, and now they knew for sure.

"Oye," Domita said to Looney, "Mariposa was almost your mami!"

Carmen blushed and laughed. "Almost," she said. "How is Flaco?"

"In Quentin for murder," Domita said. "Sixteen to twenty-five. Thirteen if he behaves."

"Shame," Carmen said to Looney. She went to the far wall in the room and picked up one of the folding chairs. Domita followed suit, and they both unfolded them in front of Diablo and Looney and sat down. Carmen looked Looney in the eye.

"*Queria a tu padre,*" she said, "a great man. When it's time to man up, Flaco mans up, *sí?*"

"*Sí,*" Looney agreed. "He stands tall."

"What about you?" Carmen said. "Can you stand tall, tell me what you know about Oscar Mike?"

"Looney," Diablo warned, "you shut the fuck up!"

A *Corona* cuffed Diablo upside his head again.

Looney shrugged and looked at Diablo, who glared back at him. Then he returned his gaze to Carmen.

"Why would I know anything about that fool?"

"'Cause," Carmen explained, "when I dropped his name the other day, Diablo was trying not to piss his pants in front of me."

"That's bullshit, man!" Diablo yelled.

"Diablo," Carmen said, "stop frontin'. I came up around harder *soldados* than you." Carmen gestured around at the *Coronas* in the room, causing them each to nod and thrust out their prideful chests. "I know the difference between scared-tough and real-tough, and the stink of fear was all over you, *chico!* That's the kind of scared you get when you know something you shouldn't. But what doesn't click is what you're scared of. One thing *la chotas* knows for sure is that Oscar's a white boy. So what if you told someone something? You think a *loco gringo* would even begin to know how to find you in your own barrio without gettin' smoked?"

"Okay!" Diablo yelled. Then he scanned the room at all of his home boys, took a deep breath and spoke. "We helped him creep away—after the City Terrace thing. It had to be him."

"Yo," Looney said, "it was *definitely* Oscar, homes."

The gangsters standing over them looked shocked, and each shouted different questions at the five young men, demanding to know why they had not mentioned it, why they would do such a thing, and what they were doing in City Terrace.

The yelling became a single, loud noise in the room, while the five young gangbangers each looked around trying to explain themselves. Domita clapped her hands and called for order.

"So," Domita said, "tell Mariposa what happened."

"We're hangin' out," Looney said, "waitin' for fuckin' *Spartan* to come pick up his fuckin' bud, right? Then way off, we hear guns and explosions and shit. We see the fuckin' smoke and everything. We wanted to get the fuck out of there, but Diablo's all like, '*Yo man, we're tryin' to get paid and shit.*'"

"Yo, hold the fuck up," Diablo said. "Your bitch-ass kept whinin'. I said we can go but when we got back without the fuckin' money *you* had to tell Spyder how some gunshots scared you the fuck off. And you were all like '*fuck that,*' so we waited, *marica.*"

"Fuck you, bitch!"

"Fuck you back, *coño!*"

"Shut the fuck up and keep talking!" Domita commanded.

"Okay," Looney said. "So the motherfucker just steps to us. And he looked like some skinny-ass pussy."

"No muscles like you?" Domita asked.

"A little bit," Looney answered. "Kinda like Kobe Bryant 'cept he was a drink of spoiled milk. But he stepped straight up, *no* fear."

"No fear," Jarhead, who had been quietly sitting, decided to talk, now that the cat was out of the bag. "Strapped like a pig."

"What do you mean?" Carmen asked.

"He didn't flash no badge, right?" Diablo said, "but he had on a fuckin' bullet-proof vest, a nine and fuckin' grenades and shit."

"So," Looney said, "we think he's *la fuckin' chota*, and we play it cool 'cause we got a fat sack of weed in the glovebox. If we knew it was *Oscar...*"

"We'da smoked his ass," Shadow rasped for the first time.

"Okay, what then?" Carmen asked.

"Dude steps to us like it's nothin'." Looney said, "Gives Diablo a big wad of dollars and gets in the fuckin' car, like he just bought it off us or some shit. Tells us to drive to the eight-one-eight and drop his ass off."

"Where'd you drop him?" Carmen asked.

"Griffith Park," Looney said. "Then we turned our asses around and went back to the crib, and there *you* were on TV, lookin' *so* fine, talkin' 'bout the cops was bangin' with Oscar Mike, like three blocks away from where we were at. Yo, it *had* to be him! But we didn't know!"

"How much money did he give you?"

"Seven-K."

"You still have it?" Carmen said. "It could have fingerprints."

"Fuck you," Diablo said, "like I'm gonna give it to you!"

Domita shot out of her chair and into Diablo's face. "I was digging bullets outta your *papi's* back when you were swimming laps around his huevos, *maricón*! You're alive because of me, and you best respect *mi hermana*!"

Diablo's home boys gave him worried looks.

At that moment, Carmen's phone rang. She withdrew it from

its case and looked at the screen. It was Gary. It could wait. She sent the call to voicemail and put it away.

"Just tell me what he looks like," Carmen told Diablo.

"Mariposa, baby," *a Corona* spoke up whose name, Carmen recalled, was *Felon*. Carmen did not know him well, but she remembered he was a great source of marijuana back in the day. He and Domita were thick. He was a tall, muscular *vato* with oiled black hair, a face chiseled with scars. "We can do way fuckin' better than that," he told Carmen. "I got *Rapto* in the party outside."

He flexed one of his large biceps, showing off a gorgeous tattoo of a raven-haired beauty with the word *Eliza* in cursive underneath it.

"He did this without a picture, eh. He can draw that *maricón!*"

Carmen wanted to give out an exhaled cry of victory, but she just giggled and covered her mouth, jumped out of her chair and threw her arms around the *Corona* who had just topped off her great day with gravy, and kissed him on the cheeks.

She looked over at Diablo. He was dejected and put-out. Realizing that he could be the future of this gang, Carmen went back around and sat back down in front of him. She took his face with both hands.

"Diablo," she said. "*Usted es mi familia.* I would never sell you out to no cops. I would never do that to you. I will prove it to you, okay? *Eres mi hermano.*"

She kissed him softly on the cheeks. He seemed to accept the peace offering. Carmen then thanked Looney and the rest in a similar, affectionate way and joined the party.

Diablo and Looney went right to work with the tattoo artist on the sketch that was going to rescue her beloved city from a monster and make Carmen Sanchaz a superstar.

58

AFTER SMOKING A bowl with 18th Street's finest, and reminiscing about the old days with Domita and her *Aristocrata* sisters, Carmen approached Diablo and Looney, sitting on the floor with Rapto, a plump, tattooed El Salvadorian with a long beard and a Harley Davidson bandana. Felon was right. He had a lot of talent.

Oscar Mike's face had taken shape. He had close-cropped, military style hair, which coincided with some of Homicide Special's notes. It could have been the Chronic, or it could have been a way for Carmen to be involved in the process, but she thought out loud. "He could have been a hero who fought terrorists," she said. "What made him become one?"

"Jarhead's a Marine," Diablo said. "He got capped in the back in Baghdad."

"Did you really?" Carmen asked Jarhead.

"Ooh rah," Jarhead said nodding. "Semper Fi baby, just like bein' in a clique, know what I'm sayin'? Always faithful."

He and his home boys gave each other five, and fist-bumped. It was a real shame. Another American hero who was probably going to die young over some drug money or spend most of his life behind bars. This gang world was such a small part of the real one, but this was the culture she came up in, so Carmen pretended to agree with them. They had her back. She had to have theirs.

From the drawing, Oscar Mike's face was gaunt and thin like a man who gets plenty of exercise but should eat more. The eyes were deep-set and intense.

How many deaths have those eyes seen? How many sick and cruel ways had he learned one could be killed? Why should people doing what they do in traffic matter so much? The question could also be asked of his victims. Why couldn't they just signal? Why couldn't they let that guy who signaled come into the lane they were in? Why not share the road, put down the cell phone, be patient, be polite?

"Why is it so hard for people to just drive safely?" Carmen said. "It costs nothing."

"Is what it is," Diablo said. "Just gotta deal. Go with it, eh. Better reasons to smoke a fool than some bullshit."

"I know," Carmen said. "It's so… *la verga, stupid chingada.*"

Domita strolled up behind Carmen, wrapped her arms around her waist, a bottle of cerveza in one hand. She gave Carmen a sisterly squeeze and looked down at the drawing.

"He should see how they drive in Trujillo," Domita said. "He'd need, like a *nuclear bomb* to fix shit down there."

Carmen and the group of vatos laughed.

"It's not funny!" Carmen giggled.

Domita kissed Carmen on the cheek and offered her the cerveza. Carmen figured one beer would not hurt and accepted it.

When Rapto was done, Felon shot a picture of the sketch with his phone. "I wanna remember this bitch's face," he said. "Take fuckin' pictures, all of you."

The others all took out their various cellular devices and did as they were ordered.

"Study that shit," Felon commanded. "E-mail that shit to your fuckin' homeboys! You cross paths with this bitch—"

"We fuckin' smoke him!" Diablo said.

"No, *maricón*!" Felon said, slapping Diablo upside his head. "Get his fuckin' plate, tell *la chota* where the fuck he is, and get the fuck out. Nobody better try and take this fuckin' bitch out them self! You smoke the wrong fuckin' white boy, just cruisin' home from his fuckin' job or some shit, it's gonna be your fuckin' ass!"

Carmen's phone rang. She looked at the screen—Gary again. This time she answered the phone and headed for the front porch outside where it was quieter.

"*Papi!*" Carmen sang cheerfully. "Where have you been?"

"That's not funny, Carmen," he replied. "We need to talk."

"Okay, okay," she said. "Chill out, I'm here. What's up?"

"A little while ago the FBI told me to hold on the exposé until Detective Wheeler is able to provide a description of Oscar Mike. It is imperative to law enforcement that we don't air this until then."

"Ooh, *Papi!* Zarah's gonna have a surprise when she wakes up!"

"What's that?" Gary said confused. "What do you mean?"

"*Mami's* about to make you very happy!"

59

IT HAD BEEN four days since Oscar Mike's tussle with Zarah Wheeler. For two days he tried without success to find out what her condition was. No one was talking, and there was nothing on the news about her death, which meant she lived. Infiltrating a hospital full of cops and feds to finish her off was risky, bordering on stupid.

Zarah Wheeler would not forget any detail of their struggle, especially his face. The media may not have known about it, but law enforcement may have had a description of him in hand. They had the advantage. Time to make a tactical retreat.

He chose to hit the road in a vehicle he owned rather than a stolen one. He paid cash for a used Toyota Tundra. All of his essential belongings were packed into the bed of his pickup, but he kept his toolkit of weapons close at hand. He had stashed a sawed-off shotgun and an AR-15 assault rifle in the back of the cab. He had installed a police scanner and radar for peace of mind.

He drove up I-5 North and was running behind. He wanted to be passing through Oregon two days ago, but it took him that long to arrange travel.

Leaving America on a plane was impractical. Airports had too many paranoid eyes, too many cameras. He decided to drive to Seattle. He had arranged to make egress on a Japanese container vessel that would carry him from Seattle along The Gulf of Alaska and then southwest over the North Pacific to Nagoya. From there he would catch a flight to Odessa, and then, maybe, he could relax.

This escape would be a long trip, but the route was deceptively erratic—odd enough to make him difficult to track. He doubted the people who were hunting him had considered that he had the resources and connections for such a meticulous getaway.

He allowed the police to think he was a psychopath, but he was a professional. Being a merc had its perks if one was good at his job, kept quiet, protected his identity, did not get greedy, knew how to use his funds and did not burn bridges.

He loved his hometown as much as anyone, but people had to be made to understand. Making something that should be simple and safe more hostile and dangerous than it had to be, just because *they can,* is not an excuse for it. People needed to be taught respect and consideration, if for no other reason than because they did not know who they were sharing the road with, or what they were capable of.

Getting on a soapbox, passing benign laws, raising fines did not work. Billboards and public service announcements were condescending words that nobody listened to. The truth that life is fragile and impermanence is a fact of nature never crosses their minds. Potentially getting killed in a wreck does not frighten anyone.

Terror worked.

All one had to do to know the truth of his mission was to turn on the television.

Oscar Mike is right.

Go on the Internet.

Oscar Mike is right.

And these people would turn around after posting how *right* Oscar Mike was, get in their cars and multi-task like they're trying to break a record—texting in one hand, holding food in the other and steering with their fucking knees. Or insist on tapping their brakes every thirty seconds even though there is nobody in front of them. Or come to a complete stop and try to cross over three lanes of traffic to turn, after realizing they've almost missed the goddam turn.

There were too many examples to be made yet. Oscar Mike could not be finished so soon. He cursed himself. If he had just let Zarah Wheeler be...

He decided to vanish for a time, remain at large, let people wonder if he was still out there—a shadow over the streets of L.A., watching, waiting for the right time to renew his mission.

If he was arrested and thrown in prison, the city would feel safe and people would go right back to acting however they pleased. He could not have that. His campaign was far from over.

60

ZARAH SAW FIRE. Black smoke and flames engulfed an empty void surrounding her. She heard whipping, crackling and snapping, unable to discern what was giving fuel to the blaze. She searched for a path to safety, but there was no way out.

The heat was singeing the hairs on her skin. She hugged herself and rubbed her forearms, trying to protect herself and soothe the itching from the rising temperature. She heard the chopping rotors of helicopters, but when she looked up she saw nothing but dark- ness. When she looked down, she was barefoot. She realized she
was naked. A man's arm shot out from the edge of the flames. The skin was on fire—red, oozing and bubbling. It seized Zarah's leg and yanked her off her feet. When she hit the bottomless ground, she gasped and kicked.

"No, no, no! Please, please…"

Oscar Mike's voice filled her ears. "THIS IS IT, ZARAH."

The grotesque hand pulled her into the fire. She wailed as the heat peeled her flesh and raced up her long hair.

Her skull was aflame. She flailed and screamed. The smoldering hand gripped tighter as another emerged and grabbed her by the arm. It pulled her sideways toward the blaze.

Zarah screamed for help, begged it to stop, struggled to free herself, but none of it was any use. The flames crept over her face and devoured her. She felt the wetness of her tongue sizzling, sputtering and vaporizing inside her mouth.

The searing heat blurred her sight, the vitreous body of her eyes burning and bubbling. Her vision died. In the dark, she felt scalding pain and heard her skin hissing within the merciless scorch. She felt the pressure building behind her irises. She howled an inhuman shriek of agony as she felt her eyes *pop*.

Zarah sat bolt upright, heaving heavy breaths. She was sweating and trembling.

"Whoa," a woman's gentle voice said. "You're okay, Zarah. You're okay. You had a night terror, but you're fine. You need to calm yourself, okay?"

Zarah found herself in a cold, bright room. Her head felt two sizes too big, and her brain pounded against the walls of her skull. She felt something squeezing her calves. There was similar pressure on her arm. She was covered in a blanket, with only a paper-thin gown and a pair of mesh panties between her and complete nudity.

"Why am I in a hospital?" Zarah asked, collecting her breath.

The nurse explained her injuries as Zarah looked around the room.

There were no windows. There were no sounds of activity, no traffic in the halls, just the humming and hissing of the two compression circulators, squeezing on her calves as they contracted and expanded. Zarah figured it must have been late at night. She felt warm and light—almost weightless.

"Am I on drugs?" Zarah asked.

The nurse nodded. "Dilaudid," she said. "For the pain."

Zarah wanted to have her wits and to be able to think straight.

"No more opiates, please," Zarah said.

Zarah tried to work out what happened. She remembered Sebastian tied to a chair, bleeding, half dead. Now she was in a hospital bed.

Sebastian!

"I need a phone. Where's my phone?"

"It's almost 3:00 am. Anyone you want to call is asleep."

"I'm calling cops. They're used to it! Give me my phone!"

"Zarah," the nurse said, "you *must* calm down."

A familiar, gruff voice said, "Let me talk to her."

"Charlie?" Zarah called out.

The nurse blocked her view, but she could see the sides of his girth and felt relieved.

"She can't have visitors right now," the nurse said, "and cellular devices aren't allowed in here."

"She won't use her phone, but we have to talk," Charlie said.

The nurse rolled her eyes, made some notations on Zarah's chart and said, "She's all yours," as she headed out the door.

"You got cops *and* feds guarding you," Charlie told Zarah as he pulled a metal stool away from the wall and sat. "The only way in here is through all of us. Even Adam Jamison is out there."

Zarah sat up and looked at the I.V. taped to her hand. She looked past Charlie, out the door, looking for the nurse who had just left."

"The only way *out* of here is through all of us, too," Charlie said, "so just take it easy."

Zarah let out a frustrated sigh and relaxed into her bed.

"How is Sebastian?"

Charlie looked away.

"He's okay, right?"

No answer.

"Charlie?" Zarah said. Tears filled her eyes and blurred her vision. "He was alive. When I got there, he was alive. He's *alive!*"

"I'm so sorry, Zarah." Charlie leaned in close and put his hand on her arm. "He coded in the ambulance before he got here."

Zarah made an effort not to lose control, but she was not sure she could manage it for long. She choked back the pain. The one person she was beginning to feel comfortable showing that kind of weakness to was dead. Sebastian was gone.

"He was a decent guy," Charlie told her.

"Oh please!" Zarah said, tearing her arm away. "Don't coddle me! I saw your interview with him, the way you treated him!"

"That was then. I'm pretty sure he went down fighting for you, but we need your statement."

Zarah did not understand. She did not remember. She did not need to give him more reasons to doubt her, did not need him asking questions she could not answer. "Tell me you got him," Zarah said, suppressing as much emotion as she could.

I'll cry later, she thought, *when I'm alone.*

But she was always alone, and would always be alone. *Sebastian...*

Charlie shook his head.

"Is Singer here, too?" Zarah asked. "I want to talk to him."

Charlie shook his head again. "No one's heard from him since the day before yesterday," he said. "He reassigned your eyeball the night you were... Sheridan called the FBI and chewed his SAC out over it, so Singer may be in the penalty box."

"Wait, what?" Zarah asked. "Singer doesn't have the authority to reassign anybody. Where's Wilster?"

"She's outside, now," Charlie said. "But Zarah...we weren't protecting you. Singer was."

Zarah's confusion had no words. Charlie must have seen it, because he continued. "Zarah," Charlie said, "when you agreed to work with the FBI, without discussion, before your hearing, the bosses decided you weren't a team-player and—"

"Hard to be a team-player without a team," Zarah said. "Not one of you stood up for me, not one of you had any sympathy for me!"

"Zarah that's not—"

"Bull, Charlie!" Zarah said. "The FBI wouldn't have been able to see through the circle of LAPD wagons around me if I was *man* enough!"

"You gonna play the sexism card now?" Charlie said.

"Oh, piss off!" Zarah said, raising the back of her hand and showing him the I.V. needle stuck into her vein. "Do I look like I'm running for office here? You cut me loose and threw me to the wolves, and if I was a man and twenty years older you'd have had my back."

Charlie threw his hands up and shook his head. He took a deep calming breath. "Zarah," Charlie said, "I didn't throw you to the wolves. *I* was on medical." He rubbed his shoulder for emphasis.

"You wouldn't let me see you," Zarah chided. "You didn't speak *one word* to me, wouldn't take *one* of my calls that whole time! What do you call that?"

"Anger management," Charlie answered.

"WHAT?"

"Look, Zarah, we ain't Starsky and Hutch. You need to seriously dial-down your *chutzpah* if you wanna be an H.S.S. dick, but—"

"I just came out of a coma, like *two minutes ago*," Zarah shouted. "*This* is how you comfort your wounded partner?"

"But..." Charlie continued, "*We have a good thing*. You may have noticed that I'm the kinda guy who runs off at the mouth when he's angry."

"Yeah, I *did* kinda notice that!"

"So I needed to cool off, and I needed you away from me for a while. I'm sorry if that hurts your little feelings."

Zarah blinked, and studied his face for a moment. Then she nodded. "Fine," she said. "Maybe one day *you'll* get suspended, you'll have the world coming down on *you*, and I'll be sure to put my *little feelings* before yours and *not* support you through any of it."

"Zarah," Charlie laughed, exasperated, "you should have been fired. We *both* should've been. And with Carmen Sanchaz out there beating the drum she was beating, all *you* got was suspended. You had support. The wagons *were* circled. You're just too pissed off and blind with guilt and self-pity to see that."

"So it's perfectly okay that my protection detail was pulled?"

"No," Charlie said. "It was fucking petty, but you never asked to be protected, Zarah, and Singer gave Torres his word that he'd put a detail on you."

"So, where was Singer's detail?"

"At the time, his so-called detail consisted of one fucking guy," Charlie said. "It turns out that Oscar Mike isn't as all-fired important to the FBI as we thought. Singer called for more people, but they needed time to get their shit together. He tells me that the two of you agreed to provide some information to Carmen Sanchaz, and he took the one guy he had off your security to find her."

Zarah wanted to jump out of bed, find Carmen, hobble her and lock her in a box until they had Oscar Mike in custody and then go to work on Sherman Singer.

"We did *not* agree," Zarah said. "When I argued against it, he reminded me of who I answered to. I need to get out of here."

Charlie shook his head. "No way," he said.

Zarah gritted her teeth, and gnarred in frustration. She was close to cursing at Charlie, but she held her tongue. She sucked in a deep, angry breath and held it a moment before closing her eyes and exhaling, a little calmer. She shook her head. It was too late anyway. What was she supposed to do with Carmen now, tackle her, live on TV in front of a million people? It made her head ache. She thought of leaving the hospital against medical advice, but Charlie was clear that no one was going to let Zarah out whether she wanted them there or not.

"Whatever," Zarah said. "There's no reasoning with her anyway."

"Well Singer assured me that Carmen'll hold the story until we have a description."

Zarah thought of Sebastian again. Once she knew that Oscar Mike was *Seth* from the dojo that one time, she should have let him go, protected him. Then it hit her.

"I need a phone."

"No, Zarah."

"I have to talk to Corinna, Sebastian's wife!"

"No, Zarah," Charlie said. "You're concussed, your face is busted and you're high on meds—"

"I'm pissed off! How high can I be?"

"You're not making *any* calls or going *anywhere*!"

"Fine!" Zarah said. She was too bereaved and too fatigued.

Charlie looked surprised that she did not press it further, but Zarah was so tired. She did want to rest, to grieve and excise the notion of having a happy life. God did not want that for her and was cruel about how He would *taketh away* if she tried.

"You should all go home and get some rest," she said to Charlie.

"No one is resting now," he replied.

She managed a weak smile. "Thanks."

He stood up and slapped the lights in her room off as he left. Now it was pitch black except for the electric medical equipment. All she could do was sit in the dark and think about Sebastian and all the wrong moves she had made. She allowed herself to cry.

61

CARMEN SANCHEZ AND Gary Sterling sat in the office of Aiden Daniels, the Executive Evening Director for Channel Six. He had seen the footage they had shot, had heard the interviews, and would either approve and decide when to air it that evening, or disapprove and send them back to the editing bay.

Carmen was not worried. The story she and Gary had put together was relevant, poignant and drenched in blood. It would be the top story of the evening broadcast without a doubt.

Daniels was looking down at Carmen's script with his glasses perched on the crest of his sharp nose. He nodded his head as he finished one paragraph—a good sign. Furrowed his brow when he read others—not so good.

Without looking up at either of them he said, "Very good, you guys. This is going to be pretty huge." He held up the sketch that *Rapto* had made of Oscar Mike. "Did the LAPD okay this?"

"No," Gary said, "but from what the FBI told me they have a sketch as well—from Detective Zarah Wheeler."

"Zarah's awake?" Carmen asked.

Gary quickly nixed her question with a wave of his hand.

"So we both have a sketch," Gary said. "What's the big?"

Daniels tossed the sketch onto his desk. "No big," he said. "You just can't use this. Talk to them and use theirs."

Carmen felt her hackles rising. That little hand-wave told Carmen that Gary was lying about the FBI having a sketch, too. But since Carmen had the only sketch of Oscar Mike... "Do you know what a miracle it is I even got that?"

"Carmen," Daniels said, "you busted your ass for all of this, and nobody takes it for granted."

"I don't get it!" Carmen said. "We should air this! People need to know what this *pendejo* looks like already!"

"I agree, Carmen, but it's not our decision."

"We're the *fucking news!*" Carmen shouted jumping to her feet. "It's *not our decision* to inform the public? What are we all doing here then? Why don't we all just raise chickens or something?"

"Carmen..." Daniels said, his voice heavy with warning. "Do you want to get busted, hard? You want to lose what few police contacts you have? Want to become a target for harassment, get put in the center of controversies you *don't* want to be in the center of—like *free speech* nuts versus *law and order* nuts—while Oscar Mike is still at large, knows he's been made and changes his appearance?

"And let's say some poor local, who *kind of* matches the sketch, commits a petty crime but is no serial killer. Say he's shot and killed by some do-gooder with a *right to protect*? Never mind that your sketch gets an innocent man killed, now a defense lawyer's got reasonable doubt when Oscar Mike *is* caught. Who's everybody gonna blame for that, Carmen?" Daniels thrust his finger straight to Carmen's chest.

"Worse than that," Daniels continued, "they'll blame this network, and this network will protect itself. So if you want to destroy your career, maybe go to jail, air the sketch."

Carmen stood there, speechless for a moment and then plopped back into her chair, folded her arms and sulked.

"What we have is more than enough," Gary assented, putting a comforting hand on Carmen's shoulder, which she shrugged off irritably. "It's still a great exposé."

"Carmen," Daniels said. "You've been ice skating uphill for a long time. You've survived here because you've got a personality that people respond to. Your work lately, this exposé, are all steps in the right direction, but if you take liberties and make the rules up as you go, then yes, go raise chickens."

"All right," Carmen huffed. "Thank you."

"Okay," Daniels said. "Now let's talk about the concerns I have about some of the language you're using here."

Carmen sighed, at her wit's end, and hung her head backwards, looking up at the ceiling.

62

ZARAH SAT UPRIGHT in her hospital bed and bit down on a Double Bacon Cheeseburger, courtesy of Charlie Slocum, who sat on a stool at her bedside. She was on a non-narcotic anti-inflammatory, which was not managing her pain well enough, and her head hurt whenever she chewed. There were obvious narcotic remedies, which the doctors seemed suspiciously eager to give her, but the tradeoff was her ability to think clearly. So she grinded through the aching and throbbing with discipline.

Every day she struggled to remember what had happened, but all she was able to summon into her memory was seeing Sebastian tied to a chair in a pool of blood. She still remembered what Oscar Mike looked like from his visit to the dojo, sort of. She asked anyone in a lab coat when her memory would return. None would say when, or guarantee that it would, but the forensic artist was coming anyway, and maybe talking about *dojo Seth* would shake something more recent loose.

She would be out of the hospital soon. Much of the swelling around her eyes had gone down, and she was set to be discharged the next day. The bad news was she would be surrounded by LAPD and FBI warders until Oscar Mike was dead or in lockup, no matter how much she protested. As far as they were concerned, Oscar

Mike had taken the last shot at her he was going to take—that was a problem.

Zarah wanted to take one more shot at him.

It burned in her mind. Everything else was irrelevant.

He had murdered Sebastian, and she would happily sacrifice what was left of her life to give him what he deserved. All of this "protection", as well-meaning as it was, would present obstacles and arguments and would slow her down. What was more frustrating was that everybody was treating her like a fluffy, little duckling that had been stomped on.

Adam Jamison, however, was brazen as hell. He brought her red roses and renewed his invitation to watch "Star Wars" with him. What nerve. Zarah's *second* true love is stabbed to death the same as her first, and Adam wants a date? Was he kidding? Suffice it to say, it did not go his way, though Zarah had been more polite about it than she had felt like being. Adam was a good guy, and did not know her history with men. Nobody did.

Sebastian…

Between her deceased husband, and Sebastian, Zarah had decided that she should not bother with romance anyway. She was no good at it. Besides, police work was a round-the-clock job, and *good* police work was not kind to relationships.

Adam was undaunted, and Zarah was grateful to have one person in her orbit who did not walk on eggshells, but the *friend zone* was as close as he was going to get.

Captain Sheridan, Lieutenant Torres and Charlie were all trying to shelter her, but there was no real shelter. Zarah could not stop thinking about Sebastian's death, and her desire to make Oscar Mike pay was unquenchable. She was not going to get anywhere lying around, and every time someone told her to relax, the hotter her blood boiled.

"Charlie," she asked, "where is this sketch artist already?"

"On the way," Charlie said. "Just try and—"

"Say 'relax' and I'll pull out this IV and stick it in your eye!"

"Jesus, I can't believe I thought this side of you was sexy."

"*What?*"

"I get that you're upset," Charlie said, "but none of your howling is gonna make time go faster."

"I've been waiting since yesterday, you fat bastard!"

Sherman Singer stuck his head through the doorway. "Sounds like she's awake," he said.

"OHH, *look* who it is," Zarah said. "Have you been looking for my hospital room this *whole time, Sherman?*"

Charlie clenched his jaw and tensed his hands as if he wanted to flip Zarah's bed over with her in it. Singer gave an abashed chuckle and slid into the room.

"Take over for me before I put her back in a coma," Charlie said.

"Whatever," Zarah grumbled.

"Turn on the TV," Singer said. "Carmen Sanchaz is on."

Zarah fished around her blankets for the bulky, eggshell colored TV remote that was integrated with the nurse-call. When she found it, she switched it on for the first time since she had awakened. It was tuned into an episode of "The A-Team," in Spanish.

"Channel six," Singer said.

"I know what channel she's on!" Zarah barked.

Zarah cursed, realizing that the TV remote did not have numbered buttons, and she had to cycle forward through all of the channels to reach the one she needed.

When she reached Channel Six, it was displaying a photo of victim number two, Ari Farhad. He was dead and mangled in his BMW, his face torn by buckshot.

"*El khara dah!*" Zarah cursed at the TV, throwing the remote. As it was attached to her bed with a half-inch thick cable, the remote did not make it far.

The original crime scene photos had been shot in color, but for the delicate sensibilities of network news sponsors, they had been rendered in black and white. A feminine, Pakistani voice narrated:

"Everything was great that day," she said. *"We had decided on the cake. We found out his sister was flying in for the wedding..."*

The picture dissolved to another angle showing the outside of Ari Farhad's BMW, the shattered, bloody glass.

"...we were on our way to have lunch with my parents, and we were running very late. Then out of nowhere, this... not a man, some kind of animal does this to us! For what? Because my fiancé didn't want to keep people waiting? Because he pulled ahead of some insane, egomaniac at a red light? That's why he deserved to die?"

Then the picture on the screen dissolved to the outside of an upper class, ranch-style house. Zarah recognized it as the Stein residence, where the most savage murders had taken place.

Carmen Sanchaz narrated: *"This was once the home of Studio City residents, Carol Stein, her husband Karl and her two young boys Jonathan, and Jacob. Carol had had a lot on her plate on January 31st, 2015. It was the day before Superbowl Sunday, and she was all over town making preparations. Her husband Karl had planned a small party with close friends..."*

The photo on the screen dissolved into a series of pictures of Carol Stein and her family, smiling, joyful, at the beach, in front of Yosemite Falls and other various locales, having good times while a different woman's voice spoke in voice-over.

"Carol was a very giving, loving, wonderful person," the woman said as the caption *STEIN FAMILY FRIEND* faded onto the bottom-left corner of the screen while the slideshow continued. *"She touched the lives and hearts of so many people,"* the voice-over said. *"And they loved her because she was just so warm and so wonderful and so filled with life and enthusiasm."*

"None of that mattered..." Carmen's voice said. The picture dissolved to a new still-shot of the house with police tape around

279

the perimeter and austere, grim looking detectives on the red-brick walkway and driveway, *"when she crossed paths with Oscar Mike."*

They cut to another forensic photo of the front door wide open with yellow police tape across it. The picture slowly zoomed in on a security keypad above the doorbell that had been pried away from the wall, hanging from a few wires.

"Carol Stein's body was discovered several days later."

"By *you*," Charlie heckled, "courtesy of the nut-sack you're shitting on!"

"Shh!" Zarah said, wanting to hear Carmen's story, though Charlie had an excellent point. The Stein murders had stood out in Zarah's mind, not so much because of the brutality of it all. It had always bugged Zarah that Carmen had been the one to find Carol Stein's body, four days postmortem, and *after* Oscar Mike had called to tell her—presumably because nobody had stumbled over the crime scene in all that time, and he was sick of waiting to hear about it on the news.

It had been Superbowl Sunday, and the Steins had planned a party. Nobody called? Nobody showed up? Nobody had gone to their front door? Nobody had noticed the security panel had been tampered with? *Nobody?*

Some friends, Zarah thought, *but that's L.A. for you.*

If Oscar Mike had not left a note at the scene, confessing to the murders, Zarah would have pulled each of the Stein's so-called *friends* into an interview room and raked them over the hottest coals she knew how.

Carmen continued. *"She had been brutally tortured and stabbed to death by a vainglorious psychopath, in her own home."*

As Carmen continued narrating, and as other voices talked about Karl Stein and their young children, more evidence photos dissolved into and out of the slideshow. Photos of Karl Stein, face down in his children's bedroom, and then the children, their corpses blurred for the most part, but still bloody. It was gruesome, and stomach-turning, and Zarah knew that the public's reaction would be acute and powerful. Finally, the picture dissolved to an evidence photo of the note Oscar Mike had left. A man's voice-over dramatically read the words.

"*She thought that she could be an entitled b<beep>ch to everyone around her and not ever pay a price. She sealed her fate the moment she convinced herself that she was better than everybody else. The belief corporate-raised Americans have that they can do as they please and trouble will always be passed to someone else was what killed this family.*"

The man reading the note was trying to sound urban, dark and evil. Zarah thought it was what Count Dracula may have sounded like if he had been from Brooklyn.

The voice continued. "*Trust me when I tell you if she had simply taken one of a dozen empty parking spaces, they would all be alive.*"

The picture cut to Carmen sitting inside what looked like Homicide Special's busy offices and cluttered cubicles in Parker Center, but it could have been any unit in any police station.

"He did this over a *parking spot,*" Carmen matter-of-factly said to someone off screen.

"Yes," a male voice answered. A graphic appeared on the bottom of the screen: LAPD CRIMINALIST, and the picture never cut away from Carmen—still protecting everyone involved in the story, except herself.

"Massacred a whole family," she said, "over a *parking spot.*"

The criminalist, whose voice sounded too much like Adam's for it not to be, answered, "*That's right.*"

"And this hypocrisy," Carmen said, "is an ongoing theme in Oscar Mike's holier-than-thou messages to us, isn't it?"

"Yes it is," Adam said.

"This is not uncommon at all."

"Not at all."

"It's rather cliché, isn't it?"

Zarah cringed. Every handful of dirt Carmen flung at Oscar Mike was coming out of her own her grave.

"Murderers like Oscar Mike grow on trees," Adam said. "A lot of them admit they committed the murder, but they never really accept responsibility. They did it, but it's not their fault. Oscar Mike is no different. *'She was being rude.' 'He didn't let me in his lane.' 'They knew I was out there and did it anyway.' 'They asked for it.' 'What did I do? I took out the trash. I made commuting that much safer. I did a good thing here.'*"

"So there's no remorse at all," Carmen said.

"None," Adam affirmed. "He'll never say, *'I'm sorry for what I've done.'* He couldn't care less about his victims."

After a few more leading questions and blandly scientific answers, Zarah tuned out. Her mind projected visions of horrific scenarios: Carmen abducted, Carmen ambushed, Carmen shot down in the street or slashed to death with her own kitchen knife. How badly would she suffer? Where would her body be found? What would the note say?

Still, Oscar Mike was a strategic thinker. If Carmen was lucky, assuming that the killer was even watching, he may think that this report was a manipulative tactic, a trap to set him up. He may decide to ignore it. On the other hand, maybe he would not. It occurred to Zarah that it could be used as a set-up. She would give the notion some thought.

"Tonight," Carmen Sanchaz said, "we at Channel Six Network News have given you the smallest glimpse into the reality and true nature of the horrific crimes committed by the cowardly, demented and derailed mass murderer calling himself 'Oscar Mike'."

"Calling himself?" Charlie heckled. "You made that his name!"

"Shush!" Zarah said. She focused on the scenery behind the reporter. Carmen was on a familiar bridge spanning the 110. The freeway was flanked by thick acacias, Chilean wine palms and avocado trees. It was a clear night. A soft breeze was playing with the reporter's wavy, auburn hair. Brilliant, red brake-lights of various automobiles below flickered with steady white head-lights and illuminated a river of rush-hour traffic that flowed like electric lava toward the scintillating skyline of Downtown L.A.

Seeing what a beautiful night it was made Zarah feel more frustrated. That gorgeous evening was just outside the building, and she was imprisoned in a drab room, surrounded by cops and feds.

The scene changed again to another macabre slideshow of black and white crime scene photos, many with the more horrible wounds blurred.

"All of our hearts go out to the families of the men, women, and children—victims who are not to blame for the inhuman violence inflicted upon them, whatever wrongdoing existed in the monstrous mind of their murderer."

"A lot of alliteration," Singer said, "from narcissistic news ladies, preaching in public places."

"And to the women and men of law enforcement..." Carmen's voice continued. The picture dissolved to images of City Terrace, cars burning, injured innocents being tended to by E.M.T.s, *"who have been hurt, who have risked and lost their lives, working relentlessly without respite to hunt Oscar Mike down and bring him to justice..."* The picture dissolved to a photo of Zarah in her dress uniform, the same photo Carmen had used to shame her months before.

"Oh, heavenly days!" Zarah said.

"You have our most sincere gratitude and steadfast support."

There was a dramatic pause in Carmen's spiel, the picture returned to a mid-shot of Carmen, and in her eyes Zarah caught the quickest flicker of the reporter's trademarked sass before she returned to her professional countenance.

"Oh no, Carmen," Zarah said. "Don't do it."

Every eye in the room was glued to the screen.

"Oscar Mike enjoys leaving messages," Carmen said. "Tonight, let us give *him* a message. You don't like how we behave in traffic? Well, welcome to Los Angeles."

Zarah could hear applause and some females cheering from what must have been the nurses' station outside, down the hall. They must have been watching, too.

"There's something you need to know about us Angelenos," Carmen said. "You don't scare us. You don't impress us. You're nothing to us, and we can't wait to say it to your face."

"Oh, poop," Singer said.

"If anyone has any information regarding the Oscar Mike investigation, please contact the FBI's Los Angeles field office or the LAPD's Homicide Hotline."

Graphics of the phone numbers appeared as Carmen read them off, but Zarah had stopped listening. She imagined Oscar Mike loading his guns and getting into a stolen vehicle to go find Carmen.

"Someone get me a phone," Zarah ordered.

64

"THIS IS CARMEN Sanchaz, Channel Six Network News."

Carmen held her expression and waited for Lamar to give her the cue.

The tally lamp on Lamar's shoulder-mounted camera blinked off.

"We're out," Lamar declared, looking pleased.

Carmen tossed her mic to Gary and took a deep breath. She knew her segment had substance, weight, and would make an impact.

She turned and looked over the 110 South from the Elysian Park Bridge. It was a cloudless L.A. evening with a bright moon and uncommonly clear air. She felt a warm breeze and inhaled another heavy breath, taking in the scents of the air, tress, metal and exhaust. She relaxed but kept her chin high, her shoulders back, and casually anchored a hand on her hip.

Lamar put his camera down on the pavement and began to coil its cables as Gary took a phone call from the network.

She wished she could have used her sketch, but she did not need it. It would be enough to give it to the cops, accept their gratitude, and if they gave her permission to air it, even better. For the first time in a long time, Carmen felt like a real reporter.

Traffic had loosened up, and the running lights on the rear ends of all of the commuting vehicles were moving without pause.

Carmen heard someone coming up behind her. When she turned, she saw the ecstatic grin on Gary's face before he swept her into a chummy bear hug and squeezed.

"They loved it!" he told her as he roughly jounced her up and down in his arms. He planted a huge kiss on her lips, and then released her.

She giggled, "*Ay, papi.*"

"They loved all of it," Gary crowed. "You were great! I mean, we're gonna catch some flak for improvising that *message* part."

Ever since Oscar Mike had recruited her to carry his message to Zarah Wheeler, Carmen was hoping for a chance to let him know that he had misjudged her.

"I don't know what came over me," she lied. "I just had to say something. I know Daniels will say it's bad reporting."

"Well, the public is all over it," he said. "The poll is climbing, and the message boards have lit up. The national affiliates are running with it. It's gonna trend—you can bet on it!" He gave her another smooch. "Come on, let's celebrate!"

Gary raised a fist in the air, and he spun away from her and toward the news van with sleek, victorious brio in his gait.

Carmen giggled again. Gary's phone rang, and he quickly answered it. His ecstatic countenance flattened. After a few solemn nods, and a humble "Yes ma'am," he gave Carmen a raised eyebrow and a grin.

"It's Zarah Wheeler," Gary said, "for you."

Uh oh, Carmen thought. She had switched off the ringer on her own phone before starting her broadcast. She had not felt it vibrate. She took it out of her pants pocket and looked at her lockscreen. No missed calls. Zarah had Carmen's personal number, but she had chosen to go through the studio, and they through Gary. Not good.

Carmen put away her phone and took Gary's, trying not to look nervous. She did not know what she could have possibly done wrong. Then she remembered *Rapto's* sketch of Oscar Mike and loosened up. That would take her off of Zarah's shit-list.

"*Hola mami!*" Carmen tried to sound light-hearted in defiance of the dread that had overtaken her mood. "How are you feeling?"

"Carmen," Zarah greeted her with the same suspicion in her voice she always had when Carmen expressed any kind of familiarity. "I'm good. Thanks. Um... so, the story you just did..."

"I know," Carmen said, not wanting to hear it. "But I needed to do it. I needed to get through to people."

"I believe you did," Zarah said, "and since one of those people is Oscar Mike, you need to get off the street and get some cops around you *now*."

"You're overreacting," Carmen said.

"The main reason he'll come," Zarah told her, "is because you think he won't."

Carmen shook her head. "What'll it say about me if I go to Parker Center and surround myself with cops, *me,* after I told the whole city not to be afraid?"

"Who said anything about Parker Center? Come *here*."

"What?"

"Come to me," Zarah said, "to the hospital. The optics will be fine. You can say you were visiting me—of course half the department is already here, so, you know, *'what a coincidence.'*"

"Zarah, I'll be fine."

"Okay," Zarah said. "What if you just went to ground tonight, and tomorrow when I'm out, I can personally keep an eye on you?"

In the background, Carmen heard a man's voice say "*What? Are you off your damn rocker?*"

"Mind your own business!" Zarah said. "Not you, Carmen, *him.* So what do you say?"

Carmen thought for a moment. Carmen may not have been

her friend, or even much of an acquaintance, but she had known her long enough to sense that something was amiss—something in the detective's voice. Zarah did not sound interested in protecting her. Then it hit her.

"Wait," she said, "You want me to be bait, don't you? You don't care about my safety at all!"

"Hey, Charlie tried to talk you out of this, remember? And trust me, I'd have been after you, too, but... Well, I was in this *coma,* see, and who did that again..? Oh, right, the psychotic, mass murdering terrorist *you* just called out on network television!"

"Charlie was just trying to scare me," Carmen said, "like you're trying right now!"

"Nobody should have to *try,* Carmen! You should be terrified! Heavenly days, are you *that* arrogant, or just stupid? And by the way, *mami,* I don't need *you* to be bait! All I have to do is go outside and—"

There was a commotion over the phone. Carmen heard Zarah yelling at someone to give the phone back to her and a man's voice telling her to lay back and calm down.

"Sanchaz," the voice said, "it's Charlie Slocum."

In the background, Carmen heard Zarah barking mean words at him.

"Zarah's not one-hundred percent right now," Charlie said. "We can't let her get excited, so let's us two talk like professionals."

65

CARMEN, GARY AND Lamar had gone straight to the Homicide Special Section's offices in Parker Center after hanging up with Detective Slocum. It made her feel like she was fronting. If Carmen was still in *el barrio* and had watched some *chola* do that exposé, and found out that she ran straight to a police station afterwards, Carmen would call that bitch a fake and never believe anything she said again.

Most people from *el barrio* were not gangbangers. Most had honest nine-to-five, paycheck-to-paycheck lives. Some were even cops, and it was not as if none of them knew how to tweet. Carmen's credibility was on the line, and if Slocum was luring her into some kind of "protective custody" trap, she would sue them for defamation of character. He better have something worth all of this.

A friendly, young, Pilipino officer led Carmen and her crew through a large, bright office with a dozen or so cubicle stations. The place looked empty, but it had an energized feel. Phones rang. Keyboards clicked and distant voices chattered, but she only saw two people.

The officer led them to Detective Slocum's work station, a grey cubicle close to a water cooler with a cluttered desk, steel-wire framed shelves with binders stacked haphazardly, and an old-school rolodex next to an office phone. There was a large computer monitor on his desk that had many post-its stuck to the screen.

On the dirty-grey cubicle wall there was a corkboard, and in the lower corner was a black and white photograph with a skinny young boy, maybe eight or nine, standing next to Walt Disney in front of the castle in Disneyland. Both were smiling, and Disney had his hand on the boy's head, having ruffled his hair just as the photo was taken.

The boy's eyes were grey and had none of the granite in them that was there now, but the boy was Detective Slocum without a doubt.

Lamar sat in the swivel chair at the desk. Gary, seeing an empty folding chair next to it, plopped down, leaving Carmen to stand.

"Really?" Carmen said.

"Hey," Gary replied, "we could all be eating at The Vine, but this day hasn't been long enough."

Across from Detective Slocum's cubicle was an empty work station with an empty chair. She put her hand on the backrest and began to pull it across to the others.

"Don't use that chair," a brusque male voice told her.

Carmen looked over and saw Lieutenant Torres. He retrieved a chair from one of the other empty cubicles and rolled it to her.

"Whose work station is that?" she asked him.

"I'll be back when Slocum arrives from the hospital," Lt. Torres said. He returned the chair that she had taken to the empty desk. Then he strode away and disappeared behind a door in the far side of the room.

Carmen looked over the workstation. Carmen peered around the outside of the cubicle and read the nameplate affixed to it. It was Detective Zarah Wheeler's. There were no pictures in the cubicle, no personal items at all.

"Zarah's all business, isn't she?" Carmen asked no one in particular. She returned to Zarah's desk and examined the cubicle.

"Carmen," Gary said, "what do you think you're gonna find?"

"Don't you think it's weird?" Carmen asked. "I mean, even Charlie, the biggest *gruñón* in the LAPD, has something personal here."

"Wheeler was suspended," Gary reminded her. "She probably took all that stuff with her the day she left in case she got reassigned."

Carmen nodded. It made sense but did not ring true. Zarah was an air-tight, private person. If anything personal about her was here, it would be stowed out of sight. Carmen opened the center drawer.

"Holy crap, Carmen!" Gary whispered.

There was nothing but some pens and miscellaneous business cards. She shoved it closed and opened the top side drawer.

"This is when Charlie-boy strolls in and busts our ass," Lamar said.

"You guys ever heard of journalistic curiosity?" Carmen asked.

Lamar decided to be the lookout. He stood up, faked a stretch and scanned the room. Gary hung his head in his hands.

Carmen moved some odds and ends around in the drawer. Everything belonged except a photograph buried under some papers. It was a picture of Zarah standing next to that guy that was stalking her. Carmen could not remember his name. It had an "S."

Stephen, maybe? Spencer? Something? Whatever.

They were both wearing martial arts clothes, bone-white jackets with big, black puffy pants, like Steven Segal in the beginning of "Above the Law", before success went to his stomach.

Zarah and Mr. S. were in a Japanese garden. Mr. S. was a hottie, too. Carmen bet that there was a delicious, hard body under all of that loose fitting karate stuff. He had his arm around Zarah's shoulder. She was resting her head on the edge of his. They could have been man and wife in this picture if Carmen did not know better. She re-buried the picture in the drawer and closed it, satisfied.

They waited a little longer, made some small talk, and after a while Detective Slocum arrived, looking as big and weather-beaten and grumpy as ever. Next to him was the hazel-eyed, black-suited FBI guy who had invaded Carmen's apartment. Carmen forgave him since he had done Carmen the biggest favor any cop had ever done her.

"He gave me all that Oscar Mike stuff," Carmen whispered to Gary.

"Sorry to keep you waiting," Charlie said, offering a handshake to Carmen. Surprised, Carmen took his hand and shook it. She did not know if this was just tact or if he had rethought his opinion of her, but she assumed it was the former.

"You know Special Agent Singer," Charlie said, his voice heavy with disapproval.

The agent ignored Charlie and offered his hand. Carmen returned the greeting and then introduced Gary and Lamar.

"We can't thank you enough," Gary told Singer. "It must have been a real risk you took. I mean really, thank you."

"Don't mention it," Singer said, "I mean it."

Lt. Torres appeared, standing in front of Zarah's cubicle.

"All right," he said, "looks like the ice is broken."

Singer pulled out the chair from behind Zarah's desk, spun it around and was about to sit, but was cut short by Torres. "Let's go someplace with a little more room," he said.

They adjourned to a large room with a wooden table, flanked with more swivel chairs. After everyone sat and was settled, Carmen felt small. Detective Slocum was always intimidating, but after adding Torres and the FBI Agent on top of that, Carmen thought they should be reminded that they wanted something from her, not the other way around.

"So what's this about, guys?" Carmen asked.

"Well," Torres began, "we all saw your story on TV tonight."

"How'd you like it?" Carmen asked, not sure she wanted to know.

"People liked it," Charlie said.

"What about Detective Wheeler?" Carmen asked, "I gotta know."

Singer cocked his head as if he wondered why that mattered.

"Well…" Charlie thought for a minute, looking for the best way to put it. "Aside from being injured, grieving and sad, she's in the meanest mood anyone has ever seen her in. And being the absolute worst patient any hospital has ever had, ever... She's complicated. Even in the best of times, Wheeler's a tough read.

"What do you mean?" Carmen asked.

"Look," Charlie said. "Oscar Mike killed a good friend of hers—"

"Sebastian Michaels," Singer added.

Mr. S! That was his name!

"Wait," Carmen said. "He's dead?"

"Bled out right in front of her," Singer said. "Not that she remembers any of it after he beat her nearly to death."

Charlie glowered at Singer.

"Oh my God," Carmen said. "I wanna... I mean, she invited me and I said 'no', but can I see her, visit her?"

"Oh, no, no, Carmen," Singer said with a wry chuckle.

"Why not?"

"If you visit her now," Torres said, "in the state she's in..."

"She'll hog tie you with IV tubes and sit on you until the cows come home," Slocum said.

"She is very anxious to keep you safe," Singer added.

"That's not how she sounded when I spoke with her," Carmen said. "It sounded more like she wants Oscar for herself."

"She does," Charlie said. "So do I, and so do all of us. You give any cop in L.A. five minutes alone with Oscar Mike, you'll be making their day."

"Whatever Zarah's motives are," Singer said, "the bottom line is you've put yourself in grave danger, after Detective Slocum urged you not to, and after I urged *you*, Mr. Sterling, to wait."

"That was my fault," Carmen said. "Gary wanted us to hold off, but look..."

Carmen reached down and picked her briefcase up from beside her chair, unzipped it and withdrew a piece of paper, and unfolded it on the table and offered it to Charlie. It was Rapto's drawing of Oscar Mike.

66

"WHAT'S THIS?" CHARLIE asked.

"This is from four eyewitnesses," Carmen said, "people who got a *very* close look at Oscar Mike, minutes after the City Terrace Shootout. I mean people who actually exchanged pleasantries with the man and didn't realize who they were talking to until later."

"How did they come to exchange these pleasantries?" Charlie asked, passing the sketch to Singer without giving it more than a brief glance.

"He paid them to smuggle him out of City Terrace."

"He what?" Torres asked. "We need to talk to these guys!"

"Never gonna happen," Carmen said. "I tried."

"Yeah, sure," Charlie said. "How hard did you try?"

Carmen snickered. "My conscience is clear, Charlie. I even asked if they had any of the cash he gave them left, thinking maybe you could get something forensic or whatever. I almost got pimp-slapped for that one."

"And why are '*they*,'" Charlie asked, "so quick to trust you?"

"You were a gangbanger once, correct?" Singer asked. "They'd trust someone like you."

"They're *familia*," Carmen said, "and *someone like me* was still lucky to get through the door. They wouldn't even have opened it for someone *like you*, especially with that *puto*, Ken-doll hair."

"Excuse me?" Singer said leaning forward with a look that dared her to repeat herself.

"No," Carmen said. "There's no excuse for that hair."

"Okay guys..." Torres said as he took the sketch from Singer.

"You wanted us to wait until you had a description," Gary said. "Now you have one. I'm sure Carmen can go back to her source and try again when you have Oscar Mike in a cell."

Carmen shook her head, "There's nothing more I can do. They won't talk to cops. Period."

"Unless they're already in a cell and want a deal," Torres said. "Then they're real chatterboxes."

Carmen gave an indifferent shrug.

"Speaking of deals," Gary said, "Detective Slocum told Carmen there'd be something in it for us if we had a discussion. So far we've been doing all the giving here."

"We want Carmen to accept our protection," Charlie said.

"If I air that," Carmen said, pointing at the sketch in Torres's hand, "he'll run or hide and leave me alone, right?"

"Maybe." Torres said. "This will help, but it wasn't done by a forensic artist which raises concerns about its accuracy."

"City Terrace happened a pretty long time ago," Charlie said. "And this kind of thing..."

"We'd be stupid if we let you put this on TV without another drawing from someone else to compare this to," Singer said.

Carmen rolled her eyes and exhaled. "I swear this is exactly how Bin Laden got away the first time!"

"Come on," Charlie said. "I have no doubts about this drawing..."

"Odd, since you barely looked at it," she said.

"Are the guys who gave this to you gonna talk to us?" Charlie asked. "Are they gonna testify? Are they gonna point their fingers at Oscar Mike in court and identify him for the record?"

Carmen was silent. After thinking about it for a moment, she understood where Charlie was coming from. She bit back a curse, shook her head in defeat and huffed a frustrated breath.

"There you have it then," Charlie said.

"Whatever," Carmen grumbled.

"We gotta do it right, Carmen," Charlie said. "And what if this isn't what he really looks like? Oscar won't run from that, if anything it will embolden him."

"And I have to tell you, Carmen, Gary," Singer said. "Zarah and I were cultivating a strategy for the media to air the descriptions that she and Sebastian Michaels could've provided of Oscar Mike, before, or even as part of your exposé. We were going to have the borders watched, all points of exit and entry covered, entire local and state police, federal law enforcement, and even civilians with their eyes open, on the lookout. All *you* had to do was wait.

"You wanna tell him how unimpressed and unafraid you are to his face? He *will* give you the opportunity, and *our* ability to stop him is no better than it was the day this whole thing started. He's coming for you, so we kind of need each other here."

"You *think* he'll come for me," Carmen said.

"We know," Singer said. "Wheeler's in the hospital and her close friend is in the morgue. It's pretty compelling evidence."

"It still doesn't mean he'll do anything," Carmen argued.

"Oh, but he'll want to," Singer said. "What if he thought you related to him? What if after he gave you all those crime scenes to report and helped your career, he feels betrayed by you? He'll want you *worse* than Zarah Wheeler, a lot worse, and this is a guy who acts on his impulses."

"It's really not about him," Carmen said. "You said it. I'm a *chola* gangbanger. You know what gangbangers think of mouthy bitches who pick fights and then duck behind a bunch of *soldados* and make them handle the business? I can't tell people I'm not scared of Oscar and then run scared from him and hide behind you, *especially* you."

"I can see the fuckin' meme on my Facebook already," Lamar said, flourishing his hand into an artist's frame with his forefingers and thumbs. "A picture of smilin', sexy-ass Carmen with the caption: *Tells Oscar Mike she's not afraid,* dot, dot, dot, *hides behind the LAPD.*"

"Exactly what I mean," Carmen said.

"We're offering *protection*," Singer said. "No one, expects you to hide. We want you out there, in plain sight, doing what you do best."

"Pissing people off," Charlie said.

"So this *isn't* about keeping me safe!" Carmen said.

"This is crazy," Gary added.

"Just listen," Charlie said.

"To what?" Gary demanded. "I'm still waiting to hear what's in this for her, besides losing her juice with the viewers and maybe getting killed."

Charlie looked at Carmen. "Do you think the viewers that you're so convinced will give you shit for coming here won't give *us* even more shit if something happens to you?" he asked.

"The offer is, if you cooperate with us," Torres said, "we'll cooperate with you."

"Meaning?" Gary asked.

"Meaning we'll all be pals," Torres explained. "The slate, clean. You think about that for a second. This is RHD, Homicide Special Section. We work the big cases, the big names, the highest profiles. That's a door every reporter in L.A. wants the keys to."

"You'll end up working on *20-20*," Singer said, "or some hour-long crime show on *Investigation Discovery* or something."

"If I respectfully decline?" Carmen asked.

"You'll sign a paper stating, for the record, that you respectfully decline," Torres said, "and we go on like we've always done. You walk away, and if Oscar Mike sees you out there, an open target..." Torres shrugged. "We'll eat a bowl of shit for it, but we can say we tried."

Not long ago, Carmen was in the same boat with Charlie, the roles reversed. This is how desperate the police have become. Carmen understood their anxiety. It was reasonable, but the thought of being a hypocrite because *maybe* Oscar Mike would come…

Lt. Torres must have sensed her inching toward "no" because he leaned forward and said, "If we're watching, and he tries anything, we'll finally catch him. You'll be the reason, and we'll make sure everybody knows that. We'll go on the air and say '*Carmen Sanchaz helped us set up the worst murderer to hit L.A. since Richard Ramirez*'. What do you think your credibility will be then? And I'm not talking about *el barrio*. I'm talking about the whole city, the whole state, shit, the whole country. The FBI is in this with you."

"Another door you want the keys to," Singer added.

"You're *not* hiding," Charlie said. "You're *not* afraid. You're *working with us*, doing what dozens of undercover cops do every day, putting yourself in the line of fire to protect and serve your city."

That was not a bad notion. Even people in *el barrio* would be okay with that.

Gary leaned toward Carmen and whispered in her ear, "They're gonna tail you anyway. May as well take the offer, get *something* out of this."

Carmen nodded. "You guys are talking about a lot of maybes here," Carmen said.

"The biggest *maybe* is that you'll survive if he comes at you and we're not watching your back."

Carmen took a deep breath. If someone had told her she would ever be offered friendship from the police department or that she would ever agree to help them, she would have laughed. But opportunities like this were too rare to dismiss. Seizing rare opportunities was how *Ojos Mariposa* escaped from 18th Street and transformed herself into Carmen Sanchaz of the Channel 6 Network News. It was also what Zarah wanted. If she placed herself in the danger zone with Zarah, she could start cutting herself some slack for putting her there in the first place.

"Okay," she said exhaling a deep breath.

Charlie smiled, probably for the first time since the mid-1950s when that photo with Walt Disney was taken.

67

T HE CLOCK SAID it was the AM, but Zarah could not
tell anymore. She was anxious. In the next few hours she
would be liberated from this freezing, antiseptic gulag.

She was finishing up with the FBI's forensic sketch artist—
Agent Brian Davis, a pleasant, patient man if not a punctual one.
He had been worth the wait. Just talking to him as they drew up
the sketch had been therapeutic. He had asked some probing questions about details that Zarah had not considered, like not just the
color of Oscar Mike's eyes but what she thought may have been
behind them. All she had to draw from was *Dojo Seth,* who had visited her jujitsu school to reconnoiter his enemy.

When Zarah thought about it, it was obvious that *Dojo Seth*
had wanted to be out of her presence when she followed him to
his car. She remembered feeling a little hurt by that, but she dismissed it as a guy who had more to do that night and a girlfriend
to do it with.

She could not believe it still put her out, but thank God for
small favors. She admitted to Brian that she thought the killer
could be considered good looking, fit and athletic, built like a cop
just out of the academy and with the posture of a confident man.
Details poured out so fast that the artist had to slow her down.

Dojo Seth may have been a hunk, but Oscar Mike was the

opposite of anything that even brushed up against attractive. Zarah knew she was at death's door the instant she looked into his eyes. She remembered how intense they were, but still, lifeless. There was nothing there—nothing good anyway. She remembered his expression—wrath, hate.

She remembered.

She remembered seeing Sebastian there. She remembered falling into the same trap Karl Stein had fallen into when he rushed to his murdered children's bedside.

If you had just looked behind you! Dammit, Zarah! You know better!

Hours passed while Zarah amended some of her earlier descriptions, and Brian interpreted them on his sketch pad. His eyes and mouth were especially important. She remembered Oscar Mike's smug, satisfied expression when he had his gun pointed at her forehead.

Officer Wilster, in a pressed, dark blue LAPD uniform knocked on the door as she entered halfway into the room. Having a Viking from S.W.A.T., and the first female in the unit, should have been a great comfort. Wilster knew that the males were watching, looking for any show of weakness or incompetence, hoping for it. Zarah remembered how that had felt when she was in uniform, all too well. Wilster *could not* drop the ball, and that made Zarah safer with her than any of the boys from the club—and that was going to be a problem.

"Carmen Sanchaz is here," Wilster said.

"I have everything I need," Brian said. "I can go in the corner and finish this up. It's no problem."

Wilster was waiting for an order. Zarah nodded and motioned for her to let Carmen pass.

When Carmen entered, Zarah was a little taken aback. Carmen's makeup was light, and her wavy, brown hair was tied into a bun. She looked pretty and natural. Her clothes were casual, vulnerable—an apricot blouse and blue denim pants. She had to be off the clock. She was holding a magazine in her hand.

"Hi," she said, regarding Zarah with sympathy and some nervousness. She also looked a little guilty. "I wanted to come when I found out exactly what happened, but…"

"It's okay," Zarah said. "The mood I've been in lately…"

Zarah introduced her to Brian. The reporter shook his hand, exchanged polite pleasantries and turned away from him without showing any interest in his drawing.

"I'm so sorry this happened," she told Zarah.

No 'hola, mami', no snarky quips or sass. Zarah wondered if this was the real Carmen Sanchaz or an act.

"Thank you," Zarah said.

"I'm so sorry about your boyfriend."

Zarah let the misunderstanding about Sebastian go, even though Carmen should have known better. She was there when Sebastian was caught in his truck outside her house. Would a *boyfriend* have done something like that?

It did not matter anymore. Everybody seemed to think that they had been a couple, and the more Zarah denied it, the less they believed her. She was tired of correcting them. The only one who needed to know the truth was Corinna, and she was not taking Zarah's calls.

Eventually Zarah had given up on a face-to-face and did all of her confessing and explaining on Corinna's voicemail. She had even gone so far as to admit that she had thrown herself at Sebastian on the night he died—and that he had bounced her like a bad check. He had loved Corinna and only Corinna. Zarah never heard back, but the confession had been made, the condolences had been sincere and the bad karma was released.

Reminded of bad karma, Zarah looked Carmen over and thought for a moment. Never before had she felt any species of sincerity coming off of the reporter, but that was the vibe Carmen was putting out.

"Carmen," Zarah asked, "why do I have the feeling you're blaming yourself for this?"

"I..." Carmen started but seemed to be having trouble finding words. "I shouldn't have blamed you, on the air... for City Terrace."

She had a point there.

"Carmen..." Zarah said. "It's okay."

"No," Carmen said. "He wouldn't know your name. I'm sorry for that."

"What's done is done," Zarah told her. "We're good, so don't beat yourself up. There's no way you had anything to do with any of this." Zarah gestured to her beaten face.

Carmen may have made it easier for Oscar Mike to find her, but Carmen did not make Sherman Singer re-task her protection detail. If she had had backup with her that night, things may have turned out far different.

"He sent that big file to me to give to you. He got your name from my report. He had to, or why am I involved? It had to be me."

"Look," Zarah said. "Whatever his twisted reasons, he put us together and now we're friends."

Upon hearing the word *friends* Carmen stood straighter and looked proud. Her eyes brightened, and she smiled. For a second Zarah thought she should have said '*allies*' instead, but she could not take it back. "Let's make him regret it," Zarah said, "continuously."

Carmen nodded.

Zarah gestured at the magazine Carmen had. "What have you got there?"

"Oh," Carmen said, forgetting that she was holding it. "I don't know what they're giving you to read in here, but..." She thrust the magazine at Zarah with a nervous chuckle. "It's just something."

It was the latest issue of *Black Belt Magazine*. Fond memories of Sebastian flooded her mind. Sebastian hated Black Belt Magazine. Zarah's eyes filled, and she laughed as she forced her tears back. No way was she going to cry in front of Carmen Sanchaz. "Thanks," she said with a sniffle. "I'm outta here in a few hours, but I'll take it home."

"Oh," Carmen said, relieved. "That's right, I forgot."

"I heard you accepted LAPD's offer," Zarah said.

"Oh, yes," Carmen said. "Not the kind of offer someone in my position refuses."

"That's good, but listen…you've been to the crime scenes, you have the photos. Think back. Remember those pictures. Look at my face, Carmen."

"I know," Carmen said. "I actually *wish* you were one of the cops protecting me."

"Oh, I wish that too," Zarah said, "you have no idea."

There were several moments of awkward silence before Carmen glanced over at the artist, who was adding some pencil strokes to his sketch.

"Well," she said, "looks like you're busy, so I'll just…"

"Actually," the artist said. "I think we're done, but you'll have to leave the room for a second."

"It's okay," Zarah said. "She's authorized. You can check with Agent Singer if you want."

Carmen straightened up and looked proud again.

The artist turned his sketch pad around and showed it to them. Zarah and Carmen both stared at the drawing. Zarah saw the same man who stabbed Sebastian to death and beat her to within inches of her grave.

"That's him!" Carmen said pointing at the drawing. "My God, that's really him!"

Zarah thought it was pretty damn presumptuous for her to make such a bold statement, having never laid eyes on Oscar Mike. Zarah must have been wearing her thoughts on her face, because Carmen looked like her sassy self, as she took her phone out of her pocket. She tapped the screen a few times, took a few steps to Zarah's bedside and handed it to her. It was a photograph of a drawing she had obtained on her own.

It was *Dojo Seth*; a little thinner, bushier eyebrows. He did not have a hood over his head, but the resemblance was still uncanny. If Zarah's drawing was accurate, so was Carmen's. Zarah handed the phone back. "It's him."

"If I'd just aired the damn picture..." she growled, as she tapped the screen a few more times.

"Okay," the forensic artist said. "I guess we're going to circulate it then."

Zarah nodded to him as she reached for the landline on a bedside tray. "I'm letting them know, Carmen," she said.

"Thanks. I gotta move on this."

Zarah nodded again, and Carmen darted out of the room.

68

IT HAD TAKEN all day, but Zarah was free at last. She left the hospital in an unmarked car driven by Officer Wilster. She would have driven herself, but her car had been impounded and she was advised not to by the medical staff. Zarah rolled her window down to enjoy the evening, but Wilster objected for safety reasons.

I swear, the sooner I can ditch these people the happier I'll be!

"Wilster," Zarah said, "I appreciate you protecting me in the hospital, but I'm out now. It's not necessary for you to keep doing this."

"If you want me to stand down," Wilster replied, "we can address that tomorrow, but tonight my orders are very clear."

"I haven't requested protection," Zarah said. "Not from the LAPD, and not from the FBI."

"You didn't mind before."

"That was then," Zarah said. *I was afraid then.*

"Wheeler," Wilster said. "I didn't ask to be sent to you, then sent back to SWAT, and then sent back to you again. Don't get me wrong, I like you, but when the bosses tell me to go somewhere, that's where I go. Being your bodyguard doesn't make you the boss of me."

"Being my bodyguard doesn't make you the boss of *me*," Zarah said, "so if I decide to open a window and breathe oxygen, I'm going to."

"Fair," Wilster said. "Stupid, but fair."

Zarah rolled down her window and took a deep breath of semi-fresh, L.A. air.

Her house in Pacoima was decidedly unsafe, but it was exactly where Zarah wanted to be. Everybody else's plan was to keep Zarah stashed in a FBI safe house. They had not told her where, and few would know. When she arrived home, officers wanted to make a security sweep of the house to make sure Oscar Mike was not lurking inside, but Zarah forbade it.

As politely as she could, she told them that she did not want any of them there and allowed them to choose between standing guard outside or going elsewhere, but what they were not going to do was violate her privacy. After they begrudgingly agreed to stay out, Zarah entered her home, locked her door and went straight to the glass cabinet of her entertainment center and withdrew a .9mm Smith and Wesson semi-automatic pistol.

It was black and silver, a little dusty, but it had not been idle for so long that it would not do its job. The recoil on it was slight enough that she can put multiple rounds into a target without having to re-aim every time she squeezed the trigger, and she can squeeze it fast.

Zarah slid out the magazine and looked at the bullet topping it off and slapped it back in place. Then she began her own sweep of the house, and was more than thorough. She checked everywhere, including places where no adult human could hide, like the dishwasher and under her kitchen sink. She checked her bedroom, the closet, in her wardrobe drawers, everything. She checked her bathroom, her medicine cabinet, her toilet tank hoping for something, anything from him just so she could prove to herself that she was not scared.

Tell me you left another "message" somewhere. See if I'm shaking.

When she had run out of nooks and crannies to inspect, she accepted that Oscar Mike had not returned to finish the job—yet.

She returned to her living room, ejected the magazine from her pistol and placed them both onto her coffee table. The weapon wanted a strip-down and thorough cleaning. Then she would make a strategy to draw Oscar Mike to her. She did not care that a gaggle of guilt-ridden cops and feds were guarding her. She did not ask them to, and they would not make her burrow into a hole and wait for that psycho to take a shot at Carmen without her being there to return fire.

She felt her pulse throbbing under the skin of her neck. She needed to relax, but there was too much to do. She had to retrieve her car from the police impound. She had to call her jujitsu classmates and tell them the awful news about their sensei, on the better-than-average chance that Corinna, who clearly never gave a damn about the dojo, had not bothered to. But first, Oscar Mike. It was not safe for anyone in Zarah's orbit until he was good and gone.

She looked at the bottle of rum atop her cherry-wood bookshelf. She doubted one shot would hurt, but if she was not going to get buzzed, what was the point? Besides, she was running on a concussion and a lot of medications that did not play nice with booze. She needed her faculties clean and sharp.

Later.

She retrieved her gun cleaning kit from the top shelf of her broom closet, returned to her living room and prepared her pistol for action. As she worked, she tried to think of ways to get Oscar Mike's attention. She could not just assume that he was still watching her, especially after that news story by Carmen, and no matter how Zarah sliced it, every road to Oscar Mike started with Carmen Sanchaz.

Zarah finished cleaning and reassembling her gun, returning

the Smith and Wesson's slide assembly to its frame, and racking it a few times to make sure it would operate smoothly.

A knock at the door gave her a start.

She snatched the ammo clip from her coffee table and inserted it into the gun's magazine well. She was going to clean the magazine next, but it would have to wait. She chambered a round

"Who is it?" she demanded.

"Singer!" the FBI agent's voice fired back.

Zarah grumbled, and she stood up. She went to her door, flipped the switch beside it illuminating her porch, and then looked through the peep hole to make sure. Wilster was still there, and next to her was Agent Singer. Zarah opened the door.

Singer was looking chipper. His blonde hair shone in the soft glow of Zarah's porch light. His eyes twinkled, and he had a satisfied smirk. He carried a bulging case and had a gun holstered on his hip. Zarah glared, waiting for the agent to give voice to his business there.

"A fed without a warrant is like a vampire," Singer finally said. "You gotta invite me in."

Zarah stood aside and allowed Singer to enter her home. As Singer passed by, Wilster asked Zarah if she would be ready to leave for the safe house soon.

"Yeah," Zarah said, "sit tight, it's gonna be awhile."

Wilster opened her mouth to speak, but Zarah shut the door before she could utter a word, and then she locked it. She turned to find Singer sitting on the couch and pulling a large folder out of his briefcase. Zarah sat down next to him and returned her gun to the coffee table.

"I feel terrible about everything," Singer said. "I hope this'll begin to make things right."

He gave Zarah the folder.

"What's this?" Zarah asked.

"See for yourself."

Zarah flipped open the folder, and the first thing she saw was a photograph of *dojo* Seth in a U.S. Marine dress uniform in front of a U.S. flag.

"My God," she said. "That's him."

"Meet Master Sergeant Drake Barrett Mitchell, formerly of the United States Marine Corp."

It hurt Zarah's face to smile, but this was astounding.

"Singer," Zarah said, "how did you get this so fast? We only circulated the drawings, like, an hour ago!"

"Biometric technology, detective," Singer bragged. "Facial recognition, databases, and some cooperation with other agencies… all things you'll have at your disposal when you come aboard."

"This is incredible!"

"Don't get too excited," Singer said. "It's only been a couple of hours, and what I have is more scary than satisfying."

"So, tell me about it."

"Well, we know he's a private military contractor for *Bluelake Worldwide*. We suspect he has under-the-table, off-the-books clientele overseas."

Zarah glanced over his dossier.

So, the pig has a human name. Wait till Carmen hears this.

"Your profile suggested he'd be higher up than Sergeant," Zarah teased.

"That, I can explain."

"Tell me."

"Here is the very abridged history of Oscar Mike: His father murdered his mother, got life in prison, and little Drake Mitchell was fed into the system. I don't have his school records yet, and I don't know anything about his tour through foster care."

"I doubt it was very caring," Zarah said.

"Actually, It may have been *too* caring," Singer said. "The nicest, most nurturing and loving foster parents… they get these kids who've been abandoned or orphaned. Or someone like Drake

Mitchell—whose dad murdered his mom—and they overdo trying to make the kid happy again. They heap on the praise and adulation, trying to bolster his self-esteem. The end result is you get this little, self-important asshole running around. You see it sometimes with the firstborn in family units and especially only-children who got way too much love and sympathy growing up, and not enough discipline, so they think they're the shit."

Zarah shifted uncomfortably in her seat.

"Anyway," Singer continued, "He joined the corps in '87, completed recruit training in San Diego and got into the Recon Indoctrination Program, the Basic Recon Course, *bada-bing bada-boom*, he's gone."

"Gone?"

"Like Keyser Söze. *Poof.* The kind of *gone* that looks suspiciously like someone saw something in him that qualified him for stuff more *hands-on* than observing and reporting, which is pretty much what recon does. So he goes off-the-grid from there. Only God and Chuck Hagel knows what he did during that time. My bet is that it involved fake I.D.s and guns with silencers, for starters. Anyway, on paper, he disappears until 1991."

"Where is he in 1991?" Zarah asked.

"The Naval Amphibious Base in Little Creek, Virginia, allegedly for more recon training, and then, *poof*, he disappears again. Pops back up in '93 during Operation Gothic Serpent in Somalia, not with the Marines, but with the Rangers—disappears again. He's dark for almost a decade before he surfaces in Afghanistan, a First Lieutenant with Force Recon, which is a decent post, but probably pretty boring for someone like Drake Mitchell.

But, in 2003 he does something bad. The records don't explain exactly what happened, but whatever it was, it ended with him beating the crap out of a subordinate, a staff sergeant, probably for some insult or *perceived* insult, I suspect. Now, the kid he beat up was the son of one of the joint chiefs."

"Oops," Zarah said.

"Yes. There was a court martial, and he was busted back to Master Sergeant."

"That's a long way down isn't it?"

"*Nine* pay grades," Singer said, "which... that ain't legal. For a marine lieutenant the max they can do is two pay grades, right? I mean after everything he did in the line of duty, and it was probably pretty horrible stuff, they took an awful big shit on him. Even *I* feel bad for the guy. He could have fought that judgement and won."

"Yeah," Zarah said, "but they would've made his life hell. I've seen that kind of thing in the LAPD. You can fight, but even if you win in court you lose on the job."

"True enough," Singer said. "Anyway my guess is Bluelake was sleazing around, whispering sweet nothings, telling him how awesome his is, and he lapped it up. Whatever the case, rather than fight the demotion, he walked as soon as he could, and before the ink was dry on his discharge he was doing jobs for Bluelake."

"And Bluelake is a mercenary group," Zarah surmised.

Singer nodded. "It pays to be well-trained, heartless and willing to kill without compassion or conviction. My guess is during his mercenary career he made contacts in other countries, fulfilled some contracts against his fellow Americans and made bank."

"So why is he here?" Zarah asked. "Why is he murdering civilians for ridiculous moving violations? What is he compensating for, his loss of authority?"

"Yes and no," Singer said. "I mean, the *real* answer to that isn't in these documents, but I think he's what the behavioral guys call an '*invulnerable narcissist*'. He *knows* he's superior, right? And he'll rage on people who don't treat him that way and take revenge. His self-esteem is in the stratosphere and he has no shame whatsoever.

"Like I mentioned, his caregivers may have treated him like

a little prince from early childhood, so he wasn't compensating for anything."

"Until his demotion made him lose face," Zarah suggested.

"Right," Singer said. "That, coupled with the way L.A. drivers dismiss the rules, dismiss each other, dismiss *him,* having *no idea* who the hell they're dealing with, and what he's capable of doing to them…"

"So, this is all about Drake Mitchell turning some need to feel powerful again into some homicidal, public service announcement," Zarah said, "as if it *isn't* all about him."

Zarah never needed an FBI profile to know that Oscar Mike's skin was so thin that he would lash out at anyone who poked at him. In City Terrace, he could have followed her, stalked her and Charlie to someplace less risky to do his murder, but after she had flipped him off, he saw red. He *had* to attack. And then, when Zarah put a bullet between his shoulder blades, his ego must have smarted even more.

But after he had soundly defeated her in Sebastian's apartment, he had taken all of that power back. He may have been denied his coup de grâce, but the beating he had given her spoke volumes. Sebastian had saved Zarah from Oscar Mike's knife the same as Oscar Mike's Kevlar had saved him from Zarah's bullet. The score was even.

Oscar Mike no longer *had* to come for Zarah, which meant that Carmen was in much deeper peril than Zarah had realized until that moment. If Zarah was going to have an opportunity to take him down, she would have to disparage his superiority again, seize it from him again, and goad him into coming to reclaim it.

"I'm calling Carmen," she said, standing up and heading for the cellphone in her purse by the front door. "I wonder if they'll let me on the air…"

"Okay," Singer replied. "I'll call Torres and, wait, what? Why?"

"Your first profile was near spot on," Zarah said, retrieving her phone, "and I don't think your current theory is far from the bulls-eye. I want him to see me alive and well, and dissing him like Kanye West at an awards show. I want him furious and careless. I want him to come at me with all he's got."

"You don't have to do this," Singer said. "We have his name and his face is all over the news. People saw Carmen's story. They're already calling in tips. We're watching the borders, the airports, and every place he can try to get out."

"Running would be the smart thing to do," Zarah said. "I want him to do something stupid."

69

CARMEN SAT BEHIND the co-anchor's desk at the Channel Six news studio. The network had decided to air her exposé again, but this time she would follow up the story with the sketches of Oscar Mike, though the bosses did not hesitate to air them as soon as they had the LAPD's okay. Things were running smoothly, so when Gary appeared in the studio with a severe look on his face, she expected the other shoe to drop. What she received was icing on the cake. Oscar Mike had been positively identified, and Zarah had asked to do an on-air interview with Carmen.

"Drake Barret Mitchell," she mouthed as she flipped through a pad filled with notes. "When's Zarah gonna be here?"

"She's here," Gary said, "talking something over with Daniels."

"I still can't believe she's going to let me interview her."

"I don't believe Daniels is just letting it happen," Gary said. "I don't like it."

"Are you kidding? This is a total coup for us, *papi!* We've arrived! I thought you'd be chilling the champagne already."

"I know, but something in Zarah's eyes," Gary said. "She's not doing us any favors."

"That's the deal we made," Carmen told him. "Zarah wants to

chum the waters and fuck with him. I'm okay with that. He might even get dimed before he even knows he's on TV."

Carmen looked past Gary and saw Zarah in the back of the studio. Her face was still a train wreck, but the rest of her was as if she had never set foot inside a hospital room. Her dark hair was fresh and clean, and she was dressed in a smart, black suit. Her entire posture said "survivor". Nothing about her energy suggested she had been victimized, traumatized or even a little cowed by her experience.

The detective was still chatting with Aiden Daniels as they approached Carmen. The tall, blonde LAPD woman who was guarding her at the hospital walked behind Zarah, scanning the room with hard eyes and a dejected expression, along with another dude in a *Men in Black* suit that screamed *G-Man*.

"Here she comes," Carmen told Gary, who turned around to look.

Daniels smiled at them, which was weird. He put his hand over Gary's shoulder. When Carmen's eyes met Zarah's, something instinctual in the reporter made her stand up. She smiled at Zarah.

"Never thought I'd see you in here," Carmen said, offering a handshake across the long desk.

Zarah returned the smile and shook her hand. "Nice to see you again," she said.

Carmen noticed some trepidation in her expression. As a reporter, Carmen had seen many interviewees deal with bouts of nervousness before going on the air. Even the most hard-boiled law enforcers had to overcome stage fright.

"You guys know what to do," Daniels said. "As soon as you're ready, you can start recording. The interview will air after we rerun the exposé tonight."

"Understood," Gary told him.

Daniels turned and strode away. When he was out of earshot,

Carmen sat back down and leaned in towards Zarah as if sharing some gossip. "So, what did you guys talk about?"

"He just wanted to know why I'm doing this," Zarah replied.

"Good question," Gary said, earning a dirty look from Carmen.

"I'll be honest," Zarah said. "I told him I thought it was important that people see that they can depend on their sworn protectors to handle this. I want them to see that yes, I was attacked, but here I am, alive and still on the case."

"Even though you're not?" Gary asked.

"I am," Zarah said, brooking no argument.

"Gary, lay off already."

"It's okay," Zarah said. "So how's this going to work?"

"Simple," Gary said. "We'll get you hooked up for audio..." Gary walked behind the desk, and pulled a comfortable looking chair with a high back across from Carmen. "You'll sit here. We'll announce that the police and FBI have obtained a photo-description. We'll display it, say what we have to say, and then Carmen will ask you questions pertinent to the case."

"We're gonna have fun, you and me," Carmen said.

Gary looked as if he was going to toss some cookies. "I guess we're ready then."

70

ZARAH FELT SATISFIED. Carmen had asked all of the right questions, and Zarah made sure to lace each answer with a veiled insult. Wherever Oscar was hiding, if he was watching, he had to be seeing more red than the devil.

"Drake Mitchell is average height," Carmen had asked, "not a tall guy, not a small guy?"

"Yes, average," Zarah had answered. "Nothing special or outstanding about him at all."

Carmen had been smart to use Oscar Mike's real name. Zarah made sure to keep her demeanor friendly, confident and not at all afraid or damaged. Question after question, answer after answer, Carmen and Zarah took turns poking Oscar Mike with a stick.

"But still detective, it looks like he beat you up pretty badly."

"His objective was to kill me," Zarah had replied. "Shows you what a miserable failure he is when the target fights back."

"Still it's best not to approach him if you see him on the street?" Carmen had said.

"Yes," Zarah had answered. "He *is* armed and dangerous…"

That interview was the most fun Zarah had since the whole Oscar Mike case started. It reminded her of her university days.

After the taping was done, Carmen left the studio to review their spot, and Zarah was hungry. Having survived on hamburgers and hospital food for close to a month, Zarah wanted something different. After she picked up her jacket and purse from behind a television camera, she asked Wilster to take her to a supermarket.

"The safe house has no kitchen," a tall, dark-haired, FBI agent said, "so it's gotta be takeout."

"Okay," Zarah said, squeezing her sinuses. "Get it through your skull. I'm *not* going to a safe house."

The FBI Agent opened his mouth to answer, but Wilster stopped him short. "Supermarket's fine," she said.

Gary had overheard and approached the group. "The Vine's not far from here," he said. "I have standing reservations. The network will foot the bill. If you'd like, I'll call them and tell them you're coming."

"No," the FBI agent and Wilster said in buzz-killing harmony.

"They mean no *thank you*," Zarah said.

"Are you sure? It's a decent meal."

"Is that what Carmen's gonna do?" Zarah asked.

"I don't know what she's gonna do," Gary said. "I wish she'd just go to ground, but 'a deal's a deal' she keeps saying."

If Oscar Mike was going to try for her again, Zarah figured she had to be easy to get to. Besides, she had received plenty of solitude in the hospital, and if Zarah sat home alone with guards posted, she would be too safe, too secure. Oscar Mike would not move against her under those conditions.

Just go.

"The Vine?" she asked Gary.

Gary nodded. "It's a good place."

Zarah shrugged and nodded back. "Okay," she said. "Thanks."

After Gary left to call in the reservation and was out of earshot, Wilster approached Zarah, and looked her hard in the eyes. "The strategy was for Carmen to be the bait, not you," Wilster said, with more anger than concern.

"I have my own strategy," Zarah snapped, "and it doesn't involve Carmen, or *you*."

"With respect, Zarah," the FBI agent said, "Our job is to—"

"Singer and Sheridan may have assigned you guys to protect me," Zarah said, "but not *once* have I requested it, nor did I ever agree to be a prisoner. Now, I honestly, sincerely *thank you* from the bottom of my heart, but I *decline* your protection. Do I need to write it down, or record it on your phones, or swear it in sacrificial blood before you just accept it?"

The FBI agent looked at the immovable hardness in her face and shook his head. He thought for a moment, and then took a deep breath. "Well," he said, "I can't force you to go to the safe house, but Braden Wade will have all our nuts in a jar if you're running willy-nilly out there without us. I'll tell Singer what your disposition is, and I'm sure he'll pass it up the chain, but we gotta go with, wherever it is, and *you* should just accept *that*."

"Yes," Wilster agreed. "Do whatever stupid thing you want, Wheeler. But try, you just *try* and do it without me."

"I was hoping you'd say that," Zarah told Wilster, "'cause you're my ride."

71

ZARAH WAS FAMILIAR with The Vine but had never eaten there. It was a quaint, two-story brick house with a white, picket fence in front and a French-countryside motif—one of those pretentious celebrity hangouts where the show-biz elite went to be seen.

Wilster pulled up to the front of the valet area and exited their black, unmarked car first, then went around the back with her hand on her sidearm, scanning every car that rolled by.

As Zarah stepped out of the car, the smell of freshly baked bread, coffee and something creamy, buttery and delicious wafted into her broken, bandaged nose in spite of the swelling.

Two more FBI vehicles pulled in behind Zarah's, and when the valet approached, Wilster warned him not to even think about getting behind the wheel. When he argued that the front of the restaurant was not a parking space, she agreed to pull forward to the end of the valet area. If he had a problem with that, he could *"take it up with Gary Sterling of The Channel Six Network News."*

The evening was warm and windless. Two thick trees stood on the sidewalk in front of the restaurant, their trunks swallowed by lush, green ivy. Diners waiting to be seated milled about.

As Zarah looked over the crowded environment she felt cold, and as she watched the two FBI cars follow Wilster's lead, she felt tightness in her chest, tingling in her limbs. A second thought about the wisdom of this move was burrowing into her thinking.

Zarah ran her hand along the outside of her purse and found the bulge of her Smith & Wesson, reassuring herself that it was there.

She scanned the outdoor dining area of The Vine. Diners were jammed together, rubbing elbows and chewing the fat. Zarah thought of City Terrace and how many innocents she had put in harm's way that bloody afternoon—the dead and injured cops, wounded civilians, the fire, and smoke, and chaos.

Zarah was being reckless, again. As much as she wanted Oscar Mike to stick his head out so she could blow it off his shoulders, there was too much risk to the innocent people here. If he spotted her and decided not to ambush her as before, if he decided to strike, right here, right now...

What if he fires into the crowd? What if he throws a grenade?

She was being selfish. Her vengeance was not worth the collateral damage, and Sebastian would never have approved. She changed her mind about dinner and headed back towards the valet area. Wilster was right. This was stupid.

As she walked toward the gate, Wilster saw her coming, and Zarah nodded, gesturing for her to get the car. Zarah's stoic guardian nodded her approval and seemed to slacken a little before she turned and headed back toward the Charger. And then Zarah's stomach did a backflip.

Carmen Sanchaz was walking along the sidewalk towards the front gate with a couple of uniformed police on either side of her. She looked collected, pleasant, and her posture was confident. She noticed Zarah, smiled and waved. Zarah approached her.

"Carmen," she said, trying not to sound alarmed, "I guess Gary told you I'd be here?"

Carmen nodded, "I was planning on just grabbing something from takeout and going home."

"Good idea," Wilster said from the street. "Detective Wheeler?" She motioned to the black, unmarked car at the end of the valet area.

"Are you leaving?" Carmen said, "You haven't even sat down."

"Yeah, Carmen," Zarah said. She lowered her voice. "I thought it'd be okay. I mean I wanted to, but—"

"But what?" Carmen said, pulling Zarah by the arm toward The Vine's hostess station. "The network's paying, and it's not like you ain't good enough to eat here. You're a star. After tonight, you'll be a bigger star."

"After that interview," Zarah said, stopping Carmen in midstride "we'll both be dead stars, and who knows who else may get hurt if we don't do the smart thing. Let's grab that takeout, and... how about you come to my place, or I'll go to your place or something? We have to get away from all this."

"Zarah, you need to chill," Carmen said. "Peep this..." She pulled the front of her purple, paisley blouse open to reveal a black Kevlar vest. "These things are hot as shit," she said, "but I feel kinda like a badass. Besides, our interview isn't going hot for another three hours. Not to mention Oscar'll flee like the Roadrunner on coca when he sees his own face on the screen and not some sketch. And *mira*, look at these cops." Carmen pointed to the sidewalk and flourished like a game show model at three uniformed officers from Carmen's detail, Wilster looking perturbed, and Zarah's three FBI agents. "*One-time*, everywhere. That's what's really scary. Come on now, let's get a table."

"What's really scary," Zarah said, "is how many people can get hurt if—"

"Excuse me," a man's voice spoke from behind, and Zarah felt a gentle tap on her shoulder.

Zarah turned and found herself looking into the kindly face of Sir Patrick Stewart. "I'm sorry to bother, but are you Detective Zarah Wheeler?"

She was never much of a movie goer or a couch potato, but she knew Captain Picard from "Star Trek: The Next Generation" too well. Zarah looked at him with her mouth open. She had been told that working for Homicide Special would have exposed her to the occasional celebrity, but until then it had never happened.

Patrick Stewart smiled. With a casual, quiet tone bordering on intimate he said, "I just want to tell you, I've been watching the news, and I think you do a selfless job and I wanted to thank you. I'm glad you're out here protecting us."

Zarah fumbled around her brain for words. Sir Patrick, used to this reaction, smiled amiably. Zarah looked at Carmen, who was also star struck. Her face wore a smile Zarah had never seen on her. Not snarky, not sassy, not arrogant, but overjoyed and happy.

There was a loud, concussive blast from the street. Carmen gasped as the side of her head tore open in a burst of blood that splashed Zarah's face. Carmen went limp and collapsed onto the floor.

Zarah did not have time to register what had happened before there was another blast. She felt something hot toss her hair and whistle past the side of her skull. She touched it with her hand and felt wetness. She looked at her fingers and saw blood. Another rapport pierced the air, and one of the white pickets cracked and splintered as a bullet passed through it.

A woman sitting at a table behind the fencing screamed, returning Zarah to her senses. Patrick Stewart dove aside to the floor and yanked the legs out from under the hostess's podium, using it for cover. He motioned for several others to join him.

Zarah reached into her purse, yanked out her gun and switched off the safety. She turned to see if anyone was hurt.

"LAPD! Everybody lie down and stay down!" Zarah commanded.

"Grenade!" Wilster's voice shouted from the sidewalk, "Hit the deck! Down, down, down!"

The crack of gunshots filled the air, followed by an explosion in the street that shook everything. Windows rattled, flower-vases atop the tables rocked and fell over. Car alarms screamed in the street.

Diners shrieked as Zarah hit the deck next to Carmen. The tough reporter was not gone, yet. Her eyes were wide open, and her stomach heaved as she gulped in deep breaths, like a fish on dry land, close to the end of its life. Zarah's stomach knotted and her heart pounded.

"Carmen!" Zarah shouted. "Carmen, you're okay, you're okay! Just hang on!"

Blood poured from Carmen's temple and Zarah could not see the extent of the bullet wound. She frantically scanned her surroundings for anything she could to stop the bleeding. She remembered City Terrace, remembered Oscar Mike wagging his shotgun at her playfully, remembered Charlie, his shoulder torn open by shrapnel, his angry voice roaring, *"Go get him you stupid bitch!"*

The pain of her own injuries lessened. She clenched her teeth and jumped to her feet with strength she did not know she had. "Someone help her!" she commanded, pointing down at Carmen. Several people crawled towards them. She looked down at her friend. Carmen's eyes were lulling, as if she was fighting to stay conscious.

Zarah was losing time. She had to go. Carmen would understand, if she survived.

"Help is coming," Zarah told her. "Just hang on. I gotta go."

Using the smoke as concealment, Zarah marched toward the street with her gun thrust in front of her. This was not going to end like City Terrace, but it was going to end. Tonight.

72

DRAKE BARRET MITCHELL had a good escape plan all worked out. He had been halfway to Seattle, and was not checked into his motel room for ten minutes before he switched on the news and was immediately convinced to turn around and return to L.A.

It was a bad idea, but he had been at tactical disadvantages before and he still finished the job. He simply would *not* rest easy, no matter which non-extradition corner of the earth he ensconced himself in. Carmen Sanchaz had brazenly called him out and expected him to, what, let her *live* after issuing such a challenge? After he had *spoon fed her* ratings, and air time, and fame on a silver plate?

No fucking way!

Still, by the time he was half way back to Los Angeles, he was telling himself that he should have ignored the reporter's taunt and just left. *Fuck her!* He almost turned around and headed north again, but instead, he sped up towards L.A. He could *not* let such an insult stand.

Rather than go on the lam, he would go to the mattresses, and he fantasized about all of the different ways he would make Carmen Sanchaz pay, and the whole of Los Angeles would shake their heads and say, *she should have known better.*

When he arrived in L.A., he set back up in Toluca Lake and then went about watching the reporter's home. Carmen Sanchaz's smartass report was bait. She had police watching her. *I knew it! Why didn't I just fucking leave?* But there was nothing for it now. He was committed.

Three houses on her street were vacant, one of which was two doors down and across the street. From there, Drake observed Carmen Sanchaz's coming and goings through high powered binoculars.

As the LAPD followed her, she tried to ignore them in an inconvenienced, bitchy way.

Good, Drake thought. *Treat them like shit and see how willing they'll be to take a bullet for you.*

The cops followed her as she drove from her home to her network's headquarters. Those shiny, blue broadcasting vans were in and out all day, but Drake surmised that when Carmen Sanchaz left to report her news stories, her police escort would make her easy to track.

The police presence did not faze Drake. He had been trained to shadow military targets with fiercely loyal, savagely violent, and far more paranoid security details than a handful of cops who had paychecks to collect and laws to abide by. He followed the same protocol to surveil Carmen Sanchaz as he would have to recon the Caliph of some Islamist militant group, but there was less stress. Policemen were not irrational, not desensitized by daily, blood-and-guts combat, and most were afraid of death.

Carmen Sanchaz had pissed him off good, but Drake was no sucker. He would not make a move until the time was right. The cops could not watch her forever. All Drake had to do was wait.

Then something interesting happened. Carmen Sanchaz went to the hospital that Zarah Wheeler had been taken. What was she doing there? Was the detective still laid up from the ass kicking he had given her, or was it something else? It was not practical for him to break off of his surveillance to find out. He stuck to the reporter's car and kept watching.

She exited the hospital looking haughty and purposeful. He tailed her, and her police escort, to her studio. She ran her studio badge through a scanner and drove in after the gate lifted. Then the two cars following her did the same.

There was metered parking on the curb, and it was easy enough to sit in his truck and watch. He expected to observe her security detail rallying around a news van, but then something more interesting happened.

A few hours after Carmen Sanchaz entered her studio, as night fell, Zarah Wheeler rode past him in a black Dodge Charger. Her face was bruised and patched up with bandages. It gave Drake an instant of joy before it made him angry.

She should be in a goddam coffin, not a muscle car!

There was a hard-looking chick with blonde hair, combed and tied high and tight, driving Zarah around. Two more unmarked cars followed behind her. The blonde behind the wheel said a few words to the guard in the booth, and the gate tilted up and let them pass, followed by the rest of them.

Drake wondered what Zarah Wheeler was doing there, but it did not matter. He would watch the news later and see what was what. All he hoped for was an opening—a small window of opportunity where those cops would be off their game, but so far they were a tight unit.

The moon was full and high when the detective exited the studio building. Drake checked his weapons, his .45, his shotgun and the AR-15 in the back seat of his truck. He made sure his grenades and ammo magazines were secure on the utility belt, and he geared up.

Then Drake reminded himself that Zarah Wheeler was not the primary target anymore. If he hit her now the odds of him escaping were nil. He had committed himself to taking out Carmen

Sanchaz, so he calmed himself and waited. He did not wait long before his prey emerged from the tinted, glass door of the studio into the parking lot.

Her LAPD security started their engines. She entered her convertible and drove away, followed by the rest of them. Keeping his distance, Drake stayed with the caravan. They did not follow the route to Carmen's home this time, and the ride ended at a little restaurant in West Hollywood. The street was narrow and crowded.

The escort cars turned on their flashing lights. The vantage from Drake's tall Tundra gave him a perfect look as Carmen exited her vehicle. There was a brief moment where she was alone, but as Drake reached for his weapon, two uniformed police quickly jumped from their vehicles, took positions on either side of her, and escorted her down the sidewalk.

Since there was nowhere on this little street for Carmen Sanchaz to go besides this restaurant, Drake decided to pull out from behind their vehicles and find a place to park. As he passed the front of the place, he spotted Zarah Wheeler's blonde cop-chauffer standing at the entrance of the little bistro. She looked suspicious and alert.

Holy shit, Zarah Wheeler's here, too!

He sped past and glanced over. Sure enough, his eyes found the bruised up detective standing behind the white, picket gate of the restaurant. He looked for parking. He reached the end of the street as a Hummer was pulling away. Coming in the opposite direction, a man driving a Kia saw the open spot and signaled that he wanted to park, but Drake sped up and stole it out from under him.

Drake exited the truck and quickly pulled on his black coat. As the Kia cruised past, the driver rolled down his window and shouted, "You're a real fuckin' asshole, you know that?"

Drake turned and marched towards the Kia with unmistakable malice in his step. The Kia sped away—another car-brave bigmouth who was lucky Oscar Mike had more important cats to skin.

He strapped on his belt and took the .45. He concealed his gun behind his coat onto a holster he had fashioned out of a wire hangar and some duct tape, making his draw time twice as fast as any cop strapped with a standard sheath.

He considered equipping the handgun with a suppressor, but it would not have been a neat fit on his homemade holster, he probably was not going to use his gun anyway, and if he did, the loud report of the .45 would startle bystanders into a scurry, and he could use it to cover his getaway.

He strolled toward his destination like any other pedestrian, reminding himself that it was just recon. He *must not* make a move if the conditions were wrong, no matter how much he wanted to.

He approached the restaurant from across the street. The cops and feds in front were having a discussion, pointing hither and thither.

Establishing a radius. Setting a perimeter. Is this a trap?

He recalled City Terrace, when Zarah Wheeler had ambushed him as he drove randomly through West L.A. He never knew how she had managed that. Did she know he was there? Hoping he would make a move? Would she expose civilians to this kind of danger? She had done it before.

As he walked past the restaurant from across the street, he saw Zarah and Carmen having a discussion outside, together.

If you're gonna go, go frosty and focused, before they're ready.

Drake was about to reach into his coat when he saw the tall, blonde cop looking at him. Their eyes met. He pretended not to care, and looked back at the restaurant. If he retreated now, she would know he was up to no good. Then the cop turned around to look at Zarah and Carmen. All of the guards did. One of them was pointing behind Zarah, who was talking to a thin, bald, old man in a grey sweater.

He looked familiar, but Drake did not waste time trying to place him. Whoever he was, he had all of the guards distracted. This was a moment Oscar Mike could not ignore.

Had it been the reporter alone, he would have been inclined to hold his position and continue his recon, but this was a chance to clip Zarah Wheeler and Carmen Sanchaz at the same time, and Drake doubted such an opportunity would present itself again anytime soon. He drew his .45.

Quick but careful, he aimed at Carmen Sanchaz and fired. He saw the round strike her temple. She crumpled to the concrete.

One down.

The guards' heads snapped toward him. He quickly fired at Zarah. He saw the round zip through her hair. She reached up and felt her head.

People panicked and ran in all directions. Drake had to adjust his aim, but he could not wait all day for a clean shot. He fired one last round but missed.

Damnit!

The guards pointed at him, reaching for their weapons.

Drake took a grenade from his belt, pulled the pin with the pinky finger of his gun-hand and released the striker lever. Four feds were drawing their side arms, and the blonde cop was taking aim; Drake tossed the grenade at the car in front of the feds.

"Grenade!" the blonde hollered. "Hit the deck! Down, down, down!"

The blonde took two rapid shots at Oscar. The rounds struck him in the chest and flattened against his Kevlar without penetrating. Drake returned fire. His round struck the blonde in the collar. She looked down at the wound in surprise, and then back at him, outraged he would dare shoot her.

That's a woman, Drake thought as he watched her take cover behind her car—more to protect herself from the grenade's shrapnel than his bullets, he suspected.

The grenade exploded, filling the street with smoke and fire. Drake looked past the flames for Zarah Wheeler, but she was obfuscated behind billows of smoke. Drake expected that when she emerged, she would come out shooting. Drake needed cover, and there were cops everywhere. He cursed and ran towards the street he had parked on.

When he reached his Tundra, he turned and saw that no one was pursuing him yet, but the civilians were gawking.

"Oscar Mike," someone said.

He looked to see who had said it. People who were not running away or moving toward the fire were inching toward him. One guy was taking his picture with a smart phone. Drake raised his .45 and shot him in the face, through the device. The man dropped dead. People screamed and ran. Some hid, and others froze in place.

He had given away his position, and the jig was up. If he had any expectation of escape, he had to go now and never stop until he was out of the country. He jerked open the door of his pickup.

"DRAKE MITCHELL!" A woman's voice roared behind him.

He turned and saw Zarah Wheeler charging up the sidewalk toward him, her weapon raised.

Pedestrians hit the ground and dove from her path. Zarah hurdled over a man crouched in front of her, stopped and raised her weapon.

Drake aimed at her.

Fire spurted from Zarah's gun. Loud, ballistic popping filled the air. A round tore the skin of his neck as if someone had run a red hot poker across it. The next shot ripped into his right ear. He felt a burning numbness. Zarah Wheeler had factored in his vest and was going for the head shot.

Drake returned fire, not bothering to aim. When she dove aside, he opened the passenger door of his truck, tossed his

332

.45 inside, yanked out his shotgun and pumped two rounds at Zarah Wheeler.

Some people in their crossfire were hit by the spread of buckshot. They screamed and bled and rolled around in agony.

Zarah rose up and fired a few more rounds at him, but they *thunked* against the open door and passed through the window over Drake's head, raining down broken glass. Police sirens were wailing in the distance.

He rested his shotgun on the back seat of his truck, pulled another grenade, armed it, stood and threw it towards her. He jumped into the driver's seat of his truck. The grenade exploded.

73

WHEN ZARAH SAW Oscar Mike toss the grenade, she took off running in the opposite direction and did not stop until she heard the explosion. The shock of it almost took her off her feet.

She had seen him get into his pickup truck and knew he was well away. Zarah ran back to The Vine to check on Carmen's four FBI guards. They were all alive. Each had tried to jump over The Vine's picket fence and escape the blast. None of them made it out unscathed.

Officer Wilster was sitting on the sidewalk, not far from the fire. She was resting her head against the door of a car, putting pressure on her bleeding collar. Zarah stood beside her, and caught her breath.

"You get him?" Wilster asked as she tried to staunch her injury, blood spilling between her fingers.

Zarah shook her head. When she opened her mouth to speak, her chin trembled. She collapsed to her knees, covered her face with her hands and cried out. Her tears wet the side of her Smith & Wesson. She wept, unable to stop the flood of despair, grief and rage.

"Are you injured?" Wilster said.

Zarah shook her head.

"Then snap out of it, you're on the clock!"

Over Wilster's radio, Zarah heard Charlie declaring that he was on route. Great. That was what she needed, more speeches about pondering and plotting. He would be right, for the second time. All Carmen had wanted was some dinner and to feel free from Oscar Mike for an hour or two. Zarah looked over to where she had left her and saw several good Samaritans crouched over where she lay, trying to help. Seeing that there was activity, she knew that there was still life in the reporter.

"Give me your radio," she ordered Wilster.

Wilster picked the radio up off of the cement and handed it over. Zarah called in the make, model and description of Oscar Mike's truck, and which way he had driven off.

"What happened to you?" Zarah asked Wilster.

"Broken clavicle, I think," she said. "I nailed him in the chest, twice, but I forgot about the armor. Stupid of me."

Several ambulances arrived along with several more squad cars. One of the people next to Carmen was calling out to the EMTs and waving desperately as they exited their vehicles. Zarah was relieved that Carmen was going to receive medical attention, but it did not squelch her worry.

Cops were also jumping out of their cars. Every unit should have been hunting Oscar Mike down. All that was going to happen here was shell case collecting, witness interviews that would not produce anything time-worthy, and tending to the wounded which did not take a hundred officers to do.

Zarah thought of Carmen again—then Sebastian. The tears came back. She forced herself to focus. She was wasting time. She sucked a breath of oxygen along with the miasma of burning rubber and gasoline, stood up and addressed all of the uniforms.

"Listen up!" she said. They all turned. Zarah was not on active duty, but a person bandaged, bleeding and covered in black soot was worth a listen. "The suspect is Drake Barret Mitchell, a.k.a.

Oscar Mike," she said. "He's in a tan pickup, I think a Tundra, last headed west down Alden Drive! The truck will have a broken rear-left window, and some bullet holes on the rear, driver's side door! If we know this guy at all, we know he's going to be looking for a new vehicle!

"Now listen! He's armed, desperate and dangerous! You have his description and info in your databases! It's rush hour, guys! You all *know* Oscar Mike's M.O.! So get on your radios! Listen for car-jackings, auto-thefts, road-rage, and motor-vehicle related violence! Scour these streets! We need everybody out there tonight! RHD, ME-C and SID will handle this scene! The only thing the rest of you have to do is be on this hunt! So be on it!"

"Who are you?" one of the cops demanded.

Zarah shot him a look that must have been terrifying because he raised his hands, said "yes ma'am," and got in his car. The rest of them followed suit.

Zarah looked for Wilster, who was being helped into the back of an ambulance.

"Gimme the car keys," Zarah said.

Wilster looked as if she was about to argue but thought better of it. She reached into her pocket, withdrew the keys and tossed them to Zarah. She snatched them out of the air and headed down the street for the Dodge Charger. As she neared the end of the valet driveway, Charlie was jogging toward her from down the sidewalk. He called her name, waving to her. She pretended not to hear him. He would only tell her to go home, or lie down. Or he would find any number of clever ways of telling her she that was a lousy cop and did not know what she was doing. She did not need to hear any of it.

"Zarah!" he shouted. "Wait up!"

She ignored him and continued to the Dodge. She was opening the door when Charlie caught up to her. "Zarah," he said, breathing heavily. "Hold up."

"I don't have time, Charlie," she said.

"Come on, Zarah," Charlie said. "You can't be the only one who gets to shoot at him."

She looked across the roof of the car at him. He looked sincere.

"Say one thing to piss me off," Zarah warned, "and you better be ready to tuck and roll, 'cause I'm not gonna slow down when I kick you out!"

"Maybe I should drive," he said. "Zarah, your head is—"

"Already you're starting!"

"Okay, okay," Charlie said, getting in the passenger side. "You're so sexy when you're like this!"

Zarah huffed and shook her head.

Charlie guffawed as they both sat into the car. Zarah peeled away, heading west.

74

THE GRAZING WOUND to his ear had taken its time to start hurting, and now Drake Barrett Mitchell was in excruciating pain. That fucking bitch damn near took his fucking ear off! And the *too-near* miss on his neck burned and throbbed. He gnarred and slammed his fists into the steering wheel. He wanted to tell himself that his grenade had done Zarah Wheeler in, but he knew better. He hammered his wheel again.

He had taken Alden Drive west for a while and then doubled back to Doheney. Then he took Melrose east and traffic was being a sonofabitch.

Fucking Melrose! Fucking hipsters, hippies and homos!

People were looking at his bullet-ridden truck, a couple of them had cell phones and were *talking while driving.* It infuriated him more. There they were, cutting each other off, not allowing each other to change lanes, honking and being assholes right in front of him, and he had to hide from Zarah fucking Wheeler!

He punched his wheel again. He wondered if the police had broadcast everything about him on the news. Well, at least Carmen Sanchaz was not going to be the one reporting it. Drake would have smiled if he was not in so much pain. He did not have a chance to examine his ear, but it must have been pretty bad considering how much it still stung through his adrenaline.

He turned down Beverly Drive and continued east until it became Silver Lake Boulevard. He found a freeway overpass. It was the 101.

He found an access gate to the fenced-off space under the onramp. He squeezed the truck into the hollow cavity beneath the concrete gradient, behind some small bushes surrounding it. Once he was nicely ensconced, he relaxed a little. It would take an effort for motorists to see him from the street, and for helicopters to spot him from above it would be impossible, assuming the LAPD did not equip infrared night vision, but it was a risk he had to take.

He would wait out rush hour, dump his ride here, find a new car, double back again, get onto the 10, then the Pacific Coast Highway, and make his way up north to Big Sur, or Yosemite, or Redwood. From any of those points, he could buy some gear, hide in the woods awhile, grow a beard and backpack all the way to Alaska if he wanted to.

No one'll be looking for a homeless backpacker.

First he had to dress his injuries. He reached into the back of the cab and pulled a fifty-five inch, roll-gear duffel bag into the passenger seat. He unzipped it and dug past his AR-15, around boxes of bullets and ammo magazines, pre-paid cellphones and car-theft gear as he searched for his first aid kit.

When he found it, he examined his ear in the rearview mirror. It looked as if a rat had chewed his earlobe off. He took a clean rag and dampened it with hydrogen peroxide and cleaned the wound. He gritted his teeth and hissed as it burned, sputtered and stung. He took the pain and dressed the ear with a bandage. That was the best he could do. Then he went to work on his neck, which was not as difficult. When he was done, he sat back and fumed.

He could have killed Zarah Wheeler so many times—at her stupid dojo, or in her bed at home, or in her stupid boyfriend's apartment, but he had to play games. He had to let her know why. And this night he had missed her frontal lobe by less than an inch!

Why didn't he just use the AR-15 and pepper the whole god- dam restaurant? Why didn't he just throw a grenade at her and watch it rain bloody bitch pieces all over the street? Why did he always choose the least simple ways of doing things?

Now there was no way to get at Zarah Wheeler, and there was no way he would allow himself to be captured. Why let that happen? So she could look at him through glass or whatever and flip him off, and laugh at him like he is nothing?

"FUCK YOU! I'll DIE FIRST!"

He pounded his fists on the steering wheel, the dashboard. He clawed the upholstery, pounded his elbow onto the armrest. Eventually he calmed down, but as the hours passed, the pickup ran out of fuel. The air conditioning died, the interior of the truck grew hot, and he steamed in his own juices. He pulled the collar of his Kevlar vest away from his chest and blew inside to cool himself.

After a while the streets were less hectic, and he felt he had better head out, though his ingrained predisposition toward minimalism, especially out in the open and on foot, grated at him.

No problem. Just a guy going down the street, breaking every rule in the low-profile operative's handbook, bleeding with bandages on him with a gigantic duffel bag that can't help but look like it has a rifle in it. Nothing to see at all.

He had to get out of plain sight. He found a side street and looked for a vehicle—nothing special or so modern that it could be tracked with a satellite, or could not be started without a key. In the parking lot of an Italian restaurant, he located a green pickup that looked like it fit the bill.

He knelt next to the truck and retrieved his Slim Jim and a flathead screw driver from the duffel. He jimmied the door, and as soon as he opened it, the alarm sounded and lights blinked. On a busy street like this, a car alarm was not a big deal.

He slid into the driver's seat, jammed the flathead into the ignition slot and gave it a violent twist. Dash lights illuminated as if the key was in the ignition. Oscar reached under the steering column and found the alarm's kill switch and disabled it. Then he returned his tools to the duffel and hoisted it onto the back seat. Inside ten seconds the truck was good to go, and it had a full tank.

Drake was beginning to think things were going his way. Then out of the corner of his eye a man and woman ran towards him.

"Yo! That's my truck!" the man shouted.

He wore a baseball cap, backwards. He was muscular and tattooed with a thin beard and some kind of strange, tribal pattern shaved into it. His jeans were baggy, and he wore them almost halfway down his legs with a black, extra-large shirt with some kind of silver skull-with-angel-wings artwork tucked all the way in.

His blonde escort was wearing tight jeans and a sickeningly colorful Ed Hardy bikini top, flaunting her fake tits as if they were the second coming of Christ.

"What the fuck you think you doin'?" The man yelled.

Don't kill him, Drake thought, knowing he would give up his position if he did. He told himself to gun the motor and speed away.

"You best get the fuck away from my ride you punk-pussy biatch!"

No, this guy has to go.

Drake stepped out of the truck. He realized his weapons were all in his duffel. The big guy rounded on him with his shoulders back and his chest pushed out like a gorilla.

Drake assumed a docile, cowed look and raised both of his hands. That filled the moron with even more of himself, but when he stepped forward to shove Drake, it was the end for him.

Drake yanked him in close by his large arms, seized him by the neck and clawed into the soft tissue, pinching the nerves hard. The man dropped to his knees to escape the pain. Drake held on tight. Then he closed his clawed fingers around the guy's larynx and crushed it.

The man collapsed, wheezing to his last breath.

The woman shrieked and ran for the street, waving her hands and crying for help. She pulled a smartphone with a hot-pink, bedazzled case from her back pocket and was dialing. Drake jumped back into his stolen truck, punched the gas and charged. She tried to dive aside, but the truck clipped her hard. She squeaked like a rat as he sped past. In the rearview he saw her drop like a puppet whose strings had been cut.

He had not killed her. She was still squirming around on the street. It was a well-lit area, and it would not be long before police were on the scene. There was nothing for it now. Drake decided to stick with his plan and double-back west toward the 10.

75

AFTER THEIR FIREFIGHT, Oscar Mike had headed west, so Zarah and Charlie cruised westward down Beverly Boulevard a few miles and then traveled northwest on Santa Monica Boulevard, listening to their radio for any activity that would point them in Oscar Mike's direction.

The word was out. His face was also broadcasting on every TV station and social media site. The FBI was watching all of the borders, every airport, bus station, train station and even seaports. Choppers were airborne, and satellites were scanning.

Zarah had inquired after Carmen on the hailer, but there was no information regarding her condition. Carmen's condition had been in a tailspin when Zarah left her. A voice in Zarah's head kept asking if Carmen would have been as worried had their positions been reversed, and Zarah kept telling herself: *It doesn't matter! Just hang in there, Carmen.*

"Everything okay?" Charlie asked.

"Fine," Zarah said, tears watering her eyes. She wiped them away.

Charlie nodded, expecting that answer. They drove in silence save for their radio, chattering irrelevant information.

"Carmen deserved better," Zarah said. "From us, I mean."

"I know," Charlie said. "She had it tough her whole life. She used to be a gangbanger, you know that?"

"I had a feeling she was from that neck of the woods."

Charlie nodded. "Her brother and uncle are both in prison. Father's dead, mother's an alcoholic."

"I wish I'd known that," Zarah said.

"That's no rebuke coming from you, Zarah. You don't tell anyone anything, and we all know you have a story."

"Nobody needs to hear my story," Zarah said, wondering if she should call her mother.

"Why not let us decide? People share with people who share."

"Okay," Zarah said, "why are you always at Disneyland?"

"Because people are happy there, and I like to see people happy."

"That's it?"

"Yeah, it's not complicated. Now it's your turn."

Zarah opened her mouth to argue when the radio issued an alert.

"8H4K 211 and 187 at 55 Fountain Ave, be advised, suspect fled scene heading east in green Toyota Tacoma—"

"Toyota Tacoma," Charlie said. "That's a pickup truck."

Zarah slammed her foot to the pedal and turned on the car's flashers. She turned around and headed back toward West L.A.

"Zarah, let's not rush all the way to Echo Park," Charlie said. "Let's cruise. He may double-back this way again."

Zarah gave a heavy sigh and shook her head.

"You don't have to be the one to get him," Charlie said.

"I know, I know," Zarah said. "You're right."

Zarah slowed down and continued east, watching the road like an eagle, hoping for a call-out, hoping that an air unit spotted the right green pickup truck, hoping that she *was* the one to get him.

76

D RAKE BARRETT MITCHELL had fled as far west as he was comfortable with in the stolen truck. Several choppers had passed overhead, and if they were looking for him, they had come too close, too many times. He had not crossed paths with any police on the way, but as long as he was in that truck, he was asking for trouble.

The silicone slut he had run down could have come to. She could have given the police a description, a time frame, a plate number. He doubted she had the brains to retain such information, but amateurs made such assumptions. He would err on caution's side.

He had made it to Santa Monica, as good a place as any to change up. He abandoned the vehicle in a parking garage. Then on foot he made his way to Ocean Avenue and crossed a concrete bridge spanning the Pacific Coast Highway. From there, he made his way to the coastline.

Santa Monica beach was closed after midnight, and it was well past. The moon was bright in the sky. Seventy yards away, mercury-bulb lamps kept the bike path and accompanying board-walk flooded with white light, sheathing the shoreline in darkness. It would be difficult for anyone to see him from there, and from beyond, impossible.

When he reached the splashing, whispering waves he placed

his duffel on the sand and washed the blood off of his hands in the cool, salty Pacific. The plan was to stick to the beach until the wee hours. Then he would find another car to steal and hopefully avoid having to crush another douchebag's windpipe and run down his whore.

He retrieved a suppressor from his duffle and attached it to his .45. The midnight curfew was not strictly enforced, but if some beach cop patrolling the sand on an ATV came along, he would be ready.

He humped north along the water. The rushed, unprofessional job Drake had done packing his massive duffel and the weight of the AR-15 and shotgun inside made it a difficult hike, but he had managed under worse conditions.

The cold, salt breeze stung his wounded ear, reminding him he *did* have some regret. One regret was out looking for him at that moment. He was certain. He felt his blood beginning to boil again.

I could have killed her! I should have killed her!

He wanted to shake her up one last time before he disappeared, so when he was gone she would lay awake at night wondering when he would come for her. He put his duffel down, unzipped it and took out a pre-paid cell phone and a notepad with his contacts and phone numbers.

77

ZARAH'S PHONE RANG. She took it out of her pocket and looked at the caller I.D. It displayed a number she had never seen before. She touched the answer button and put it to her ear.

"Wheeler," she said.

"Tell me you're not driving, Zarah," A man's voice said.

Zarah's eyes widened, and she shot an alarmed look at Charlie. Then her hackles rose. "Yes, *Drake*," Zarah said. She engaged the speaker function on her phone and tilted the small mic toward her lips. "You gonna do something about it?"

Charlie withdrew his notepad and pen from his jacket pocket.

"It's cute how you ask me that," Drake said, "as if I haven't done enough already."

As Oscar Mike spoke, Zarah turned the phone's caller ID display toward Charlie, who scribbled the number from the caller ID onto his notepad and then nodded when he had what he needed.

"Oh?" Zarah said. "Shouldn't I be dead then?"

"When it suits me."

Charlie quickly swiveled the Charger's small notebook computer towards him and began a reverse-lookup and trace to track the number to the cell tower it was using, and he had to act fast while Oscar Mike's phone was still active. When Charlie had entered everything he needed, Zarah switched off the speaker and returned the phone to her ear. She needed to buy him time, so she decided to try and engage her enemy in a verbal judo match.

"Give it a rest," Zarah said. "You missed the last shot you're ever gonna get. How's the ear, by the way?"

"Excellent," Drake said. "Since I'm such a poor shot, tell me, how's Carmen? And that jujitsu teacher you were fucking? Did you get to share an ambulance, or was it a bag for him, too?"

Zarah wanted to roar obscenities at him, but this was the game, to see who could trip whom first. "Too bad you didn't have the guts to stick around and find out," Zarah said.

"Yeah, too bad," he said. "We wouldn't be having this talk."

"I know. All of L.A. would be pissing on your grave."

"Excuse me," Drake said, "but which one of us put the other in the fucking hospital?"

"Which one of us runs like a scalded dog every time we meet?"

"Without backup, you'd have lasted a fucking minute!"

"That's longer than you would have without Kevlar."

"You carpet kissing, rag head, whore!" Oscar Mike hissed.

"Ouch," Zarah said. "That's language unbecoming an officer. Oh wait. I mean, *Master Sergeant.*"

"I'm gonna kill you with so much pain!" Drake said. "You're gonna beg me to stop I'm gonna make it hurt so much!"

"You can't see it," Zarah said, "but I'm flipping you off as hard as I can."

78

"**Y**OU'RE FUCKING DEAD!!"

Drake threw the phone onto the sand and stomped on it until it was buried. His blood boiling, imagining all of the ways he wanted to end Zarah Wheeler's life, he continued along the beach.

It was not long after when, far in the distance, Drake noticed blue and red flashes strobing from a boat on the water and a beam of while light piercing the blackness as it swept over the waves. It was searching for him.

He could have been overreacting, but he needed to play it safe. He ran inland. As soon as he reached the boardwalk, a helicopter thundered over the beach, scanning the darkness with a spot light. It was no coincidence. Zarah Wheeler had tracked the call.

Fucking bitch! Then Drake cursed himself. *Why did I call her? Why didn't I just stick to the goddam plan?*

He crossed the boardwalk and made his way toward the street. The Santa Monica after-hours nightlife was still in full swing beyond the boardwalk. Restaurants were full, their little white lights twinkling away in the trees outside. Pedestrians were walking up and down the sidewalks. Traffic was thick but flowed smoothly. There were vehicles parked everywhere on the curbsides, and one of them would be his.

He was half way there when he spotted two Santa Monica Police cars cruising down Ocean Avenue, taking their time. Drake casually leaned across the back of a palm tree, out of their line of sight, until they had passed. Motorists behind the cops were cruising, none of them having the balls to pass the slow-moving police cars, and none of them daring to blow their horns.

Why couldn't people behave this way all the time? If it had been a pair of tourists, the road would be a din of horns and curses. If it had not been cops slowing things up, people would be jockeying from one lane to another trying to pass them, creating one dangerous situation after another.

Fucking hypocrites! Fucking cowards!

It was not long before Drake found an inconspicuous car worth stealing: a brown, boxy Honda Civic that must have been built in the '80s. It was parked on the curb in full public view, but the longer he stayed on the street the likelier it became that he would be discovered. He had to risk it.

He discreetly removed the jimmy from his bag and opened the Honda's lock with no trouble, no alarm and no interference. He placed his duffel in the back seat and then bypassed the car's ignition interlock. As he closed the door, he heard a female voice.

"Oh. My. God."

He looked to where the voice was coming from, and a curvy blonde female, with two equally curvy girlfriends were looking at him. Drake glared at her, and she froze.

"I'm not him," Drake told her. "I look like him, that's all."

She did not look like she believed him. Another woman in the group turned and took her cellphone out of her pocket and acted as if she was making a phone call, but the angle of the phone suggested she was trying to photograph him.

Drake drew his suppressed .45. The blonde screamed. Most of the spectators scattered like bunnies from a fox, and the rest were deer in headlights. He sat into the car without taking his weapon off of the girl, closed the door and sped away.

He merged into one lane and out of another, trying to make headway, like that LESTAT1 jerkoff whose hand he had chopped off and delivered to that fucking bitch Zarah, but he needed to get moving.

As he reached the ramp for P.C.H., he spotted something he never thought he would see. Two lanes away there was a black Dodge Charger. In the driver's seat—with yellowish-purple bruises around her eyes, a soot-stained adhesive bandage applied to one of her high cheekbones, and another on her forehead—was Zarah Wheeler.

Her black hair was dry and frayed. She looked alert, but tired. Drake was about to take aim with his .45 when behind him— *BWEEP bip bip BWEEP!* Police.

Through the rear view mirror, he saw the flashing lights of squad cars. Traffic was heavy, but the vehicles behind him were getting out of their way. Soon they would be upon him. He heard a helicopter approaching.

Shit!

He wanted to pull the trigger so bad! She was right there! He should not have to run! They should all be running from him!

"FUUUUCK!"

He put his gun down on the passenger seat and took the ramp to the Pacific Coast Highway. Traffic was thin and moved quickly. He kept checking his rear view. If the police were still behind him, he had a great head start. He heard no sirens and saw no lights— even the helicopters were absent. He was going to make it.

Then, an ocean of red brake lights appeared in front of him. He slowed, then stopped. Traffic crept. Vehicles of every shape and size jammed behind him. There were no open lanes, no off-ramps, no way out. If he tried to turn onto the shoulder and bypass the jam, he was sure to be noticed.

He roared. He cursed. He grabbed the steering wheel and yanked it front and back as though he were trying to strangle it.

Traffic crept forward.

A helicopter chopped through the air and passed over him. It wheeled around and made another pass. Far behind him, he saw the police lights inching through the crowd of jammed-up vehicles.

Traffic crept forward.

Drake tried to snake his way ahead. He was concerned that the helicopter would notice, but he dismissed it because other impatient assholes were doing the same thing.

When he reached the end of the jam, he gunned his motor, ready to race ahead and get off of the highway. Then he saw what had caused the jam.

A Triple-A tow truck was parked on the shoulder with its amber warning light flashing in front of a navy-colored sedan with its red hazards blinking. A road-side assistance mechanic was twisting the lug nuts onto a spare tire as a young man, dressed as if he was on his way to an identity-confused, *wigger* convention, with a ball cap sideways on his head, a puffy black jacket with faux-fur trim and baggy jeans leaned against his car, goofing off on his smartphone.

Drake could not control his breathing. The rage built up in him.

This is what is causing a traffic jam? People have to LOOK at someone changing a tire as if they've NEVER SEEN IT BEFORE?

Drake roared from the depths of hell. He pulled over behind the crippled sedan, slammed on his brakes, put the car in park, and stood up out of his little, stolen Honda. He jerked open the rear passenger door, ripped the duffel bag open and filled his pockets with ammo magazines and removed the AR-15.

"WHAT ARE YOU ALL *LOOKING AT*?"

Drake took aim at the first people he saw gawking at the scene. It was a middle aged couple in a silver Lexus. Drake squeezed the trigger, and the assault rifle thundered, spitting fire and bullets. The Lexus was shredded with holes. Blood splattered the windows as they cracked and collapsed. The Lexus listed to the side of the road like a dog that had been clipped crossing the street, driver and passenger both leaning limp over their shoulder straps.

Drake strode into the middle of the Pacific Coast Highway, took aim at a random windshield in front of him and fired into it. He repeated the process over and over, aiming, and bursting rounds into everyone in his path.

"IT'S JUST A GODDAM FLAT TIRE!"

Drake clambered up the bullet-riddled hood of an SUV and stood on its roof. He howled like a demon and opened fire into the traffic jam. The hot lead pierced metal, broke graphite, shattered glass and bloodied the helpless, trapped motorists and passengers.

"YOU WANNA SEE SOMETHING? HERE, *YOU RUB-BERNECK MOTHERFUCKERRRS!*"

The police helicopter made its way over and began to circle. Its spotlight shone on him, but Drake did not care. He ejected the clip from his rifle, retrieved another and shoved it into the magazine well. He yanked back on the charging handle and fired again, destroying every windshield he saw.

Motorists on the other side of the highway slowed to watch.

"IT'S NOT EVEN ON YOUR SIDE OF THE FUCKING STREET!! ARRRRRRRGH!!"

He unloaded across the across the divide. When his weapon was empty, he jumped down from the SUV and reloaded.

Cars that raced forward to make it past the jam were shot at. Some escaped; others, strewn with bullets, lumbered into the thick, concrete center divider or lulled up the road until their car's momentum died with its driver. People who left their vehicles and tried to run were shot in the back.

"ALL YOU PEOPLE HAD TO DO WAS JUST DRIVE! DRIIIIIVE!"

Drake sensed someone coming up behind him. He spun and saw the Triple-A mechanic charging him with a tire iron. He was a bald, athletic Latino. He swung for Drake's head, but Drake blocked it with his rifle and rammed the mechanic's face with the butt. The mechanic stumbled backwards and fell. Drake pointed his weapon.

"No, no," the mechanic begged. "Don't!"

"YOU DON'T GIVE ME ORDERS!"

"WAIT!" the mechanic cried.

Drake fired four rounds into his chest, and the AR-15 was empty— no more magazines.

The mechanic wheezed, sputtered and expired. Drake heard more helicopters. He looked up. The dark sky was a baby's mobile full of choppers, circling him from above. His chances of getting out of this were falling towards zero fast. He was not sure if the choppers would open fire on him. If they could, it would not be long before they did. It was time to go.

The young man who was having his tire changed cowered by the rear of the tow truck. Drake yelled, "Here's a souvenir, asshole!" and hurled his rifle at him. The kid whimpered as the AR-15 bounced off of his crouching body and clattered onto the asphalt.

Drake looked down the Pacific Coast Highway at the bloody pavement, the groaning motorists, many running away, many writhing on the street in their own gore.

Message sent. They'll remember to keep their fucking eyes on the road next time.

Down the highway, police were on foot, running toward him through the mess of bullet-strewn cars. Their guns were drawn. They would be firing on him already if civilians were not panicking and muddying up their line of sight. Oscar Mike was not bound by such rules.

They keep falling for this.

He yanked a grenade from under his coat—he had to make it count. After this, he would only have one left. He pitched it at the police and turned toward his stolen car. He decided to retreat into the hills. The darkness and serpentine canyon curves would make him a harder target to hit.

He was about to get into the old Honda, but he thought that the little car would not have the power to race up hills. He looked at the tow truck. It would not be much faster, but at least it had armor.

The grenade exploded, rocking the highway. People on the streets screamed. Black smoke rose from the point of impact. The cops were either dead or taking cover, because he did not see them anymore.

He hefted his duffel bag from the Honda and ran to the tow truck. The keys were in the ignition. He sped down the highway, approaching Sunset Boulevard, but he could not turn there. That street would be too crowded. It had to be Topanga Canyon. It was a dark road that winded and slithered up the hill with less traffic.

He stepped on the gas. The tow truck grumbled as it sped up. He looked out onto Sunset Boulevard. As he passed it, he saw a black Dodge Charger coming straight at him, and at this speed, it would ram him as soon as they reached the highway.

Zarah Wheeler!

79

ARAH AND CHARLIE cruised down Ocean Ave, on the lookout. Then they heard the call: Oscar Mike located on the Pacific Coast Highway, westbound, and firing on civilians. They knew they would never catch up to him if they tried to come up the P.C.H. from behind.

Planning to head him off, Zarah took a roundabout route, following Ocean Avenue to Marbery Road, around Rustic Canyon to Sunset Boulevard and then straight towards the P.C.H. like a cruise missile.

Another call-out came, detailing how he threw a grenade at officers and made off with a Triple-A roadside assistance vehicle.

"Al'ama!" Zarah cursed in Arabic, earning a confused look from Charlie. The radio advised everyone listening that the suspect had a propensity for throwing grenades. "Ya *think?*" she yelled.

Zarah's speed picked up with her anger—ninety-seven miles per hour down a crowded street. Motorists barely had time to pull off to the side and get out of her way, and Zarah swerved around the ones that did not. She knew it was making Charlie uncomfortable, but he kept his mouth shut.

Zarah saw the helicopters buzzing around the scene. She saw Channel Six's *Action in the Air* chopper and thought of Carmen and how much she would have loved to be in on this. It enraged Zarah more.

She stomped on the accelerator, and the Dodge barreled down Sunset. As they neared the turnoff to P.C.H., Zarah saw the white tow truck approaching. Charlie pointed and yelled, "There he is!"

"I see it!" Zarah said. "Hang on!"

Zarah charged like a rhino, trying to smash into the tow truck's rear to spin it out.

"Zaraaaaaaaaaahhh!!' Charlie squealed.

Zarah turned the wheel, aiming the Dodge's fender at the tow truck's rear tire. Drake Mitchell saw her coming and accelerated. Zarah reached the P.C.H. and shot past the rear of the tow truck, missing it by inches. She cursed as she jerked the wheel hard to the right. The Dodge skidded into the large intersection and nearly crossed over into oncoming traffic before Zarah righted its course.

"What the fuck!" Charlie demanded. "Are you trying to kill us?"

"No!" Zarah said. "Just him!"

"You know, with a cracked head and shit, you shouldn't even be—"

"Tuck and roll, Charlie!"

The tow truck swerved to the side and pulled onto Topanga Canyon Boulevard. Zarah was glued to his tail.

"Ohhh God!" Charlie moaned. "I hate canyons at night!"

"Well, pretend it's Space Mountain!"

"Space Mountain doesn't have fucking mountains!"

"Then the Matterhorn," Zarah said. "Pretend it's the Matterhorn!"

"The MatterHHAAAGH?"

Zarah sped around a sharp turn. The car's rear fishtailed into the dirt shoulder, the Dodge's rear end missing the base of a sandstone rock formation by a whisker. Zarah stayed on target.

Charlie covered his chest with his hand. "Okay," he said, his breaths short. "I gotta get out now."

"*Permanecer sentados, por favor,*" Zarah quipped, as she slammed her foot onto the accelerator and bashed into Oscar Mike's bumper.

"That wasn't funny!" Charlie said. He picked up the radio. "He's heading north up Topanga Canyon Boulevard," he said with heavy breaths. "How about some back up?"

"*Affirmative, we're right behind you,*" a voice cracked back through the radio. "*Air-one, where's a good place to head him off?*"

"North Topanga and Old Topanga," Charlie said. "Both cross Mulholland, so those turnoffs are the places to be."

"*That's affirm,*" Air-one said.

"We'll set up there," another unit responded.

Zarah rammed the truck again. It swerved but stayed its course.

"Back off, Zarah," Charlie said. "Let's drive him to our boys."

80

WHEN DRAKE HAD turned onto Topanga Canyon
Boulevard, he did not realize his mistake until it was
too late. It was a steep, narrow route, one lane in each
direction, winding through faults and folds concealed by dense
vegetation, full of wide curves and hairpin turns.

Treetops peeked over the steel guardrails, indicating the dicey
elevation he was climbing. When the sheer drops appeared to level
off, it was because of large caprock boulders and slanted buttes lin-
ing the roadsides, courtesy of the Santa Monica Mountains.

The alternating perils between taking an ugly tumble into a
gorge or plastering himself against a giant rock seemed like a high-
wire act with the added threat of having Zarah Wheeler behind
him in muscle-car that could take the canyon at high speed
with aplomb.

She had stopped ramming him, which convinced Drake that
she was driving him toward spike strips, barricades, and a fully
armed and armored LAPD Tac-team with *shoot to kill* orders
up ahead.

One grenade, a shotgun with two rounds left, and a silenced
handgun that was also low on ammo were not going to present
much of a challenge. His only chance was to get off the road, take
to foot among the trees, hills and rocks inside the canyon, and fade

into the moon-cast shadows. He slowed down, rolled down his window, reached outside with his sawed-off, and fired a random blast at Zarah Wheeler's car to distract her from the chase long enough to surprise her with what he planned to do next.

81

BEFORE ZARAH COULD begin to understand why Drake Mitchell took a shot that had no chance of hitting anything, he slammed on his brakes, and Zarah had to swerve left to avoid folding her car on the tow truck's bumper like a soda can.

She eased down on her brakes. If Drake Mitchell's plan had been to force her to overtake him, it was not going his way. Now the two vehicles sped over the canyon alongside each other, but it was a short matter of time before oncoming traffic would force Zarah to return to the tow truck's rear. She had to make a move. When she looked over, she saw Charlie, Glock in hand, rolling down his window.

He reached out with his gun as Drake Mitchell stretched out his arm with his. Charlie aimed at the truck's tires. Drake Mitchell aimed at Charlie's head, and with a sawed-off shotgun he would not miss.

"Charlie!" Zarah shouted. She jammed the wheel right. Charlie yanked his hand back in the car as Zarah broadsided the tow truck's flank, shoving it into the guardrail. The sound of grinding metal made a cold tingle flow over Zarah's skin. The tow truck swerved and slammed Zarah and Charlie back into the oncoming lane.

"Zarah, back off," Charlie yelled. "I wanna take out his—holy shit, Zaraaaaah!"

The two vehicles sped toward a sharp hairpin turn. Zarah stayed glued to Drake's side, determined to drive him over the edge into the steep canyon below.

The turn was imminent. Charlie screamed for Zarah to stop, but she refused. The truck smashed into the guardrail. Then Zarah's Charger careened into its side with enough impact to kick the car's rear end into the air. The power of the collision and the weight of the massive tow truck were too much for the steel rail to contain. It wrenched away from the street and bent under the truck. Zarah could not be sure if it was a smirk she saw on Drake Mitchell's face in the white beams of her headlights, but she was certain there was no fear on it as he and his getaway truck spilled over the edge and out of sight. She heard it rumble into the canyon.

Charlie gripped his chest again and breathed heavy.

"Grenada wasn't as scary as your fucking driving!" he said.

Zarah unbuckled her seat belt. "Is the radio still working?"

"I think so," Charlie said.

"Tell them where we are," she told him as she opened her door.

"I think they know," Charlie said, gesturing his thumb upwards that the three helicopters above them.

"We need people in that canyon," Zarah said. Charlie nodded.

Zarah slid out of the car and ran to the edge of the road and looked over. She saw the headlights of the tow truck. It was steep, but not a big enough drop to kill someone like Drake Barret Mitchell.

Charlie winced as he limped from the Dodge and joined Zarah. They both saw the wrecked truck. It had rolled onto its side, its crash stopped by a thick tree. The door opened upward, and Drake Mitchell climbed out. Zarah aimed her gun. "Don't move!"

Drake Mitchell raised his shotgun. Zarah and Charlie jumped back from the edge. The blast reverberated through the air. Zarah and Charlie returned to the edge. Charlie raised his Glock as Drake Mitchell threw aside the shotgun and rolled over the upended side of the truck. Zarah fired a shot and hit nothing. Charlie did not bother to squeeze the trigger. They watched him run from the wreck and fade into the cover of the dark, wooded canyon.

The three choppers circled the canyon sweeping their spotlights over the thick canopy of trees. Little light would reach the ground, and all they were doing was lighting up the treetops.

Zarah holstered her weapon and scanned the terrain at her feet for a way into the gorge.

"You're not thinking about going down there?" Charlie said. "He's a commando, Zarah. That's his fucking wheelhouse down there!"

"He can't get away again," she said. "He just can't." She noticed Charlie favoring his right leg. "You gonna be okay?" she asked.

He nodded and gave an affirmative grunt.

"Just let everybody know where we are," Zarah said as she lowered herself onto her stomach.

"*You* be careful," Charlie said.

Zarah nodded and pushed herself, feet first, on the ground and slid over the side, carefully clambering into the canyon, using branches, stones and indentations as handholds and footholds.

When she was more than halfway down, she moved faster. Her head began to ache, reminding her of what happened the last time she confronted Oscar Mike. As she lowered herself, her weight pried loose a sandstone handhold, and she slipped from her purchase with a yelp. As she slid down, she snatched at stones and brush and bushes— anything to slow her fall.

The ground was coming up fast. Zarah kicked away from the wall, spun and grabbed for the trees. The twigs and branches were desiccated by heat and drought. They snapped and fractured as Zarah tried to grip them. Zarah felt the blood rush to her head. She blacked out for a split-second before she hit the ground.

When she regained her senses, she scrambled to her feet and

whipped her .9mm from its holster. She leveled it in front of her, scanning the shadowy woods with wide eyes.

Get it together! You're a razor!

She heard the helicopters overhead, still searching. Thin blades of light pierced through the branches, and flickered through the canyon as the spotlights scanned as much of the ground as they could. It was not long before the sound of their rotor-heads grew fainter, and the search lights moved further away.

As Zarah approached the tow truck's headlights, the woods around her seemed to grow darker with an edge to it that made her skin goose up. She stopped. The closer to the headlights she came, the easier she would be to see—and shoot dead. A warm breeze blew from the east and made the pines, eucalyptus and acacias rustle. Zarah sensed something watching her. Something cold and implacable—hostile.

She listened. She heard distant footfalls in the dead leaf litter. Drake Mitchell should have been far away, but he had waited.

Zarah continued walking, away from the bright headlights, weaving through the tree trunks and bushes for cover. After several yards, she stopped and listened again. She squinted into the dark and caught a faint outline in the moonlight—a man peeking from behind a tree ahead of her. She fired at him. The report of her gun bounced off the canyon walls and filled the air.

"Here I am, Zarah!" Drake Mitchell called out. "Near!"

Zarah waited to catch another glimpse of him.

"Almost as near as when you watched Carmen *die!*"

Zarah heard a metallic *ping,* and she saw Drake Mitchell's figure step out from behind a large tree and throw something toward her.

Grenade!

Zarah knew if she ran she would lose him, so she raced towards his outline in the moonlight. Something *thudded* on the ground behind her. She picked up speed.

From behind, a loud *BOOM* thundered through the canyon. The shockwave took her from her feet, and she slammed onto the dirt and dead leaves and needles. The darkness lit up, and a several yards in front of her stood Drake Mitchell. He aimed a pistol with a suppressed barrel at her.

Zarah rolled aside as he fired. She heard the round strike the ground beside her as she took cover behind a large boulder and pulled herself to her feet. The light dimmed and flickered and then became bright again. The grenade had ignited the foliage. After months of Southern California heat with no rain, the small fire had plenty of fuel and was strengthening, growing fast.

Zarah saw Drake Mitchell trying to escape farther into the canyon, slithering around trees and hurdling rocks. She shot at him, grazing his leg. He hissed, spun and returned fire. Zarah dove to the ground.

The brush fire snapped and popped. Sparks went airborne like angry hornets, helping the fire rise higher and sweep farther along the canyon floor, filling it with black smoke and hellish heat. The shadows performed a demonic dance with the flickering, orange light.

Zarah pushed off the ground and took cover, but she did not hide for long. The fire was advancing, and she could feel its intensity from forty yards away. She ran at Drake again, leveling her gun. She fired. One round left, and then—*clink*—the slide sprang back. She was empty, and had no extra magazines. Drake returned fire. The hammer struck the pin without a sound. His weapon had also dried up.

Zarah threw down her gun and charged at him with all of her energy. Drake charged as well, and like two rams, Oscar Mike and Zarah Wheeler collided. With strength on his side, Drake took Zarah down onto her back. She felt the wind leave her as she hit the ground. He mounted her and put his weight on top her stomach and abdomen.

"Fucking bitch!" he growled as he raised his fist and punched her in her bandaged temple.

A colorful explosion of dancing phosphenes filled her eyes like fireworks, and Zarah's vision blurred. She threw her arms around his waist and yanked him forward, pressing her head into his chest so he could not reach her with his fists.

"What the fuck is this bullshit?" he said.

Zarah knew she could not stay there forever, so she reached up and grabbed his shoulders, hoisting herself upward so that her feet were flat on the ground. Drake raised up to bash her again, but this time Zarah was ready. As Drake brought his fist down, Zarah threw her forearm up and wrapped it around his arm. Using his downward force, she yanked his shoulder to her and thrust off of the ground with her heels, tossing Drake aside.

Zarah jumped to her feet at the same time as her enemy. The flames thrashed closer and closer. Zarah felt a spread of warm wetness running down her cheek—the cut on her temple had reopened, inundating the loosened gauze bandage. Blood seeped through its adhesive tape in a thick, red curtain down the side of her face as it ran free from its dressing. Oscar Mike's ear was dripping blood from his ear through his own hastily applied bandage like a leaky faucet.

They faced one another. Hellfire raged in their eyes as they circled the empty ground between them, slow and guarded, like two alpha wolves in a turf war, closing the distance with each step as the flames devoured the canyon floor, growing larger and coming closer.

Drake's jaw trembled. He looked energized and wrathful. Zarah forced herself to relax and breathe. She inhaled through her nose and smelled the burning woods around her. The smoke was thick, and it was all she could do to keep from coughing, showing weakness.

Drake smirked. "I shouldn't have killed your pussy-ass jujitsu teacher and that spic whore as quick as I did! I should have tied them up and cut them into pieces and *cooked them* in front of you!"

Zarah shrugged. "You're gonna die for it either way," she said.

Drake looked as if he could not believe her impudence. He chuckled the fakest laugh Zarah had heard in twenty years as a police officer.

"You stupid, *stupid*, bitch," he said. "I *gutted* children! I shot women, and strangled men, and killed who I pleased! I butchered your colleagues, your friends and your lover *right in front of you*, and never even *came close* to catching me! You think *this* is gonna be—"

Zarah snapped a kick full of dirt, pine needles and leaves into his face. It was not enough to blind him, but when he flinched, Zarah sprang forward and slammed his wounded ear with her fist. He roared in pain and staggered backwards. Zarah stayed on top of him, rocking his temple with a solid punch. She threw another, but Drake blocked it and threw his own. It did not have much power, but it hurt.

Now he was on the attack. He came at Zarah. Hissing at her, he threw a series of hard blows at her head. Zarah blocked, ducked and weaved, but she had not seen the one thrown at her midsection. It struck with force. Zarah grunted and bent over.

With one hand, Drake seized her by her hair and yanked her up toward him. She gritted her teeth against the pain and thrust both hands out, clawing his face. With both hands, she raked down the skin over his eyes like a cat sharpening its nails. Drake's eyes slammed shut as he released her hair. Zarah shot a powerful side kick into his abdomen, sending him staggering backwards.

Zarah could taste blood in her mouth and was having a hard time breathing, but she wasted no time. She advanced and threw a strong fist at his temple. He ducked under it and delivered a vicious combination to her midsection, followed by a wide, round haymaker to her jaw. Zarah staggered backward toward the fire.

Drake gnarred, lunging toward her, his shoulders thrust out as if he were going to tackle Zarah and shove her into the flames. For a split second, she was a deer in headlights, but as soon as she was within his reach and he had stretched out his arms, Zarah twisted her back to him and dropped straight down on one knee, curving her spine into a hump. Drake could not stop in time. He could do nothing but dive over her to avoid tripping. He rolled onto the ground behind her with half his body landing in the crackling, thrashing flames. With a terrified croak, he scuttled away from the fire.

Zarah leapt off the ground and rammed her knee into his spine. She lashed out with her hands and wrapped an arm around his throat as she buttressed his back with the side of her body. Placing her free hand over her fist, she pulled her arm tight against him, wedging her forearm deep under his chin. She squeezed and constricted his throat with everything she had.

The fire ate its way up his legs. Flames whipped over his head and licked Zarah's face, burning her cheek and singeing her hair as Drake struggled. Zarah remained braced, her arm locked around his throat like a band-clamp. She lowered her head and pressed it behind his to give her at least *some* protection from the fire.

He reached behind him to try and grab her, but his arms could not bend back that far. He clawed at Zarah's arm around his throat. He kicked and tried to hitch his body up as his legs smoked and smoldered, but Zarah would not be budged. Without leverage, all he could do was buck and squeal like a pig in a snare as Zarah cut off the blood flow to his brain.

The fire was already close to consuming them both. The heat seared Zarah's arm. She embraced the pain as she suffocated him with all of her remaining strength. After the fire had reached his stomach, he stopped resisting and went limp. Zarah released him and pushed herself away. Drake Mitchell dropped backward into the dirt.

Zarah's jacket sleeve had caught aflame. She yelped, jumped to her feet and tore the jacket off. She flung it into the fire to avoid creating a whole new blaze to worry about.

She shook her head and cursed herself, realizing her phone was still in the jacket pocket. Backing away from the fire, she looked to see where her car had been. Everywhere she looked there were tall flames and no way back. There was no time to climb up to Charlie—if he was still there. She heard choppers approaching once again, but could not see them through the smoke and trees.

Zarah turned away from the fire. Ahead, she saw a slight, distant twinkle of lights through the branches atop a steep, round hill covered with large rock formations and vegetation. The lights seemed to be moving to and fro, like fireflies. Zarah did not bother trying to figure out what was causing them, the bottom line was rocks could not catch fire. Zarah's best chance of survival was to outrun the flames, reach that hill, get behind the formations and keep going until she hit a road. On wobbly feet she stepped toward the hill.

Behind her she heard an inhuman shriek, and she spun around to see what it was. Drake Mitchell sprang at her from out of the flames— his smoldering, red flesh blistered and glistening, and his scarred eyes burning with rage. Zarah screamed and stumbled away as he hit the ground in front of her. He seized her legs and yanked her from her feet. He hissed as he pulled his way up Zarah's body. She tried to kick him away, but he held on.

The heat scorched her pant legs. The fibers fizzled and seared Zarah's skin. Her shrieks filled the canyon.

She balled up her fist and slammed it into his temple. He grunted, gnashed his teeth and kept crawling on top of her, pulling himself by her clothes, handful by handful. His Kevlar had protected his insides, but the heat it gave off on the outside was burning through Zarah's blouse. She punched him again as hard as she could manage, but he did not stop. When he reached her neck, Zarah could feel his breath on her skin, then his teeth on her throat. She jammed two fingers into his mouth and fish-hooked the inside of his cheek. He roared at her.

She tried to wriggle out from under him, but all of his weight was upon her. He grabbed Zarah's wrist and yanked. Her fish-hook slipped out of his mouth. He pushed himself up onto his knees and was about to straddle her. Zarah lashed her legs around his midsection. She grabbed his smoking vest and tried to pull him into her as she had done before. It burned her, but she held on, only this time he thrust his hand onto her chest and braced himself with a straight arm.

Drake Barret Mitchell, his face blistered and black, looked at Zarah Wheeler with an insane, lascivious smile that caused her stomach to twist. She felt his thumb slip a deviant caress around her nipple.

She clamped his hand onto her breast, trapping it. Zarah snarled. "That is *it*..." With a teeth-gritted, primal grunt, she snapped his elbow inward with her free forearm. There was a dull pop as his elbow joint separated and his humerus tore away from the rest of his arm.

Drake let out an agonized, high-pitched wail and yanked himself away. That injury, on top of what the fire had already done, must have overloaded whatever it was in his brain that had allowed him to push through the unimaginable pain of his burns. Shock took him, and Zarah saw that he was teetering on the edge of consciousness. She released his trunk from her legs and kicked him away. He tumbled back.

Zarah felt horrible burning on her face, arms and legs. Adrenaline had kept the pain at bay as she fought, and she knew that if she did not run fast she would be well-done in minutes. She felt her breath shorten. She coughed from inhaling the smoky air.

She heard a ghoulish groan. Drake was awake, writhing and twitching on the ground like a squashed insect that refused to die.

The fire was close to him, and he had to be broiling worse than Zarah was. She was fine with that. He deserved to burn.

Still, *Oscar Mike* was defeated. Now her duty was to save him if she could. She reached down and pulled him away from the fire. She imagined Sebastian approving of her honorable decision. Over Zarah's other shoulder, the voice of Carmen Sanchaz was telling her to let the *maricón* cook.

As she dragged him away, the flames seemed to become faster and more aggressive. She heard sirens behind the flames and more choppers in the sky, but still could not see them. The small hairs on her forearms were singed all the way up to her sleeves. She had to move while there was still someplace to run.

Zarah tried to hoist Drake across her shoulders, but the burns to her legs had seared her quadriceps, arms and chest. She could not lift him without intense pain. The fire was upon her, singeing her clothes. She could feel the skin of her face burning. The tip of her nose felt as if it would melt off. If she tried to drag Drake with her there was no way she would escape. The fire was picking up speed and strength. Zarah turned and ran as hard as she was able, surrendering *Oscar Mike* to the inferno.

As she puffed and coughed and struggled to focus through her dizziness, she pressed forward, between the trees. She thought she heard screaming behind her, but Zarah told herself that it was the fire trucks and police. She forged onward in defiance of the pain and dizziness.

She tripped over brambles and roots. She scrambled over rocks and ridges. Without looking back, Zarah pressed forward, out from under the woods, toward the tall hill with the large, sandstone tor, and the small, dancing lights—which looked more and more manmade the closer she came.

It could have been minutes or hours before she had outpaced the fire and was heading uphill. A long way across from her, she saw the flashing lights of fire trucks and police vehicles on the road above, but there was no way to reach them. In the sky helicopters circled the burning canyon.

The flames were still coming her way, though the firefighters coupled with the rockiness of the canyon must have slowed it down. When she reached the hill, she was tempted to take a breather, but the fire was not resting, and she would not be able to carry on if she stopped now.

Her muscles ached, her head throbbed, and her stomach begged her to double over and vomit as she pulled herself up the hill. When she made the summit, she discovered a mesa, hosting a make-shift campground with a half dozen teenaged campers. The lights had come from their lanterns, flashlights and vehicles, and judging from the scramble of activity, they were readying to make themselves scarce before the fire reached them.

Several campers stopped what they were doing and looked at Zarah with alarmed expressions. A young, blonde girl wearing a lime colored t-shirt and grey nylon capris dropped the cooler she was carrying and ran to Zarah. "Oh my God," the girl said. "Ma'am, are you okay?"

Zarah answered with shaky laughter and wept in release as she dropped to her knees. The girl wrapped her arms around Zarah and braced her to keep her from collapsing onto her face.

"I need help!" the girl cried. It was the last thing Zarah heard before she surrendered to exhaustion and fainted from pain.

82

ZARAH GASPED, AND her eyes snapped open, already filling with tears. One more night terror, courtesy of her concussion. She had dreamed of Sebastian, tied to a chair, pumping blood out of his wounds… Carmen struggling to stay alive, bleeding from her temple and sucking oxygen, her eyes wide in shock and fear… Charlie screaming invective at her while his shoulder bled, and panicking civilians scrambled for safety… *"Man down! Man down!"* Then Oscar Mike's hate-filled voice: *"THIS IS IT, ZARAH."* She dreamed of flames again, roaring out from nowhere, consuming her.

Zarah gathered herself and looked around. More IV machines and PCA pumps. Another heart monitor. Another gown as thin as rice paper. Something about it was funny, and through her tears, Zarah laughed and shook her head.

I'm out of the hospital for less than a day…

She looked at the needle inserted into the back of her hand and laughed harder. She felt hazy, and sticky. Her arms and chest were swaddled and patched in bandages covered with some kind of ointment. Her skin had a reddish hue.

Zarah knew she had been burned badly, but she felt no pain. She attributed it, and her giddy state, to opiates. She tried to read the labels of the IV bags to see what was dripping into her bloodstream, but it was too dark and she was too far away to make it out.

When she tried to sit up for a closer look, the drugs lost their grip. She let out a quick shriek as searing pain in her chest forced Zarah back to proneness.

A blonde nurse wearing turquoise scrubs entered the room. "Hey there," she said.

"Hey back at ya," Zarah said. "Is Charlie in the hallway again?"

"I doubt anyone knows you're here," the nurse said as she checked the roller clamp on the IV tubing. "Can you tell me your name?"

"Where's my phone?" Zarah said. "I need to make a call."

"You didn't come here with a phone, or any I.D.," the nurse said. "Some young people rescued you from a forest fire in Topanga, and you were rushed here with second and third degree burns."

"Where's here?" Zarah asked.

"LAC USC Medical Center. Now may I please have your name?"

Zarah chortled. "Detective, no wait, Special Agent, wait, not that either. It's just Zarah. Yeah..."

"Well, Zarah, most of the burns you sustained are a mild second degree, but your right arm is severe, third degree," the nurse said as she punched a few numbers into Zarah's IV machine. "But we're gonna dial down on your pain meds a little. Is it Zarah Wheeler?"

"Yes, Wheeler."

The nurse nodded. "You're all over the news. About a day and a half ago we told the LAPD we thought we had you, but no one's followed up yet."

Zarah chuckled. "That sounds about right."

"Everybody's looking for you. I have to tell someone to call them again. Holler if you need something." The nurse left the room.

"A phone!" Zarah called after her, doubtful that the nurse really meant that last part.

83

THREE WEEKS AFTER being discharged from the hospital, Zarah sat in a red vinyl, tufted button booth, smack in the middle of a darkened Studio City deli that hearkened to the Hollywood of the late 1940's and was noted for its celebrity clientele. Her mother would have lost her Islamic mind if she found out. Zarah savored that thought as she contemplated ordering the matzo ball soup.

Her burns were healing well, but she still felt as if her skin radiated heat like a flat iron, so Zarah decided that since it was a hundred-degree day, she needn't heat things up on her insides as well. She ordered a Ham and Swiss on Rye instead—that would have pissed her mother off good, too.

What induced Zarah's mind to drift to her mother was the delightful excitement to be seeing her father. In the parking lot of the deli, her car was clean, packed up, gassed up, and ready to hit the long road to Chicago. While she and her dad had never lost touch, she had not seen him, or her Illinoisan family, in close to a decade.

Zarah had come to California to be as far-removed from her old life as she could and yet remain an American citizen. But the beaches, mountains and palm trees had lost their charm, and her father's spacious condo off Lake Michigan, with North

Chicago's cooler, moister air seemed like a good place to heal, reflect, confront painful memories and put the past out to grass—to start again.

On a flat-screen TV bolted to a brass and wood column raised high for all to see, Zarah watched the image of herself being helped down the three, wide concrete stairs leading from LAPD's Parker Center. She was surrounded by LAPD colleagues, Charlie, Adam, Woodley and Pérez, Lieutenant Torres and Captain Sheridan and several other detectives who had shown up to watch her hearing and testify.

A familiar voice narrated. "...*in the weeks to follow, Deputy Police Chief Marcus Padilla explained the findings of the LAPD's Board of Rights' disciplinary hearing in response to the questions raised regarding Detective Zarah Wheeler's role in the City Terrace Shootout...*"

Zarah's black hair was clean and neat, tied in a smooth pony-tail. She had worn a peach and black pantsuit that day, to look tough, and to hide the mess of spoiled-looking skin. Her gait was stiff as she was helped into a black sedan.

The picture on the TV screen cut away to the stout and serious Deputy Chief standing at a podium bristling with microphones in front of a mob of reporters from every species of media.

"It has been determined by the investigating body," Padilla studiously said, "that Detective Wheeler responded appropriately to an urgent situation according to her sworn oath as a police officer."

A tawny-haired woman in an eggshell blouse raised her hand. "Can you address the accusations that Detective Wheeler acted without backup as a reckless, glory-seeking opportunity?"

"Aay, *puta!*" Carmen Sanchaz yelled at the TV from the opposite side of Zarah's booth, producing curious glances from the diners surrounding it. "Why'd you have to go there?" She shook her head and looked at the detective. "Some people have no parameters," she said.

Ridding Los Angeles of Oscar Mike had earned Zarah the

gratitude of the city and her citizens, and with it, a measure of fame. But tearing heroes down trended and made headlines. The media did not have any ammo left, but some of them dry-fired at Zarah anyway.

Zarah had emerged from *Oscar Mike's Inferno,* as the media labeled it, with a sharp longing for the days when she had loving family close by, and true friends. Such people did not exist in Los Angeles, where the premium was placed on having friends, not on being one. Carmen seemed to be taking a sincere shot at a real friendship, and Zarah welcomed it, but she had a hunch that there was more to this *"girl's luncheon"* that Carmen had invited her to.

Zarah snickered. "If you didn't like the question," she asked, "why'd you keep it in the story?"

Carmen smiled. "I didn't do the editing," she said. "I narrated and wrote some copy. Everybody at the studio is treating me like any pressure is gonna make me fall out 'cause I got shot."

Carmen looked good, Zarah thought. Oscar Mike's bullet to her head seemed to have given her an optimistic glow, and made her a hundred times prettier than she had been. She was wearing a crisp, blue blazer with a cream-colored blouse, and her hair was tied in an auburn bun. She had kept her makeup simple but alluring and had obfuscated the scar on the far left side of her forehead with concealer.

She would be applying concealer there for the rest of her life, but Carmen had nothing to complain about, though she did anyway. If Oscar Mike's round had struck her directly in the temple, it would have killed her, but the angle of her head and the trajectory of the bullet had only chipped a small piece of her skull away, causing a great deal of soft-tissue damage and bruising, but nothing life-threatening. The real danger came when the hydrostatic shock had caused her muscles to go limp. She had dropped like a wet towel, and banged her skull on the concrete sidewalk.

After Zarah had left the scene with Charlie, Carmen had been stabilized by EMTs. Brain damage was a concern at first, but she had recovered fast—faster than the time Zarah had spent in searing pain, smeared with ointment and swaddled in hydrofiber.

When the story hit the street—how Carmen was injured, while voluntarily putting herself in harm's way and baiting Oscar Mike—her name had become as big as Leon Mandel's, if not bigger. It was a spin, of course. Other reporters, from other networks, did not hesitate to suggest that Carmen, and the LAPD, had deliberately put innocent people in harm's way. Carmen called it *jealous bias*, Zarah called it *karma*. Thankfully, Sir Patrick Stewart declined to comment.

"They're just pampering you," Zarah said. "You're not just a reporter. You're a story."

"Detective Wheeler called in a Code Two," the Deputy Chief on the TV said, *"well before they attempted to affect an arrest."*

"This decision," Carmen's voice narrated, *"comes swiftly on the heels of Zarah Wheeler's pursuit of Drake Barret Mitchell, the domestic terrorist better known as 'Oscar Mike', which led to his death and Detective Wheeler's extraordinary story of survival…"*

"Check it out," Carmen said, gesturing around the room at the many eyes pretending not to be watching the two of them. "There are producers here. Directors. You know how much money you could get for your story?"

"Is that why you wanted to eat here?" Zarah asked. "Because I'm not interested."

"Fine," Carmen said, "but I'm telling you now, if someone comes asking me, I'm sellin' out and moving to a beachfront in Malibu."

Zarah smiled and shook her head.

"So, listen," Carmen said. "I'll tell you why I asked you here. You're a celebrity, *mami*. This is where celebrities go to eat expensive baloney sandwiches, to be seen, and… to talk business."

"You brought me here to talk business?" Zarah said. "You've interviewed me two dozen times."

"Twice," Carmen corrected. "And twice was enough for anyone with eyeballs to know you oughta be in pictures. You have a communications degree. You took broadcasting in—"

"Okay, what are we doing here?"

"I'm here to see you off to Chicago," Carmen said, "and to see if you'd like to co-host a national panel show when you get back."

It would have been a nice surprise if Carmen had just wanted to have lunch to say farewell, but Zarah knew there had to be an angle. She expected to be asked to give one last interview, but never had she considered to be offered something like a TV show. Zarah regarded Carmen with a tilted head and narrow eyes.

"Aay," Carmen said, "I have no dog in this hunt. I was asked to *gauge your interest*. That's all."

"You're saying there's nothing in this for you?" Zarah asked.

"Maybe, maybe not," Carmen said, "but when bigshots from cable TV ask for a favor, I'm *doing* it, *chica*. To tell those guys 'no' is asking to be assigned to human interest, bake sale, bullshit for the rest of my life. I'm hot right now, but they've buried better reporters than me for getting a big head and forgetting who runs shit up in this piece."

"Relax, Carmen," Zarah said. "I totally understand that."

"Then don't give me that *look* you do."

"What look?" Zarah asked.

"Like I'm some *puta estafador* trying to trick you or something."

"Okay, Carmen," Zarah said. "I'm sorry... I just... I don't know what I wanna do, all right?"

Carmen's face softened. "Look... If you have trust issues with me, I don't—"

"Carmen," Zarah said, "I have trust issues with my own reflection, so that's a given, but do you honestly think I'd be here if I was holding a grudge?"

"I guess not, put that way."

"Then *stop* trying to make me think I should be."

Zarah admitted to herself she had always liked something about Carmen Sanchaz, even when she hated her. It was what made her easy to forgive. Then she thought back to her final conversation with Sebastian, about trusting that most people were good. There was a font of honesty and kindness within the reporter. Perhaps when Oscar Mike's bullet struck her it awakened the person Carmen Sanchaz should have been all along.

"So," Carmen said, "what do you want me to tell them? About the offer? The show?"

Zarah thought back and remembered her days at the University of Chicago, remembered dreaming of travelling the globe for CNN, covering world events. But that was not what Carmen's *big-shots* were asking for. They wanted a cop's perspective, and a hero cop's perspective counted for more somehow. She still had a job at the FBI waiting for her, but nothing was chiseled in granite, yet.

"I don't know," Zarah said. "I just... I don't know, really."

Carmen nodded and dropped the subject. Then the two of them had lunch, talked about things girlfriends talk about and lost track of time in each other's company. As the hours slipped away without notice, and neither of them wanted to leave, Zarah knew she had a friend. Carmen walked her to her car and hugged her gently, aware of her burns.

"If you don't do the show," Carmen asked, "will you come back to L.A.?"

Zarah wanted to say no with absolute certainty, but she could not. "I don't know," she said. "But let's promise not to lose touch."

"I promise," Carmen said.

Zarah sat into her car and took a deep breath. The road ahead was long, and the future was clouded—full of tough questions and hard decisions. As she pulled away, with Carmen waving goodbye in her rearview, she headed toward the 101 South.

As she merged onto the freeway, a speeding SUV barreled up from behind her, barged into her lane and cut her off. Zarah cursed, leaned on her horn and blared at the illegal lane change. The lone driver flipped her the bird and then bullied his way across the road, into the carpool lane—another violation. He sped away and vanished into traffic.

Zarah smiled.

ABOUT THE AUTHOR

Paul J. Hale was born in Chicago and raised in Los Angeles. A graduate of California State University Northridge, he is an amateur folklorist and has written several short stories in the action, fantasy, science fiction and supernatural genres, has co-written several produced screenplays and is the writer, producer and host of "The Disney Story Origins" Podcast. "OSCAR MIKE" is his first novel.

He is an avid martial artist who holds Black Belts in Budoshin & Danzan-Ryu Jujitsu and studies a variety of martial arts.

He lives in Southern California with his wife Teresa and two children, Lincoln and Brienne.

Paul's website can be found at pauljhaleauthor.com. You can e-mail him at pjhauthor@gmail.com, like his Facebook page at facebook.com/pauljhaleauthor, and follow him on Twitter at @pauljhaleauthor.